W9-CHM-041

Living Other Lives

Caroline Leavitt

Living Other Lives

WARNER BOOKS

A Time Warner Company

FIC

Warner Books, Inc., 1271 Avenue of the Americas, New York, NY 10020.

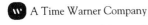 A Time Warner Company

Printed in the United States of America

First Printing: May 1995

10 9 8 7 6 5 4 3 2 1

Library of Congress Cataloging-in-Publication Data

Leavitt, Caroline
    Living other lives / Caroline Leavitt.
        p.   cm.
    ISBN 0-446-51705-4
    1. Grandmothers—Pennsylvania—Pittsburgh—Fiction.   2. Women—
Pennsylvania—Pittsburgh—Fiction.   3. Pittsburgh (Pa.)—Fiction.
I. Title.
PS3562.E2617L56   1995
813'.54—dc20   94-19750
                                                                    CIP

Book Design by H. Roberts

For Jeff, with love

Living Other Lives

August 1990

They're speeding. Lilly's air-conditioning busted miles back, and now the wind skids into the car through the open windows, slashing back her lengthy hair, ruffling Dinah's, which is so short and wispy that it barely breezes. Music filters from a passing car, a song about loving someone forever, about never ever letting go. "Oh, babe, you are my everything . . ." They hear a vaguely familiar wail, and then another car beeps and squawks and narrows the sound right down into nothing.

Lilly drives like a crazy person. She weaves dangerously in and out of lanes; she almost never signals if she can help it. It's a wonder none of the cops they've seen squirreled up behind the billboards have jammed out into the road and stopped her. Lilly edges recklessly toward the shoulder of the road, wincing when she clips it just a little too close. She swerves back into the lane, and Dinah sees the small red sedan almost the same second Lilly does. Dinah tenses, gripping the soda she bought at the last rest stop. She braces herself near the door, but she doesn't say "Watch out!" to Lilly. She doesn't even meet her eyes in the rearview mirror. The driver of the sedan smashes on his horn, a sound that reverberates deep within Dinah.

"You trying to get killed?" he screams at Lilly.

Lilly speeds up, passing him by four cars. "Put on your seat belt," she tells Dinah, who doesn't move, whose heart skips and crashes against her ribs. Dinah looks out at the wash of sky, dark and damp, like it needs to be wrung out. She puts the cold soda can up against her forehead, cooling herself a little, calming down. "Maybe we should listen to the weather," Dinah says. Actually, she's hoping for some music.

"Why?" Lilly says, and leaves the radio alone. Lilly doesn't talk much, not about the car or where to eat and certainly not about herself or Dinah, and no, never, ever, about the funeral or the future—or especially about Matt. But it's all right. The silence is safer. At least that's what Dinah thinks, anyway. If you don't think about it, it doesn't exist, it didn't happen. She tells herself this over and over, until it almost loses its meaning and becomes a hypnotic, like any words would, like samsara, the mantra they gave her the two weeks she briefly got involved in TM, an interest that lasted as long as her crush on the leader of the group. She's fifteen to Lilly's thirty. Matt was her father, and a month ago Lilly was almost her stepmother, a subject neither one of them even wants to touch.

The front seat is fairly empty, but Dinah prefers to hunch, long and ungainly, in the back, apart from Lilly. Her arms hoop her bare sunburned legs, which are already beginning to peel. Dinah fools with the loose pieces and thinks of a bad voodoo movie she once saw. *Night of the Zombie Women.* Skin. Hair. Nails. It's really bad luck to let anyone have a piece of you. There's one of her short blond hairs, drifting onto her left knee, and she carefully picks it up to pocket it, but the wind catches it and flings it out onto the dangerously moving road.

All this past month Dinah's been staying with Lilly in New York City. It had started out as a vacation: Dinah and her father coming all the way from Ohio to Lilly in New York—one long special visit because Lilly was going to give it all up to live in Ohio with them. But now no one's going home to Ohio. Now, no one's staying in New York.

Dinah has no real choice where to go. Dinah's mother, Maggy, is still alive, but she left when Dinah was barely two and never tried to keep in touch.

Instead Lilly's driving Dinah to Pittsburgh, to go live with her grandmother Dell, and then Lilly's moving on alone. Lilly hasn't asked Dinah to go with her, and the only reason she's driving Dinah at all is because Dell said there were papers about Matt that Lilly might have to sign; there might be personal items to go through.

Dinah would rather eat nails than go live with her grandmother. Both she and her father had a terrible relationship with Dell, but you'd never know it from the way Dell's talking now. She treats Dinah like her long-lost friend.

"I can't wait!" she cries over the phone to Dinah, her voice all runny with emotion. "Tell me what foods you like and I'll go buy them." She told Dinah she's already bought butter crackers and imported cheeses and sodas and Pennsylvania Dutch pretzels; she's already stayed up half the night baking a chocolate cake that smells so delicious that she can't help but swipe some of the frosting every time she passes it sitting on her kitchen table. She's arranged everything so Dinah can attend the local high school, so Dinah can feel at home. She's even repainted the spare room pink, which was Dinah's favorite color—but last year.

Nothing can wait now that Dell is no longer so sick. She's sixty-eight, and before this she had never missed so much as even one day of work. "And I won't again," she insists. She's at home now, out of the hospital nearly two whole weeks this Wednesday, with a bill of health so clean it ought to have a Good Housekeeping Seal pasted to it, and Dell says that all she can think about is that for a while she was so ill, she didn't even know the funeral had happened, something that, depending on the time of day and her own fragility, she will consider either a blessing or a curse all her life.

Driving had been Lilly's idea. The rhythm of the road—the humming white lines, the wink of the lights—all soothe her, get her all hypnotized so everything inside of her seems somehow cauterized. Sometimes injuries heal that way, helped with a little fire. And sealed off, you don't really feel much. You can pretend that the heart doesn't bleed, that it doesn't break—oh no, it merely bends, as supple as a sapling.

Dinah's amazed how much Lilly seems to love her car, the one thing she's paying any sort of attention to. She never stops touching it. It's not even that nice a car, to Dinah's mind, just some old heap with a chipping blue paint job and torn vinyl upholstery. There's an old Saint Christopher medal hanging from the rearview mirror, although Lilly is Jewish, and anyway, everyone knows Saint Christopher's sainthood was recently discredited. He's the protector of nothing—you might as well hang up a picture of your cat.

"Why do you have this?" she asks Lilly.

Lilly rubs her thumb across the medal thoughtfully. "He has a kind face," she decides.

Lilly must be seeing something Dinah's not. Lilly readjusts the medal. She smoothes the ripping seats; she tissues clean all the spots on the windows. She always wants the car within her sight. It astounds Dinah that she thinks nothing of sleeping in it. The first night they had left, they hadn't even been on the road two hours before Lilly pulled off the road to take a quick nap. The sky was black ink, the side road was almost deserted. "Just an hour," she said, and then she burrowed along the front seat, while Dinah sat up in the back, hearing werewolves and vampires in the thickening night and wondering how much force it might take a maniac's crunched-up fist to crash through one of the closed car windows.

New York to Pittsburgh should only take nine hours tops, especially with the way Lilly's speeding, but they've already been driving a day and a half and they still aren't there. They keep losing time because Lilly has to stop so often. Her head sways and droops, and then she pulls over and naps, and there goes another hour. And they lose time, too, because of Dinah.

Dinah readjusts her legs. She tilts back her head and finishes the soda and then realizes with a start that she has to pee again. She looks at Lilly's face through the rearview mirror.

"I think I need to stop," Dinah says. Lilly's eyes in the rearview mirror hood over.

"We just stopped a half hour ago."

"I can't help it."

"Maybe you shouldn't drink so much soda."

"I wouldn't need to if it wasn't so hot."

Lilly sighs. She swerves in the exit lane and heads toward the rest stop. She parks the car.

Some rest stops are cleaner than others. This one has four stalls in the ladies' room, and three are flooded, carpeted with sopping brown paper towels. Dinah is disgusted and hot and sweaty, and she'd leave if she didn't have to pee so badly. Instead she grabs more paper towels and layers them on the floor, then clumsily makes her way to the only stall that works.

On her way out, she's thirsty again. She hesitates only for a second before she puts her quarters into the machine for a can of berry soda. She finishes it in long breathless gulps, then she buys another can and hides it under her shirt.

Lilly is almost sleeping when Dinah gets back in the car, the soda frosty against her bare stomach. Two minutes more and Lilly probably would have been out for another hour. "Hey," Dinah says, and slams her door. Lilly yawns and blinks and jerks the car into motion.

They're not on the road for more than ten minutes when Dinah's thirst is so great, she doesn't care how angry Lilly's going to be that she got more soda. She pops open the top. Lilly's eyes, through the rearview, snap at the sound. Dinah's hand freezes. She waits.

"Can I have a sip of that?" Lilly finally says, and Dinah

takes one long gulp of soda and then hands her the can. They pass the soda back and forth, and it's gone quickly.

Lilly pushes back her hair. The car is making a funny sound. The brakes grind so often, it begins to worry her, and she pulls off the Pennsylvania Turnpike into a service station. A boy, almost as young as Dinah, dressed in greasy white overalls, lumbers over to the car and glances at it with disinterest.

"The brakes are sticking, and it's making a terrible sound," Lilly says. Her hair is matted. Her shirt is pasted to her back with sweat.

"Ask him to fix the air-conditioning," Dinah says. The boy looks at Lilly, who is plucking her shirt from her body. Lilly looks at Dinah for a moment, and then Lilly nods at the mechanic. "Check that out, too," she says finally.

He yawns. "I'll take a look," he says. "Could be something's worn out. You want to wait? There's a diner." He points next to the service station. "The Busy Bee," the sign says. Next to it is a small gift shop.

Lilly looks around. "Maybe I'll get something to eat. You want something?"

Dinah shakes her head. "I'll be in the gift shop." She hopes Lilly orders four courses. She hopes the auto mechanic looks at every gear and piston and wire before he finds anything wrong. She knows the longer Lilly takes, the longer it'll take before they get to Dell's, and the more time Dinah will have to think about what it is she's going to do, which is anything but live with Dell.

Any plans Lilly's made, she's keeping to herself, and when Dinah asks, Lilly simply looks distracted and changes the subject.

Dinah spends a good hour just standing around in the gift shop, trying to think what to do. She picks up the porcelain dogs with tiny gold chains around their necks. She studies the T-shirts with snappy sayings printed on them, and then, gradually, she's reduced to reading all the greeting cards.

Nothing is giving Dinah any ideas. It's so hot she can't think straight. She is suddenly so panicky, she's ready to scream.

Dinah moves to the map rack and scans. There's Ohio, where she lived with Matt up until a month ago. It makes her queasy just to look at it. Maine. Texas. And then she spots one of New York City, and she looks around casually, heart thundering, and then quickly stuffs it into her bag.

It's so simple that she's astonished she didn't think of it before. She doesn't have to go forward. She can go back, to New York, and be gone before Lilly knows it. She'll get a room at the Y, and then, immediately, she'll get a job. She figures she can lie about her age and get a waitressing job. They like them young and pretty in New York City, she bets, and at least she's young. She can live on less than anybody. She doesn't need much. She'll work her fingers to the bone and eat peanut butter from the jar for dinner. She can wash her clothes out in the sink. If she has to live in a hovel, then she'll do it. She'll tide herself over until she turns eighteen, and then she'll see, then she'll figure something out. She'll be able to have her life, busy, forgetful, so ordered that there's no room for thought—a new life as free as she can get it.

Leaving the city is a dangerous thing to do, Dinah decides. If she and her father had stayed in the city that muggy Sunday when they were visiting Lilly, if they had gone to a SoHo flea market the way Dinah had begged and begged, if they hadn't gone upstate where Lilly promised it was cooler, none of what had happened would have happened. Dinah wouldn't have had to go swimming. She wouldn't have made her father come in the water with her. You're rewriting the script, Dinah imagines Lilly responding. You're trying to change the ending. Well, who wouldn't? That's what Dinah would say back.

The whole last month she was at Lilly's, Dinah didn't eat, she didn't sleep, she couldn't concentrate on a book or TV, and she didn't want to go out of her room.

Now she has a plan. She can get a cab to a train at one

of the rest stops. Or maybe she can hitch. She's so excited that she can hardly stand it. She goes outside, toward the back lot, where it's empty, and stands there reading the map as if all those names were entrées on a menu, and she's ravenous.

"Dinah!" she hears, and abruptly she stuffs the map in her purse and comes around back front, where Lilly is now arguing with the mechanic. "How can it be that expensive?" she says, but she hands him a credit card and then looks over at Dinah in disgust. "The pads and shoes had to be replaced," she says, but Dinah hasn't a clue what she's talking about. "I couldn't afford the air-conditioning, too." Dinah immediately feels ten degrees hotter. She gives Lilly a disgusted look. "The car just has to run," Lilly says defensively.

They drive back onto the turnpike, the car running clean and silent, and when it's almost dark again Lilly decides they should stop for the night. "We lost so much time, we might as well lose some more. Maybe with a whole night's sleep, I won't need to nap. You should get some sleep, too." Lilly tells Dinah, but Dinah's wired. "You tired?"

"No," says Dinah, but Lilly's not listening.

Almost as soon as they enter the hotel room, Lilly flops fully clothed on the twin bed closest to her. She doesn't even bother to pull back the covers, which are stiff bumblebee plaid and smell faintly of all the other lives they've held, lives that, like theirs, are just passing through. "Dinah Was Here," Dinah scribbles on the inside closet wall. She turns to see if Lilly's seen this bit of petty vandalism, but Lilly's instantly asleep, her breathing evened out, her face untensed. She suddenly says something, and Dinah stops. Lilly, deep asleep, makes indecipherable sounds. "Ruffl. Whirr. Slasz." She sleeps with her mouth open. You'll catch flies, Matt used to say. Lilly once told Dinah she could read the future, that she knew things. Dinah crouches right down next to Lilly, but Lilly now is mute. Any secrets she has, she's keeping to herself.

Dinah tiptoes around the hotel room, delaying Lilly's reluctant swim back up to consciousness as best she can. She sits and reads the hotel room service menu so many times, she's got it memorized. Peach cobbler with butter brickle ice cream. Roast beef on rye. Cobb salad. Nothing sounds good to her, especially the things that used to, like the fresh raspberries in cream. She stares into a horizon of cars in the parking lot and watches a soundless, boring TV. She sits in the hotel room while Lilly sleeps and tries to remember what she saw of New York City with Matt and Lilly. Important and cool streets. Macdougal. St. Marks Place. Bleecker. She doesn't care that Lilly once told her that those were the most touristy places in the whole city. She laughed when Dinah insisted on reverently touching the Bleecker Street sign. Dinah likes thinking of herself as a native New Yorker. She knows the score. She's hard and tough and fast, bouncing back from defeat with a certain style everyone would admire. "You live in New York!" her friends in Ohio will say. They'll envy her, tacking up the postcards she sends them on their bulletin boards, and Dinah will be generous and send them lots. Maybe she'll be a writer, a New York thing to be. She'll write about romance and flight, and even if she falls in love with someone, she'll still dedicate every book to her father.

Dinah knows to pronounce "Houston" as if it rhymed with "cow," she knows how to order coffee regular, how to walk like she owns the streets. She'll grow out her horrible ragtag hair, wear earrings so long that it'll be a wonder her lobes aren't pulled out of shape, and all of her wardrobe will be black, even her underwear. No one would suspect she was from Ohio, a place they probably made fun of routinely. And lucky for her, New York City streets are easy. The subways are filled with maps. Everywhere there's direction, and all you have to do is find it and then follow it. She'll keep track of every dime, of every pair of woolen winter gloves. She'll keep a tight hold on her money, her wallet, and herself. She'll never lose anything or anyone else again.

Lilly mumbles in her sleep, and Dinah suddenly realizes

that it's nearly morning. Quickly she gets up. But at the exact moment when Dinah's hand reaches the door, poised for flight, Lilly stands unsteadily. Lilly looks at Dinah in surprise, as if she doesn't know why Dinah is still there with her. "Dinah," she says, but she doesn't finish the sentence.

"That's my name," Dinah says.

"Ready to rock and roll?" Lilly says finally.

"I have to pee first," Dinah says, and Lilly's mouth tenses.

No one should be able to tell Dinah what to do now. No one should be able to tell her how to live her life, how to try to continue. Certainly not someone who doesn't seem to be doing such a hot job herself, someone who's even admitted as much. She sneaks a peek at Lilly, who brushes back a long ribbon of hair from her flushed cheek. All Dinah has to do now is wait for another chance. She could wait for Lilly to need to sleep again, but now she's really anxious.

Pittsburgh looms closer and closer. Already she's spotted green exit signs. Her head feels stitched up, and it seems as though things are contracting about her, closing up her possibilities. She'd better do something and fast.

They pass one, then two exit signs. Pittsburgh, one says. Ninety miles. Dinah sits up abruptly.

"I need to stop."

Lilly flashes her a look, but she begins to dart toward the exit lane, her head bent, her face pale and unreadable, a face Dinah's been trying to figure out since the day she first saw it.

Well, Lilly doesn't even look much like herself now, either. It's as if a layer has been peeled from her. You wouldn't even notice her on the street if you saw her. You'd walk right by. Lilly's hair is beautiful, but she hasn't combed it in two days, and it's tangled and dark with dirt. She's in the same black T-shirt and jeans she wore in New York, the same white Keds, torn at the toes. Dinah's brought five black tank tops from the Gap with her, and she wears a clean one every day with her cutoffs. She shores back what hair she has with a length of black leather. If her blue high-tops make her feet feel sweaty and smashed, she just takes them off.

Lilly swerves around a Ford. "Whoops," she says.

"Will you fucking learn to drive!" screams a voice. Lilly ignores it. She pulls into the bright rest stop, slowing only when she has to, and as soon as she does, she sees it's packed with cars, that the only space left is a standing one, right in front of the restaurant. "Holiday's," the neon sign says.

With the car stopped, the heavy moist air hangs on them like wet wash. Dinah gets out, stretching her body like elastic. But once on the sidewalk, she's suddenly more scared than she ever counted on being. Where is her courage? Her purpose or her plan? She tells herself that she can't be timid all her life, especially if she plans to live in New York City. Now Dinah, she tells herself, suddenly yearning for her father to be there saying it for her. That thought hurts, so she rallies. She has to do this. There's no alternative. The house in Ohio is already up for sale. Her father's gone. Lilly's going. Dell wants someone she doesn't even know.

This is her future staring her right in the face, and all she has to do is grab it. She has all of fifty dollars to her name right now, stuffed inside the back pocket of her cutoffs. There's more, probably, but that means she'll have to wait for the lawyers, and anyway, she's still considered a minor. Now that the reality of her decision is setting in, the questions start. How easy is it to find a job or an apartment? There's no time even to find out about buses or trains or airports; she's going to have to hitch, to trust someone other than herself, and suddenly she wonders how easy it is to ruin a life, even one that as far as she can see might be already ruined anyway.

She looks tentatively at Lilly. Lilly never hitches, though she told Dinah she had in the seventies up until the time the driver pulled a penknife and offered to cut her nipples off for her. Dinah thinks of this and suddenly promises herself she'll check out the cars she gets into. She'll make sure the seats are intact and that the doors all have working handles—or better yet, she'll accept rides only from slight-bodied women. "Be right back," she says.

She walks in the restaurant and out the side door. Families are wandering past. Dinah sees a young woman in startlingly white shorts and a T-shirt getting into a car, and tentatively Dinah approaches, but when the woman sees her coming toward the car, something moves in her face and she smartly snaps down the locks. She guns her engine, frowning at the wheel, the windshield, at anything but Dinah, whom she means the expression for. Behind Dinah, a man is hoisting himself into his truck. He looks young and strong, and Dinah thinks maybe he's funny, too. Dinah starts to smile, and his dark eyes are suddenly hooded. His body snaps up. "You looking for me?" He laughs, and Dinah's stomach pinches in fright at the way he's studying her, leisurely grazing, eating her up alive. She starts back into the restaurant, trying to look casual, in complete control.

"Hey, hey, where're you going? You need a lift?" He laughs. He's wearing a T-shirt the color of a black eye. His jeans pull across his hips, so tightly that Dinah can see an outline of keys in one of the pockets. He hooks his thumbs into his belt loops, waiting, and when he takes a step toward her, she bolts like a gazelle into the chilly restaurant again. She feels like she's being followed, like his eyes are pasted on her back. She looks behind her, through the glass of the automatic door. Her gaze spins from car to car. Doors slam and pop open, voices call and connect, but she can't see an opening for herself, she can't see any sort of lead. Defeated, panicky, she goes out the front door, and there is Lilly, half sleeping, propped up against the steering wheel, her hair lazy about her shoulders. The car hums. Lilly spots her and twists to open up the back door for her. She settles back onto the front seat, waiting impassively, one hand playing with the worthless Saint Christopher medal. Sweat prickles along Dinah's spine; she can't bear being inside her own skin right now. The thought of getting trapped into that backseat makes her crazy.

"What?" Lilly says. "Don't you feel good?"

"I love eight-thousand-degree weather," Dinah says.

"We're almost there," Lilly says. "You won't be this hot much longer." Dinah stares out her window. Lilly opens her door and gets out.

"I'll run in and get a better map," she says. "Be out in two seconds, then we can go. The front's really cooler if you want to sit there."

"Fine," Dinah says. Nothing matters to Dinah anymore, and at least she can listen to the radio. She gets in, resting her head on the steering wheel. The seat's positioned perfectly for her. Her toes tap against the gas pedal, and then suddenly Dinah knows what she'll do. Her heart's beating so hard and fast and free again that she can't imagine Lilly can't hear it.

Dinah reaches over the seat to click on the radio. She needs something to drown out her fear, which has become audible, grown so loud that she's surprised the whole parking lot hasn't turned around to see her. There's a static hiss, and then there's a voice, soft and insinuating, wanting to let the listeners in on a secret about bad breath. "Brush it, floss it, Breathalyze it!" the voice sings.

"I'll turn it off when you get back," she assures Lilly, who looks as if all this sudden sound hurts her. Dinah's head is pounding. From the corner of her eye she thinks she sees the man who offered her a ride, and she contemplates snapping the door shut and turning up the windows, but it's so hot.

The radio music hums in Lilly's head. Despite herself, she's thinking about that mouthwash jingle. Breathalyze it, Lilly thinks. She hears the melody, and she can already tell she'll be hearing it miles down the road.

It feels funny to get out of the car. Lilly hasn't wanted to stop, hasn't wanted to think about anything but the pull and flavor of the road, and now suddenly she realizes how badly she has to pee, how badly she wants coffee. Now here's this girl, almost a stranger, making her notice herself, and she hates it, she's angry at Dinah for it. She wishes time would stop. She used to be in such a hurry; she couldn't wait to wake up. But why not, when the first thing she saw when she opened her eyes was Matt. He hated New York, but when he was there he still managed to be full of New York plans, and all of them included her—he wanted to explore NoHo and the Lower East Side, he wanted to go to Coney Island that very minute. "Every moment matters," he told her, but of course he meant only that he had just the weekend, then he had to fly home to Dinah—until that one last weekend when he had brought Dinah up with him.

The automatic door slides open as soon as Lilly moves toward it. Inside is a blast of air so icy, Lilly feels flash frozen. She looks around and approaches an older-looking man who's carefully needlepointing two yellow cats on a white background, the whiskers in bright red. He grins at her. He's wearing a blue bowling shirt that says "Mabel" on the pocket, and he's so openly friendly that it startles Lilly, who's used to service without any smile. Behind him he's got a red, framed picture of a woman in a blue dress, and it doesn't take Lilly long to see that the woman has his features. She thinks about that, and she thinks how funny it is that Dinah doesn't look like Matt at all. Dinah carries his genes, but there's no part of her that can make Lilly look in recognition and say, Ah, yes, there you are. Is that good or bad? she wonders. Does it make things more or less painful? She doesn't know; she knows only that she wants to get Dinah—who is usually sulky and rude to her—to Dell's so she doesn't have to think about that question at all anymore, so it won't have to torment her. She suddenly misses Matt so much, she's practically doubled over with bottomless longing. She's sickened by the depth of her need.

"Now, what can I do for you?" he says, and Lilly wishes for a moment that she could tell him. She wonders what he'd do, but instead she points to the maps. "Pittsburgh," she says. "And coffee."

He gives her the map. "Nice city," he says. "Not what you'd think at all. Surprisingly green and pretty."

She looks outside, sees Dinah resting her chin sullenly against the vinyl front seat, and then she turns to pay the man, who's followed her gaze to the car. "Your daughter?" he says, nodding. "Pretty girl." He points to the photo behind him. "My girl Adelle."

"She's not my daughter," Lilly said slowly.

"No?" he says, and then Lilly turns around to see her car, the battered blue sedan she's had in New York for nearly ten years without a single break-in, full speeding out toward the open road, Dinah braced tightly over the wheel.

Her hand never catches the paper cup of coffee he's stretching out toward her. She's dimly aware of it toppling, splashing forward, milky tan staining across, but she's running, out past the electric door into the flat glare of the heat. She's almost there, dodging cars trying to park, swerving around people lazily making their way to lunch. She shoves past a man in a black T-shirt. Even from this distance Lilly can see how Dinah's shaking, how she's gripping the wheel so tightly that her fingers are white. Thank God for the bottleneck at the exit, or Dinah would be on the highway already.

Lilly's a runner, ten miles a day in Central Park, even after that terrible incident with the jogger, when her mother called her every day to make sure she was alive. Lilly thought nothing could ever hurt her, nothing could happen, and ha, look how wrong she had been. Now, she sprints, jamming herself right in front of the car. The car smashes to a stop, and Lilly thuds against it, hard. Pain shoots up along her leg. Her right hip wrenches. Her shoulder, her side, are burning up, and her breath stitches up tight. She grabs on to the car, partly for balance, partly to feel it's still there. She feels faint, but she walks over to Dinah and leans toward the open window and grabs her with so much force, Dinah's head snaps back. And for the first time since Dinah's been with her, Lilly starts to cry.

Dinah takes her foot off the gas. Her mouth trembles. Behind her a driver blasts his horn and edges around the car, rolling his eyes dramatically.

Lilly pants. Her head feels as if it's expanding. She has to touch the car, the hood, the rusting chrome trim. "What were you thinking!" she finally cries, her voice scraped raw. She swipes at her tears. It's so hot out, anything could happen. Maybe it's all a mirage, she thinks. It feels that way. Maybe if she wanders over to the pay phone by the Coke machine, something different will happen. She'll wait for the woman in the pale pink jumpsuit to get off the phone, and then she'll call Matt. Come and get me, she'll say. She'll carefully spell out the directions.

"Where were you going?" Lilly says finally.

"Anywhere," Dinah says, determined not to say "New York," not to give it away. She slowly gets out of her side of the car and stands for a moment out in the pulsing heat.

"Are you going to do that again?" Lilly asks.

"Why? It's nothing to you," Dinah says.

Lilly looks startled. "How can you say that?" she says.

She waits, breathing in Dinah's stormy silence, and then finally gets back into the car and starts it up. The motor coughs. Her thighs stick to the hot seat. Her own hands feel as if they couldn't grip anything more substantial than air. She rubs at her hip, which is already feeling better. Tonight, bruises will flower across her pale skin, marking her for weeks. In some strange city she'll look down at her bare legs and see a bruise yellowing toward pink, and she'll think of Dinah. She swipes at her nose. Dinah suddenly looks so young to her, exhausted, her face bleached of color, that Lilly's anger cools a little. She's only a girl.

"Come on," Lilly says wearily.

Suspiciously, Dinah opens the car door, getting into the back again the way she has since this trip started.

"Last time I checked, there was no law about riding in the front," Lilly says.

Dinah slumps against the door. "I like it back here," she says.

"Okay," Lilly says tiredly. "But I won't hold it against you if you change your mind."

Lilly pulls back onto the highway, nipping off the path of a red Toyota, which beeps at her energetically. "Here we go," she says.

She figures she's going to need to sleep again soon, deep and dreamless, a relief up until the moment she has to wake again, but she's worried now about Dinah—and about her car, which she's going to need. She'll have to hide the car keys and hope Dinah doesn't know word one about how to hotwire. She'll have to hope Dinah won't hitch. Soon, soon, she tells herself. It's like a lullaby. Soon. Soon, soon. But after soon, what comes next?

If she's lucky, they can make Pittsburgh in two more hours and Lilly can settle Dinah with Dell, then maybe Lilly can move on. Two hours isn't such a long time. Lilly has enough friends, and maybe she can go visit them; she has enough money, so maybe she can stay on the road for six months, maybe more, before she has to stand still again and figure what to do now.

It's so funny. Life had always been so planned out, so ordered. She used to predict the future. The dead spoke to her, talking, talking, talking in a vocabulary so rich it was dazzling, but the dead don't speak to her now. None of them—not even the one she wants so badly her heart is tearing in two.

She used to make good enough money talking with the dead, looking at the future. It was a precarious gift, though. Sometimes it worked and sometimes it didn't. When it did, she could look at a woman sipping tea at a fountain and suddenly tune her in, just as if the woman were no more complicated than a transistor radio. She'd take one look, she'd *feel* a future, and then she'd just know that by next year that woman would be living with her sweetheart in California, that in two years that woman would have a new job. She could look at a waiter and a message would filter in. His father, felled from a heart attack, wanting to be heard, wanting to reassure his son that everything was all right.

Sometimes Lilly told people the things she picked up, sometimes she didn't. It depended on the people. Lilly used to think that she could shape her own future, too, that the things she picked up like radar, the messages that sometimes came to her gave her some control, but now the future looms in front of her, mindless, like a huge lumbering adversary that's taking its sweet time before striking. She tunes in on herself and draws a blank.

This morning, when they were checking out of one of Lilly's rest stops, she had tried to read the desk clerk, a young woman in a fussy floral suit, but all she had picked up was the fizzy pop and hiss of static from the woman's black-and-white TV, a soap opera, a sound blatantly in the here and now. Everything's gone. Every door she ever had opened seems sealed shut. She's so unprepared. She doesn't have a clue what she's going to do.

Her friends are sure she'll want to come home, that she'll think of New York as a safe haven. Lilly doesn't know. Home. Slanted Manor. Two tiny rooms with wood floors so old, they inclined. Drop a pea and it would roll toward the door. Walls so thin that she heard the asthmatic sneezes of the cat next door. The first week she had moved in, a neighbor had slipped a note under her door: "Could you please not walk after 10:30 at night? Your footsteps disturb me." She had taken off her shoes; she had taken to wearing socks. Below her, a married couple warred continually over who shouldn't have married whom more. Across the street, as soon as she woke up, when she came home for lunch, and when she came home to sleep, for hours at a time, a young, thin man masturbated languidly in front of his window, only his face hidden by a partially lowered Venetian blind. Johnny Jerkoff. She got used to all of it. It became comforting, familiar, a story to make her friends laugh. Her first apartment in the city and she had loved it, but now she doesn't know how she feels about it or about anything. All of her senses seem to have gone dead.

Lilly slams into the rivery roar of the highway traffic, and for the first time in her life the feel of the road seems dangerously unfamiliar. Ground is giving way. It wouldn't surprise her if there were suddenly an earthquake, right in the middle of the Pennsylvania Turnpike. The car lists to the left. The sky tilts. She imagines the highway splitting open into a ragged seam, tumbling cars and people into the chasms. She imagines a tidal wave frilling up out of nowhere, crashing down, cars desperate and giddy, surfing across rolling eighty-foot walls of water. Anything could happen. Above them a jet plane speeds so fast, it splits the sky with a sonic boom. Dinah jumps in surprise. "Hold on," Lilly says, and then, lifting her chin, she punches on the gas.

chapter 1

Lilly had always loved cars. When she was a baby, small and colicky and growing up in a Detroit suburb, her parents swore the only thing that would comfort her crying was the sound and speed of a long drive. As soon as she heard the motor, the swell of her sobs would soften. Her breathing would even out, and after a few miles she'd finally sleep, deep and dreamless. "Like you were barely there," her father said in admiration.

Lilly got over the colic. She grew into a restless, dreamy child. At five she could read. At seven she was writing her own stories. And by eight she knew that her parents weren't happy. Her father, Bob, was pale and silent and wore glasses. He was an accountant, a fact he continually regretted. He was almost never home, and when he did arrive he was always laden with work and in no mood for conversation. "Let's go to a movie," said Nora, Lilly's mother. She was slender and lovely and kept the same long red hair that she swore had won her her Miss Detroit title in her twenties. Bob waved her away. He held up his briefcase. "I'll be lucky if I can join you ladies for breakfast," he told her.

"Party pooper," Nora said, stringing her arms loosely around Bob's neck, pulling him to her for a kiss. He shook her off. He ruffled Lilly's hair and carried his work into the den, which he was setting up as a minioffice.

"Off limits," he told Lilly when she tried to wander in. "Not now," he told her when she waved two badminton rackets toward him, wanting to play. Some Saturday mornings, when Lilly would wake up, she would see him sleeping on the couch in his office, a blanket tossed over him, hiding his face. Nora would be out on the porch, chain smoking angrily.

Nights when Bob called to say he was going to be late again, Nora roamed the house. She picked up and put down countless magazines. She flicked channels on the television, and once she went to find Lilly, who was avidly reading *Charlotte's Web* in her room. "Hey," Nora said brightly. "What do you say you and me make Toll-House cookies?" She waited, smiling expectantly. Lilly held her book tightly to her chest. The pages seemed to breathe against her.

"I've got butterscotch chips," Nora coaxed.

"Charlotte's going to have babies," Lilly said.

"Oh, babies," Nora said impatiently.

"I want to see what happens. The pig's in trouble."

Nora folded her arms. "Wouldn't you like some warm cookies to go with your book?"

Lilly hesitated. She pressed her nose against her book, darting a glance at the colored illustration of Charlotte in her sparkling web, and in that moment her mother unfolded her arms and turned from her.

"I give up," Nora said. "I might as well just buy myself a poodle."

Lilly kept reading. She was almost to the end, fighting sleep, when she heard her mother slamming around the house. The radio was turned up high. She heard Bob coming in and Nora's tight, angry voice, and then there was the silence, and that was the hardest of all. She put her book down and burrowed under a cocoon of covers. She whispered stories to herself about spiders. "Charlotte," she said, rocking herself, willing herself toward the distance of memory.

As she got older, her parents fought more and more, and it was harder to blot out their anger. Lilly crouched in her bed, burrowing under the covers, clapping her hands to her ears. She sang to herself, she whispered stories, but still she heard.

"You're never home!" Nora shouted. "I never see you!" Lilly leaped up from her bed.

"I want, I need, I want, I need," Bob said. "That's all I hear from you. I love you. Isn't that enough?"

Lilly raced barefoot out the back door, her parents' words trailing her, filtering out. "Failure . . ." "Never should have . . ." And always, always "money." In the distance she could hear the Bramstones' collie barking hysterically. The crickets rasped in the night.

Lilly walked over to the car, a turquoise-and-gray Plymouth that was always open, and climbed into the back. The leather smell intoxicated her. She curled against the seat. Lilly sighed and shut her eyes.

Bob jerked open the car. He slammed the door so hard that it reverberated, and then he turned and saw Lilly, blinking on the backseat, and his face softened for a minute.

"Hey, let's go inside," he said, half smiling.

Lilly saw the keys in his hands. "Don't go," she said.

"I'm just going for a drive. Just to cool off." He sighed. "Why don't you go inside. Your mother will be worried sick."

Lilly shook her head. Bob looked at the house. The lights were blazing on in every room.

"All right, then, come with me," he said.

He drove and drove until he was almost out of the state. Lilly didn't know where they were going or if they were ever coming back, and she was afraid to ask her father. He didn't speak to Lilly or turn on the radio, and she contented herself watching the other cars from her window, watching the back of his head or his eyes, narrowed in the rearview mirror, staring at the car beside them. It was a snappy red convertible. A young woman was sitting so close to the man driving, she could have been buckled into his seat belt. She knitted long pale fingers into his hair, and he laughed and kissed the side of her mouth, and Bob looked away abruptly.

He swerved the car toward a rest station. "I'll be just a minute," he said, and then he stopped. "Do you need to go?" he said, pointing to the bathrooms, and Lilly shook her head. She watched him walking, his gait heavy, over to the pay phones. Lilly sat up, watching his face as he talked. He kept washing one hand over his forehead, and when he got back in the car his shoulders were hunched.

"I thought I'd pick up ice cream," he said to Lilly. "What flavor do you want?"

"Peach," she said.

"Let's get strawberry," he said. "Your mother likes strawberries."

They came home, the ice cream still frosty, and Nora met them at the door, her robe tied about her hips, her red hair spread across her back. "Hey," Bob said, hesitating. "Don't you look pretty."

Nora tightened her robe. She frowned, and then she looked at Lilly, and something in her seemed to loosen. "Hey yourself," she said. "You'd both better come in. It's getting cold out." She looked at Lilly. "And you," she said. "You had me worried. Don't you do that again."

But the fights continued, and Lilly did do it again. The best times, she would wake up and the car would be already moving, her father would be driving. He'd drive for a few hours, neither one of them breaking their unspoken code of silence, and then he would come back and park in the drive. Before he was even out of the car, Nora was at the front porch. He bounded up the steps, and he and Nora would act as if nothing unusual had happened between the two of them, and Lilly didn't know why, but she felt comforted.

* * *

The Sunday Lilly turned twelve, Nora was fuming be-cause Bob had gone off the day before to play golf with clients when he had promised to take them on a long drive to see the fall foliage. She was scrubbing the kitchen, complaining bit-terly. "And you, too," she screamed at Lilly, who was reading, her little white transistor blaring David Cassidy. "Improve your mind, improve your chances!" she said.

"I'm *reading*," Lilly said, lifting her book.

Nora dashed a dish rag into a soapy bucket. "You can't read with that noise!" she snorted. "David Cassidy! Did he graduate? Did he go to college? He did terribly in school! He got horrible grades!"

"I give up!" Bob shouted, and dragged his plaid jacket from the closet. Lilly looked up from the book she was read-ing. *A High Wind in Jamaica*, the chapter where a young girl was living it up with pirates, far away from parents. She looked at her father expectantly.

"Come on if you're coming," he said, and stalked out.

She had been asleep on the front seat, and he had stopped short when a red VW had plowed into the wrong lane. Lilly had hit her head hard against the window, and for a moment the pain was so great that she didn't feel it at all. The air sprinkled into a dazzle of silver lights that circled mer-rily around her. She made a weak grab for them, and then her stomach squeezed and she threw up all over the front seat.

"Oh, God!" Bob said. He was almost crying. "Sweetie," he said. He put one hand on her lap, damp with vomit, and he drove like a crazy person to the hospital. He scooped her up and carried her into the emergency room.

They gave her a clean johnny to wear. She had X rays where a doctor made her move her head in four different posi-tions, and afterward he made her put her fingers together, and touch her right ear, and then he ruffled her rumpled hair. "You're right as rain," he told her. He let her change back into her soiled sweater, and he brought her out to Bob, who was pacing anxiously. "Her X rays were fine," he said. "She just banged the old noggin."

The car still smelled of vomit, but Bob pretended nothing was out of the ordinary. He pulled into a gas station and tried to clean it up a bit, but the smell stayed, like a stain. "Well, what do you care, right?" he said, though he was breathing through his mouth. "I'll get some Lestoil and it'll be something to laugh about later."

The whole way home, Bob talked. "You all right, honey?" he said. "You want ice cream, or a soda, anything at all, you just say so."

He walked with his arm around her into the house, where Nora screamed when she saw the vomit crusted over Lilly. "Everything is under control," Bob said.

But that evening Lilly had a terrible headache. Nora gave her chips of ice wrapped in a blue washcloth for her head. She gave her two of her own carefully hoarded stash of Valium, and when none of that worked, she gave Lilly a small tumbler of rum.

"The way you drive!" Nora shouted at Bob.

"Keep your voice down," said Bob. "Keep everything low." His hands descended an imaginary curtain.

Lilly was feverish. Her face held a faint patina of sweat. In the other room she heard Nora shouting into the phone, badgering questions at a doctor. Lilly pressed her fingers deep into her temples. She pressed her forehead along the wall and pushed, trying to dislodge the pain. Nora came back into the room. "He won't come, he says to call tomorrow," she whispered to Bob.

"He can call my ass," Bob whispered back.

Nora rubbed her back. Lilly clamped her eyes shut, and suddenly she heard a voice, a man calling to her as if from a distance. She strained, but the words were muddy.

"Baby doll," Lilly said, and Nora stiffened.

"She's delirious," Nora told Bob.

"What's she saying?"

Lilly heard the voice again. "He went to sea," Lilly said. "Baby doll."

"Migraine, I'll bet. Audio disturbances," Bob said. "Visual, too. Like shots of light, am I right?"

Lilly squinted. "It hurts," she said.

"Into bed," Nora said. She raised her daughter up and settled her under the covers. "You sleep," she said.

When Bob found Nora, she was leaning along the living room wall, staring out at the blank street, and she looked so sad and lost that he walked over to her and touched her hair.

"My father used to call me baby doll," Nora said. "When he was alive."

"He did? You never told me that."

Nora turned slowly and faced him. "I never told anyone," she said.

Lilly's headaches went away, but the voices didn't. She'd be walking into class and look up at the teacher expectantly, and suddenly she'd hear a woman's voice, the sound garbled, as if it were under water. She clapped her hands to her head so many times that Mrs. Moregenstern, her teacher, sent her to the school nurse to have her hearing tested.

One day, in biology, while the teacher was droning on about cytoplasmic streaming, an image suddenly flashed into Lilly's mind, so real and vivid, she jolted upright, as if shocked. She saw her uncle Ted mowing the lawn, but the blades of grass were flying out from the mower and not in. He shut off the mower and headed toward the house. "Nap time," he said.

She thought it was funny. She told Bob that morning, and nobody thought anything of it until two days later, when they got a phone call that Ted had died. "Was he mowing the lawn?" Lilly asked, terrified.

Bob studied her. "He was eating dinner, lambie. He choked." Then he turned away.

Lilly was sure there was something dreadfully wrong with her. Leukemia. A brain tumor. No one normal heard the dead speak. Her English class had already had to read *Death Be Not Proud*, and most of the girls had cried. Her best friend, Irene, had gone to her family doctor and begged him to tell her the truth about her own leukemia, convinced that he was trying to be gentle when he shooed her away and told her not to waste his time with such nonsense. Lilly now remembered the cold certainty of the book's ending. She remembered how she had loved it, how she had read the whole book twice through and clasped it against her own brave, beating heart. Things were wonderfully sad and moving when they weren't happening to you.

She couldn't tell anybody what was happening to her. She didn't want anyone to know. She took three buses to the local medical library and dragged down a foot-high book on the brain, flopping it onto a long wood table. "Pretty heavy reading," a man said to her, grinning. He was hunched over a book himself.

"It's for a report," Lilly said.

"Do you want help?"

Lilly stared down at a picture. A cross section of the brain. Her stomach pulsed. "No," she said. "It's okay."

"Okay, well, all you got to do is ask," he said cheerfully. He returned to his books.

Lilly read about three different kinds of tumors and one degenerative disease before she closed the book, disheartened. Anything could be happening inside of her, taking more concrete shape and substance. Schizophrenia. Aneurism. There was no control, but she decided to fight for it anyway.

At night she stayed up as late as she could, terrified disaster might take over while she slept, before she had a chance to call for help. She turned on all the lights in her room and forced herself to read. Nora, walking by, sighed but moved on. When Lilly grew tired, she bundled up under the covers, poking out her nose to breathe. And when she woke in the morning, it was always a surprise.

She watched herself. She didn't tell her parents that she heard voices, but she knew they were watching her. Her father never forgave himself for the accident. He bought a huge prominent Saint Christopher medal. "Uh, the last time I looked, we were Jewish," Nora said, but Bob still hung the medal on the rearview mirror. Even so, he wouldn't take Lilly driving with him anymore, and in truth, the pleasure had gone out of the drives altogether.

"But I want to go," Lilly insisted. "You fall off a horse, you get back on. And there's Saint Christopher—"

"Oh, please," Nora said. "He should have got Saint Jude, the patron saint of hopeless causes. That's *his* protector."

Bob shook his head. "We'll see," he told her, which of course had always been a safe way to say no. He studied Lilly at night. When he saw her staring into space, he shook her wildly.

"Leave her alone, for heaven's sake," Nora said.

Lilly sometimes felt as if the messages she received were interrupting her own life. Now we pause for a word from— from whom? Nine times out of ten she didn't know. And why did they pick on her? She was barely in junior high. She had no interesting kinds of power, and she still had to answer to just about everybody, but the voices came, clamoring to be heard. And the worst of it was, they never said one thing about her. She certainly could have used help. It would have made her feel better knowing that maybe now she wasn't popular, but in four years her phone wouldn't stop ringing. But the voices never showed her her future. They sidestepped her. They gave their information for other people. Always for others.

She was in third period French class with Mr. Carion. He was French and so young and handsome, half the girls in Lilly's class scratched his name across their notebooks. He was usually teasing and funny, but two of the girls, Alice Moroz and Jean Matur, had irritated him with their whispering and giggling.

"What?" he said. "No secrets in my class."

Alice flipped back her long, lank hair and snickered. *"Voulez-vous couchez avec moi?"* she said. Jean smothered her laughter behind her fingers.

"What is wrong with you people, you are so immature?" Mr. Carion said, flushing. And then Lilly looked at him, and a voice parted her thoughts, strong and female and insistent. *"Il épouse Marie,"* the voice said, and suddenly Lilly knew Mr. Carion had lost his mother two years ago, and she knew his mother had called him Jules.

The bell sang out, and kids tumbled out from class. Jules, Lilly thought, dazed. She braced her hands against her desk. She rubbed at her temples.

"Okay, Lilly?" Mr. Carion said.

"Is your first name Jules?" Lilly said, and he started. He stepped back from her.

"No one calls me that anymore," he said quietly.

"Are you getting married?" she said, and he frowned at her.

"Now, who told you a thing like that, a confirmed bachelor like me?"

She shrugged. But two months later he ran off with the gym teacher, a tall, elegant blonde whom everyone hated because she was so strict, a woman whose name was Marie.

Nora knew something was wrong. Lilly often came home as white as a piece of paper. At night sometimes she heard her daughter moving in her bedroom. You didn't have to be blind to see that Lilly wasn't sleeping, to hear her in the kitchen or see the light under her bedroom door. When she woke up she had faint, smudgy circles under her eyes.

"What's wrong?" Nora demanded, but Lilly just stirred her oatmeal and lowered her sleepy black eyes. "Okay," Nora said. "You don't want to tell me, that's fine. But tell someone else, would you?"

Nora packed her up and took her to an expensive child psychologist, who looked narrowly at Nora. "Why would you ever want to tamp such a wonderful imagination?" he said to Nora. "It's just puberty, that's all. And everyone grows out of it."

"So you'll grow out of it," Nora told Lilly on the ride home. "Whatever it is," she said meaningfully. "Whatever you can't tell your own mother."

Lilly bunched against the window, frowning.

"Are you listening to me?"

Lilly looked up. "I'm listening," she said, but she thought that that might be the trouble.

The summer Lilly turned fourteen, some of her friends began to date. Irene cut her hair into a shag and began wearing lipstick and gold hoop earrings. She was out more and more when Lilly called, and once when Lilly was exasperated and just showed up at Irene's house, it was to find Irene lolling on the porch with Dan Folez, who sat behind Lilly in French class and who was so stupid, Lilly had to feed him whispered answers when Mr. Carion called on him.

"Hi, Lilly," Irene said. "Just passing by?"

Dan saluted Lilly. Neither one of them made room on the porch for Lilly or made a move toward her, and Lilly just kept on walking. All that night she waited for a call from Irene, an apology or something, but none came.

Lilly was home more and more. She hung around, listless. "Everyone dates," she told her mother.

"It's ridiculous," Nora told her. "You're not dating until you're sixteen and that's final." Lilly didn't bother to tell her that not only hadn't anyone showed the slightest interest in her, but two boys in her math class had called her Stick, and it wasn't a compliment.

"And when you do date, you be careful," Nora continued. "The Bronstein women are not known to choose wisely," she warned.

"I'm not you," Lilly said.

Nora laughed. "Ha," she said. "Let's hope not, but darling, your future's in your genes, and your genes are half Bronstein."

That summer, too, Bob lost out on the vice presidency to a younger man, and Whitley Latozzo moved in next door. Whitley was young and thin, with unruly black hair that he was always taming back with his hands. He lived alone. He didn't move in much furniture, and already he had started to dig up a large rectangle of dirt in his backyard. "Oh, Lord," said Nora, inspecting Whitley. "What have we got here?"

Whitley was a lawyer who hated lawyering, who had schemes of something better. "I want to open a restaurant," he told Bob. "Start it small, just serve lots of fresh, simple things, maybe some of them I grow myself." He looked at Bob, mopping pinpricks of sweat from his face. "You know, you've got the same good soil I've got. You ought to start planting, too." He grinned. "Maybe come in the restaurant business with me." "Maybe," said Bob, and then Whitley told Bob to get in the car, that he was going to pick up some gardening stuff and he would be more than happy to get Bob started.

Nora and Lilly watched both men drive off in Bob's station wagon and come back with gardening gloves, spades, pruning shears, and seed. It took them two whole weekends to finish digging up rectangles of dirt in the back. Another two weekends to argue what seeds to plant, always with an eye to the restaurant they fantasized over. They argued how to plant the seeds, a task they did with such delicacy that Nora laughed at them.

Whitley loved to tell stories, and Lilly's family was a good audience. He talked about the time he tried to be an actor, and the time he hitchhiked cross-country and got derailed in Ohio. He didn't stop telling stories until after midnight, and long after Lilly's bedtime, and when he left, Nora stretched.

"He's nice, isn't he?" she said.

Every weekend he and Bob gardened. He would amble over to the house, and while waiting for Bob to get out of the shower, he'd have his coffee with Nora.

"I want to help," Lilly said, fussing with her cereal.

"Don't you go encouraging either one of them," Nora said, but she smiled at Whitley.

They would be at it all day, and at dinnertime Nora knew to make dinner for four. "Hey, guys!" she called. "I have dinner for the both of you, so get in here!" They tromped in, taking off their muddy shoes in the hallway, sitting at the table, grinning like boys. Whitley was loud and funny at dinner. He toasted everyone with the ginger ale Nora poured into their glasses. He complimented Nora on everything, even the way she had mashed the potatoes, and he asked so many questions, he made Nora breathless. "I'll help with the dishes," he said.

When Bob went to shower, Lilly sat in the kitchen, listening to Whitley sing sailing songs as he washed. "Singing makes the work fly," he said to Nora.

"Oh, no, I can't sing," she said.

He held up a soapy dish over the floor. "Uh-oh, my grip feels slip-per-y." He grinned, and Nora began to sing, tentatively at first and then in such full throat that Lilly was amazed.

"I didn't know you could sing," Lilly said to Nora after Whitley had gone home, some apple pie wrapped in tinfoil in his hand.

Nora smiled to herself. "Oh, I can sing."

As Whitley began coming to dinner more and more, Nora began to change. She cut her hair in a shag like Irene's. She stood out in Pucci-print shorts that she had gotten on sale at Shady Lady and a sleeveless tank of Lilly's that she prided herself on fitting into. She wore platform shoes. Lilly was embarrassed. Her mother hung Japanese lanterns along the porch to give the men light, a thing that made all the neighbors talk. Her mother wore the shortest skirts and the reddest lipstick, and sometimes she sang Neil Diamond, belting out "Song Sung Blue," even though it was no longer a hit. What did she care? She sang as she hung up the wash on the line in the backyard. She swayed her hips and kept time with a jab of a clothespin, and watching her, Lilly wanted to die with shame.

Both men grew squash, cucumbers, zucchini, and radishes, but only Bob grew raspberries, bushes he was so proud and careful of that he would slap Lilly if he saw her sneaking near them. As far as he was concerned, her mouth was always suspiciously red.

Woodchucks ambled down from the back woods and squatted in the center of the garden, impervious to Bob's shooing. They had moles with no eyes that Lilly found fascinating. "But how can they know where they are?" she asked Bob.

"They just know," he said.

They had rabbits Lilly wanted to keep as pets and one raccoon that tipped over the garbage a few times, and then Bob bought a cat that did nothing but lie lazily in the sun.

Nora stood in the garden wearily. She was tired of zucchini, tired of raspberry jam. "Whit," she said. "Tell Bob to give it up, would you?"

Bob ignored her and went on filling jars with kerosene to catch and drown the Japanese beetles. Whitley tugged at Nora's hand. He made her crouch down beside him. "Listen," he said, and lowered his head to the grass. "You can hear things grow if you listen hard enough."

Nora laughed and slapped his hand from her. Lilly, though, bent down and listened to the ground. "What things do you hear?" she said, wanting to compare notes, but Whitley was looking at Nora.

Lilly got up and approached her father. He handed her a

jam jar full of oily kerosene. The smell would stay on her clothes for days. "Here, go get some Japanese beetles," he told her.

It was her favorite job. She carried the jar from bush to bush, shaking the hard shiny insects into the kerosene. There were millions of them. She never told her father, but she liked them, she liked the iridescent colors. They floated in the kerosene like a million glimmering buttons. They never fought, which amazed her. Sometimes she found herself holding her breath. She waited until she saw Bob digging in the radishes, and then she went to the front of the house, to the vacant lot that was alive with grasshoppers, and there, on the pavement, she splashed the kerosene down. Hundreds of shiny bugs fell to the ground like coins. She waited, and then, gradually, there was a sudden buzz, and all those bits of light and life rose up again, humming back into the sky, resurrected. She didn't know what it was, but suddenly she was freezing in that July heat. The air felt different. Rough against her skin. And the sky, dense with bright beetles, suddenly thickened and grew dark. She thought of her father—she heard a voice—and suddenly she knew something terrible was going to happen. She turned and ran back to the backyard, and there was Bob, lying in the garden, the hose splashing water above him in one long arc, a woodchuck already starting to climb lazily back down toward him.

She shouted for Nora, who came out of Whitley's next door, Whitley beside her, her face flushed. Nora ran out into the middle of the garden and spooned her body around Bob's with a wail.

"Call an ambulance!" Whitley called. He pushed her out of the way, lowering his head, the way he read the ground sometimes, and then he lifted up. "His heart is still beating," he said.

Bob's heart continued to beat. He lived. And no matter what Nora or the doctors or Bob himself said, Lilly was convinced that she had saved him, that if she hadn't felt a chilly warning that something was wrong, it might have been too late. And suddenly she felt she knew why she heard the voices. Suddenly there was a reason and purpose to it. And she began to pay attention.

"That's my girl," Bob said. He went out and bought small hand weights he exercised with every morning.

"You don't have to do that," Lilly told him authoritatively. "This won't happen again."

"Oh, it won't, won't it?" he said, struggling with the weights, lifting them high over his head. He puffed and lowered his beefy arms. "Glad you think so."

"I know so," Lilly said. "I have a feeling."

"Have a feeling about cleaning your room, darling," Nora said, sweeping into the room and lowering Bob's arm. "Not too much now," she said.

Lilly didn't care. She was happy now for the images, for the voices. If something or someone wanted to let her know ahead of time that she might fail a Spanish test, then she considered it a gift to make use of. She studied harder; she got a B plus, a grade that made the teacher raise one of her bushy brows in surprise. She took guilty pleasure in eavesdropping. If she had saved her father, she could save others, if she were only around them. Saint Lilly, she thought, and laughed.

She was still careful not to tell anyone outside her family. If she wanted to roam in the woods behind her house with her friends or if she wanted to be picked on a team for ball at school, then she knew it wasn't good to call attention to any difference.

Bob's illness made him the kind of man Nora had always wanted. He didn't worry about Lilly anymore. Now he was the one who wanted to go out dancing every night, who wanted to stay up late going from club to club. "Come on, come *on*," he kept urging. He came home from work and walked past Nora's table set with china, a roasted chicken steaming in the center, and reached for the phone. "I bet we can get reservations at that new Chinese place." He winked at Lilly. "Chinese, Lilly?" he said. He liked to tease her. "So what do you know?" he asked her. "If we order the wonton, will we all get food poisoning?"

Lilly turned thoughtful, refusing to be kidded. "No," she said generously. She didn't mind ordering in, but she was embarrassed to be seen with her parents.

"Ah, wonton it is tonight, then," he said.

Nora leaned along the refrigerator, a plate of green beans in her hands. She was motionless for a minute, and then she got the waxed paper and began winding it about the beans, settling it over the chicken. She changed into her good shoes and swiped her mouth with lipstick. "Get your sweater," she told Lilly, her voice flat.

"I don't want to go," Lilly said. "I'm getting too old for this."

"We're trying to be a family here," Nora said. "Don't even think of picking up a book. Get that sweater."

He took them to bowling alleys, where the manager came over and warned Lilly about throwing the bowling ball down like that. "You could damage the floors," he told her. Bob took them ice skating and to movies and once to a play, but when Lilly thought about it, the thing she most remembered was the roar and wall of sound around all of them, but with nobody really talking except to ask if you wanted another Coke or popcorn or because you couldn't hear a line of dialogue in the movies. Bob wanted to come home only when he was exhausted, and then he'd fill up the silences in the car with his yawns, and as soon as they were in the house, he stretched. "I just want to check the garden," he told Nora.

"It's midnight," she said.

"Well," he said, "the garden doesn't know that."

He went out back still in his good dress shoes and his good jacket, leaving the door unlocked so he could get back in. As soon as he was out the door, Nora turned brusque.

"Okay, get to bed, it's late," she told Lilly.

Lilly took her time. When she finally got into bed, she could hunch herself up and look out the window, and she could see her father, just standing there in the center of his garden, his hands at his side, staring impassively. She was asleep when she felt a body, warm against her. Lilly, dreaming of dinosaurs, woke with a start. Nora soothed her. "You were having a bad dream," she said.

"I was?" Lilly said. "No, I wasn't."

"It's all right now. I'm here."

She waited, wanting Nora to leave. She was about to nudge her mother when she heard her even breathing. She saw she was asleep. She was still wearing makeup. Lilly got up and peered out the window again, but this time all that was out there was the moon, rising in the sky. She went and got *One Flew over the Cuckoo's Nest* and went into the extra room, where she read on the couch until she fell asleep.

And then suddenly Bob began coming home later and later, and every time Lilly looked at him, he seemed to be fading. It felt as if he had a layer of waxed paper in front of him, and it made her scared. He still gardened and talked to Whitley, but he wasn't as interested anymore. He let the zucchinis overrun the carrots. He let the raspberries be eaten by birds. If Nora wanted salad greens, she had to go out in the dirt in her Pucci-print shorts and pick them herself. He didn't ask the family to go on outings anymore, and he seemed to Lilly to be like everyone else's father now. A ghost who left early in the morning before you were even fully awake and a ghost who came home with the paper under his arm. Even at dinner, when Whitley talked about the restaurant, Bob studied his green beans.

Something was wrong, but Lilly didn't know what it was. One night Lilly went out to the car and got the Saint Christopher medal and began wearing it, buttoning her shirt collar over it so Nora wouldn't see. Safe journey, she told herself every morning when she lit out the door. She touched the medal and relaxed, but two weeks later Bob announced that he was the one who wanted a divorce now, that he had things he had to do.

Nora fell apart. "There's nobody else," he told her. "Just me. That's all I want. I'm getting out of business. I got an offer to teach."

"Teach," Nora said, numb. "What about the restaurant?"

He gave a half smile. "I was fired," he said. "I didn't want to tell you."

"Didn't want to tell you?" Nora said. She repeated it like a refrain while he packed his good shirts and his pants and a few of his books.

"I can send you money," Bob told Nora. "The house is paid for, believe it or not. And you can have it. And you won't starve. Not with the garden."

"I'll get a job," Nora said.

"And you can visit me," he told Lilly. "Anytime."

Lilly was silent. She didn't believe he would really leave. She had known he was having an attack. Why wouldn't she also know if he was really leaving, too? He might get in the car. He might even stay in a hotel for a week or so, like some of her friends' fathers. But he'd be back.

The day he left, Lilly refused to kiss him good-bye. "Please, honey," he begged, "don't make this harder than it is." He stooped toward her, but Lilly stepped back from him. When he drove slowly away, Lilly watched him from behind a neighbor's bushes.

That night she woke up to hear noises in the backyard. She pulled aside the blind. There was Nora in her baby blue robe and fuzzy slippers, digging up zucchini and radishes, swatting raspberry bushes flat with the edge of the spade. She was crying, talking to herself loudly. Lilly got up to get her slippers. She made one last check out the window. Her heart rose. In the shadows she saw two figures. Someone was rocking Nora. I knew you'd be back, she thought. Exhilarated, she pressed closer to the window. She saw Nora lift up her face, and then in the light Lilly saw the other face, lifted for a kiss. Lilly saw Whitley.

Bob sent them money every month, and he had given Nora the house. He usually just put the check in an envelope with a short note. Teaching is great, he said. He wrote out the names of movies he saw, books he was reading.

"Two can play this game," Nora said.

She went out and tried to get a job, but the only one she could get was with Avon. She brought home the red patent-leather sample case to show Lilly, spreading out tiny gold lipsticks, small bottles of foundation in four different colors ("Perfect for any complexion," the label said). Lilly looked doubtfully at the cosmetics. The reds were a little too brassy, the pinks so pale you had to reapply one lipstick four times just to get a tint.

"Come on, be my customer," Nora said. Lilly got up and went behind the door. "Hey, I need help!" Nora said.

"Knock on the door," Lilly said. "This is my house."

Lilly tried to be the worst possible customer. She rolled her eyes when Nora insisted the day cream could rid her face of her worst wrinkles. "Is red my color?" Lilly asked sternly. "Should I put the day cream over or under the moisturizer?"

Nora pursed her lips. "Over," Nora insisted doubtfully.

Every day Nora went out, and when she came home at night she was tense and exhausted. "How did it go?" Lilly asked. "Did you sell anything?"

"That Mrs. Martin is a real moron," Nora said. "She took the samples and didn't buy a thing. And Peg Botanski, down the street? She was irritated at me just because I said she had dry skin."

At night, when she had calmed down a little, she and Lilly played with the samples, making themselves up. "Two glamorous doll faces," Nora said.

Lilly wore makeup to school, and Nora instructed her if anyone asked, she should be sure to mention it was Avon and that her mother could get it for them. She studied Lilly. She draped her best silk blouses about her daughter. She let her rumple her suede skirts.

"Did you know when you were born, I thought you were an alien?"

"No, you didn't," Lilly insisted.

"No, really," Nora said. She propped her feet up on the bed. "We had a midwife. Bob's idea, everything so blasted natural. I called her at three in the morning because I thought I was going to split open. But does she come right over?" Nora shook her head. "She says, 'Call me in a few hours. It's not labor.' Not labor!" Nora snorted. "I got in the shower, and then I felt something wrenching at me. I thought my water was breaking. What did I know? I sat on the toilet, and all of a sudden, you were born. 'What is it?' I kept screaming, and your father was shouting back, 'It's a baby!' as if I had thought you were an alien."

Lilly thought of herself as an alien, floating down through space. She thought of the messages she sometimes heard, and she suddenly felt afraid.

Nora reached over and brushed back her bangs. "You hit your head on the toilet, but I scooped you up. I made Bob promise we would never ever tell you that story."

"But you just did," Lilly said.

"Well, you're older. It's funny now," said Nora. "We're two women now, we can be friends." She stared dreamily at the window. "Isn't it strange, you think you want one kind of life, but when you get it, you always want another."

Lilly thought there was something wrong with her because she didn't really miss her father. She felt he was with her the same way he had always been with her—always a bit beyond her reach. She hadn't been completely wrong, because he did come back in a way. He sent her postcards inside envelopes with a quarter so she could call him and talk to him. She called him every week, and although he said he was having a fine time, he never asked her to come see him, and after a while there was nothing to talk about.

Nora was upset Bob wasn't calling. "What did he say?" she demanded.

"Nothing, really," Lilly said.

"Ha. That's my Bob," Nora said. She fiddled with her shag. To save money she had tried to do it herself, and now it looked like roofing shingles. "Did you tell him how well we were doing? Did you tell him I have a career?"

"Sure, I told him."

Nora studied her. "And what did he say?"

A dime of pain was forming behind Lilly's right eye. "He said he missed you," she said.

Nora lightened. "Ha," she said. "Let him."

Nora stared out the back window, where Whitley was puttering in his garden. His chino pants were ribbed with dirt. There was a woodchuck ambling down toward the house. She rapped at it through the glass, and Whitley turned and saw her, and his stern face fractured into a smile.

Gradually the letters came less and less frequently, and then they stopped completely, but by then Lilly was eighteen and all she wanted was to be on her own anyway, and when she went to college, she went to Boston University, a place far away enough from Detroit and Nora so she would have to live there.

Nora cried that she missed Lilly, but her own life was full of surprises. She told Lilly she had stopped going door to door and had talked her way into the only job she thought she could get—as a saleswoman at Hudson's cosmetics counter. It was easier than at Avon because she didn't have to seek out the women; they came to her. They crowded at the counter, wanting lipsticks and expensive eye creams and perfumes she was delighted to sell them. "Your mom's a success," Nora said. Behind her, Lilly heard a man's voice.

"Who's that?" Lilly said.

"Whitley," Nora said. "He's come for dinner."

* * *

Lilly didn't ask anymore what was wrong with her. She went to the college library and read everything she could about clairvoyance, surreptitiously keeping one hand over the book so no one would make fun of her. She hadn't come by her gift the usual way. She hadn't been born with a caul. She hadn't been blessed. Maybe it was the bump on her head from the car drive with her father. Maybe it had dislodged something, shooting electrical impulses across newly tangled wires. Sometimes she thought her mother was right. She was crazy. She needed medication. She managed to lie well enough to Student Health about nervousness to wrangle some Valium. For four whole days she heard no message. It was as if someone had put on a white noise machine in her head, a welcome blur blocking the noise.

Other times she told herself it was very scientific. She had gotten an A in physics, and she knew as well as anybody that all thoughts were nothing more than energy, that energy wasn't destroyed. So didn't it make sense that she was just acting as radar, picking up energy?

And then one day she read about studies going on at a university in France. Scientists were studying a phenomenon they couldn't explain. The voices of the dead, coming through like static, filtered through layers of white noise, from the recently deceased. "This is a new age," the scientist said. "Get used to it."

Get used to it. Lilly sat down and wrote to the scientist, but although nothing came back, she began to feel better. She told herself that knowledge like this was available to everyone, even the worst skeptics, and that the only reason she was hearing the dead was because she had better receptors.

Still, she kept it to herself. And she made use of it. She was asked out by a pleasant architectural student named Brad, but on the ride home she suddenly looked at him and knew he didn't really like her. She knew he was going to turn down a lonely road and pretend that he did. "Take me home," Lilly said.

During her junior year of school, Lilly met a group of girls who called themselves the Waltham Witches. They consulted the I-Ching before they went on dates, they read the tarot for important exams. Even her roommate, Ann, brought in tarot cards and consulted them for everything. She fanned them across her narrow bed and stared from the cards to the complimentary booklet that came with them, trying to decipher her future.

"You ought to do this, Lilly," Ann said. "This is major cool we're talking here."

"I'm too straight for major cool," Lilly said. She didn't like the way the girls giggled over the cards, the way they manipulated them until they came out the way the girls wanted.

"Whooo!" Ann made her voice sound spooky. "Barry's gonna ask me out!"

"And cows can fly," said another girl.

Lilly, lying on her bed reading, said nothing. She didn't have to look at the cards to know Barry would indeed ask Ann out. She felt it. When Lilly looked at Ann, she heard Ann's grandmother singing something low and soft. She saw Ann's grandmother, a faded image like an old photo. She was wearing a flowered apron. Lilly couldn't stand to look at the cards.

"Well, maybe we could go to a psychic or something together," Ann said. "I know one who charges only thirty-five dollars. She's supposed to be too ignorant to be a fake."

"I think I'll pass," said Lilly. She hated anything that had to do with the occult. She hated the gypsy storefronts where the women sat lounging on hard metal chairs and beckoned you from the street. She hated Witches Brew, a store on the edge of campus that sold spells and wax candles you could melt into effigies. She hated it that people made it into something bizarre and mystical, but even worse was when people made it into a joke, something only morons believed in, gullible people who needed to cling.

Only sometimes was it intrusive. Only sometimes did she wish she didn't always hear these insistent messages or see these bright, flashing images, things telling her something.

One night she was in bed with Pierre, a French exchange student she really liked. They had been to a movie. He had held her hand and tickled her, and he had been a considerate and careful lover. He was asleep, his mouth faintly open, and Lilly leaned toward him carefully. Asleep, everybody's layers fell right away. You could get to the depths and see it, as new and clear as a baby's skin. A voice rippled up to her, and Lilly waited, stroking one finger across Pierre's soft, downy hair. "He loves Emily," Lilly heard, and she saw a face in her mind she recognized, a curly-headed blonde who sat in front of her in algebra. Lilly stiffened. *"Emmie,"* the voice whispered, and Lilly slowly got up and got her clothes. She dressed, not looking at Pierre, not wanting to hear another wounding word.

She began to think of the universe as a kind of fatherly figure who'd reward you for good and punish you for bad. Sometimes she'd do something really good, like call Nora when she didn't really feel like speaking to her, because she just knew that if she did, if she could manage to carry on a whole conversation without being irritated once, the math exam the next day would be multiple choice. She'd be rewarded. And if she didn't, not only would it be problems to figure out, but there would be only four, so that only a perfect score would do. She knew it was a ridiculous way to behave, that probably the universe could care less what she did, but it gave her life a framework.

One evening Lilly was trying to make cocoa on her hot plate when Nora called her.

"I'm marrying Whitley," she told Lilly.

"Whitley!" Lilly said.

"Well, I always liked Whitley," Nora said. "And you don't know everything."

Lilly knew enough to graduate magna cum laude in English. She didn't know, though, how difficult it was going to be to find a job, even when she moved to New York City, where she thought she'd have a better chance. She had some money Nora had been saving for her, and she spent two months living at the Y while she looked for an apartment she could afford. At the end of the two months she cursed herself for not taking the first apartment she had seen, a single room so tiny you couldn't even fit a bed in. She had laughed in the realtor's face. "Who could live in that?" she insisted.

"People do," said the realtor. What did he care? There were ten others who would grab up the apartment.

Lilly was in tears wandering Forty-sixth street when an old woman sweeping her steps waved the broom at her angrily. "Go cry somewhere else," she suggested.

"I would if I had somewhere else to cry," Lilly said, weeping.

The woman squinted. She must have decided that Lilly wasn't a murderer because she lowered the broom.

"You know of any apartments?" Lilly said.

The woman did—a place that Lilly would end up living in her entire time in New York. Her husband was a super at a building right on Twenty-ninth Street, and for a small fee (one hundred dollars, which would be much less than a broker's fee) he rented her a small, noisy studio with a window that looked out on an air shaft and another that looked out into another apartment building. Lilly was thrilled. An old woman hung out of the bottom window, glaring at the people who passed by. The neighborhood was seedy and lively, and at night she took to carrying an umbrella, swinging it so people knew she meant business. She didn't mind the acoustics. It comforted her to hear the couple downstairs fighting about who tended to whose needs more, to hear the man upstairs singing off-key Verdi in his shower. The noises of people would keep danger away, she reasoned, and only once was she frightened, when she heard a voice calling out, "Stop! It hurts! It hurts!" She bolted up in bed. The voice stopped.

She looked for work, but the jobs that were offered her—entry-level positions in publishing or advertising—paid slightly more than minimum wage to start, and Lilly began to worry. She thought about going back to school, if only she could figure out what it was she wanted to go back to school for. In the meantime she began waitressing at Clyde's, a tony Chelsea café that specialized in California cuisine. She didn't mind waiting tables. The tips were good; the hours were better; and as soon as she walked out the door, she forgot about the job.

As a gimmick Clyde's had a palm reader, a Yale graduate named Susan Budelli. Susan was tall and lanky with a scrambled head of dark curls she liked to twist in her fingers. She dressed in expensive, brightly colored suits and polished, matching high-heeled shoes, and she always polished her nails. She arrived in time for the after eight crowd, people who had had hard enough days to be more in need of a reading, and she kept to herself. She hadn't said more than two words to Lilly, though Lilly, hungry for friends, had once invited her to a movie after work. "Let me get back to you," Susan had said, but although Lilly had lingered after work, Susan had simply waltzed right out, oblivious.

Susan charged ten dollars. She looked at her sign-up sheet and then she walked right over to her client's table and made herself at home. She read for twenty minutes, and although she spread out a deck of tarot elaborately, it didn't take Lilly long to see that Susan was merely telling people exactly what they wanted to hear. Lilly didn't know anything about the cards, but it didn't seem to her that a heart stabbed through with ten swords meant happiness. It didn't seem that a castle tumbling to the ground could possibly mean a raise.

Lilly walked by, balancing a plate of lard-free refried pinto beans and rice. "Ah-ha," said Susan, leaning forward, one curl dipping into a question mark against her cheek. "You're going to find love at work."

The woman, a blonde with the shortest haircut Lilly had ever seen, leaned back and grinned. "Is it that new guy in clerical?" she asked.

Susan merely smiled, calm and even as a Cheshire cat.

Susan predicted good fortune for nearly everyone. A man in a funny plaid suit was going to get a raise. An elderly woman was going to inherit the money she needed to pack out of this god-awful city and move to Florida. "Buy yourself some white shoes," Susan whispered. The one time Lilly heard her tell a man he would always live alone, that he would never have children, and if he did, they would be deformed, the man turned out to be Susan's cheating ex-boyfriend.

Susan had a small following. Her blue sign-up sheet grew longer and longer. Susan was even written up in *New York* magazine, which touted her as "the society seer" at Susan's request, because she wanted to upgrade her clientele.

Lilly didn't have to read people's tarot cards to know how they were feeling. It was as simple as the way a man might pick at his food, rearranging it endlessly on his plate but never once tasting a bite, or the way a woman had upswept her hair carefully with a chipped rhinestone clip, or even the halting, angry way a businessman might order nachos. And sometimes, too, she heard the messages.

One Friday she was serving avocado frijoles to an older woman who was being read by Susan.

"Plate's hot," Lilly said, but the woman didn't seem to notice. Susan, sitting across from her, fingered a small spread of cards.

"Oh, my, yes," Susan said. "I see a new job."

"A job?" the woman said, confused.

"A romance!" Susan said. She stabbed a finger down into a card showing two lovers. "See that?"

Lilly straightened, and then she heard, clear as glass, a voice, a name. "*Doug,*" Lilly heard. Lilly picked up the woman's teacup and refilled it. The woman kept her eyes down. Lilly saw a boat, water, and then she suddenly got so cold, she had to put the cup back down again.

"Are you all right?" The woman suddenly looked up at Lilly in concern.

Lilly's head was reeling. "He drowned," Lilly said, her voice so dry she couldn't get out the words.

The woman looked panicky.

Susan jerked her head from her client to Lilly in real annoyance. "You know each other?" Susan said. "Because I can do this reading later."

The woman leaned forward. "Yes," she said. "We know each other."

"Great," said Susan, her smile stiffening. And as she stood up, Lilly sat down carefully. She took the woman's hands and began to talk.

Lilly developed her own sort of reputation. You could never book Lilly the way you did Susan. You could never tell when Lilly would wander over to your table and in a low, quiet voice whisper a message to you, but sometimes it was at exactly the time when you needed it the most. Clients began to talk among themselves about Lilly. They said she had contacted their dead son, they said she had made contact with a missing daughter, and some said that even as Lilly was contacting them, she began to look differently. Her face lengthened. Her hair seemed somehow lighter, somehow blond. Once, when she was doing a reading for a woman whose son had been killed in a fire, the whole left side of her face looked burned, and for two days afterward she couldn't stand for even the soft white cotton of her pillow to touch her cheek. One woman swore that for a moment Lilly had looked exactly like her fourteen-year-old daughter who had died of cancer. The restaurant began to double its clientele, and Lilly not only began collecting tips, but she got a much needed raise.

"More power to you," Susan said, but all Lilly had to do was look at her to see how annoyed she was with the competition. Susan began coming to work with a small pouch of Viking rune stones. She brought I-Ching sticks and a small crystal ball, and she expanded her readings now to forty minutes. And then, abruptly, on the first warm spring day of the year, when the scent of the lilacs outside was so strong that it almost made you swoon, Susan quit. "I'm moving to Colorado with my boyfriend," she announced. The manager promptly gave Lilly another hefty raise. "Your workload's about to double," he told her, smiling. "And we'll just forget the waitressing."

Customers asked, but Lilly didn't do tarot. She didn't know what any of the lines in a palm meant; she didn't feel anything from holding a ring that had belonged to someone's father. She didn't go into a trance and speak with the voice of someone's dead loved one. She was a receiver, that was all. She sat quietly with a customer and waited for the messages to come. Sometimes they came, but when she was tired or irritable or sick, well, then sometimes they didn't. And the more open she was, the more they seemed to come, so many she sometimes couldn't untangle all the voices. "The dead are always with us," she told people.

She got more and more customers. People were so grateful to hear the names of their dead coming from another person that they sometimes wept, but they wouldn't let Lilly stop telling them every word of every message she got. Sometimes people didn't understand that the messages the dead gave her were garbled, that Lilly had to struggle to make sense. And, too, sometimes the messages were no more profound than the messages of the living. Fathers wanted to tell wives they loved them and not to worry. Kids wanted their parents to buy the right kind of dog food for their dog. And mostly people just wanted to tell their stories, again and again, the way they had in life. People still wanted to be heard.

The thing was, Lilly didn't know who was hearing her. All these people were depending on her, pulling at her, but she felt a little empty. She had a boyfriend named Robert, whom she had met in line for a movie, and for a long time they had been in love, and now, while she was still in love, he seemed to be in something a little different. There was something new around him, something that kept her from being able to read him the way she used to, and it made her worried and insecure. "What do you say we rent a summer house?" she suggested, trying to nudge him into the future with her.

"Leave New York?" he said. "Everyone I hate is gone to their summer houses. Why would I want to follow them?"

"Because it's cooler. Because there's water."

"Summer's the only time you can get into any movie you want," he said. "You don't need reservations to eat."

He was tall and so handsome that all her friends kept telling her how lucky she was, as if his looks were any of her doing. He dressed in antique suit jackets over dark T-shirts and black boots, and he allowed her to cut his long, thick hair if she promised she wasn't saving any to make up wax effigies.

"Would I do that!" Lilly said, though in truth, sometimes on nights when strange women came up to her and asked if Robert Winthrop was "her" Robert, she thought about it.

Robert was a filmmaker who kept trying to get the stories of her clients out of her. "It's confidential!" Lilly insisted.

"But they'd make great stories," he said. He didn't really believe that Lilly was psychic, a spot of contention between them. "Come on, you look at a woman whose eyes are red from crying, and ten to one it's man trouble. You see an older man all upset—it's his job or divorce. You have *clues*, Lilly, you can key into a wedding band or a bruise."

"You do it, then," Lilly said mildly. "And anyway, if it's so hokey, why do you want to film it?"

"Film is sometimes hokey," he said. He wanted to hide a

camera above Lilly and film a night of her readings. Cinema vérité, he said. People would line up for blocks to see a film like that. His friend Ester, a high school teacher who came regularly to Lilly for readings, had already agreed to be filmed. "But I didn't agree," Lilly said.

"Why are you trying to sidetrack my career?" he said.

Robert was gone for a month now, filming a documentary about monkeys who were being specially trained to help paraplegics. The monkeys could feed the humans they were paired with. They could answer the door and put a ringing phone up to a waiting ear. They could offer the comfort humans might shy away from. And they could bite, too, Lilly thought. They could get malicious. You couldn't trust them.

She missed Robert, but when he called her, their conversations were short and sharp. He seemed exhausted. "It's not the film I really want to make," he told her. "The monkeys are more difficult than you can imagine. They don't like the lights. They get so protective of their charges, if you so much as blink at them, they rush you."

She thought of him with an angry monkey clinging and clawing at his sweater. He never wanted to talk very long, and when she got off the phone with him, all she could think of was the first few months they were going out, when he was so soft and sweet to her, when they sat up every night until three because there was always something else they wanted to say to each other. It was a time, too, when she couldn't wait to see him, when sometimes she had shown up at his editing room because she couldn't go on another second, wanting him the way she did.

"Why, you must be psychic," he'd said, laughing and unbuttoning his shirt. "I was just thinking about this." Well, that sort of thing was happening less and less. Now when she came to his editing room, he told her he had to *edit*. "Later," he promised, but later he was exhausted and cranky. Later he wanted to talk about how he had just read in some magazine about a film school friend of his who was already making *fea-*

tures, not some documentaries, another friend who was writing a script for Scorsese, for Christ's sake.

"So you do it, too," Lilly said to him, but he looked at her as if she had just got off a plane from Mars. "Write a script," she said encouragingly. "Make the time."

He looked at her as if she had struck him. "How supportive," he said bitterly, and then grabbed his leather jacket. "I'm going to a movie," he said.

It was one thing to be lonely when you were away from someone, it was another to be lonely while you were with them, and that was beginning to be the case. He was a million miles away—he barely spoke to her over brunch at the Cupping Room because he was dreaming that he was making films so great they would win Oscars, he was in Cannes, he was the toast of Hollywood and the New York Film Critics Circle. But what Lilly couldn't figure out was where she fit into all these reveries—or if at all. When she dared to read him—a real breach of privacy she couldn't help—she saw and heard nothing but fog. The future unfolds as it should, she sometimes told clients when she saw them wincing from their lives. It was the kind of statement that didn't make her feel any better, either.

She didn't know what it was. You'd think with all the advice she gave other people about their love lives, she could advise herself. She sat in her tiny studio and listened to the couple downstairs arguing about who was the worse lover, and then she called her mother; but Nora didn't want to hear excuses.

"Marry that boy before someone else snaps him right up from under your nose," Nora said.

"I don't think he wants marriage," Lilly said.

"You make him want it," Nora said

Lilly studied her floor. The slant seemed more pronounced. "I don't know if *I* want it with him," Lilly said.

Nora paused for a moment. "Honey bunch, happiness never hurt anybody."

In September Lilly went to her mother's wedding without Robert, who was shooting monkeys and couldn't get away. Even though it was a second wedding, Nora insisted on wearing white anyway, a linen suit with white satin shoes and in her hair white flowers that Whitley had grown himself.

"So let them talk," Nora said. "I'm the one getting married."

Lilly wore a black velvet dress that didn't fit right, and the whole time her relatives milled around her not one of them asked her when the devil she was getting married, and even though she had warned Nora to tell them to keep their mouths shut, it depressed her that not one person asked.

Nora kept scanning the crowds, peering from face to face so anxiously, Lilly finally asked her whom she was looking for.

"Your father," Nora said simply.

"You invited him?" Lilly said, looking askance.

"A wedding's the best way to let bygones be bygones."

He hadn't shown up, although every time Lilly looked at Nora, even when she was waltzing with Whitley, her mother seemed to be looking.

When the time came for Nora to throw her bouquet, Lilly was standing far along the wall, and Nora simply marched right over to her and placed the flowers in her hand. "You caught it," she informed Lilly. Then she leaned forward to embrace Lilly.

"Love comes when you least expect it," she said.

chapter 2

Matt Renfield always hoped love would be different for his daughter, Dinah, than it had been for him. He had married at twenty-three, so crazy about his wife, Maggy, that he sometimes called her ten times a day just to hear her voice. The marriage had lasted less than three years. He had bought her a used car, hoping it would allow her to give vent to her restlessness, but all that had happened was she had run off with the mechanic who had worked on it, leaving him with a brutally scarred heart and a two-year-old daughter. She'd kept in touch for a while, and then the letters and the calls had scattered to a stop, and the last he had heard was that she was married to a computer salesman and living in Texas.

Dinah hadn't known her mother well enough to miss her, and Matt did everything he could to make sure she didn't feel deprived. He was going to vet school on scholarship, but he had a healthy amount of savings, and he didn't scrimp when it came to Dinah. The house was always filled with toys and, later, with books on dinosaurs and astronomy, with biographies and literature. She almost always had a book in her hand, or an animal, and he was used to finding a Nancy Drew mystery by her ant farm, biographies by the garden outside where her turtle Big Joe liked to burrow. He took her with him to work, letting her play in his private office. Weekends they went to the lake or the zoo. He told her there was nothing she couldn't talk to him about, and he meant it. And when she became a teenager, he began to read *Sassy* magazine and *Seventeen* so he would know just what it was girls liked and cared about, and sometimes he just wandered through the malls listening to the packs of girls, catching the cadences, high and sweet and yearning toward the lives they were going to have.

He would have done anything to save her from the restless longing for someone who just wasn't going to be there for her. Another person missing in action. Another life going on without you knowing anything about it. *Are You My Mother?* was the title of one of her favorite books when she was a little girl, but Dinah never once in her whole entire life ever asked that question of anybody, and he was glad.

He had grown up under the shadow of someone who wasn't there, and he didn't want that for Dinah. His father had gone off to the Korean War months before Matt had been born and hadn't come back. Missing in action. He hadn't known what that meant back then. Had his father been tortured or killed, or was he still alive somewhere and they didn't know it? He knew, though, because his mother, Dell, was always so angry with him, so impatient, that somehow his father's not coming back had something to do with him, that it might even be his fault. "If your father were here to see this!" his mother shouted at him when he was caught stealing baseball cards at Pizzi's store down the street. "You're lucky he's not!" she shouted, and then, stunned by her own words, she would burst into tears.

He remembered his mother didn't have time for him when he was growing up. She looked at him as though it pained her to see him. She shooed him out of the house because she said she had to nap and he was too noisy, but he sometimes hid outside the window to spy on her, and he saw her pouring wine into a juice glass, sipping it, and swaying to

Pat Boone singing "Love Letters in the Sand," her eyes damp and dreaming. She sent him to overnight camp when he was just five, and even though he cried and begged and regaled her with stories of how he hated it, how alone he was, she sent him every summer after, too. "Mummy has to work," she said.

She did work. Hank's, his father's shoe store, was a thriving business, and Dell was determined to keep it up for the day Hank came home. "I want him to be proud of me," she insisted. She left Matt with baby-sitters who watched TV or talked on the phone and noticed him only when it was time for them both to eat lunch or dinner.

She was there by six, and some nights she didn't leave until seven. When she came home she had another, even more important job. "Don't disturb me now," she told him. She got out two pens, in case one ran out, and a ream of creamy white paper and envelopes, and then she spent the evening writing angry letters to the government about finding her Hank. She started a Wives of MIA group in Pittsburgh and held meetings every Thursday night, his night to play basketball, his night when all the other parents except for her came to the school gym and watched their kids. "Don't you want me to find Daddy?" she asked him, exasperated.

"I don't know," he said, because in truth he didn't know what that would mean, finding Daddy. It took Dell two steps to reach him, to strike him so hard against his face, he would feel the bruise for days.

She belonged to a Military Book Club simply because she thought one of the photos in the books might show a picture of her husband. Maybe, too, the long and tedious texts might mention Hank. They never did, but she became something of an expert about Korea. Matt was twelve before he realized the places they vacationed were always near another MIA group, always near another set of meetings.

"You don't remember your father at all, do you?" she sometimes cried, and it would drive him crazy.

"I wasn't born yet!" he shouted at her, and she flinched.

"Well, don't you think I know that?" she said.

He grew up, and outwardly his mother seemed the same. Preserved in her yearning for her past. She had to take two different buses to find a beauty shop that still finger-waved hair. She sometimes had dresses made, styled from photographs of her when she was barely nineteen. She was still attractive enough to have offers, but she refused to date. "No one compares to your father," she said, "and besides, you think I should be married when he walks back through that door?"

Matt got used to being by himself. He was smart. He could be funny, and although he knew how to be by himself, how to spend an entire day reading or studying or walking, he also yearned to feel as if he belonged to something—or someone. He fed stray cats yowling outside the house, falling in love with them for the short time they let him. He sometimes spread a little sugar out in the backyard to encourage the ants. And he began to court other people.

His friends' families got used to setting an extra plate for dinner for him. They liked him because he was an A student, because he was well scrubbed and so polite, a mother could die of happiness. And he, in turn, was happy being loved, happy when a friend's mother cheerfully rubbed his hair and said, "Oh, don't be so formal, call me Ann. Bob does." The happiness followed him, right up until the moment he returned to his own empty house and a note Dell had left him. "At the store. Back by ten. Dinner in fridge for you, sweetie!" Dinner. Tuna casserole. Cheese sandwiches. He ate listlessly, reading, blasting the radio.

When he was seventeen he came home to find Dell standing perfectly rigid on the front porch, a letter crumpled in her hand. She looked right through him. "Dead!" she cried.

"Who's dead?" he said.

She wavered, and when he touched her, she gave a small hurt cry. "Come on," he said, his voice low, and brought her inside. He had to unpeel the letter from her hand. And then he saw. Hank, his father, was dead.

But he hadn't died in the hands of the enemy. He hadn't died of wounds on a battlefield, his last dimming thoughts of his young wife. He had died in a small apartment in the south of France, of a heart attack, and the only reason anyone thought to contact Dell at all was because the authorities had gone through his things and found her picture and a letter he had started writing her. He had carefully addressed it at the top, he had gone so far as to write "Dear Dell, I—" and then after that the letter stopped. There was no money. He had lived under an assumed name, but he had kept a diary, and in it there were many discoveries. He hadn't really been missing in action at all. He had gone AWOL. And no one knew why.

Dell had been devastated. "He loved me," she insisted. "There must be some explanation." She went through all his old love letters, over and over, searching for clues. She looked at the photos of the two of them together. When she went to an MIA meeting and told them, the other women were sympathetic. They urged her to keep coming to the meetings, but Dell felt something had changed irrevocably. She was no longer really the wife of an MIA, because after all, while these other women's husbands were God knew where, hers had been running a tidy little business in France. Hers had neither danger nor drama about him, and hers had had no desire to find her. After a while she stopped going.

His father's death changed everything. Dell hired help at the shoe store. Every day he came home from school and she was in her white full-length lace slip, weeping. He made her supper, grilled cheese and a salad and a diet Coke, and sat with her while she picked at the food. She had never paid much attention to him, but now suddenly she grew frantic. "Where were you?" she kept saying.

He was used to being by himself, to tending to his own needs. There weren't many kids in the neighborhood. He had grown up in love with the library and in love with the mailman, who let him go door to door with him, who even now sometimes still sat down in the shade and read the backs of postcards out loud to Matt. "Florida is peachy," he read. "We swim every day and Lynn already has quite a tan. Wish you were here, Love Tim." The mailman winked at Matt.

Dell, walking by one day, saw Matt reading the cards, and walked over and slapped him. The mailman looked stunned. "People have a right to keep their lives to themselves," she said, her mouth trembling.

After that her life became the shoe store. Matt left home to struggle on with his life, and sometimes she came and visited him, or he visited her, but the store was the only place she felt happy, if only because it reminded her of her early days with her husband, a time when she had been happy, when she had thought the happiness would linger and last.

Matt had always hoped he might find a mother for Dinah, and that he might find someone to share his life with, but lately he thought that maybe when you got older, there were just too many complications. He had been so busy raising Dinah, so busy building his vet practice, that he hadn't started dating until Dinah was twelve. He felt rusty and stupid, out of practice, but women liked him; they sometimes fell passionately in love, and sometimes he loved them back, but ordinary life always intruded. He had to break dates when Dinah was sick, and a few times simply when she was crying and lonely. He broke dates, too, to be at his clinic, where he was sitting up nights with a dog recovering from chemo or carefully monitoring a cat with fever. His relationships drifted apart.

Matt kept dating. Sometimes he told himself it was a matter of time. Sometimes he told himself that it didn't matter, that he didn't know many couples who seemed to genuinely like each other anyway. But he never stopped thinking it was possible. And he did know animals who mated for life. Parrots were the most romantic of all. In the wild they were always within inches of their mate. They were never alone.

Wrenched apart from their beloved, kept alone and caged in a household, they found surrogates—the man who fed them or the man's wife, and when that surrogate left for work or even for a long hot bath, the parrot felt betrayed and acted out the only way it knew how—by biting and putting up a fuss so loud, only a human being would ignore it. Geese mourned when their mates died. Lobsters had nuclear families.

He watched his daughter, herself on the cusp of dating. He thought that if a boy could love and appreciate her half as much as he did, she would be okay in the world. She would be safe, because love like his would never run out, it would never ruin.

It was evening. Matt was out to dinner with a new woman, the daughter of one of his clients. Dinah had made up an excuse not to join them. "Algebra exam," she'd said, but as soon as they were out the door, she put "Summer Blonde" bleach in her hair. It came out thatchy and unlovely. She had thought it would make her look different enough for several boys to fall helplessly in love with her. She shook her head, and bits of hair sprinkled down into the sink.

She felt prickly with anger and guilt. Why wouldn't a woman be in love with her father when half the girls in her class were, too?

"*That's* your father?" Terry McBain, who sat behind Dinah in math, had asked Dinah in astonishment when he showed up at parent/student day. "He sure doesn't look like a father."

The other fathers were in baggy gray suits and ties and scuffed wing-tip shoes. The other fathers were balding or wore crew cuts and were so serious, you didn't dare get near them. Matt was wearing black jeans and cowboy boots, and his hair was as long as that of some of the older boys, only on him it still looked cool and natural and not as though he were trying to still be young. He was frank and funny, and he looked at each of Dinah's teachers as if no one in the world were more interesting or intriguing.

Miss Magrogan, Dinah's young, single English teacher, stood a little too close to him, but he didn't seem to notice. She flipped her hair; she flirted. "He couldn't be your father," Miss Magrogan said to Dinah the next day at school. "What, did he have you when he was sixteen?"

"He's my father," Dinah said evenly.

Dinah knew how her teacher felt. When she was little, she had been madly in love with her father herself. "Will you marry me?" she used to ask him, and he always laughed.

"Ask me in twenty years," he told her. "You'll feel differently then."

But as the years passed, she hadn't felt too differently, and the only change she could pinpoint was that she had stopped asking him.

At first it didn't scare her. She knew enough of her friends' lives to know, first, how mother-raised they were, a luxury she had never experienced, which on second thought didn't seem like such a luxury at all. She had never felt deprived. She had never missed her mother. How could you miss someone you had never known? Besides, she didn't see what was so great about a mother. Her friends' mothers were always sniping at them because they didn't like their daughters' hairstyles or clothes or smart, fresh mouths. Her friends' mothers went on cleaning rampages just for excuses to read a well-hidden diary whose secrets they sometimes betrayed right at the dinner table.

The closest thing she had to a mother was her grandmother Dell, who was bustly and distant, who called on her birthday and sent her shoes for presents, and who almost always had to cut her visits to them short so she could get back to her shoe store.

Matt wasn't your traditional father, either. There were more than enough reasons for her to adore him. Her friends' fathers were silent, seldom home men, who wandered through their own homes like strangers. Her friends' fathers bought their daughters exorbitant gifts sometimes and other times yelled at them for wearing too much mascara. Matt was different all right. He was home and available. He let her eat what she liked and go to sleep when she liked and choose her own clothes, even when she was in kindergarten. He listened to every story with interest and respect, and he never failed to tell her how special she was, how lovely, even when she suspected that she was not. Matt was the one who first introduced her to films and books and art and animals, and he talked to her like an adult, the two of them sitting out on the porch until all hours. He told her his worries about his practice, about money, and, sometimes, about love. "We can always tell each other everything," he said. "Right?"

"Right," she said, but she hadn't been able to tell him that sometimes she thought that her family history was skewed, that sometimes she imagined that he wasn't her father at all, that maybe her mother had just told him that because she needed someone to care for the child she didn't want. Maybe Matt was a friend, and no relation at all. He didn't seem like a father. Dell didn't seem like a grandmother, so maybe they really weren't her family at all. She rented *Daddy Long Legs* three times just to watch Leslie Caron fall in love with her older guardian, Fred Astaire.

As she got older, she worried that she was sick. It wasn't natural, was it, to love your father this way, to imagine always being with him? Her friends dismissed their fathers, calling them "the old goat" or "Mr. Has Been," ridiculing what their fathers wore and thought and said. They wouldn't be caught dead walking around the reservoir late at night with their fathers, the way Dinah did with Matt every chance she got. She even went to a free clinic and saw a sliding-scale counselor, who listened to Dinah and then shook her head.

"Honey," she said gently, "does your father sleep with you?"

Dinah grew heated. "What, are you crazy?" she said.

"You want to sleep with him?"

"What's the matter with you?" Dinah cried.

"Things are never about what you think they are." The counselor tapped a colored pencil across her desk. "What are you afraid of? Boys are as scared as you. You go on and date, and your feelings will take care of themselves. You watch, your father will slide right into the background."

Hah. She knew she'd have it easier if she could fall in love with someone other than her father, if she could find someone who might compare. She was more than willing to try, and she was enough of a scientist to know you had to experiment a little to find a solution, but she was tall and gangly and unlovely, and no one in her entire school wanted to date her, much less talk to her. She had screwed up her courage and written a note to Billy Hamilton, a blond artist who sat in front of her in math class: "Would you like to go to the freshman dance with me?" She had slid it into his notebook, and she had even watched him open it. She'd shivered, planted to the wall, watching him read, and when he'd carefully refolded the note and put it in his pocket, her heart had sung. She'd waited all day, lagging behind after lunch, taking so long to get to the bus stop that she'd missed her bus, but three days later he still hadn't said one word to her, and she hadn't heard until after the dance how he had come with another girl, how they had stood so close to each other, they'd looked seamed together.

Something's wrong with me, she thought. She studied herself in the mirror. She wondered for the first time in her life about her mother, how she had been able to leave Matt so easily. "She just left," Matt had told her. She sat out on the porch with her father nights, the two of them sipping lemonade and cheating at Scrabble, and she thought, Well, maybe she'd just have to go away, like one of those dramatic heroines in a 1940s movie. Maybe she'd just have to transform, the way Bette Davis did from spinster to siren in *Now, Voyager*. She'd go to school someplace. Oh, she didn't know exactly where yet. College somewhere distant and exciting, with so many people it might make you dizzy. Maybe Europe. Someplace where boys would appreciate the fact that you read books, that you could tell the sex of a turtle just by the color of its eyes. She wanted to be a vet like her father. And she wanted, too, more than anything to stand outside on a soft summer night and tilt her face up for a kiss that might be the one thing to transform her.

She wasn't completely evil, was she? She didn't want her father to end up old and alone and odd like Miss Rafferty, who lived in a tiny Cape Cod down the street with sixty-five cats, some of them six-toed, some of them so grimy, the neighbors had once called the board of health.

She tried to be pleasant to her father's girlfriends, to help things along. She thought maybe they could be friends, maybe that would make everything easier for her. She had even fallen a little in love with his last one, an architect named Elaine, whom he had gone with for nearly three years.

Elaine taught Dinah how to ice-skate, how to apply mascara without poking the wand in her eye, and how to highlight her hair with just lemon juice and water. Elaine rocked Dinah in her arms when Dinah cried over a boy who had slighted her, and Elaine insisted Dinah come with her and Matt when they went out to the movies. They were friends, Dinah thought, and she continued to think it right up until the time Elaine broke up with Matt to go live with her ex-boyfriend in Maine and didn't even say good-bye to her. Dinah found out her address and sent her a funny postcard, but even though she watched for the mail for nearly two whole months, she never heard from Elaine again.

After that Dinah's heart seemed to telescope inward. She kept her feelings close against her chest. Girlfriends, she thought, were quick to be your friend and just as quick to forget you when the relationship was over.

She was like her father, she supposed, in that she had trouble bonding to other people. Like Matt, she lived in books a lot, and like Matt, she liked and understood animals better than she did people. Her father had made sure right from the start that she had respect and wonder for even the smallest forms of life.

"Look," he whispered, pointing out to her how ants left scent spots on the ground to find their way, how butterflies emerged from silky cocoons. As a little girl she had frogs and cats and puppies and birds. She had always liked and appreciated even the mosquitoes that brightly jeweled her arms and legs with bites.

She had always had a kind of sixth sense when it came to animals. She could tell just by the way a cat moved whether it was hungry or hurt or bored. She could look at a Dalmatian and swear she knew what was wrong with it. "It's her leg," she'd tell Matt, and sure enough he'd find a fracture. "She's scared," Dinah said, and cooed something low under her throat. She read her father's books, she knew the medicines, and sometimes he'd let her administer a needle because her touch was so gentle.

She was a common sight at the office. She would pet the dogs and cats in the waiting room when the owners would let her, when they weren't so distraught and worried that they had balled up half the Kleenex tissues in Ohio in their laps.

It was terrifying, the things that could go wrong. Snakes had renal failure. Cats got leukemia and had chemotherapy. Dogs had legs amputated. Her father had once done a successful cataract operation on a lizard. And her father watched owner after owner cry in relief or frustration or pain, some of them sprawled prone on the linoleum, and each and every time it completely broke his heart. Love was love. It wasn't only dotty old ladies who doted on their pets. It wasn't only the single or the lonely or the bedridden whose heart might take flight coming home to a living thing that loved you whether you fed it or petted it or dressed it up in frilly doll clothes on a regular basis.

Her father's office was lined with photographs of the animals. "Thank you, Doctor, Love Milton," was scrawled over a huge color picture of an iguana sunning on a kitchen table. "The best doctor in town is you! I mean it! Love, Clyde," was scribbled over a picture of a frog. But on Matt's desk was a picture of Dinah, in a bathing suit at the beach, her hair frilling across her face, her finger pointing at him to stop, not to dare take her picture. "It captures you perfectly," he told her. "And that's why I love it."

They had been planning a trip together, to New York City. Matt had a symposium on feline leukemia he had to attend, a paper he had to give, some funding sources for the clinic he needed to see, and he thought they could take a week, see the sights in between his business. It'd be fun for her.

"New York City!" Dinah said. She was terrified and excited. She stayed up late trying on outfits and discarding them in a puddle on her floor. She took the nail scissors and tried to spike her hair and ended up despairing of it altogether. She marked the days on her calendar. Every night she called her friend Tonette and talked about the city.

"Watch out for lockup rooms," Tonette said soberly. "They grab you and chain you right to the bed. Anyone with enough money can do whatever they want to you."

Both girls were silent for a moment. Dinah struggled with a clip of fear, then fought it down. "How do you know?" she said.

"I saw it on a TV show," Tonette said. "It was very realistic." She heaved a sigh. "Look, just do me a favor, carry a nail file. The metal kind."

Dinah didn't realize she was getting sick until she started looking for the nail file. At first she blamed it on overexertion, all that running up and down the stairs. She put on an extra sweater against the chill she felt. She flung water on her face, and by the time Matt came home from work, she was running a fever so high, he called one of his doctor friends, who came right over, evening or not, and said Dinah had a mild case of the flu.

Dinah refused to believe she would be sick for long. She drank so much tea, she was barely in bed before she had to get up and pee again. She chewed vitamin C's, and she practiced positive thinking, sure she could will the flu away. In the end, although her fever was gone, her ears were still clogged up, and she was still too weak to go.

"I can rest in New York," she protested.

Matt sat at the edge of her bed and took her hands. "I know, pumpkin," he said. He sighed. "Look, I'm canceling."

"Don't," she said. "I'll be mad if you do." She struggled to sit up. "The animals will be furious if you don't get their funding," she said, trying to grin.

He reached down and held her. "I'm going to call Darcy, from the clinic. She'll stay with you, okay? And I'll call you every night." He stroked back Dinah's hair. "We'll go again soon. And we won't combine business with our pleasure, either. How about that?"

Dinah forced a smile. "Bring me back something wonderful," she said.

chapter 3

Matt felt guilty. He should have been looking over the paper he was supposed to deliver or meeting with other veterinarians, but instead he prowled the streets looking for gifts that a girl getting over a fever might cherish. He combed the outdoor vendors, buying dangling bell earrings he could imagine chiming against Dinah's long, pale neck, silky scarves she could cinch about her waist. He bought her a T-shirt with the word "SoHo" scribbled across it in purple ink, a cap with "The Village" spelled in sequins, and his favorite—a green rubber Statue of Liberty headband she'd never wear but would surely laugh at and love.

At night he called her. "Wait until you see what I have for you," he teased.

"Is it alive?" she said hopefully.

"I miss you," he said, which was the truth, and he told her he was lonely, which was even truer. As soon as he hung up, he thought about what she might be doing. Reading, probably, or calling her friend Tonette and tying up the phone for hours. Thinking about her warmed him; calling her had been fuel. He was happy she hadn't reached that difficult stage he sometimes saw with the kids of his clients. Teenagers hanging back sulkily from their parents, rolling their eyes, jittering their legs. He didn't know how he had gotten so lucky with Dinah. He kept waiting for her to turn away from him, to refuse to go out walking with him at night, to suddenly want to keep her life secret. It was natural for kids to separate from their parents. It would probably be better for both of them if she did, because as it was, every time he thought of her going off to college, or falling in love with a boy who might usurp him in her affections, he felt a crumpling in his heart.

He tried to be less lonely in New York. When the symposium broke up into small discussion groups of five (and his seemed to be the most serious minded—not one of them cracked so much as a smile), he did his best to be friendly. "Why don't we all get dinner together tonight?" he suggested to his group.

A woman in a red suit shrugged apologetically. "Oh, I'm so tired, I can barely manage to ring up room service," she said.

"There's great jazz clubs here, too," Matt suggested.

The others in the group were silent for a moment. One man shifted on his seat. "Maybe tomorrow," he said to Matt finally. "I think we're all a little beat."

That night Matt went out into the city by himself. He had no idea where to go, so he walked. He traveled from the Upper West Side across to the East, down to Chinatown and over to the West Village. He prowled in the shops and looked at the people. He stopped at a drugstore and bought one of those disposable cameras and snapped pictures, even when he saw people giving him amused, hard looks. He knew he was acting like tourist, but he didn't care. The pictures would be funny, and he knew Dinah would love them.

He was making his way back to the hotel, his film used up, his desire for movement spent, when he saw the café. It was still early. He could stop in and have coffee. A lovely young woman in a black coat passed by him and smiled. Matt, pleased and surprised, smiled back. He turned to find that smile again, but she was gone. And then he looked at the café and pushed open the door and went inside.

He sat at a small chipped wood table, surrounded by couples hunched over coffee, and singles, their eyes meeting like magnets. He ordered espresso from a waitress who was young and coltish. "The reader's here tonight," she advised him, pointing to a very beautiful woman with the blackest hair Matt had ever seen.

The reader was wearing jeans and a man's white shirt, and beside her, on a chair, was a battered paperback copy of *On the Beach*. She was leaning across the table, holding the hand of a middle-aged man, who was weeping quietly.

"A reader?" Matt said. He looked back at her book. For a bookmark, she had wedged a napkin between the pages.

The waitress held up her hand, palm side up. "Yeah," she said. "You know, the future?" She grinned at Matt. "Lilly only charges ten bucks. It's not very private, but she's really good. She told me I was going to get into Brandeis. Everyone said I wouldn't, that my SATs were too shitty, but she was right." She scratched one of her legs. "She talks to the dead, too," she said. "She got me through to my grandmother. Not my grandfather, though."

"Waitress!" someone called, and apologetically she turned from Matt.

Matt looked over at Lilly. Silly, he thought. Just another superstition. He didn't cross the street when he saw a black cat (in fact, he went toward the animal to pet it, to gauge its health by the feel of its coat), he didn't avoid ladders, he didn't even have a lucky number. He didn't believe the dead spoke or the future was set enough so that you might see it before it happened. He studied Lilly. She looked sincere enough, but that could be part of her charm. She was doing her reading right out there in the open, which seemed strange to him. He would want privacy, he thought. He wouldn't want anyone else to hear. He looked around the café. No one else seemed concerned. Everyone seemed involved in their own lives.

He moved his chair closer to Lilly. He tried to hear.

Lilly felt someone staring at her, shoving away her concentration. She looked up for an instant. A man at the far table was watching her. She sensed him listening. Bad manners, she thought, and she tried to ignore him, to not let him waver her focus. She concentrated on her client, who had told her only his first name, which was Tony. She sipped in a breath, going inward a bit, until the present wavered and then opened up like a ragged seam, and then she saw Tony's daughter, a pale little girl in a white dotted Swiss dress, shimmering in front of a blue sedan, calling out something that Lilly leaned forward to hear.

"What?" Tony said. "What is it?"

"She says to tell you it didn't hurt. She died quickly," Lilly said.

Tony shut his eyes. "Christ," he said. "Oh, dear Christ." He raced one hand over his face.

"It's okay," Lilly said, even though she knew it wasn't. She felt sudden heat on her face, and she looked up. That man was staring at her again. She shook it off as she would a mosquito. Tony grasped both her hands in his again and nodded at her, speechless, and as soon as she felt his touch, his daughter vanished like a small shock.

"That's all I'm getting tonight," Lilly told Tony. "Sometimes it doesn't all come."

He nodded, then he dug into his pocket and pulled out an envelope. "God love you," he said, giving her the envelope, her pay, and then he walked heavily toward the door.

God love me, Lilly thought. She was tense and exhausted, and she still felt the man's stare. She looked up and gave him a frank and hostile glare. He gave her a weak half smile, and she sighed. It was too late for this nonsense. Sometimes men came over and wanted readings simply because they wanted her. She always wanted to tell them that they'd have six kids by next year, that they'd be transferred to a job somewhere in Alaska, but she never did. It was too easy to be a charlatan. She told them the truth, because she knew they weren't listening. They were studying her eyes or her hair or simply watching her hand and wondering what it would feel like spread on their stomach, their thigh, their groin.

The starer got up and came over to her table. He was probably the kind of man who was handsome sometimes, she thought. His hair was a bit too shaggy, his nose a little too broad. He hesitated in front of her table.

"You talk to the dead?" he said.

"Sometimes they talk to me," she said.

"So, do I have a future?" he said. He sat down.

"Everyone has a future," Lilly said. "Let's see how much of it I can see." She looked down at his hands. He had written across one of them, in blue ink. "Buy Dinah earrings." Dinah, she thought. Okay.

"Let's see," Lilly told him. She shut her eyes, and suddenly she felt his future storming toward her, gripping her like an undertow. She felt herself tugged under, losing control, and then she jerked herself upright. She tried to grab on to the garbled images rushing past, to remember a face, a color, and then she heard a man's voice, low and guttural, warning, "Don't," and then there was a kind of loud hissing, and she heard "Look," but were they two separate words or did they mean "Don't look"? She felt dizzy, as if a hand were clapped across her mouth and nose. She gasped for air, and then an image exploded outward and slowed, so clear and crisp and real, it was dazzling. She saw a wedding band in the palm of someone's hand. It was round and blindingly shiny. Sparks glinted from it, and it rolled from the hand, falling, sizzling with sudden new fire. There were trees and a car racing along the highway, so fast she couldn't see who was in it, and then she heard "Dinah!" roared at her so loudly, she started. She scraped back on her chair. She was sweating.

"Hey," she heard Matt's surprised voice, dimmed, as if under water, and then she saw blond hair and blue eyes staring at her, and then she saw water, the silky shimmer of a lake, and the image snapped off, as abruptly as a light, slamming her back into the present. She had a headache. She was sweating, and she felt vaguely uneasy.

Lilly touched the wood of the table, her hair, her face, grounding herself back. Her hand trembled. She looked up at Matt, stunned.

"What?" he said. "What was that?"

"I saw a wedding band," Lilly said. Dinah, she thought. His wife. "And water." Her tongue felt thick and heavy in her mouth. Her head pounded. "I heard someone say Dinah."

Matt shook his head. He pointed to his hand, where he had written Dinah's name. "Hey, no fair," he said, smiling.

Lilly shook her head. "You really love her," she said.

"Again, no fair," he said, but he smiled again. His face warmed with color.

Lilly tried to read more on him, but something was off. She couldn't get anything except a circuitry of voices, the sound knotting together. *Di-nah.* The sound scraped in her head. *Dinah.* Lilly recoiled from it. She made the sound push back. She shook her head and stared around her. There was the table. There was the night waitress she liked. She was back in the present. "I'm sorry," she said. "Sometimes it just shuts off."

He nodded, and then suddenly she saw something: a man in uniform whispering to her. Suddenly she knew who it was. "Your father was in the army," Lilly said, "wasn't he?"

Matt started. His father. "How'd you know that?" he said.

Lilly smiled.

Matt looked up. His eyes flickered. Behind Lilly, a woman was leaning along the wall, waiting for her turn. Hesitantly Matt got up. "I never knew my father," he said.

"Well, he knows you," Lilly said. Matt frowned. "Don't

you want to know more?" she asked. She followed his gaze and saw the woman, then turned back to Matt.

"I don't know," Matt said. He was embarrassed by the other woman. "I guess not."

"Well, you can always come back," Lilly said. "It's all right if you do." She turned from him to the waiting woman, and Matt, a little disconcerted, went home to call his daughter.

When he told Dinah he'd seen a fortune-teller, she begged him to go back. "That's so cool!" she said. "Ask her about my future. Ask to speak to Fred."

He laughed. Fred was a tiger snake who had died of nothing more dramatic than old age.

"Who's to say animals don't have souls?" Dinah said, and coughed into the phone.

He hung up and lay across the bed. Animals with souls. Imagine that. He dealt with death all the time at his practice, and he treated each death with respect. When animals died, he called their owners and came out and spoke to them personally. "You might want to go to an animal bereavement group," he counseled. "Don't let anyone tell you an animal's life isn't worth grief." He was willing to dispose of the pet if that was what the owner wanted, but he also recommended pet cemeteries and priests or rabbis who might say a few words, and he knew florists who would give discounts. He held hands and dried eyes, and afterward he wrote a carefully thought out sympathy card for the owner. "I am so sorry that Diane didn't make it through the operation. She was a magnificent cocker spaniel and I know she will be sorely missed, but rest assured that all the love and care you gave her helped make her declining years comfortable and peaceful."

And sometimes, six months or a year later, flowers would arrive at the house for Matt. Attached would be a note, thanking Matt for caring. "You made Binky's passage easier for me," someone would write. "I feel I can go on." Sometimes owners said they felt the animal's presence still around them. Ghostly visions of a guinea pig in the kitchen that woke someone up. A food dish that felt warm when you picked it up. "I can go on," the letters always said. Matt saved every one of the notes, carefully putting them in a light blue box that used to be Maggy's, pulling them out when he felt blue, because every time he read one of those letters, he felt better. Love never dying. Ah, yes.

Matt spent all the next morning listening to lectures on feline chemotherapy and mortality rates, looking at slides, and thinking about the dead speaking and the future. "He knows you," Lilly had said about his father. He thought how ridiculous that was. His father had died not knowing one thing about him, including his existence. Anyone his age probably had a father in the service. It was a good guess, that was all. Lilly was smart. She picked up cues.

He walked around Chelsea that night, thinking about Lilly, and when he wound up at the café that evening, he told himself it was simply because he liked their coffee.

She was there again, this time in a short black dress, hitched up higher with a leather belt, her shoes kicked off under the table. Her hair was tangled up on her head, held in place with a silver clip, and he thought, with new surprise that he had never seen anyone more beautiful. She was sitting across from a young girl with an angry crop of acne. Lilly was gesturing passionately. She leaned forward and touched the girl. He checked the book in her bag, a new one, *Sons and Lovers*. He didn't know why it should matter, but it made him feel better that she read, that she was intelligent. He turned around and motioned for the waitress, and then he watched Lilly. She looked so suddenly luminous to him that he thought he'd ask her to dinner. He watched her, and he waited.

* * *

"Dinner?" Lilly said. "I don't know. Do you think that's such a good idea?" She didn't want to say "You have a wife."

"I have a boyfriend," she said, watching his face, but his gaze was still steady.

"I'm just here for the week," he said. "I'd just like to talk to you, that's all."

Lilly studied him for a moment, trying to figure out what it was he really wanted. He was married. He loved his wife. But he said he just wanted to talk, and he was leaving soon. There was no danger. All she would be doing after work was going home or taking herself to a movie. She thought of Robert, who hadn't called her once in four days, and then she looked up at Matt, his face alive with an interest so strong, it seemed to wash over her.

"All right," she said. "Dinner tomorrow is fine."

That night Lilly wandered restlessly around her apartment. Downstairs, the married couple was arguing.

"Well, even if you didn't have such *intense* personal problems, a kid would be out of the question," the man shouted.

She peered outside the window. Johnny Jerkoff was chinning himself nude on the edge of his loft bed. Experimentally she waved at him, and he quickly ducked his head from sight, leaving his body white and exposed before her. She sprawled on the couch and thought about Robert, and the more she thought of him, the more his image dissolved, the more it shaped itself into Matt, a stranger whose features she didn't even really have clearly in her head. A married man from Ohio who was interested enough in her to ask her to dinner, but she didn't know why she had agreed except that it would be nice to have the attention. It didn't matter. In less than a week Matt would be gone.

She met him in Washington Square Park. He didn't see her at first, and she took her time, watching him. He was wearing jeans and a sweatshirt and cowboy boots, and he was taking such exuberant joy snapping pictures that she felt charmed. She thought of Robert, snarling and hunched over his videocameras, setting up shots for hours before he'd film anything that he said was worthwhile, anything that he said might be called art; and here was Matt, crouching down to get a pigeon, balancing on a ledge to snap a skyline. She watched him, smiling, for five minutes before he spotted her, and then he slung the camera back around his neck, embarrassed.

"I know. 'Tourist' is written all over me, isn't it?" he said. "Dinah was supposed to come with me this trip. I want to make her a photographic travelogue." He grinned and snapped two more pictures of the park.

"Come on, tourist, let's walk," Lilly said.

They ambled along, stopping for pretzels, looking at all the cheap socks and sunglasses and jewelry the street vendors were hawking.

"Oh, look at these," Matt said, holding up black T-shirts with scenes of New York on them. "She'll love it," he said. He pulled out shirts, frowning at the sizes. "These can't be right," he said. "This medium looks tiny.

"She's your size," he said, holding up the shirt toward Lilly. "Can I just look at it against you?"

"Be my guest," Lilly said. She reached for the shirt, but he took it and smoothed it along her back, so slowly and gently that for a moment Lilly felt an electric current. She didn't want him to pull the shirt away.

"Perfect," he said, and she turned toward him. She looked at his hands. She remembered the feel of them on her back.

"You like the shirt?" he said, but he was looking at her, not at the shirt.

"She'll love it," Lilly said.

"Sold," he said, and handed the vendor a fistful of crumpled bills.

He bought her dinner at a little Italian place in the West

Village that he said he had discovered himself, just by walking around. It was a dark hole in the wall, and he looked so handsome and at home with himself that Lilly was surprised to feel a twist of expectation in her stomach.

"So," Matt said, pouring her some wine. "Tell me everything."

"Everything?" Lilly laughed.

"How did you start doing readings? You don't really like New York, do you?" He sipped some wine and leaned toward her. "Tell me about your childhood. Tell me about your boyfriend."

"Why do you want to know all this?" she said. She thought of Robert, who said you could know all about a person by the things they didn't tell you, who valued images and silence, who liked the way a mouth moved more than the words it might say.

Matt rested his head on the cups of his palms. "I just do," he said, and Lilly flushed.

They talked all through coffee, all through dessert. She told him about Nora and Whitley, about her readings, and about Robert. He told her about growing up, about his vet practice, and most of all about Dinah, and when he spoke about her his whole body seemed to let off a sheen.

"I wish she could have come here," he said. He looked at Lilly. "What, why are you looking like that?" he said.

"You're so in love with your wife," Lilly said. "It's so nice. It makes me yearn a little, I guess."

Matt laughed. "Dinah's my *daughter*," he said.

"Your daughter?" Lilly said. She felt the air lightening around her, the colors growing sharper.

"I thought you were psychic," he said.

"Not always," Lilly said.

"Good," he said. "We still have the element of surprise here."

He walked her all the way back to her apartment, and

this time when she heard someone whisper, *"Dinah,"* she laughed the voice away. God, she thought. It's his daughter.

But when they got to her apartment, he didn't hesitate, he didn't ask if he could use her bathroom or the phone or have a cup of tea. She felt a pinprick of disappointment. "Well," she said awkwardly.

"See you tomorrow," he said, happily, and she felt instantly better.

Lilly knew she was being silly, but all that week, when she was dressing for work, she chose her softest silk shirts, her most delicate skirts and earrings. She brushed her hair a thousand times with a natural-bristle brush from Italy until her hair seemed burnished, she daubed perfume on her pulse points and hoped for the best, hoped that Robert would suddenly appear because he had needed her more than he needed his movie.

"Something's going on," said her clients, talking among themselves. They didn't really care that Lilly's readings had grown sloppy just in the space of a few days. She was more intense. Sometimes it seemed as if a light shone out of her, and they flickered around it as desperately as moths. They told one another that Lilly had mystery, and now there was over an hour's wait to get a reading.

That afternoon Lilly took off early so she could show Matt Central Park. "My God, look at the dogs!" he said. He ignored the statues and the kids showing off on Rollerblades and pivoted to watch a standard poodle with a rhinestone leash trot by. He walked right up to the horse-drawn carriages and studied the horses, touching their coats, patting their long, sad faces. "Poor guys," he said. "This can't be fun for them."

Lilly led him by the water, waiting for him to admire five or six different dogs and one Siamese cat perched on its owner's lean shoulder.

They sat down. Matt stretched. "Sky and grass in New York City," he said. "Isn't that something." He beamed at Lilly. A young couple walked by them and plunked down on the grass nearby, spreading out a worn Indian blanket. Matt glanced over and smiled at them happily. The boy braced one hand against the girl's head and tipped it back. They began kissing passionately.

Matt looked away. He was quiet, studying the grass, and Lilly was suddenly embarrassed.

Abruptly, Matt picked up his camera and started taking shots. He got the horses and, laughing, got a shot of a man walking by with a mannequin cradled in his arms. Lilly basked in the sun, and then suddenly Matt turned toward her and snapped her picture.

"Hey," she said, holding up her hand, shielding her face. "You think Dinah's going to want that?"

He laughed and snapped another shot. "This isn't for Dinah," he said.

"Let me comb my hair," she said. She grabbed for her bag, the one Robert was always yelling at her was so large. She was searching for her comb when she heard the camera, and she looked up, startled, and he clicked again. "Hey," she said. "Hey—"

"It'll be the most you," he told her.

Next to them, the boy lowered his girlfriend to the ground. "Come on," Matt said, "let's go."

Lilly could read Matt. She saw his wide grassy lawn. She knew what his clinic looked like. She knew his daughter was pale and blond and had eyes the color of slate. She knew too that he was going back to Ohio, and that she was staying here. This is dangerous, she thought, eavesdropping on a life you have no business in, a life no one's invited you to share in. This is how people get into trouble. This is how lives are ruined. She told herself she had better tend to her own garden. Matt had taken her picture, but he was leaving. And she had a boyfriend. She had her own life. She'd tell Robert he could film her; she'd do what she could to get back the relationship.

Robert called that evening to announce he was coming in. "How about a movie?" Matt asked later, and when Lilly told him about Robert, she thought he looked disappointed, but he simply nodded. "Oh," he said, "well, another time," and left the café.

That night Lilly wore a new pale pink dress, pearly blue earrings, and so subtle a touch of perfume that it surprised her when she caught its scent.

Robert breezed in, flushed with the night. After unzipping his leather jacket, he flung himself down on her couch, his long legs outstretched. "The film's going to be *great*," he told her. "I edited those crummy monkeys so they look like goddamned royalty—they've got a real majesty about them. It may just be a documentary, but I could still win awards."

"I bet you do," Lilly said. She felt relieved. He was in such a good mood, maybe she wouldn't even have to offer to let him film her. She tried to see if she could read him tonight, gave him a quick once-over. Two hands clasping. Relieved, she rubbed her arms across his arms.

"I've missed you," she said, but she was missing Matt. She missed the crackle and glint in the air when she spotted him coming toward her.

He looked at her curiously. "Really? That's—that's kind."

"Kind?" she said, perplexed. He stood up, suddenly awkward. Matt floated into her mind, and, instantly guilty, she moved toward Robert.

"I don't know," Robert said.

Lilly reached to touch his shoulder, but he moved past her. "What don't you know?" she said.

"Look, I don't know about us." He hunched his shoulders and heaved a sigh. "Look—it's so ridiculous, but honestly, the thing is I met somebody. In the editing room," he said.

Lilly swayed on her feet. She looked at the corner of the room, and when she looked back at Robert he looked like a stranger to her. The air hummed around her. She suddenly noticed a crumpled pair of his sweat socks, small white fists gathering dust in the corner.

He followed her gaze and then went over and scooped up the socks. "Lilly, don't you want to discuss this?"

"No," Lilly said. Robert looked at her with new interest, but Lilly felt suddenly exhausted.

"I feel so bad," he said, getting up, trying to hold her, but she sidestepped. "I keep remembering all the wild times we had. . . . Jesus, I'm getting all nostalgic now," he said. "You know, who knows what this will be? Maybe it's just a—a thing. It'll burn out, then we can start fresh."

"I don't think so," Lilly said. She was proud of herself for not crying. It seemed really important that she not cry, so she kept the reins tight. She studied him. She felt like saying, "You will never be a great filmmaker, you will never be famous," intoning it as if it were some psychic prediction that even he, an unbeliever, might wonder about worriedly, lying awake at night in his new girlfriend's arms; but instead she walked to the door and opened it. Instead she was right, she was fair, she was one with the universe. "You'd better go," she said.

Robert was gone, but he had really been gone a long time before they broke up. When she told Matt, he frowned.

"I'm sorry," he said. He ran one hand through his hair. "I'm sorry, too, that I'm leaving tomorrow."

"Tomorrow?" Lilly said.

"If you ever get to Ohio . . ." Then he laughed. "No one gets to Ohio if they can help it," he said.

Lilly smiled. She was sad that he was leaving, but she had never really seen a future with her and Matt; she had simply daydreamed about one, and she was smart enough to know that the two things were entirely different. She knew all the ways a person could fool himself.

He reached into his jacket pocket and pulled out a packet of photos. "Hey, I had these developed," he said. He showed her New York scenes. "Dinah'll love it, don't you think?" He had punks with safety pins in their shirts. He had dogs romping in Central Park. Then he leaned forward and she saw a photo in his shirt pocket. Her own face flashed before her, and she looked at him, but he was pointing out the skyline in a photo to her. She moved closer to him, pretending to look at the photo but instead looking at the shaggy, shiny line of his hair, the curve of his ear.

That day, while he was at his meetings, she kept thinking that she saw him. It was simply nerves, it was a phenomenon. She knew theoretically that anyone could hear the dead or see the future, that anyone could probably talk to the dead; but this was something different. She had had clients swear to her that they had seen their dead husbands sitting on the bed, but they were women who hadn't slept in four days or eaten in two. They were women so desperate for connection, they would have seen aliens landing on their front yards if they had wanted to. She wished she had a photo of him, but she couldn't think of any easy way to ask for one or take one.

She thought they should be enjoying their last bit of time together. They should be exchanging addresses for postcards that would probably dwindle right into nothing. Instead, though, he seemed as restless as she was, and on Matt's last night they had dinner at a new French bistro on Twenty-second Street. They didn't talk much, and they both kept ordering more wine. "We'll have to keep in touch," Matt said finally.

They lingered over dinner, and then, abruptly, Matt stood up. "Please," he said. "Can we just walk a little?"

He looked as if he needed to talk, but she couldn't hear a word he was saying to her because of all the voices that had abruptly started clamoring in her head, crowding her with whispers and veiled threats. *"No. Careful."* She felt like swatting them out of her way. She glanced at him, his head was down, and then she followed him out. He looked miserable, and then the voices moving inside of Lilly grew louder and more insistent. *"Careful,"* they said. Matt took her hand. *"Dinah,"* a voice said.

She tried navigating them toward the Village. They could sit in the Peacock and have dessert in a dark corner. They could just walk, right through to SoHo, but no matter how she turned, the streets were somehow always heading for Lilly's. She let the streets lead them, right up to her door, and as soon as they were inside, he stopped talking.

They didn't talk anymore that first night, but they didn't have to. Lilly pulled the sheet and the comforter from her bed down onto the floor, and as soon as she reached to touch him, the voices in her head grew louder and louder, but she kissed his neck anyway, she kissed his mouth, and then all she heard was his breathing, and the steady beat of his heart soared up against her own.

When she woke up in the morning, she knew it was the beginning of something. He was already in her kitchen, making pancakes. The sheet was torn, the comforter bunched up around her. Lilly got up and padded into the kitchen. The table was set. He had tea in a pot, warm and fragrant.

"I can't believe this," she said.

"What, you thought I couldn't cook?" he said.

"That's not what I mean," Lilly said.

He put down the spatula for a moment. "I've always known you," he said.

She sat down at the table, watching him moving through her kitchen comfortably. A voice was hissing in her head, but she ignored it. "Ditto," she said.

He turned and grinned at her.

"Oh God," Lilly said. "Can we take this slow?"

"Absolutely," he said. "I have to go back to Ohio in less than two hours."

"Oh," she said. The days stretched and pulled ahead of her. "So how soon can you come back?" she said.

"How soon can you come there with me?" he said.

Lilly, flooded with attention, gave more and more attention to the people she read. She usually read for an hour and then grew exhausted, but now people said she read for an hour and a half or sometimes two hours if the dead had a lot to say, and she never once charged extra.

"Well," Nora said when Lilly told her about Matt. "I just want you to remember that if he can fall in love so soon, he can fall out of love that much sooner."

"Oh, for heaven's sake," Lilly said, annoyed. "What would ever possess you to say a thing like that to me?"

"The Bronstein women don't have good luck with men," Nora said mildly. "That's all I'm saying."

"You don't call Whitley good luck?" Lilly said.

"Well, of course I do," Nora said. "But luck changes."

Lilly didn't believe in luck, but she did believe in fate, in destined love.

"This is happening too quickly," Matt said on one visit.

"Ha," Lilly said. "That's what you think."

Still, it was always a shock to see him again, tall and beautiful and the air humming around him. She wanted to know everything about him, but she wanted him to tell her. She didn't want to hear it from the dead, who had opinions of their own, who were not, contrary to popular opinion, always one hundred percent accurate but filtered everything through their own experience. *"Take it slow,"* some said. *"Speed it up!"* a voice shouted. Lilly swatted the voices away.

Matt made her stand up beside him. "You want to know how I can tell we belong together?" he said.

"Fate," Lilly said.

Matt laughed. "No," he said. "It's because your head fits right here along my shoulder."

One night they went to the sixplex, and after the first movie he grabbed her hand. "Hey, I want to see the credits," she said.

"No, you don't," he insisted. "Trust me."

Trust me, she thought. She got up, and then he quickly edged her into a line, and they were filing into another movie, sneaking in like kids. It was a terrible movie, but he laughed. He reached across and took her hand and laced his fingers with hers. And this time he stayed for the credits, still holding her hand.

He saw possibilities in everything. When she complained that she hated her apartment, he bought wine and cookies and made her come up to the top of her roof and look at the stars. While Robert was aloof, while Robert had stared and stared at the friends she had introduced him to, always evaluating them for film, Matt genuinely liked people. He charmed strangers on the street, stopping them to compliment them on their pets, to give expert advice. He charmed Lilly, too, disappearing into a Woolworth's and presenting her with two goldfish in a small plastic bag, the only pet he thought belonged in New York City. "Everyone needs an animal roommate," he said.

They stayed in some evenings, lost in bed, making love, talking, making plans. They'd buy a big new house in Ohio.

"We're impulsive," Lilly said, but he shook his head.

"No," he said seriously. "Sometimes I think it's fast, but I told you, I've always known you."

"What about Maggy?" she said. "You married her."

"She fit me," he said. "But I didn't fit her."

"I miss you," he said. "Sometimes I think I see you, all over Akron. But you know, if I concentrate really hard and want to see you over there by the window, I bet I could." He toyed with a lock of her hair, swinging it like a jump rope. He lifted her shirt and kissed her stomach, pulling her toward him.

Lilly lifted herself up. "What would you do if I just died?" she said.

Matt looked at her, stunned. "Why would you ask me a thing like that?"

"I don't know. I'm with people dealing with death all day long. And I'm with the dead. And I can't imagine being away from you."

"I'd live a horrible, haunted life," he said.

"I'd haunt you," Lilly said.

Matt shook his head. "No," he said. He let the hank of hair drop from his fingers. "There's no question of that one. I'd be the ghost."

Lilly stretched. "Well, I'm not going to die," she said. "I'm too happy and too much in love."

"Well, in that case," he said, and kissed her again.

Dinah's father's courtship of Lilly was different from his courtship of any other girlfriend Dinah had known. For the first time in her life her father seemed a little unhinged to her. He flew to New York another weekend to see Lilly, promising to take Dinah next time, arranging for her to stay with Tonette, and when he came home he was so exhausted and jittery, it made her nervous to be near him.

He lunged when the phone rang at night. He left work to race home and fetch the mail, and if there was even a postcard from Lilly, he was delirious. He called Lilly nearly every night, tying up the line that Dinah had been thinking of using for an hour or so herself, and as soon as he got off the phone he would pass by Dinah as if she were a ghost. She stood in front of him, making him see her. "Hey," he said, pleased.

"Isn't it awfully soon?" she said meanly.

"No," he said, thoughtful, "probably not soon enough." He ruffled Dinah's hair. "You two have got to meet."

"Sure," Dinah said, but she had fifty reasons why the next weekend wasn't good, or the weekend after. He didn't talk to her as much anymore. When she went out to the porch, he was spinning in dreams. She was only fifteen, but she left her college catalogs right on her bookshelf; she allowed words like "San Francisco" and "Boston" to enter her conversation at dinner, and when she tentatively stole a glance at her father, he was smiling, a million miles away.

"What's she like?" Dinah demanded during dinner one night. She couldn't tell much from the photo Matt showed her. All she saw was a lot of black curly hair, a face in shadows. She knew Lilly didn't care that Matt lived in Ohio, she knew Lilly loved to read and loved animals. "What does she do?" Dinah asked.

Matt looked vague. He took a long swig of his wine. "Well, she's clairvoyant. A medium. She was the one who told my fortune when I first went to New York."

"A what?" Dinah said, astonished, suddenly interested despite herself. "She's a Gypsy?"

"I didn't say that," he said. "She's not a Gypsy at all. She works at a restaurant. She has *clients*. She's very well respected," he said. "The people who come to her are artists and writers and teachers and doctors, too, I think. She's really educated and funny and . . . well, you'll have to meet her. You'll see for yourself."

"You don't think it's weird that that's what she does?" Dinah said. She tried to imagine the face in the photograph, hunched over a crystal ball, peering into the glass. "What'd she see in your future?" she asked. Matt laughed. "What'd she say about me?" She suddenly felt a little exposed. Something clipped at her stomach.

"She doesn't read people unless they ask," Matt said. "That's invasion of privacy."

"I still think it's weird."

"No, it's kind of wonderful," he said.

Dinah was looking at Matt so doubtfully that he finally got up and started clearing the table. Balancing plates and glasses, he went into the kitchen. The water splashed into the sink. Steam rose. And he began to hum, tapping out the rhythms against his thigh.

Dinah watched her father. Love changed people. She had never seen her father this happy before in her entire life. She couldn't explain it, but although he was as loving and devoted as ever, there seemed to be a new and sudden force field around him—a Lilly field—she thought, and no matter how much she tried, she somehow couldn't break through. It began to scare her a little. She could ask him for fifty dollars three days in a row, and he would give it to her. She could walk out of the house in a skirt so short that she wouldn't dare sit down in it, and he wouldn't say one thing to her. She was late to school at least three times a week, and that wasn't counting the days she sometimes didn't show up at all, and still he seemed oblivious of anything but Lilly.

"I want you to meet her," he kept saying. He kept trying to schedule a visit to Ohio for Lilly, but something always went wrong. Lilly's apartment flooded, and she had to be there. She got called to jury duty and was sequestered all weekend. "I'll write you a note and get you out of school so you can come with me to New York," he said to Dinah.

"I have a test," Dinah said, even though she secretly ached to see New York City. She thought it must be the coolest place in the whole world, but if it meant meeting Lilly, she wasn't so sure she wanted to go. It was hard enough watching him change when he was missing Lilly. She didn't know what he'd be like when they were all together. She kept thinking of the force field Lilly had somehow set up.

"I'm really serious about this woman," Matt told Dinah late one night when the two of them were sprawled out on the porch. Dinah concentrated on a scab on her knee. "What would you think about my getting married, about Lilly coming here to live with us?"

"I don't know her," Dinah said. It was the kind of thing people said when they didn't dare say what was really moving in their hearts. She tried to reassure herself, to tell herself that this was what she had wanted for her father, and that in any case she was leaving for college in a few years.

"I know," he said. "I know this is so rushed, but neither one of us can help it." He threw an arm about Dinah. "Do you think it's stupid, me being so daffy in love at my ripe old age?"

"It's fine," Dinah said, but she felt doubtful.

He tried to fix it. He kept trying to arrange a visit. He kept showing Dinah photos of Lilly she didn't want to see, staring deep into them way past the time Dinah lost interest.

Every time Lilly called, he made Dinah get on the phone, but as soon as Dinah heard Lilly's voice, her mind numbed. She couldn't concentrate on anything Lilly was saying to her. She couldn't say anything more than a few syllables. She only felt her father standing beside her, waiting for the phone, and as soon as he took it from her, she became invisible to him once again.

"What she like?" asked Dinah's best friend, Tonette.

"Like the others," Dinah said. "It'll never last."

"Is she pretty?"

"She's disgusting," Dinah said. "I saw a picture. And she's really weird, too. She talks to the dead."

"Really?" Tonette looked interested.

"She's probably a fake," Dinah said. "My Dad's too blinded to see it yet, that's all."

Tonette stretched. "Well, your father's really cute. I bet he'll find the right one soon enough, if that's what you're worried about."

Dinah, staring down at the bitten half-moon of nails on her hand, curled her fingers forward. "I want to marry her," her father had said. "I wasn't worried," Dinah said.

Lilly called almost every night, and it really bothered Dinah. She and her father knew each other better than anybody else in the world, but on the phone with Lilly, Matt became a stranger to her. He was wired. He had marathon conversations, where he gestured wildly. He whispered and shouted and laughed so loudly, Dinah couldn't concentrate on anything but the longing in his voice.

Grabbing his jacket, he grinned at Dinah. "I gotta take a walk. Be right back," he said, and then he was gone for hours, gone before she could ask if she could go with him.

The phone began to make Dinah nervous. When she picked it up, she could tell it was Lilly even before she spoke because of the force field, creeping right through the wires. "Dinah!" Lilly said, and even though Dinah knew it was better to act sweet, she felt as if she would drown if she didn't get off the phone.

"I have to study," she said.

She got to hate the ring of the phone. It was always Lilly. "Tell him to call me right away," Lilly said breathlessly. "He can call me no matter how late it is."

"I'll tell him," Dinah said.

That evening Matt came home starving. "Let's go get Italian food," he urged. Dinah pulled on her jacket. "Anyone call?" he said as they were at the door.

"Phone was dead quiet," Dinah said.

She didn't feel guilty through dinner. She and Matt toasted each other with sparkling water that she pretended was white wine. They had two desserts each, and she even convinced him to go to a movie. "Let me just stop at the house for some more money," he said.

As soon as he got inside, the phone rang. Dinah leaned along the doorjamb. "No, she didn't," she heard Matt say, and then he turned and frowned at Dinah.

Dinah lifted one hand. "I forgot to tell you!" she whispered. "Lilly called!"

"Tomorrow's fine," he said. "I'll call you at one." He held the phone closer. "Oh, me too, Lilly," he said. He hung up the phone slowly.

"I forgot," Dinah insisted. "I'm sorry. I'm really sorry."

Matt hesitated for just a moment. "Well," he said finally. "We'd better hurry if we want to catch that movie."

The next time Lilly got Dinah on the phone, Dinah felt a new prickliness in Lilly's voice, which made everything worse. "Write it down that I called," Lilly insisted. "You got a pencil?"

"Sure," said Dinah, her fingers motionless.

Lilly sighed. "I'm dying to meet you," she said.

"So you talk to the dead," Dinah blurted.

"Well, yes," Lilly said.

"So did Joan of Arc, only it was an ear infection," Dinah said. She was surprised when Lilly laughed.

"When I see you, I'll give you a reading," Lilly promised. "Wouldn't you like to see your future?"

"No," said Dinah. "I wouldn't."

Dinah felt her father slipping away from her. He even looked different. Leaner. Paler. His hair grown so long now, it worked its way into the collars of his shirts. Her spring break was coming up, and she began to stop at the travel agency on her way home, bringing back brochures of beaches and mountains and deserts. Package deals so cheap they could stay away for the whole two weeks. Without Lilly, all he'd have to do is look at her and know how lonely his relationship was making her feel. "I don't want you to break up," she could say. "I just want us to be the way we were." He'd say that he didn't for one moment realize—that of course they could work things out.

"We should go away," Dinah said.

Matt looked up at her. "You read my mind," he said.

"I vote for the Rockies," Dinah said, grinning.

"I have something more special," Matt said. He hesitated, his smile starting to spread. "New York City."

"New York City?" Dinah said.

"How'd you like to be a witness at your father's wedding?" Her grin changed a little. "What's the matter?" he said. "Why that face? I told you we were thinking about this, right?"

Dinah shrugged, helpless and angry.

"Is it Lilly?" he said.

"You don't know each other," Dinah said.

"That's where you're wrong," he said. "I know everything about her, even the things she hasn't told me yet." He pushed out a breath. "And you'll get to know her. Do you really think I'd fall in love with someone I didn't think you'd probably love, too? We're father and daughter, kiddo. We think pretty much alike, don't we?"

"I don't want to go to New York," Dinah said.

He looked at her with surprise. "I thought you were dying to see the city," he said. "I thought this could make up for the last time, when you got sick."

"I thought we could have a vacation."

"It *is* a vacation," Matt said. He cradled her head along his shoulder. "Come on," he said. Then he looked beyond her, at some point she couldn't see. "It's something, happiness," he said, stroking her hair. "It's incredible to look forward to your own life."

All that next afternoon Dinah wandered around the shopping mall. She phoned Tonette to meet her, but Tonette's mother answered. "Tonette's studying if she knows what's good for her," she told Dinah.

Aimlessly, Dinah drifted in and out of stores. She tried things on and took them off and couldn't remember the color or style or anything she had had on. She wandered through Macy's housewares on her way to Juniors. A couple was giggling over flatware, and Dinah suddenly felt undone, as if she were the only person in the world who was destined to be alone in life. Destiny. Lilly's word. She felt like bumping into people. She felt like saying something mean about what they were choosing.

Brides. No one said "old maid" anymore, but everyone knew what it meant. What made Tonette think that if boys didn't want her now, they might want her in college? Looks didn't change that much. People were pretty much fully formed by the time they were five.

She tried to act normal. She picked up a teapot and pretended to be examining it. If a clerk came over to her and accused her of shoplifting, she would deserve it. If she were arrested, it might be too good for her. As penance, she finally bought the teapot for Lilly; it was ten dollars more than she could really afford, but even when she had it gift-wrapped, it didn't make her feel any better.

chapter 4

They left for New York in record-breaking heat, and Dinah thought the weather was a bad omen. The Akron weatherman, Pat LeRoy, who was known for his foolish gestures and foppish costumes, had done the weather in green Bermuda shorts and a bright yellow T-shirt, a hat with a whirling propeller perched on his head.

By the time they got to the plane, Dinah's sleeveless white dress was pasted to her back. Matt bought a *Daily News*, and on the cover under the headline BAKED APPLE! 104 DEGREES IN THE SHADE was a picture of three half-naked kids cavorting under a spumy fountain. Dinah touched the picture of the water, and her finger came away smudged with ink.

"What, are you nervous?" Matt said as they settled onto their seats.

Dinah pulled the shade down over the window. "I just don't like planes," she said.

She pretended to sleep through most of the trip. She didn't tell him she was scared. She remembered stories someone at school had told her. Men grabbed girls off the streets and chained them to beds, and for a certain sum of money any man could do anything he wanted to them. People were shot for no reason at all.

She lagged behind while getting off the plane. "Wait," she called to Matt, who was rushing ahead. She grabbed on to the handle of his carry-on, tugging on it, making him see her.

"Hey!" A woman waved. She was in black jeans and a faded black T-shirt, her hair tugged into a ponytail, and as soon as Dinah saw her, she felt the force field creeping in, threatening and alive. Lilly. This was Lilly. Dinah grabbed for Matt's sleeve to steady her, but he was already moving toward Lilly.

"Remember me?" said Matt, and Lilly laughed, and when they kissed, Dinah looked fixedly at the blinking sign by the food concession. HOT DOGS, it said.

Arms surrounded Dinah. "I bet anything you're Dinah!" said Lilly, hugging her excitedly. Lilly smiled, but even Dinah could see how tentative she was, how unsure, and for a minute the force field weakened, right up until Matt took Lilly's hand and Dinah was left to trail behind.

The ride home was fast and noisy. Matt sat beside Lilly, and Dinah curled up in the back. Lilly blasted the radio and darted in and out of lanes, making Dinah so nervous, she clutched at her seat belt. The highway gradually turned into cityscape, with streets that seemed dirty and crowded with screaming people, and Lilly pointed out the sights. "Look, Dinah, the Empire State Building!" she said.

The car careened down one street and then another, flinging Dinah hard, up against the door. "Ouch," she said.

Lilly squinted along the road. "A parking place!" Lilly cried, and squeezed triumphantly into the spot.

They walked two blocks to a brick apartment building. It was so hot and humid, Dinah felt faint. The stoop had a hole in the top step. Across the street, an old woman in a flowered housedress was hanging out of the bottom window, staring in a kind of stupor. Below her, a filthy white cat stretched languidly and then spat. The air, thick and heavy, tasted metallic on Dinah's tongue.

"Welcome to my humble home," Lilly said. She pulled

open the door. The dark foyer smelled of burned popcorn, and Dinah could hear someone singing operatically from upstairs. "Jesus, shut up!" Lilly shouted, but the singing soared.

Dinah was horrified by Lilly's tiny slanted apartment. She had seen countless New York City apartments in the movies, and every one of them had seemed larger and more dramatic than the next. Lilly's apartment looked nothing like any of them. Dinah motioned to a door. "Another room's in there?" she said.

Lilly laughed. "Closet," she said.

In the bathroom, Dinah saw a water bug the size of her thumb skittering across the bottom of the tub, which was gray and glazed with soap. She scooped in a breath and bolted from the room, her heart bumping. "You've got bugs the size of dinosaurs!" she said, and Lilly laughed again.

"Welcome to New York," she said grandly.

Dinah wandered into the bedroom. Two goldfish were swimming in a big bowl. You and Me. That's what Lilly had named Matt's presents to her. She frowned at them and then felt guilty because you couldn't really hate an animal. Stuck in Lilly's mirror were four photos of Matt, pictures Dinah had never even seen before. Most of the pictures were taken in New York, in front of places she had never heard of. In a small gold dish were three silver pins, one of a dragon, which to her own thrilled amazement Dinah brazenly pocketed.

"Come on, let's take a walk," Lilly said.

Dinah, hand over the pocketed dragon pin, was nervous about going out into the city. It seemed dirtier and more crowded than she had imagined and stifling with heat. The people seemed deranged. Matt and Lilly and she walked all the way to the Village. At first Dinah was terrified. She refused to make eye contact. People were talking much too loudly. She saw a man spit less than six inches in front of her, and two blocks later a man grinned at her as he zipped up his fly, a line of urine curling into the street in back of him.

Dinah kept her purse clutched so closely to her chest, she could feel her heart beating right through it.

"You'll get mugged that way," Lilly said. "Walk like you own the street." She demonstrated, swaggering a little, but Dinah was unconvinced.

"Dad . . . ," she said, but he was saying something to Lilly, looking beyond her. "Dad," she said again, and he looped his arm about Lilly. The air seemed to shiver. It was the heat, or maybe it was Lilly's force field, but for one second Dinah was blinded; she couldn't see her father and, panicked, reached out for him. *"Dad!"* she said, and finally he turned.

"Don't shout," he said simply. "What is it?"

But by then she had forgotten, and as soon as she shrugged her shoulders, he turned back to Lilly.

New York City wasn't anything like she had imagined. Her eyes skated from one place to the next. Lilly, perfectly at home, was laughing. "Are you going to miss this?" she asked Lilly.

"Nope," Lilly said, taking Matt's arm.

Dinah moved slowly ahead of them as they walked down toward SoHo. Lilly and Matt were sipping kisses, tangling hands. "Come on," Lilly said to Dinah as they passed a store filled with nothing but earrings. Now Ear This, it was called. "Buy something," Lilly urged.

"Dad . . ." Dinah hesitated, but Matt laughed and shrugged.

"I'll wait this one out," he said, waving her inside with Lilly.

Inside were walls of cork, full of glittery earrings. Dinah stared, enraptured. She had never seen such earrings—silver, gold, ceramic, and glitter, in the shapes of appliances and toothbrushes and people.

"Take your time," Lilly said, and wandered over to a display of glass necklaces.

Dinah reached out and tentatively touched a pair of silver teapots, and she wanted them so badly that a line of pain coiled in her stomach. She looked at the price tag. Twenty dollars. She had never bought earrings for more than ten. As it was, she had just five in her purse now.

"Now those are terrific earrings," Lilly said, coming up behind Dinah and startling her. "I told Matt we'd have to take you here." She touched the teapot earrings. "Like them?" she asked.

Dinah wanted more than anything to put on the earrings and she would have, too, but she looked up at Lilly and saw that Lilly was gazing past her, out the window at Matt. Dinah turned away. "They're okay." She shrugged. Dinah walked away from Lilly, toward the door and her father.

"Hey you," Matt said. "Buy anything?"

"It's not my kind of place," Dinah said, stiffening. She thought of the earrings, and a wave of yearning hit her so hard, she placed both hands over her stomach.

"It isn't?" Matt said, and then Lilly came out of the store, grinning. She walked over to Dinah, who was looking intently at a crack in the sidewalk.

"Hey," Lilly said, and stretched out her fingers. Dangling from them were the teapot earrings. "Present," she said. "Go on, put them on."

Dinah hesitated.

"What, you don't like them?" Lilly said.

She started to curl her fingers around the earrings, and Dinah suddenly reached for them, feverish with longing. She felt them in her hands, weighty, smooth. She tried to hide how excited she was. "They're fine," Dinah said. She threaded the earrings into her lobes. She glanced at her reflection in the store window, shy and pleased, flushing with delight.

"Told you," Lilly said.

Dinah began to feel a little better. She walked behind Matt and Lilly and touched the teapot earrings, and a boy, passing by her, grinned.

"Nice earrings, beautiful," he said.

Dinah, who had never been called beautiful before,

started. She turned around to look at him again, and when she saw he was still watching her, she blushed and hurried to catch up again with Lilly and her father. Beautiful. He'd called her beautiful.

They didn't stay out very long. "I'm beat," Matt said. Although Dinah was just as happy to get out of the city streets, she kept thinking about the boy who had called her beautiful. She kept wondering if they might run into him again.

That evening Dinah was too keyed up to sleep. She kept hearing sounds from the street. All she had to do was look outside the window at the fire escape and think how easy it would be for someone to crawl right up. She wouldn't sleep, she told herself. She'd stay awake. It didn't matter that Lilly had assured her that the apartment was too high up for any-one to risk it, that it faced the street and only a fool would be so blatant. Matt slept in Lilly's tiny bedroom, with the door closed, giving Dinah the sofabed and a fan to cool her off.

For a while Dinah lay rigid. Car alarms screamed outside the window. "Ramona!" someone shouted. "Ramona! Fuck you, you bitch, Ramona!"

Dinah got up and peered out the window through the blinds. Across the street a man peered back, and it took Dinah only a second to see that he was completely naked. She shut the blinds, her breath stitching up, and climbed back into bed.

There were *Bride's* magazines lying in the corner. Lilly hadn't even asked Dinah if she had any ideas for the wedding, not that she had, but still, she would have liked to be asked. All Matt had told her was that they were going to have a small ceremony in Akron in two weeks and that then they were going to go to France.

"France!" Dinah had said, getting excited until she'd re-alized she wasn't invited.

"You can stay with Tonette," he'd said as if it were a treat. "We'll take you the next time."

Dinah peered out the window. The air still smelled,

strange and heavy and foreign. Four in the morning and people were strolling casually around the street. Not as many as during the day, but there were still people, many of them young. In her neighborhood, if you weren't in your robe and pajamas and watching TV by ten, people thought there was something wrong with you. In her neighborhood, she hadn't liked taking the bus after ten because the streets were so dark and deserted, the shadows so ominous; but here, when she looked out the window, she saw kids wandering down into the subways.

She heard rustling from the other room. She got up. She wished she had one of the dogs here. She'd go get it and curl up against it for comfort. She crept toward the door. Lilly's laughter belled out. "Shhh," Matt said.

Dinah heard the bed creak. She imagined them rolling together. She thought about desire. She had heard girls talking in the girls' room about taking their clothes off in the backseat of a used Chevy, about lying to their parents about a sleepover at a girlfriend's when really they spent the whole time at an abandoned ski slope with a boy.

Dinah knew about desire. She could look at a boy she had a crush on and imagine kissing him, imagine him unbuttoning her blouse, maddeningly slow, a button at a time, and although it made her crazy to think it, what scared her the most was the possibility that there was no way in the world anything like that was going to happen to anyone like her. She sighed, and then she suddenly heard Lilly moan, and it made her feel as if she were about to jump right out of her skin. She got up and went into the bathroom, splashing sheets of cold water on her face.

She snooped through Lilly's medicine chest, examining the pills, taking her time. "Take one every two hours for cough," one said. Aspirin. Three different kinds of skin cream and Dinah tried them all, and then a round pink diaphragm case. Dinah took it out. Girls at school took the pill. No one wanted to be bothered with something as disgusting and cumbersome and leaky as this. She snapped the case open and held up the diaphragm for a moment. Her father was adamant about birth control, especially for animals. He had told Dinah about the pill, about condoms and diaphragms, as soon as she'd hit puberty, and he had made sure she understood what a responsibility it was. Outside, Lilly laughed, and Dinah suddenly hid the diaphragm in her robe.

Back in the living room, she slid Lilly's diaphragm into her purse and crept back into bed. She heard the bed from the other room creak, and then the door opened and Lilly padded out to the bathroom. The medicine cabinet squeaked open. A pill bottle fell, and then suddenly Lilly came out. Dinah felt her standing over her.

"Dinah?" Lilly whispered, but Dinah kept still. She remembered this movie, *Children of the Damned*. The children could read every person's mind but one man foiled them by thinking of a brick wall every time one of the children was around, and it made an impenetrable shield, as impenetrable as a force field. Brick, she thought. Brick.

"Dinah," Lilly repeated, but Dinah kept still.

She heard Lilly go back in the room. She heard her father's murmuring voice and then Lilly's. The bed moved and sounded for a while longer and then was suddenly silent, and at last Dinah slept.

In the morning, Dinah, wearing her new teapot earrings, heard Lilly rummaging around in the bathroom. When she came out, Lilly watched her. Brick wall, Dinah thought.

"Were you in the bathroom late last night?" Lilly said.

"I was dead asleep," Dinah said.

Matt flashed Lilly a look. He walked over to Dinah, and for a moment she flinched, but then he put both arms about her. "Are you having a good time?" he said seriously.

"Sure," Dinah said. She looked at her father.

"I'm glad," Lilly interrupted. She came toward Dinah, close enough to touch her, and then she stopped suddenly. She smiled again. "Let's go get breakfast," she said.

They were sprawled at an outside table at Bruno Bakery, sipping iced coffee and eating mammoth butterfly cookies that were ribbed with sugar. The weather was even hotter than it had been the day before. People moved sluggishly, as if they were stunned. Dogs on leashes plopped down in the center of the sidewalk and refused to budge.

Her second day out, Dinah started to feel more relaxed. In the bright daylight the city seemed less dangerous. She ventured in and out of a few stores by herself, and when Lilly and Matt ignored her, she didn't feel quite as slighted.

A boy with long, shaggy hair grinned wickedly at Dinah, and for two seconds she was in love, until she passed another boy, who whispered, "Hey, baby," to her.

Dinah began to wonder what it might be like to live here. She watched the girls who seemed to be her age. They looked exotic to her, in heavy black shoes and socks even though the weather was steamy, in two and three sets of earrings. She watched a girl in a blue minidress and a diamond nose earring circle her arms about a boy with a ponytail and get him slow dancing with her, just for a moment. They stopped and kissed, slow and languid, and Dinah yearned toward them. She felt ridiculously babyish. She wished she wasn't wearing shorts and a T-shirt like some little kid. Like a hick. When the waitress, who didn't look much older than Dinah and was wearing an antique dress, came by, Matt, laughing, had to get her to explain some of the items. "We don't get all this in Ohio," he said, and Dinah suddenly flushed. The waitress was perfectly pleasant, but Dinah felt shamed. She rubbed at her hair, trying to make it look a little spiky, like some of the cuts she had seen. She stretched her legs out onto the sidewalk, trying to look as though she belonged.

"I could live here," she said a little defiantly.

Matt looked at her with surprise. "Kids grow up too fast here," he said.

"What's wrong with that?" Dinah said.

Lilly smiled and lifted up her heavy hair, twisting it into a knot. "Yuck, this weather is truly disgusting," she said.

Matt's face gleamed with sweat. "Let's head for air-conditioning."

"What about a museum?" Dinah said.

Lilly stirred her drink. "I know," she said. "What if we go upstate. I know this lake. It's really pretty. I can drive us."

"Sounds good to me," said Matt.

Dinah shifted. Across the street was a street fair. "Why can't we stay here?" she said.

"It's just so hot," Lilly said.

Dinah felt edgy and agitated. She didn't want to be tagging along with the two of them anymore. She didn't see one other person her age who looked as though they were with their parents. Going to a lake was boring.

For a moment she thought of suggesting that she just stay here by herself. She felt a thrill of fear. She bet she could find that boy who had called her "babe." "I'll stay," Dinah said abruptly.

"Bad idea," said Matt.

"Why?" Dinah protested. A woman wearing only a bikini whizzed past her on skates, and no one but Dinah even looked twice.

"Because this is New York," Matt said. "Because I'd like you with me." But he was looking at Lilly when he said it.

They stopped for food, and then they stopped at Macy's for swimsuits. Matt had bought the first trunks he could find, but Dinah pulled a black bikini off the racks.

"Where's the rest of it?" Lilly said.

Dinah, back at the dressing room mirror, pulled on the suit. When she turned around, she felt paralyzed. She was practically naked. The top was cut so low, it barely hid her nipples, and the bottom, held together by black strings, was so scanty, she felt ashamed. She stared at herself, frozen, unable to move. How can I wear a suit like this? she thought. How can I go out in public?

Someone knocked, and Dinah jumped. A saleswoman called out, "Do you need another size?"

Dinah hesitated for only a second. "I'm taking this one," she said, and turned for her clothes.

The whole drive up she had stayed silent, refusing to talk, but no one had twisted around and asked her, "What's *wrong* with you?" Matt and Lilly had been talking so rapid-fire that they hadn't even noticed the silence she was weaving about them determinedly.

So there they all were, at the lake. It was heavily wooded, and deep green, and a few other people were sprinkled around, some of them in the water, one man fishing from a far corner. We could have stayed in Ohio for this, Dinah thought. It was so hot that the trees seemed to be losing their shape. It was weather where people saw mirages, where lovers fought and broke up for no reason at all.

"You're not wearing a suit," Dinah said to Lilly.

"I can't swim," admitted Lilly. "But I like to wade." She looked around, and an image prickled into her mind. The lake. The first time she had read Matt. She turned to tell him, but Dinah was tugging at his arm, pulling him toward the water.

"Race you," Dinah said to Matt.

"Go ahead," Lilly said. She looked at Dinah, who was still wearing the earrings. Lilly pointed to them. "You don't want to lose those," she said.

"I won't," said Dinah, checking the fasteners.

Lilly watched Dinah and Matt plunge into the water. She was suddenly angry with herself that she had never learned to swim. She didn't like Dinah's coolly appraising stares. Dinah didn't like her, and she wasn't quite sure why. Most young girls loved the whole idea of knowing their futures, and certainly she would have been glad to sit Dinah down and tell her future, spilling out the names of boys, the places, the sparkle of the unknown that could blind you with its promise. But Dinah was as shut as a slammed door. Dinah was certainly too old for Lilly to try to be a mother to her, but there didn't seem to be any real reason why they couldn't be friends. She stood up. Matt was a spot way out, Dinah behind him. Go into the water, she told herself. Don't be a baby.

She waded, feeling like a fool. She was getting colder and colder. Her feet were planted in the muck. She wouldn't drown. It was easy to let yourself float if you relaxed enough. Easy to drift. She knew how to cup her hands into fins, how to kick her feet. Babies swam at the local Y. She saw them, smelling of chlorine, grinning and squirming in their mothers' arms.

She flung herself into the water, clothes and all. The shock of it stunned her a little. She moved her hands and stayed in place and then sprang upright again, water in her eyes, freezing. She looked out to Matt. He was waving at her and she waved back, but he kept waving. Shielding her eyes, she tried to find Dinah. There, white arms flashing, Dinah swam. She looked back for Matt, but the water was empty. Show-off, she thought. He had held his breath in the bathtub for her once, for five full minutes, coming up, his hair slick as a seal's, laughing.

"Here!" Dinah called. She was on one of the rocks, puling at a swinging rope. She grabbed it and swooped over the water, skimming across the surface, dunking into the deep end, coming up splashing. As she sprang up, her hair sluiced against her skull.

Matt splashed Lilly. "Well, look at you!" he said to Lilly, who was dog-paddling gamely.

"Hey!" Dinah called. She was on the rock again, tugging at the swing. She swung out over to another rock and landed gently. "I bet I beat you!" she called to Matt.

"Want me to swim you out to the rock?" Matt said. "You can sun on it."

Lilly looked doubtful. "It's too deep," she said.

Dinah waved long white arms in the air at Matt.

"She doesn't like us together," Lilly said.

"She will," Matt said. Dinah beckoned to him. "Just a few times," he said to Lilly.

Lilly stood in the water and watched him swimming out to his daughter. He stood up and grabbed the rope and swung, up over her head, skating over the water, landing on the rocky landing. "Lilly!" he called delightedly, and she waved at him. Already the skin on her hands was freckling from the sun. She couldn't help it. She missed Matt and wanted him to roam in the shallows with her. She waded to shore, sitting on the blanket they had brought, a soft square of blue that she had made sure was big enough for three. She pulled out the basket of food, and suddenly she was hungry. "Hey!" As if they were signal flags, she waved two chicken wings at Matt and Dinah. "Let's eat!"

Matt grinned, readying to dive, when Dinah stopped him with the rope swing. He hesitated and then grabbed on to it, and Lilly felt a stab of annoyance.

Then he looked over at Lilly and bowed dramatically, his wet hair flopping. "Last time!" he called to her.

Lilly pulled out a piece of cheese. Tonight they'd get back to the city by nine. They could have Italian food on Carmine Street, with good cheap red wine, and Dinah could have some, too. That should loosen her up, make her easier to know, maybe even easier to like. She'd tell Dinah's fortune whether Dinah asked or not, and she'd be sure to fill it with handsome boys and fast cars and lots of adventure.

She looked up at Matt. He was showing off for her. He ran three steps, gripped the rope, and threw himself out over the water. He landed and dived and came back up, laughing. "I'm teaching you to swim," he had told her. He had access to a pool in Ohio. They could be the only ones there if they went early enough, and he could start her off in the baby shallows, building her confidence. "What's a vet's favorite stroke?" He laughed, not waiting for her to guess. "Dog paddling," he said triumphantly.

Lilly clapped and then held up the bottle of wine. "Lunch!" she called.

Dinah leaned against her father, whispering something to him. He cocked his head. He listened intently, then he nodded and held up one finger in the air to Lilly. One more time. Once more. He heaved himself onto the swaying rope. Dinah stretched up and held on to her father's neck, turning him so his back was toward Lilly.

Matt looked toward Lilly, and then she waved again, and he hesitated and then stopped for a moment, resting back on the balls of his feet. He was saying something to Lilly, calling, but she couldn't quite hear him. And as she stood up to try to make out his words, Dinah suddenly, roughly, pushed him off in midspeech, hurling him into space so that he swung across the water with a nearly dizzying force. Little creep, Lilly thought, and then instantly hated herself for thinking it.

Lilly tried to follow his arc, but the sun was blinding her for a moment. Shading her eyes, she stood up, and then Matt suddenly sprang into view, his body a long speeding blur against the sharp blue of the sky, one graceful line until he struck against the rocky landing, his head smashing against the wet rock with a soft, surprising sound, and then all his body tension was gone, and limp, he was sliding, slowly, slowly sliding, back into the water.

Lilly heard Dinah screaming, she saw people moving toward the rock. A man was running in the opposite direction, so fast that for a moment she thought he was running away, until she saw him grab at the pay phone by the road. And then the fear, new and sudden and as shocking as the sound of the water, as Dinah's screams, began to hit Lilly, washing over her like a great tide.

He had died instantly, the doctor told Lilly.

Lilly sat with Dinah in a small, harshly lit waiting room, staring up at the doctor, a tiny, dark woman with glasses. "A blow like that," the doctor said. "If he had survived, he would have returned to you in a very altered state."

Lilly, stunned, didn't ask what that meant. The doctor kept looking everywhere but at Lilly's face.

She didn't know what time it was. She couldn't think what to do, how to walk or breathe or anything, and although she kept nodding at the doctor, she had stopped hearing anything. She couldn't feel the floor beneath her when the doctor led them out. Lilly kept straining back around, moving toward the closed doors. Any minute Matt would get up, woozy, and follow her out. Any minute he'd call out for them to wait a minute.

"Shhh," said the doctor, though Lilly wasn't aware she had said a word.

Dinah sat huddled in Lilly's tiny apartment, and Lilly moved as if dazed. Lilly hadn't spoken once, but people kept coming into her apartment, introducing themselves to Dinah when they came in. Clients of Lilly's. A few friends. And Robert, who had heard about Matt's death from the restaurant and come with a bouquet of flowers. Trembling, Dinah picked up Matt's suitcase, and one of Lilly's friends gently removed it from her arms and led Dinah back to a seat again. The phone rang repeatedly.

"Who's your doctor, Lilly?" a woman said. "I want to get you some Xanax."

Lilly reached for Matt's extra set of glasses on the table and burst into tears.

A man approached Dinah. "Dinah, right?" he said. "Now, that's a pretty name." He sat beside her and then patted her arm awkwardly.

She blinked at him. "You tell me if you need anything," he said, getting up again, patting her shoulder. "Anything at all."

"What's your name?" Dinah whispered, but he was gone.

Lilly's apartment became more and more crowded with

food and flowers. The people sat awkwardly, and sometimes they looked carefully at Dinah and then away again.

"Let me do the calls," said Janis, a friend of Lilly's who worked at the restaurant. "Dinah, honey, you tell me who to call," she said. Dinah, mute, sank into the couch. "Well, when you think of it," Janis said.

Janis ticked off names on a list, and she never once let Lilly get on the phone. She called and called Dell, and finally called the shoe store, where someone told her that Dell was in the hospital with pneumonia, that she was in intensive care.

"What am I supposed to do, then?" Lilly said, her voice dulled.

Robert sat down in front of her. "I'll make the arrangements," he said. "Let me do that for you." He took the phone from Janis.

"Nora's on the next flight," Janis said to Lilly.

People stayed until nearly three. Robert had arranged for a funeral in Ohio two days later. "I booked you both a flight," he said. "And one for your mother, too. A car service to the airport." He looked over at Dinah. "And I didn't know what you wanted to do, but I booked you a hotel suite of three rooms in Akron. I didn't know if Dinah wanted to stay in the house. You can always cancel it."

Lilly rested her head along his shoulder. He stroked back her hair, murmuring something into it she couldn't hear. "Do you want me to stay?" he said. "I can sleep on the floor."

Lilly shook her head. "You're being so kind," she said. She half smiled. "You weren't this kind when we were together."

"My mistake," he said. He shook his head. "You call if you need me. Any time."

He left with Janis, and then the others spilled out until it was just Lilly and Dinah, and neither one of them could look at the other. Lilly went to the closet and pulled out an extra blanket, some clean sheets, and a pillow and handed them to Dinah. She nodded to the couch. "Get some sleep," she said.

Lilly, in her room, her door shut tightly, tossed in her bed. The house was so silent, she grew scared. She padded barefoot into the kitchen, which was clean and empty, and then toward the bathroom. The cabinet door was open, and inside was her missing diaphragm. Lilly shut the door.

She went back to her bedroom and opened the window. The air, clear and cold, stung. She hunched on the fire escape, staring intently at the sky, rocking on her haunches. She heard steps, and then she turned, and there was Dinah, in a T-shirt and panties, quivering, her eyes red and swollen.

"I heard noises," Dinah said helplessly.

Lilly slowly climbed back inside the house, and as soon as her feet touched the floor, Dinah relaxed visibly. "It's all right," Lilly said. "You can go back to bed."

"What were you doing?" Dinah said.

Lilly dusted off the bottoms of her feet, which were branded with the iron bars of the fire escape. "Listening," she said quietly. "I was just listening."

Lilly couldn't tell Dinah how scared she truly was. She had spent most of her life listening to other people's dead, and she couldn't hear her own. Matt didn't come. He didn't come in dreams. He didn't come casually, the way the dead sometimes did, with a particular phrase of his cropping up in the mouth of a stranger, a gesture uniquely his brandished by someone else. She didn't sense a presence.

She shut her eyes, but all she heard were the thoughts in her head. She didn't hear Matt. But her clients had. Her clients looked expectant. They kept giving her these secretive, knowing looks. One of them, Hal Linley, a man who came to talk to his dead wife through Lilly every year on her birthday, patted Lilly on the shoulder.

"He's all around you," Hal whispered. "He misses you as much as you miss him. I *feel* him."

Lilly started. Hal looked at her as if she had secret knowledge that she just wasn't telling. All her clients treated her as if she were special, an initiate, and every time someone reminded Lilly how much she had helped them over a death, she flinched.

"Give it time," someone said to Lilly, and despite herself, Lilly laughed. "There's no such thing as time," she said.

Lilly was lucky she had savings, lucky too that Nora sent her money and her job gave her three weeks paid vacation.

"You come back when you're up to it," the owner said. He didn't listen when Lilly said she probably wouldn't. "You have no idea how much people are asking for you." He handed her packets of business cards from customers. People couldn't wait to talk to her, to see how she would handle this.

Lilly, Nora, and Dinah arrived in Akron in time for the funeral. As soon as the plane landed, Dinah tensed. She kept her eyes shut the whole ride to the hotel, her hand balled tightly into her lap.

The hotel suite was spacious and quiet, with three large rooms that each had a lock on the door. "We have time to shower and then go," Nora said.

Dinah shook her head. "I'm not going to the funeral," she said.

"Oh, honey," Nora said. "We'll be there with you."

Dinah looked around. "Is this my room?" she said, pointing to a smaller room to the side. "I just want to sleep. That's all I want to do." She dug in her jeans for a ragged bloom of pink Kleenex tissues and crumpled it in her hand.

"It's okay," Lilly said, as if she could give anyone permission to do anything.

Lilly was hot and tired and exhausted from the funeral. All these people she didn't know had been there. Friends of Matt's she had only heard about. Colleagues from the vet clinic. "Where's Dinah?" people asked. Arms wrapped about her. Hands pressed warmth along Lilly's back. When it came time for Matt to be buried, Lilly froze.

"Come on," Nora whispered to her. "We'll stand right by the car. We don't have to see this," Nora whispered, almost as if she were giving her instructions. "It's not him," she said. "It's just his body."

Lilly took Nora's hand and held it. She felt numb. People were slowly making their way away from the grave. "Come to the house," a woman said to Lilly, and Lilly shook her head. "Make her come," the woman urged Nora, but Nora was guiding Lilly back to the rental car. "Lilly," someone called, and Lilly kept walking.

"The worst is over," Nora said. She drove carefully back to the hotel. "I'll draw you a hot bath."

"I can't sit in a bath," Lilly said.

As soon as they went into the suite, Lilly knew something was wrong. She saw a white piece of paper, fluttering on the window, pinned in place by a piece of tape. "Dinah?" Lilly called, and pulled the note from the window. "BE BACK SOON. DINAH."

"She'll be back," Nora said. "She probably went to take a walk."

"That's what I'm going to do, too," Lilly said. Nora reached for her purse. "No, I just want to go by myself," Lilly said, ignoring the stubborn, hurt look on Nora's face. "It'll make me feel better," she said, and Nora untensed.

Lilly walked only as far as the cab stand, and then she got into a cab. She wasn't sure where she was going, not at first, not until her mouth opened and she heard herself saying, "Twenty-four Maplewood Lane." Matt's house. She knew the address from all the letters she had written him, and she didn't know why, but she wanted to see it.

"There you go, lady," said the driver.

Lilly paid him and climbed out. It was a big white house, with a lawn that needed tending. She stood out front for a minute. The house would be sold. Movers had already been hired to pack up everything but the furniture the day after to-morrow. Then they'd ship it all to Dell's, where Dinah and her grandmother could go through it.

Lilly didn't have a key, she had no real rights to this house, but she peered in the windows. Matt, she thought, but all she heard was the buzz and hum of insects. She sat down on the porch, and then she heard something and snapped up-right. She felt suddenly freezing. She felt suddenly alive.

The front door opened and Dinah walked out, and for a split second Lilly had a glimpse of Matt's house. Dinah was wearing a leather jacket that was too big for her, that must have been Matt's, and she was carrying a single silver-framed photo. She was crying, swiping at her nose. She stopped when she saw Lilly, who was edging to a standing position, who was staring into the house, at the old couch, the brass table lamps. Dinah stopped crying. She looked at Lilly, and then, deliber-ately, she locked the door behind her.

Lilly felt as if she had been struck. She was too tired to fight Dinah, to ask to go inside. What did it matter, anyway? None of the memories inside the house were hers. Dinah clutched the photograph closer to her, hiding it inside the jacket.

"What are you doing here?" Dinah said.

Lilly felt suddenly weary. A cab prowled by, and she lifted up her hand for it. She looked at Dinah. "Come on," she said, and walked toward the cab. She knew Dinah was fol-lowing her only by the sound her sneakers made, slapping against the pavement.

They all left the next day. "Come back with me," Nora begged, but Lilly shook her head. She and Dinah were flying back to New York, just until Dell was well enough, and then Dinah would go live with her. Lilly had already called the hospital twice, and each time the doctor had told her that Dell was being released any day, that he was putting off telling her about her son for fear of a relapse.

Lilly and Dinah were in New York for only another two weeks. It was difficult. It felt strange. Unreal. This hasn't happened, she told herself.

Lilly took a sleeping pill her first night back and fell into a sleep so deep and drugged that she felt as if she had been buried underground. She was grateful for the oblivion, but sometime toward morning a sound woke her. It was hard to wake under the weight of the drug. She was disoriented, and suddenly she couldn't remember where she was or what had happened.

Something moved in the kitchen, and Lilly, still half dreaming, thought, Matt. Matt's cooking. She smiled and got up, robeless, padding into the other room. She saw him, in the darkness by the table, and then she clicked on the light, and there was Dinah, crying, drinking juice from the bottle, and Lilly felt something smash inside of her.

She was suddenly awake with fury. Her helpless instinct was to strike Dinah, to tear the bottle out of her hands and crash it to the floor. It's your fault! she screamed inside. A scene shot into her mind: Dinah urging Matt to ride the rope one more time, always one more time, Lilly beckoning from shore. She didn't want Dinah to ask for comfort because she didn't know what she might do. She couldn't trust herself.

Dinah put the bottle back into the refrigerator. "Don't put that back after you drank out of the bottle," Lilly said. Dinah froze, and Lilly moved toward her, careful not to touch Dinah. She grabbed for the bottle, and Dinah, confused, hands trembling, put it on the counter.

Lilly waited until Dinah was out of the kitchen. She gripped the edges of the counter. Dinah's presence was overwhelming. In the other room Dinah started to cry, and Lilly suddenly jerked the juice bottle off the counter, smashing it onto the floor, the pieces skipping to the dusty corners, where they'd hide and collect light for days.

The next day Lilly went out and had an extra key made and gave it to Dinah. Dinah dangled the key from her fingers, unsure. "So you don't have to wait for me if you want to go out," Lilly said, and then she left Dinah alone. And lucky for her, Dinah kept her distance, too.

She sat up in bed nights, wondering what it was she hadn't thought to do, why the dead were silent. The dead were always telling her all manner of trivialities to pass on— they wanted a pet they had left behind to be walked three times a day instead of two. They wanted a daughter to study harder, a son to cut his hair. She had been their conduit, and although they had shown her the blue lake where Matt had died, the way they had shown it to her had made her think that that lake was a blessing that belonged to someone else and not a place she would curse all the days she would have to go on and live without him. Where were all those voices now?

Neither Lilly nor Dinah did much. Lilly sometimes talked to Robert on the phone, but she didn't go to work. Dinah sat and stared at the TV for hours on end and began reading Lilly's books, taking two or three down from the shelves. She couldn't seem to finish any of them. Lilly would find the books with their pages bent back to mark Dinah's place, under the pullout sofa or in the kitchen. She left them where they were.

Lilly had no appetite, but she forced herself to eat. She bought cheese and bread and yogurt, nutritious foods, and enough for two. "There's vanilla yogurt," Lilly said. "There's Swiss cheese. Please. Have some."

"I'm not hungry," Dinah said, reading.

"You have to eat something," Lilly said.

"I will if I want," Dinah said.

Lilly felt a flicker of anger. She looked around the small apartment. She felt cramped. "I'm going for a walk," she told Dinah, who didn't look up from her book.

Lilly walked for miles. She was already in midtown, hyp-notized by the rhythm of the walk, cheered by the snap in the air.

Lilly walked. One hour. Two. As if moving could keep thought at bay. She was in the West Nineties when she happened to glance at the Chock Full O' Nuts there and saw Dinah hunched at the counter, clumsily wolfing a sandwich. A large vanilla milkshake was beside her. Lilly stood outside, watching Dinah eat, waiting until she had drained her milkshake and another had been put before her, until a slab of chocolate cake appeared, too. Dinah started to turn, to look out the window where Lilly was, and Lilly pivoted quickly and began walking her way back downtown.

A week after they had returned, Dell called, her voice cloudy. "How did it happen?" Dell wanted to know, and then she wanted to speak to Dinah. "You'll have to live with me," Dell said.

"I don't know," Dinah said.

"You can't stay with Lilly," Dell said.

Dinah hung up the phone carefully. Lilly was sitting in the kitchen, a cup of coffee steaming in front of her, her hair freshly washed. When Dinah came in, Lilly started.

"I wish I didn't have to live with Dell."

Lilly nodded. "Do you want to stay with your mother instead?"

"My mother," Dinah said in disgust.

"A detective could find her," Lilly persisted.

"I guess you think I can't take care of myself," Dinah said. "I guess you think I'm incapable."

"Don't be silly," Lilly said. "The only one who can't take care of herself is me."

"I have a home," Dinah said. "It's not sold yet! My father had a practice he was going to hand down to me!"

Lilly put down her coffee cup. "You can't live there by yourself," she said wearily.

"Don't tell me what to do!" Dinah said, getting up. "You're not my family." She grabbed at her purse. She started for the stairs.

"Hey!" Lilly said.

"Why should you decide what happens?" Dinah said. "You don't know anything!"

"Hey, you're here with me—I've been taking care of you, I've been buying you food—"

"Who wants you to!" Dinah shouted.

She yanked at the door. Lilly grabbed furiously at the back of Dinah's shirt, tumbling the girl roughly against the door. Good, Lilly thought, good, good. And then Dinah fell, her head thudded along the wall, and Lilly felt numb with shock. She reached for Dinah. Dinah's hands flew up to her hair. They stared at each other, stunned, when the buzzer rang.

Lilly peered outside the window. Three people were there, their arms laden with food, with magazines, their chins tilted up toward Lilly's windows. One of them waved energetically, her smile encouraging. Clients. Dinah stood up, as still as stone.

"I can't do this anymore," Lilly whispered. "I can't talk about it. I can't listen to people talk about it or tell me how sorry they are. I have to get out of here."

She looked at Dinah. "I'll drive you to Dell's."

The next morning Lilly drove to Pittsburgh. She had given the goldfish to Janis, who nodded, who said she'd take good care of them. "Keep them," Lilly said.

Lilly blinked at the sun. She had been driving since she was fifteen, always with her father's old Saint Christopher medal hanging from the rearview mirror. She was glad she was driving. She had to concentrate all her grief down to a pinpoint so she could leave room for the road, for the signs. It reminded her of her father, filling up the time with business, anything so you didn't think. Dinah, in dark glasses, stared out at the road. They stopped at diners, but neither one of them really ate. Silently they picked at the food. Lilly heard nothing but the conversations of the people around her. It was just as well. She didn't want to hear other people's dead if she couldn't hear her own. Behind Lilly, a mother was diapering her baby on the blue Formica table, crooning something low in her throat. "What a big mess you made!" she said, and for a moment Lilly thought she must be talking about her. Lilly cut her egg neatly into quarters and then positioned each slice to the edge of the plate, a trick she used to do with Nora, who would remind her of the starving children in India, who would tell her that hungry or not, you had to eat.

Lilly kept seeing her grief as a living thing that she could let loose as soon as she got Dinah back home. She didn't want to cry at night because she didn't want to set Dinah off. She remembered the night she had tumbled her against the door. I could have killed her, she thought, a fact that made her hug her arms about herself. The sooner she got Dinah to Dell, the better for everyone. She couldn't be depended on to be of any good to anyone, even Dinah. She didn't want to think. She drove recklessly. She bought new maps and tried new routes. The night was hard. She left Dinah sleeping in the next bed and scribbled her a note in case she woke up. "Gone to get a burger," she wrote, although she couldn't have kept anything in her stomach, that was how nauseated she felt. She went outside, where the only noise was the river of cars flowing past and she felt like the most alone person in the world.

She picked up a flat stone and skipped it along the edge of the motel. Inside, Matt's daughter was sleeping, dreaming a life, and Lilly put her hands as deep into her pockets as they would go, and then she went back inside to her.

chapter 5

Dell had always been the kind of person who loved people at a distance, whether she wanted to or not, and because of it, she thought of herself as the kind of woman who found distant ways to thread lives together. She had written volumes to her husband, Hank. She had sometimes interrupted her crowded days to call her son and granddaughter. It didn't take much. A half-hour call. A visit once every few months. A card. And then she'd feel refueled, as if she had put her affairs in order. Her life had seemed so busy then, but now it seemed to yawn open into chasm.

Her own doctor, Dr. Lallo, tall and bearded and someone's son, was the one who had told her her son had died. Two days before she was to be released from the hospital, he came in and sat at the edge of her bed and took her hand in between his two beefy ones, and he looked so sad and serious that before he had even opened his mouth she knew that something was wrong. And then, as soon as he told her, she had a relapse. Her body didn't want to know. She got so sick, she had to stay in the hospital another three days. "You see what happens when you let yourself get all agitated?" an overworked nurse fussed at Dell, but Dell knew it was far better to sleep away three days on a tide of fever than to be awake and thinking endlessly of the death of your only son.

Dell woke, despite her best efforts not to. And she came home. She never realized how tired she really was. The hospital had given her a clean bill of health although the doctor told her to be careful, and at first she attributed her weariness to keeping the sorrow at bay.

She went back to work immediately. She made herself so tired, the exhaustion squeezed out the space left for mourning. If she dusted the entire store, she didn't think so much about being in a hospital hooked to an IV while in another state her son was being buried and she hadn't even known he had died. If she took out and rearranged the new shoes in the spring stock, she didn't feel a nudge of jealousy that Lilly, a slip of a thing who had neither borne nor raised nor lived so many years with her son, had known Matt better than she ever had and had probably been the last face he had seen.

She remembered when Matt was very little, a towhead with a mouth of teeth like little white Niblets and fingers like clothespins clamping at her. What was wrong with her that she hadn't been a better mother? Why hadn't someone stopped her and shaken her and forced her to think that there might come a moment, just like this, when she might need to remember all the small and lasting kindnesses she might have done if only she had thought to do them—milkshakes at night, rock candy for fever, a warm, loving hand to stroke the hair back from his brow?

She had never planned on children, had never wanted or planned on anything but a life with her husband, Hank. "He makes my heart buzz," she used to say. He had been small and wiry with bristly blond curls and eyes like chips of blue sky. Dell had met him at a dance, back when she was twenty-eight and still beautiful and so slender he could fit both his hands around the waist of her flowered dress when they danced. They had gotten married after only a six-week courtship. And already he had his shoe store, Hank's, and plans for the future, and every evening when he came to pick her up, he brought her shoes, the way other men might bring bouquets of flowers. Hank sat beside her nights on her parents' porch swing and talked to her about kidskin and high arches, and when he embraced her he smelled faintly of new leather. The first time they made love, he kissed each one of her toes.

After they were married, she had clerked in the store just to be beside him. Neither one of them wanted or liked kids. Hank kept kids' shoes in the stock simply because kids grew out of shoes so fast, he could make a tidy profit. But when children came in, he was stiff and impatient and so watchful, they seemed to cower right under him. Well, Dell wasn't much different. When she thought of babies, she thought of someone coming between them, she saw her neat little figure distended and unattractive. She saw his fingers spreading awkwardly, trying to circle her thickening waist.

They were perfectly happy, but in the first three months of their marriage, two disasters happened: she got pregnant, and Hank was drafted into the Korean War.

They had exactly six weeks before he left, and during that whole time, Dell never once told him she was carrying his child because she thought it would be just one more misfortune for him to worry about.

"Don't worry about anything," she soothed him. "I'll watch the store. I'll make sure everything is wonderful."

His smile wobbled. "Everything's going to be fine," he told her. But at night he woke up shivering, tangled in a thicket of sheets, slick with fear and sweat that he couldn't seem to wash off, no matter how many showers he took. He told her he had dreams about artillery fireworking across the sky, cannonballs whizzing past his head. He dreamed he couldn't feel his body anymore. He woke up frantic, thrashing, pinching at his arms and his legs.

"Where are they!" he screamed.

"It's a dream," Dell said. She rubbed his arms and legs

until he felt them again, and then she pressed her body along his until he felt her, too.

When he left, he took only one picture of her with him, his favorite, Dell in high heels and a white dress frilling in the wind. He left at six in the morning, and the whole day Dell sat at home and cried. Every day she wrote volumes, six- and seven-page letters filled with news of the shop and her own hammering need for him, but although she was growing bigger and bigger, she never once mentioned to him that she was pregnant, she never wanted to worry him. He wrote her one page at most, and he almost always said the same thing: "I love you. I'm very scared." They were letters she saved, tied in a red satin ribbon, but she never told anybody what he said to her because she didn't want anyone to know how little he wrote her. "He's so brave," she said.

She began to get lax. She let the help watch the store because her legs were too swollen for her to stand on, and her feet no longer looked pretty in the shoes she wanted to be selling. She knitted Hank socks and one sweater with a too long left arm, and when he asked for photos she was always careful to send him only the ones from the shoulders up. She saw a photo of Betty Grable in a bathing suit, twisting around from the back, and she read where they had taken the snapshot that way because Betty had been too pregnant to face the camera in a bathing suit. She tried for days to copy the shot herself, persuading a neighbor to take the shot, but every time the pictures came out, she still looked pregnant. Finally she just got a copy of the picture and attached her face to it and sent it to him.

The day Matt had been born, she finally sat down and wrote him a letter.

> I know this is strange, but you have a beautiful new son who I would like to name Matt, after my father. I couldn't tell you because I was afraid how you would take

it, and now I can't not tell you. Please be happy. I love you more than life itself. Your wife, Dell.

Dell posted the letter, feeling sick with anxiety, and then went home to watch the baby nurse she had hired tend her son. She didn't know why, but she knew something must be the matter with her because although she was fond of her son, she didn't feel that overpowering love she had read about.

"Don't you worry," the nurse had told her. "Sometimes it takes a little time to get used to a baby. You'll grow to love your son so much, you won't be able to stand to be away from him for a minute. Just you wait."

So Dell waited. She named her son Matt, a name she loved, and she told herself that everything about her son seemed a miracle. Look at his ten perfect toes! Look at his fine black hair, his damp, open mouth. She looked at him and looked at him, but nudging through her admiration were thoughts about all the diapers he used up, all the formula he cried for at two in the morning when she was dreaming she was making love with Hank, that he was just about to whisper something important to her.

She waited two weeks, and then another, and then when the mail finally came, it was a telegram saying Hank was missing in action, and then her whole life tore open. How could she not be a wreck, barely married, newly a mother, and a confused one at that, and now maybe on her own for God knew how long? How could she not have depended on babysitters? Hank's was her store now. She worried that the help was robbing her blind; she worried if she didn't get out in the world, she would make herself crazy.

Dell worked so hard at Hank's that she didn't have time to think about growing to love an infant son. She didn't have time for anything except for kidskin leathers and pumps and how to size a foot. She was barely home, and every time she looked at Matt, all she could think about was the fact that she hadn't told Hank about him, she had kept that life to herself, and now she was being punished for it by having to raise a baby all on her own.

She steeled her heart, and when Matt was five she sent him to sleep-away camp so she could spend the summer working straight through till nine o'clock, which was the best way she knew to get through a whole day without crying. And when the counselors called her to say Matt was crying so hard that they thought he might rupture a blood vessel, she came only for a short visit, bringing him chocolate and Zazu, his favorite stuffed buffalo. She was all dressed up in a pale blue suit and matching Italian leather heels. She wore a veiled hat and looked so beautiful that some of the older counselors stopped and stared. The other children laughed when they saw the buffalo. "Baby! Baby!" they cried, but Dell didn't see how Matt cringed, how he forced himself to throw the buffalo down on the ground so Dell would have to take it home with her, even though Zazu was exactly what he wanted.

"Look at this wonderful lake!" Dell cried. "Look at the woods! Aren't you Mummy's lucky boy!"

She spent the whole day with him, and when it started to get dark she took him by the hand and led him to the car, and for a moment he thought she was going to let him come home. She crouched down beside him. "Mummy has so much to do," she said. "Mummy has to work at the store until very late, and isn't it nicer that you have all these friends around you instead of baby-sitters?"

"They're not my friends," he said, but she bent and kissed him. She held up Zazu.

"You sure?" she said, and defiant, he shook his head. She casually tossed Zazu onto the backseat, where he liked to ride, and she got in the car herself. And for miles afterward all she could think of was the way he had stood there, watching the car and Zazu depart. She turned the radio up loud. She sang along so she wouldn't think about it. What can I do? she asked herself.

She hadn't time to be a better mother. Matt got older,

and then he married that Maggy girl she hadn't much liked, and then she had the store to consider. She couldn't take weeks off to visit him or Dinah, not with a new shoe store opening up in the mall, just two stores away. She invited them to visit, but still, she had to work. She couldn't take more than an hour off here and there to see them. It hadn't been her fault, had it?

Dell had never even had time to make any close friends except for Letty, who worked in Lorraine's, a discount dress shop in the mall. Letty was deeply sympathetic when she heard of Matt's death, but she urged Dell not to have all of Matt's personal belongings shipped to her. "Why torture yourself?" Letty pleaded with her. "Do yourself a favor and give everything to Goodwill." She told Dell when her husband, Burt, had died, she used to replay a video she had of their fiftieth wedding anniversary party, fast-forwarding it until their kiss, the moment when their mouths seamed together. She froze the kiss into a frame, until one day, seeing it, she cried so hard, she passed out. "When I came to, I destroyed the video. Enough is enough," she said. "Sometimes I can't even stand my memories."

"I have to do this," Dell said. She didn't dare tell Letty that the reason she needed to go through her son's things was because she felt she needed to collect memories, because if anyone had asked, she couldn't have told them what Matt most wanted in the world, or what he liked to do on his time off.

Dell had no idea what it might be like to have a girl as young as Dinah around. She had forgotten how much energy it took to be around kids, how they played their music too loud even to hear the words, how the beat made the floorboards vibrate underneath her feet. Matt had been hard enough raising, but Dinah, a girl, might be worse. Girls said they were going to the library and then wound up on the backseat of someone's car.

What did girls eat? She racked her brain, but she

couldn't remember the dinners she'd cooked for Matt, she couldn't even remember sitting down at the table with him, though she knew they must have, and she knew they must have talked and laughed and argued. So why didn't she remember much of it?

Her mind tripped and tumbled over her past. All she thought about was Matt, and every memory seemed barbed in her heart, making small jagged tears in her when she remembered the times she had sent him away to play so she could be by herself, the times he had come to visit and she had spent more time at the shop than with him. Matt, she thought. How could a whole life pass by you without your even noticing?

She thought about her granddaughter, about Lilly, and she wondered about all the things Matt had loved about them, she wondered how it was possible that these two probably had known her son better than she had. She ached to know what they knew. She had never thought of herself as alone, but that was exactly the way she felt now, and it made her feel strange and sad and really as desperate as if she were the last person on earth. If she could have warmed herself with their memories, she would have. The two of them seemed to her like a second, desperate chance, like just another missed opportunity she might be able to do something about—a connection she could make with another human being—if only they would let her.

Dinah and Lilly finally arrived at Dell's at ten at night. Squirrel Hill, the dark, wooded section of Pittsburgh where Dell lived, was practically empty. Lilly slowed, shoving her heavy hair back off her shoulders. She squinted at the numbers, hunching forward, but Dinah wasn't going to tell her which one it was. "Here," said Lilly.

Dell's house was a small green clapboard with a rickety porch and flowered hedges that were always thick with black bees. The house was brightly lit, and as soon as Lilly pulled up, Dell came running out in a thin floral nightgown, her hair in pink sponge curlers. "I didn't know when to expect you!" she said.

Her house was filled with new photographs. There was a rose-printed slipcover over the sofa and on a chair, and piled in both chairs were boxes of shoes. "Just push those off," Dell advised. Her fingers tugged the curlers out of her hair, which coiled into beige springs.

Dell went to make tea, coming back with three china cups and a plastic bear filled with honey, with vanilla tea cookies she set on the coffee table. "You'll stay for a while, you said," she said to Lilly, who nodded.

Dell leaned back onto the flowered armchair, looking from Lilly to Dinah and back again, and then she sighed. "Have some of those cookies," she said to Dinah, who stared at the plate and then took two. She balanced them carefully on the edge of her saucer, beside her untouched tea. Dell frowned and stared at Dinah.

"She's the image of her father, isn't she?" Dell said. "The eyes, a little around the mouth—" Dell looked at Lilly carefully, wondering what her son had liked the best about this woman—her dark eyes, that jumble of hair? Had he held those small balled-up hands of hers in his? Had he swayed her by her waist to him?

"I don't know," Lilly said, looking at her cup.

"Sure she is," Dell said uncertainly.

Dell leaned toward Lilly. "So where will you go?"

Lilly shrugged. "Friends. Maybe I'll find some work."

"Work is good," Dell said thoughtfully. "It's the best thing." She looked over at Dinah. "School'll be starting up soon, and that'll be the best thing for you."

Dell rose, lifting herself from her chair, hovering there for a moment. "I feel fine," she protested when Lilly leaned forward and took her hand. She stroked Dell's palm, and Dell felt a sudden prickle of energy before Lilly abruptly let her go.

Dell watched the stiff, silent way Lilly was moving, the

sullen awkwardness of Dinah. "Come on, let me show you your room." She opened the door to the flowery room. Lilly trailed behind them.

"Well, everyone's exhausted," said Dell. She got out fresh linens from the cupboard, a new soft blue blanket and a fresh pillow, and she would have slept on the couch and given Lilly her bed if Lilly hadn't protested, if Lilly hadn't threatened to go sleep in a hotel.

"You were sick," Lilly said.

"Well, all right," Dell said doubtfully.

"I don't mind," Lilly said. "Really."

"If you want anything in the night, consider my house your house. You help yourself," Dell said.

Lilly spread out the blue blanket. She had dark circles under her eyes like bruises. Her skin looked smudged, and when she looked at Dell, it seemed to Dell that Lilly was looking right through her.

"Anything at all," Dell said, and left the room.

It was terrible, Dell thought, and it was lucky, that Lilly hadn't had a chance to marry Matt, that she wasn't his wife. It made Dell the executor of her son's will, not Lilly. It made Dell Dinah's guardian. All of her son's belongings were hers now, and all she needed was for Lilly and Dinah to tell her their meanings.

At first she thought Dinah might help her convince Lilly to stay on a while, but it didn't take long to see how wary Dinah and Lilly were around each other. Dinah stayed in the flowery room Dell had worked so hard to make pretty. Dell made dinner every night, setting the dining room table for three.

"I'm not hungry," Dinah said through the door of her room.

"I already ate," Lilly said.

Dinah was staying on. Dell knew she could take her time with that one, but Lilly, now Lilly was something else. If Lilly left, there would be no real reason for them to see each other ever again. And if Lilly left, every single thing she knew about Matt would leave with her.

Dell slept in as late as she could, using up the morning because she knew Lilly wanted an early start, and she knew Lilly wouldn't leave without saying a proper good-bye.

She took her time, slowing her steps, yawning when she walked into the kitchen. "Tomorrow, I need to take you to the bank," she told Lilly. "There's some papers you need to sign."

"What papers?" Lilly said.

"I'm not sure," Dell said, "I'm just telling you what my lawyer said," and then she excused herself to take a shower.

The next day Dell dallied so long that the bank was closed before they got there. She looked at Lilly. "Let's you and me go get some tea then," she said, which was what she intended anyway, and Lilly nodded.

The two women sat at Dixie's Diner, and the whole time Dell waited for Lilly to tell her something about Matt. Dell hesitated, and then finally she couldn't help herself. "You know, my Matt . . . ," Dell said, and Lilly spilled her tea.

"Sorry," Lilly said, mopping the yellow Formica table with her napkin, but her voice quavered, and she looked so shaken that Dell felt ashamed. "Listen," Lilly said, "is it all right if we head on back? I'm just so tired."

The house was chilly when they got home. Dinah was closed up in her room. Lilly kept rubbing her arms as if she were cold. "Want to borrow a sweater?" Dell asked her.

"Would it be okay?" Lilly said apologetically. "I don't really have all my things."

Dell went to her drawer and sifted through her sweaters. She had only seen Lilly wear two different outfits, and both of them had been dark. She pushed aside a pale yellow sweater and then saw a corner of navy. Cashmere. The soft new sweater her friend Letty had bought her as a birthday present. She hadn't even worn it yet.

Dell brought out the sweater and draped it over Lilly's shoulders. Lilly touched it, surprised. She stroked it as if it were a cat.

"Oh, you don't have to give me something this good," Lilly said.

Dell shook her head. She watched Lilly pull the sweater over her head. "Look how the blue picks up the color of your eyes," Dell said. "You should always wear blue."

Lilly smiled, shy and pleased. She smoothed her hands over the sweater. She couldn't stop touching it. "This is so nice of you," Lilly said.

"You keep it," Dell said.

"No, I can't do that," Lilly said.

"It's done," Dell said. "Please. It makes me happy to see you in it. And anyway," Dell lied, "it really doesn't fit me at all anymore."

Lilly slid her hands over the soft sleeves. "I can't," she said finally.

"Well, at least wear it while you're here," Dell said.

That night, Dell couldn't sleep. She swore she heard noises in the house. Prowlers trying to break in. Ghosts. She got up to make herself some warm milk, going the long way so she wouldn't disturb Lilly, who was sleeping in the living room. She was passing the dining room when she saw a figure standing in the darkness, holding up the Chinese figurine she kept on the end table. Dell sucked in her breath, freezing, blinking, and then the figure turned and she saw it was Lilly.

"I'm sorry," Lilly said. She put down the figurine. Dell snapped on the light. Lilly blinked at her. Her nose was running faintly. Her eyes were puffy. "I couldn't sleep," Lilly said apologetically.

Dell went to the table in the living room and pulled out the few photos she had of Matt when he was little, and she handed them to Lilly.

"Oh, my God," Lilly said. She picked up every photo.

"He's still got the same smile," she said, pointing to Matt in his cowboy uniform in grade school. "Who's this?" she said. "Is this you?" pointing to Dell in a favorite primary-colored check dress she had worn to a PTA where Matt was singing in a chorus. Lilly traced a finger over one picture: Matt in baggy plaid pants and a plaid bow tie, not more than three. She couldn't let it go. She kept coming back to it. It was an image Dell remembered. She looked at the picture, and it moved. She saw Matt scampering in those pants, tripping over the hems that were too long. She blinked at the photo and the image stopped, frozen in time.

Dell put one hand over Lilly's. "There's so many more photos coming. All those boxes," she said. "We have a lot to talk about."

But, Lilly, silent and as distant and unfathomable as the moons of Jupiter, sipped a breath and looked at her picture of Matt.

All that week Dell watched Lilly. All it would take would be time for Lilly to free herself of her grief a little and then she might talk; she might tell the same stories over and over, the way Jacqueline Kennedy did, until everyone must have been so sick of it they could have screamed. You knew my son better than I did, Dell thought.

"Next week, can you take me to the doctor?" Dell asked Lilly, although she was perfectly capable of going there herself.

"I've really got to leave," Lilly said.

"Don't do that," said Dell. She reached out and touched Lilly's bare arm. "His things will be coming."

"There are some personal things," Lilly said. Dell's interest was like a living thing, waiting.

"I'll go through everything," Dell said, and Lilly fell silent. "I'll save a few things."

Lilly nodded.

"I'd like you to stay," Dell said.

"You're very kind," said Lilly. She looked beyond Dell, past the glass of the window, and out at the road.

That night, while Lilly and Dinah slept, Dell crept down to the kitchen. She measured out the last of her fresh eggs. She used the rind of three lemons, real ginger, and real honey from the greengrocer's, and she stayed up two full hours to make Lilly a gingerbread to take with her. She always felt you should be careful when you cooked, because whatever you were feeling would go right into the food, just as if emotions were an ingredient. Dell baked in warmth and need, and the possibility of forgiveness, and then she carefully wrapped the bread in waxed paper so it would stay fragrant, so even after it was eaten there would be a scent in the air, and a memory right along with it.

When Lilly left, Dinah was standing on the sidewalk, wearing black shorts and a black tank top, her eyes lined heavily with kohl. Her eyes were so dark, you couldn't read what was in there, and Lilly thought, Well, that was just as well. She let Dell hold her for a moment. "I wish you'd change your mind and stay," Dell said.

Lilly turned to Dinah, whose eyes were hard and shiny. "I left a number so you can reach me if you need me." Lilly reached out one hand, but Dinah stepped back.

"I won't need to," Dinah said, and turned away from her, going slowly into the house.

"She doesn't mean it," said Dell, and embraced Lilly tightly. She handed her a red floral tin. "Gingerbread," she said. "I made it last night when you were sleeping. It's compact enough so you can eat it right on the road."

Lilly looked at the tin, at the simple kindness that made her feel suddenly undone. "Thank you," she managed.

"If you get tired in your travels, there's plenty of room here," Dell said. "Don't be stubborn about it."

"I know," Lilly said.

She got in the car, and for a moment she felt Dinah,

hunched in the backseat, her eyes boring windows through Lilly. Startled, she twisted around, but the only thing on the seat was her suitcase, and outside, alone on the sidewalk, was Dell, waving, stretched up on tiptoe to get the last bit of view of Lilly before she disappeared into a horizon of highway.

As soon as Lilly was on the road, she began crying. She was sobbing so hard, she couldn't navigate the streets anymore. The lights, the signs, were filmed and blurred by her tears. She saw halos around everything. She had to pull over. Resting her head on the wheel, she cried.

A few cars beeped past her, and then abruptly there was a sharp rapping on the glass. Lilly struggled up, swiping at her face.

She saw a vertical line of blue. She blinked into focus, and then there was a cop standing outside, frowning in at her. He was younger than she was, with razor short blond hair, and as soon as he met her eyes, his expression changed. The fierceness evaporated, and he looked stricken. His mouth fumbled, and then he motioned for her to roll down the window.

"What seems to be the trouble, ma'am?" he said.

"Trouble? No trouble," said Lilly, trying to sweep her damp hair from her face. She composed herself.

"Are you sure?" he said, and his voice was so soft and polite that she burst into tears again.

"Ma'am," he said, "you're making me worried here."

"You don't have to worry about me." She looked up at him. He still looked stricken. "I—I just . . . ," she stammered. "The thing is, someone died."

The cop studied her for a minute. "Wait here," he said. He turned, and Lilly saw him going back to his car. He's probably calling in my license plate number, she thought. A crazy woman crying in the middle of a highway. Why should he believe something she couldn't bring herself to believe, either?

He straightened and ambled back to Lilly's window. He

thrust a small black thermos at her. "Coffee," he offered, nodding at her hopefully. "You go on and have some."

Lilly, still crying, took the thermos.

"I'll have some, too," he said, showing her a paper Dixie cup. "No one should drink alone."

Lilly opened up her back door so the cop could sit and carefully poured them both some coffee.

"My wife made it," he said. "She's a teacher. Third grade, and do those kids love her." He took a long sip.

Lilly glanced down at Dell's tin. "I have cake," she said, and opened it awkwardly. "Gingerbread."

He smiled. "I love cake. I always want doughnuts, but . . . well—you know all those jokes about cops and doughnut shops. I hate to be the one to give credence to them." He broke off a piece and handed it to Lilly, who shook her head.

"You work?"

"I will," Lilly said. "I was a kind of counselor, I guess. I just don't think I can counsel anybody."

"Well," he said, draining his cup. "You will." He got up. "You keep the thermos," he told her. "And don't drive if you're crying. You did the right thing. Pulling over like that. The absolute right thing."

He brushed himself off. "You all right to continue?" he said.

Lilly nodded. She watched him getting into his car, and then she started up her car, but as soon as she was on the highway, he was right there in back of her, her own police escort. It tickled her. Every time she glanced in her rearview mirror, there he was, his face small and serious. She bet his wife was young and pretty and worried every night that maybe tonight was the night she had been fearing since the day she had met him, that maybe tonight was the night her husband wouldn't come home. And she bet that every night he did, and that he was as glad and delighted to see his young wife as she was to see him.

He followed behind her for nearly forty minutes, trailing

her on the lonely black stretch of road. It surprised her how much of a comfort it was. She began nibbling on Dell's cake, surprised at how delicious it was, how fragrant and sweet. When he finally pulled away from her, she half expected him to hail her good-bye, like the Lone Ranger, and even after he disappeared she felt his presence, and all she had to do was look at the black thermos he had given her and feel comforted.

She went as far away as she could go. To California, and an invitation from her friend Merry, who had lived upstairs from her for almost two years in New York before marrying and moving out west to Berkeley. Merry was a chiropractor, married to another chiropractor, and she had just had a baby, which Lilly thought would be a wonderful kind of distraction.

Every day of the drive, Lilly stopped and called Merry from a pay phone. "Just wanted to check in," Lilly said. Lilly remembered Merry's husband, Jack, a redhead who went to tanning parlors almost every day, leaving him tinted a strange hot pink that hurt just to look at him. He had laughed at her when she'd suggested that maybe it wasn't such a good idea to go to the suntanning parlor every day. He had held up three small translucent pills. "These destroy free radicals," he said. "They make sun safe."

He made fun of what she did. "Some people think chiropractors are charlatans, too," Lilly said, but Jack just laughed.

Merry and her husband had wanted Lilly to stay with them for as long as she needed. "Let someone take care of you for a while," Merry said.

Now, when she saw Merry, her blond hair was cut short and straight to her chin, her eyes were like sparklers. She chattered at Lilly. Her house was roomy and carefully coordinated all in yellow. Sunny yellow, Lilly thought. Baby toys were everywhere. Merry told Lilly the practice was going great, that they had the best equipment, and in fact, they had already started giving Sunny adjustments.

"The baby?" Lilly said, shocked.

Merry maneuvered past a red truck. "Sure," she said. "It's good for her. We'd give them to the dog if we had one. Anyway, wait till you see her. She's at the clinic with Jack."

"Oh," Lilly said doubtfully.

"I'm so glad you're here!" Merry said. "Now stop that face! This is going to be a good vacation!"

"A vacation?" Lilly said, but Merry bustled her into the kitchen.

"Come help!" she cried, setting out vegetables and a cutting knife.

A stew was simmering on the stove by the time Jack came home, his carroty hair slicked back with oil, his sunburned skin peeling faintly. He had a bottle of wine on one arm, baby Sunny, fat and beaming, on the other.

"Lilly!" he said, stooping to kiss her. He set Baby Sunny down in her high chair, and then he rummaged in the kitchen cabinets for vitamin pills, slapping out six of them for Lilly to take. "Grief depletes your vitamins," he said, patting her hand. "There's megadoses of A, C, and E."

He was brusque with Merry and even rougher with Sunny, whom he bounced a bit too vigorously. "We'll have to do an adjustment on you, Lilly!" Jack said. He flexed his hands, grinning. "Ha, ha, ha, the mad doctor!" he said gleefully.

It was good to be so busy, to be in the middle of the kind of commotion a baby creates. Sunny had to be changed and washed and fed and changed again and played with, and Lilly insisted on doing all of it because of the way it all distracted her from her grief. She bent over Sunny and blew on the baby's belly until she laughed. She stared into Sunny's slate-colored eyes, so like an ocean at night. She listened idly to Jack and Merry explaining to her how to bring the baby up.

"We don't believe in vaccinations," Merry said. "It's a ruse by the government. How can you protect a child from a disease that's just about wiped out by injecting that child with the watered-down virus?"

Vaccinations, Lilly thought. Protection.

"We believe in punishment," Jack said. "Cause and effect. Sunny spits, I give her a little love tap, then she learns not to spit out her food anymore."

Lilly felt dazed. Cause and effect. What was the cause for a life spinning out of control? Maybe Jack and Merry were wrong, maybe they should be giving Sunny love taps for no reason at all other than to prepare her for the randomness of life.

She was exhausted by nightfall and more than happy to share a room with the baby. She didn't want to be alone, and Sunny's soft, simple breathing lulled and comforted her, just enough so she could sleep.

Lilly didn't feel staying with Merry was really a mistake until the next morning, when she woke crying and Merry came into the room.

"Hey," Merry said, and Lilly threw herself into her friend's arms, and as soon as she did, Merry stiffened. "It's all right," Merry said, but then she extricated herself briskly.

"Wait," Lilly whispered.

Merry turned and picked up the baby, balancing her on one hip. "Come help me with breakfast," she said, averting her gaze while Lilly swiped helplessly at her tears.

In the kitchen Lilly chopped strawberries while Merry blended something thick and green for the baby. "Jack already went to work," Merry said. "We don't want to make you feel bad, so we aren't kissing like we usually do. He can't keep his hands off me."

Lilly stopped chopping. Merry had a bright new smile on her face. "Really, we're embarrassing the way we go at it."

After breakfast Lilly piled in the car with Merry and Sunny, thinking they were going for a nice, mindless ride, but instead Merry took her sight-seeing. "I can't concentrate," Lilly said, but Merry grew insistent.

"You can't say you haven't seen Berkeley!" she said.

"It's all right," Lilly said.

"Isn't it pretty around here?" Merry coaxed. "You know there are tons and tons of single guys living around here." She nodded at Lilly, who ignored her.

Merry took her to Fisherman's Wharf and bought her a chilled red crab that Lilly threw out when Merry wasn't looking. Every time Merry saw another mother wheeling her baby in a stroller, she insisted on stopping and exchanging information, while Lilly grew frantic hearing about babies and marriage and all the things that had been taken from her. She waited until Merry went into a book shop and then went to the nearest pay phone and called Nora collect, weeping into the phone.

"Come home," Nora said. "Come stay with me." She started crying on the phone, too, which startled Lilly.

Merry, the baby strapped papoose style to her belly, found Lilly crying by the phone. "Oh, now," Merry warned.

Lilly held up her hand. "Don't tell me not to cry!" she said.

Merry was silent for a moment. The baby looked at Lilly with fresh interest. "Everything's not over," Merry said gently. "Don't you dare think that." She put one hand about Lilly's back. "Come on," she said gently. "Let's get out of here. I just thought it was better for you not to dwell on memories, that's all." She sighed. "Look," she said. "We can go to the clinic, you can lie on a table and just rest."

The clinic was filled with people. In the waiting room, a woman in a print sundress beamed at Merry. "I brought you a carrot cake," she said, setting a box on the counter.

"I can take you in ten minutes," Merry said. She led Lilly to a room with a long flat black table. "Jack'll come in and fix you up," she said. She patted Lilly on the arm.

Jack, newly sunburned, came in. "Well, now," he said briskly.

Lilly let Jack set her up on the table, though she didn't like the feel of his fingers pressing along her spine. "Lilly," he said, "I see some problems developing. Adjustments that need to be done." He probed gently along her neck, making Lilly wince. "I'd be happy to do them for you now. Free of charge, of course."

"No adjustments," Lilly said, moving from his fingers.

"You don't have to do them now, but if you don't do them within this year, I can't guarantee that you'll be walking by next year."

"No adjustments," Lilly said.

"Suit yourself," he said curtly, "but I'm telling you." He placed a small vibrating rod under her neck, arching her head back uncomfortably. "This'll help," he said sternly.

Lilly lay there listening to the noise underneath her. As soon as he was gone, she removed the rod and placed it by her side. Every once in a while she saw someone wander past in a dressing gown, Merry chattering at them or Jack giving instructions gruffly. The baby stayed in the main office and was so quiet, Lilly almost forgot about her. She finally got up to find Merry.

Merry was in the main office, talking to a man with a neatly trimmed beard. He had no shirt on, and embarrassed, Lilly started to turn away.

"No, wait!" Merry said. "This is Ted Thremmer. Ted— Lilly. She lives in New York."

Ted nodded at Lilly. "I get to New York," he said.

"Oh," Lilly said, wishing Ted would pull on his shirt.

"I'm going to a conference there next month," he said.

"That's nice."

"Maybe I could call you."

Lilly felt out of breath, as if she were suddenly alive in a bad dream.

"I bet you know some good places to go eat."

Lilly looked at Merry, who smiled. "She's clairvoyant," said Merry. "She knows them before they open."

"I won't be in the city then," Lilly said, and abruptly left the room. She was almost out the door when Merry grabbed her.

"What did I do?" Merry said.

"Maybe he can call me?" Lilly said.

Merry's face changed shape. "Listen," she said, "what is so terrible about a little company?"

Lilly pulled away. "I came here for *your* company."

Merry pursed her lips. "It's not good to just cry," she said. "It damages the body. It changes your body chemistry. Throws your hormones out of whack." She pushed at her hair. "I know you loved Matt, but I don't know if it's good to dwell on that. What if I dwelled on the fights Jack and I used to have? What would that be like?"

"I don't know, what would it be like?" Lilly said.

Merry shook her head. "Not everyone is going to be as perfect as Matt. You know that?" She shook her head. "Quick change is the best thing. I'm trying to help you be happy, Lilly. That's all."

Lilly left the next day, telling Merry there was an emergency back home. Merry's face folded for a moment. Lilly tried to remember how at one time they had been such good friends, they had promised each other they'd rent a house together when they were ninety, that they'd sit out on the porch and swap stories.

"Well, you know best," Merry said lamely.

Jack gave Lilly a hug. "You remember what I said about those adjustments," he said. He threw one arm about Merry, and the two of them waved at Lilly as her car pulled out back onto the highway, again.

She moved around. She was now so thin that she had to belt her jeans on the last notch of her belt to keep them up. Her belly was completely gone, and she could count all the ribs beneath her flesh. She looked at herself in the mirror critically, the way strangers would, and she thought, as they might: Something's wrong.

She criss-crossed back east. She drove for two hours, and before, where she had wanted silence, now she found herself blasting whatever radio station she could pull in, filling her car with sound and music. On her third hour on the road, she started to talk back to the radio. Her voice sounded raspy and hoarse, as if she had been screaming for hours, and she was suddenly panicky with her own loneliness.

She swerved onto an exit and pulled over at a rest station. She made a beeline to the phones. Hands shaking, she fed quarters into the phone. She dialed Nora, and as soon as she heard her mother's voice, she started to cry.

"Honey, come home," Nora told her. "Get off the phone and come home right this instant. Stop being so stubborn."

Lilly's fingers gripped the phone. Her heart rocked in her chest. In the background she heard the doorbell. "Oh honey, I've got to call you back. Someone's waiting for me," Nora said. "You come home—"

"No wait!" Lilly said. Her breath clipped shut.

"What? What is it?" Nora said. Lilly heard the doorbell again. "Sweetie, I've got to go. I'll call you tonight. Just tell me where you'll be—"

"No, wait—"

"What is it, darling?" Nora said.

"I don't know—I just—"

Someone tapped her shoulder. A man in a business suit. He gestured toward the phone, and Lilly ignored him.

"Mum," she said.

"Baby, I'll call you tonight," Nora soothed, and hung up the phone.

The second the dial tone came on, Lilly dug in her jeans for quarters. "Jesus," said the man waiting for the phone. Lilly dialed.

"Lilly?" Robert said.

She was on the phone with Robert for over an hour. She

wasn't aware of anyone or anything except the voice connected to her. Robert was quiet and patient. He didn't care what she said, and he let her talk until the knot of panic had loosened up.

"In case you're wondering, I'm not doing a film about you and grief," he said. "I've missed hearing you talk. Isn't that something?"

"Hey," she said, "I think I can sleep now."

"Are you sure?" he said. He yawned. "What's your number? I'll call you in the morning."

"I don't know," Lilly said. "I'm just at a pay phone."

"Well," he said, "you call whenever. I don't care what time. You hear me?"

"Loud and clear," Lilly said.

She hung up the receiver as gently as if it were a lover. Her ears hurt. Her voice felt strained and raw, but the panic was gone.

A woman in a blue dress, waiting for the phone, glowered at her, but Lilly ignored her. She felt fueled. She could drive for another two hours, she was sure of it. Long enough to get to a hotel.

In Denver she treated herself to an expensive hotel room—the room and a small refrigerator stocked with four kinds of cheese, bread, wine, and fruit, enough for a small dinner. There was a TV with three different movies she could pay to see. She wouldn't have to go out if she didn't want to, she wouldn't have to see people.

Lilly flopped on the bed. The room was dead silent. She was used to hearing people arguing next door, to the sounds of drawers opening and closing. A curl of panic formed in her spine. She grabbed the phone and set it on her chest. Robert, she thought, and dialed, but when she got his machine, she hung up. Nora would be home now. She could call her friend Tess in Santa Fe. Through the thin walls she heard a woman's laughter belling out. She looked out the window and saw a couple tossing car keys back and forth, playing, and then abruptly she got up and grabbed her jacket. She walked out of her room and out of the hotel, striding, swinging her arms as if she were a person who knew how to be happy, too.

She walked toward the diner across the street. It was half empty. The waitress started to lead Lilly to a booth, but she shook her head. "Counter," Lilly said.

Only two people were at the counter, a very old woman and a man in his fifties. Lilly sat beside the man in his fifties. He gave her a sidelong glance and moved three seats away from her, shoving his plate down after him.

She liked the loud country music chiming through the place. She liked the sound of the dishes. She wished it were noisier. The waitress, who couldn't have been much older than Dinah, leaned toward Lilly with a menu. "Hi," she said, her accent so flattened, it sounded like "Hah" to Lilly. Lilly looked for a name tag. Gertie. She wanted to call the waitress by name, to bring her close as a sigh.

"French fries," Lilly said, though she wasn't really hungry.

When the waitress brought them, Lilly touched her sleeve. "Are there movie theaters around here?" she said.

Gertie laughed. "You're not from around here, are you?" she said. "There's one theater, but it's a twenty-minute drive, and they've been showing something like *That Darn Cat!* for a month now."

"I'm from San Diego," Lilly said cheerfully. She smiled. She thought of Nora suddenly. "Smile, and people will want to be near you," Nora used to tell her. Nora used to practice her own smile in front of the mirror. "I sell cosmetics," Lilly said.

"Really?" The girl leaned across the counter. "You know, I never can get the right shade of blush."

Lilly felt herself floating out of her body. "Pink," she said, and even though she was smiling, she burst into tears.

"Goodness," Gertie said. She waved to the other waitress

and came back around the counter and wrapped one arm around Lilly. "Come on," she said.

She led Lilly to the back room and sat her on a chair. Her voice was smooth and sympathetic. "Hey," she said. "Whatever it is, it'll get lighter if you speak it."

"My husband's seeing another woman," Lilly blurted.

The girl sucked in her breath. "You know what you do, then," she said. "You buy yourself some fancy red high heels and a really tight dress." She nodded at Lilly. "I know it sounds crazy, but it always works with me. Makes him so jealous he could spit nails."

Lilly stood, trembling. "A red dress," she said. She suddenly wanted to ask the waitress if she'd go to a movie with her that night. She wanted to ask the waitress if she wanted to drive and drive and drive with her.

"It's going to be all right," Gertie said. "I know. Things like that, they happen all the time, and they don't mean nothing."

"You're probably right," Lilly said.

Gertie cast an anxious look back at the counter. Two men were tapping their menus, looking around. "Hell," Gertie said. "I got to go." She looked at Lilly. "You'll be *fine*," she promised.

Lilly walked back to the hotel, counting her steps. Thirty-five steps from one place to another. Thirty-five pieces of a life. From the café, she could hear someone laughing. As soon as she got back to the hotel, she called Nora.

Nora said, "Honey, I'm so sorry about this afternoon—"

"I want to come home," Lilly said, cutting her off.

Lilly went to stay two weeks in Maine with her mother and Whitley. Nora let her cry as much as she wanted. Trying to fatten her up, Nora cooked the foods Lilly had loved the most when she was a little girl—mashed potatoes pooled with butter, chocolate pudding served warm—and although Lilly couldn't be coaxed into eating more than a bite, it still soothed her to see the food, to smell it. It reminded her that she had ties, that someone still loved her.

It didn't take her long to turn into a daughter again. She turned twelve, whining and restless and needy all at once, and no matter how horrible her behavior, her mother looked at her as if the prodigal girl had returned at last.

Whitley went out early every morning to the woodworking shop he had opened. He was polite with Lilly, so distant that Lilly finally was moved to remind him how he had once taught her how to plant cucumbers, how he had shown her how ants herded aphids.

"Certainly I remember," Whitley said, then he kissed Nora, gently stroking a circle on her back, and went out the door.

Nora persuaded Lilly to come fishing with her. "Wait until you see how they bite!" she cried.

Lilly felt trapped in the boat with her mother. She felt pudgy and uncomfortable in her orange life jacket, and all she really wanted to do was talk about grief with her mother. She hadn't thought she'd react like this, but just being on a lake again made a line of ice race along her spine. You're afraid, face it, she told herself. Every time she looked across the surface of the lake, she half expected Matt to come floating up to the surface. She thought suddenly of Dinah in her black bikini, measuring the distance of lake between Lilly and Matt.

"You okay, honey?" said Nora. "You're shivering!"

Lilly was in long pants and long sleeves to keep the mosquitoes and the ticks at bay, and she had borrowed a white cotton hat of her mother's to keep the sun from her face. She twitched the rod her mother insisted she carry. She didn't even like fish, and she certainly didn't like fishing.

"What did you think when Daddy had his heart attack?" she said.

Nora pulled down her fishing hat and frowned. "I thought he had died," she said. She pulled back her rod and flung the line deeper into the water, swaying the boat. She looked at Lilly. "You know things hadn't been good between us for a while, but for a moment, I made all these bargains. I would be the best, most uncomplaining wife there was if Bob would live. I would stop seeing Whitley. I would cherish each and every minute." Her rod twitched, and she leaned forward into it. "Then he got well, and how could I be different when everything else was the same?" She lunged with her rod. "Got a bite!" she cried.

Lilly cringed as her mother grappled with the line, pulling aboard a silvery, flopping fish. "Ah, there's a beauty!" Nora said. "Look at that beauty!" She quickly unhooked the fish and then held it in her hands, just for a moment, admiring it, before she released it back into the water.

"Why'd you do that?" said Lilly, astounded. She peered over the rim of the boat at the ripples of water.

"I never keep them," Nora said calmly. "The sport is to hold them, then I let them get back to their lives."

"But that's unbelievably cruel!" Lilly said.

Nora looked at Lilly mildly. "It's a sport, dear."

"I bet the fish doesn't think so."

Nora suddenly put down her rod. "I think he feels damn lucky. I think he probably thinks he got off easy, that a wound that heals is a small price to pay for staying alive. That's what I think." She started fiddling with the gear, getting ready to head back to shore. "This is a terrible thing to say, Lilly, but honey, at least you're young."

Lilly laid her rod flat in the boat.

"A horrible thing happened to you that I wouldn't wish on anyone in the world, let alone my own daughter," said Nora. "But it was a fluke. You're young. You're lovely. You can find someone else to marry if you want."

"Stop," Lilly whispered. "It hurts to hear that."

"All right," soothed Nora. "But I'm just telling you."

"Tell me something different," Lilly said.

Nora didn't want Lilly to leave, but Lilly felt as if she were rushing against the grief, that the more things she did, the more places she went to, the less real her life might seem to her, and the less she might have to remember. She left on a Friday morning for Santa Fe, promising her mother she'd call, promising that she'd eat although the thought of food still made her ill. She hugged both Nora and Whitley, and everybody cried when she left.

She was planning to stay with her friend Tess, an actress who used to waitress in the New York restaurant where Lilly worked, who had given it up to manage a theater in the heat. She lived with three cats in a small adobe house on Calle Ojo Feliz Street, set under the stars.

Lilly drove. She stopped at a station for directions. "You can go two ways," he told her. "Route Eighty west'll get you there faster, but it's really crowded with cars. If I were you I'd take Forty—one long stretch you can probably go eighty on and no one will ever see you but the birds."

Lilly took Route Eighty west. It comforted her to see the other cars speeding beside her, other faces intent and hunched over the wheel or singing to themselves. Alone together, Lilly thought, and for a moment she felt comforted.

Tess let Lilly cry. Tess didn't say one thing when she woke up to find Lilly sitting in the living room whispering to the air, talking as if Matt were there. Tess bent and held Lilly. She walked Lilly out to the Indian reservations and sat with her while she wept. Tess stayed up in bed, booting out her lover, Frank, for the whole time Lilly stayed, wrapping her arms around Lilly and rocking her when she cried. Tess worked evenings as a masseuse and days as a drama teacher at a college. Every evening Lilly had a massage, and every morning she went with Tess to the college. She didn't understand why all the students were watching her, why they flocked around, until Tess finally told her that they knew what had happened.

"They think it's romantic," Tess said apologetically. "Look, they're young."

"I don't feel him," Lilly told Tess that night at home. "I don't hear anyone anymore."

Tess was chopping tomatoes for guacamole. Her hands were damp with lemon juice. She stopped her work for a moment and looked at Lilly. "Lilly, you're just blocked with grief. That's perfectly natural. Why don't you let someone else do the work for a change?" she said. "This is Santa Fe. The mystic capital of the world, Lil." She smiled. "You could . . . uh, consult," she said finally.

"If he isn't coming to me, why would he come to someone else?" Lilly said.

Tess tossed up an avocado and caught it in one hand. "I don't know. Do you?"

Lilly felt like a fool, but the next day, while Tess was teaching a drama class, Lilly took a walk. She picked up a local newspaper and turned to the classifieds, and there in the listings, as long as her hand, were mediums. Sister Sarah. Madame Diane. She didn't have to be clairvoyant to know those were the charlatans, the ones who would have pictures of Shirley MacLaine on their walls or tables inlaid with crystals, the ones who might prattle on in a phony voice, hoping Lilly was grief-stricken enough practically to hallucinate what she wanted to hear. Donna Minstein, one ad said. If I don't succeed, you don't pay. Lilly ripped out the ad.

Donna Minstein lived in a small adobe house within walking distance of Tess's college. She was Nora's age, but she was in a short blue dress and her long white hair was clipped back with an Indian beaded barrette. "Well, hello," she said, taking Lilly's hands, rubbing them with assurance that made Lilly relax a little.

"I want to reach someone," Lilly said.

Donna nodded. "Black hair," she said. "Tall. Right?"

Lilly started, and then she nodded.

"Well, honey, I saw him," Donna said. "Now you just sit. This is going to be easy."

Lilly felt ridiculously and suddenly happy. She waited. Oh, please, she thought. Please. She heard Donna shift.

"Hmm," said Donna, her voice leveling down, becoming falsely boisterous. "Lilly, baby, I miss you."

Lilly felt all the blood in her veins turning right into ice. Matt had never called her baby. He had never sounded boisterous, and he had never waved his hands around or dipped his head the way Donna was doing. As grief-stricken as she was, as much as she wanted to believe, she could recognize someone pretending.

"I'm having a good time up here with all my pals," Donna began, her eyes widening, and then Lilly, shaking, stood up.

Donna blinked. She started to say something and then, thinking better of it, shook her head. "I'm sorry, honey," she said finally. "Sometimes you connect. Sometimes you don't."

Donna fed Lilly tea even though she refused to take her money. "You'll find what you're looking for," she told Lilly, and Lilly continued to look.

She spent five hundred dollars going to mediums, and not one of them was able to do what she herself had been able to do with her eyes closed. They told her all sorts of things about herself, and almost all of them were wrong. She loved the beach. She loved the mountains. She was going to hear from Matt, but when she least expected it. "And I know you won't believe this, but you're going to be *psychic*," one woman said. Lilly's eyes flew open. She started to laugh, and then she was crying so hard, she was nearly blinded by her tears.

"No good, huh?" Tess said when Lilly told her she had finally given up. "Come on, let's fill up some time."

Tess put her to work, filing index cards at the theater, typing address labels, and Lilly began to put herself on automatic. She worked through lunch and when she saw the students beginning to leave, when she began to panic at the night spread out before her, Tess leaned over Lilly's desk and told her they were going to the gym.

Lilly ran six miles, until she was so exhausted that she longed for sleep. She climbed twenty flights of stairs on an artificial machine, and the only place she stayed completely away from was the pool.

"Listen, I'm going to start paying you," Tess told her. "You're the best secretary I've ever had."

"Come on, I'm staying with you for nothing—"

"You eat nothing, you hardly take up space. I'm paying you and that's that." Tess smiled. "Besides, I'd like it if you'd stay a while. I've been lonely, I admit it. I haven't missed Frank all that much, which makes me think I'm out of the boyfriend business for a while. Don't look so alarmed," Tess said. "We'll just take it day by day."

"I don't know," Lilly said.

"That's all right," Tess said. "You don't have to."

chapter 6

Every time Dell looked at her granddaughter, she felt a little desperate. She didn't know what she was doing, only that she didn't want to remember how alone she was.

When Dell cried at night, Dinah got a stricken, pale look on her face and then got up and went into her room and closed the door. It was a mistake to give her a room with a door that locked.

Dell listened carefully when she passed Dinah's door. Only once did she hear Dinah crying. "Dinah?" she said, knocking at the door. But then the crying stopped. "Dinah?" she repeated, knocking harder. This was her house. No one should be able to lock the doors against her.

"I'm all right," Dinah called, but her voice was slower, sludgy sounding.

"Come talk to me," Dell said.

"I'm sleeping," Dinah said, but Dell could hear her pacing the floor, creaking the boards under her weight.

Every evening Dell asked Dinah about her day. She tried to be as breezy sounding as she could, to act almost as if she didn't really count on an answer, as if every part of her weren't yearning for contact.

"My day was fine," said Dinah.

"Do anything interesting?" Dell asked.

"Not really," said Dinah. She shut her eyes, rubbing at them. "I'd better go to sleep," she said politely, and Dell's heart sank.

Dell kept as busy as she could. Every morning she exercised. In a new red jogging suit, she did twenty-five situps and five minutes on the bike. She put on a radio station that she thought a young person like Dinah might like, half hoping it'd draw Dinah into the room to listen. She gritted her teeth at the music. She hated the fake, familiar tone of the disc jockey, but she told herself, over and over, that if Dinah even stopped at the door, snagged by a pop tune, it would be worth it.

As she exercised, she thought about her son. She was almost twice the age Matt would have been if he were alive, and the very oddness of that thought made her shiver. She was sure a thought like that would never cease to amaze her.

It pained her. She couldn't remember a moment when she had ever looked at him and thought, I'm the luckiest woman alive. She hadn't been like other mothers she knew, trying to keep their child a baby as long as they could, not wanting him to leave and go out into the world.

No, she had encouraged him not to need her, to leave. In junior high school he spent so much time at his friends' homes that he fell in love with their families. The Robertses, she remembered. He was always talking about Mr. Roberts this, and Mrs. Roberts that. And then one day a Mrs. Toledo, a woman Dell didn't even know, called her up and asked for a recipe of a cake Matt had brought over to dinner and had credited to Dell. Pineapple cream cheese. "My husband just raved," Mrs. Toledo said. "Tell me, what was in it, sweet cream? Powdered sugar?"

Dell fluttered her hands on the receiver. "Family secret," she said finally.

There were lots of family secrets. She was too embarrassed to confront her son, to find out what bakery he had brought the cake from or even if he had somehow baked it himself. She didn't know her own son, and she realized she had never really known her husband, either. She couldn't say why Hank hadn't come home, why he hadn't written more than a few letters. She never understood how he could just give up the shoe shop that had been so much his pride and joy, and of course, how he could give her up. "I love you," she had written at the tag end of the letters she had written him. "Come home before I miss you so much I completely fall apart."

She never knew why Matt had fallen in love with Maggy, a vaguely trashy girl who wore too much makeup and wasn't polite. And although she had liked Lilly when she'd met her, she never knew, either, just what it was that had made Matt fall so head over heels in love with her. He had never gotten the chance to tell her, and she had never gotten the chance to ask. She had never even thought to.

She had never been good with children, not with Matt, not with Dinah when he had brought her by. She had loved a memory of a husband. She loved her son now, but he was dead. Lilly was gone. The one person left who might be hers to love, who might forgive her, was her granddaughter, if only her granddaughter would let her.

When Matt's boxes came, Dinah looked stunned. They piled up in the living room, breathing dust, and Dinah picked her way past them, and finally she took the boxes marked with her name and shoved them in her closet, far in the back.

"Do you want to help me go through these things?" Dell said to Dinah. Dell carefully slit open the first box with the edge of a scissors. Dinah flinched at the tearing sound.

"I gotta go to the library," Dinah said, and left the house with a jacket Dell was sure wasn't warm enough.

Dell spent two whole days going through the boxes, and the whole time she felt shocked. She didn't know what to keep or what to throw out. She had no idea what was important, and all the clutter made her dizzy. There was a red sweater so bitten with holes that she was sure it must have meaning or he would have thrown it out. A notebook full of sayings she couldn't decipher. "Fur and nails," he had written. "Oh, God, I love you," was on the last page, but was that to Lilly or Maggy or Dinah or someone she didn't even know? She riffled through all the pages, but she couldn't find mention of herself. She saved a ticket stub and a date book full of names and places she didn't recognize. Could she ask Dinah what these things were, or would the girl hate her for not knowing, for never taking the time even to try to find out?

She found Lilly's letters in a small blue box, and although she knew they were personal, one day when Dinah was out of the house, Dell read them. She didn't understand a lot of what Lilly talked about, the places, the films they had seen, the books, the references to people she had never heard him mention. "I miss your hands," Lilly wrote, "I miss your taste. Oh, you. Oh, love." Dell shut her eyes. The intimacy was like a door slamming in her face. "You have no idea how much I love you," Lilly wrote. "I crave you like a drug." Dell read half of the letters and then put them back. Lilly was right. It was private. It wasn't for her to know. Dell sighed and wept and struggled.

As Dell worked, she took to wearing an old watch she found of Matt's, the time stopped at three exactly. If someone asked her later, she'd tell them it was her son's watch. She'd say that it had been his favorite, because she had bought it for him for his twentieth birthday, and even after it stopped he hadn't been able to toss it out. The story warmed her. She placed the watch up against her ear, and for a moment she swore she could hear it ticking, as faint and stubborn as a small heart.

She stored them in Matt's room. She put Dinah's things in the guest room to let her unpack them as she pleased. She registered Dinah for school, and she urged her to come to the shop with her.

"I'll be fine here," Dinah said.

She was reading in the backyard when Dell left, and when Dell called to check on her at lunchtime, she was distant and polite. "I'm fine," she said, as if that told Dell anything.

Dell kept busy. She went to the shoe store and climbed into the front window and redid the display, skipping up so much dust that she was sneezing all afternoon. She talked to customers. Lunchtime she usually liked to walk down to the mall and have a bite at Ellen O's, where the waitresses knew her, but the thought of sitting down, of stopping long enough to think about her life, terrified her. She ate while she worked.

At least once a day, though, Letty came by the shop to see how she was doing. They sat and chatted, and then Dell showed her some of the photos she had found in Matt's things. Her eyes grew wet and salty. Letty pulled out a picture of Matt and Lilly in front of a building.

"Where's this?" Letty said.

"Matt and his fiancée in Chicago," Dell said, though she had no idea what city it was. "You should have seen the string of pearls they brought me from the Miracle Mile."

"Oh," said Letty. "You look so nice in pearls."

"He was always doing things like that," said Dell. "He never forgot Mother's Day or Valentine's Day or my birthday. Every holiday I got a card or flowers or a present like you wouldn't believe." She fingered the edges of her sweater. "We were so close," she said. Her voice chipped. There was a hollow burning in her stomach. "So very, very close, it was almost unusual."

"He must have loved you very much," said Letty.

Dell kept trying to get close to her granddaughter. She secretly bought teen magazines and read them in the back room at the shop, trying to decipher the lingo, to figure out what would please Dinah. Every time a young girl came into the store, Dell followed her silently, trying to see which shoes she picked up, studying her dress. She herself never ate break-fast, but for Dinah she made peanut-butter muffins from a recipe in *Teen*.

Dell set them out triumphantly in front of Dinah. "I made them myself," she urged. When Dinah hesitated, Dell put the fattest muffin on a blue plate and positioned it in front of Dinah. The muffins were fragrant and still warm.

"I used a whole two cups of peanut butter," Dell said. "I had the health food store grind it up fresh." She blinked at Dinah, who was pushing the plate away slowly. "What is it?" she said.

"I'm allergic to peanuts," Dinah said.

Dell blinked. "Don't be silly—"

"When I was ten I was hospitalized because I ate a peanut-butter sandwich," Dinah said. Dinah looked at Dell as if she had done it on purpose. She scraped her chair getting up from the table.

Dell watched Dinah leave, and then she dumped all the muffins into the trash.

Dell was proud of her store, and the first week Dinah was living there, she took her to see it. The store was all polished wood, and in the window was a fall display, plastic pumpkins and leaves scattered around red slingbacks. Dinah smiled.

Dell always dressed up to go to work, perhaps a bit too formally, but she thought it was important to make a good im-pression. She wore low heels and a good rayon dress and a string of pearls that Hank had given her for their fifth date, two dates before he proposed. Dinah was in cutoffs and a black top.

"Isn't it too hot for black?" Dell said.

"They wear black in New York," Dinah said.

"Whatever for?" Dell said doubtfully.

Dinah drifted around the store, picking up shoes and putting them down.

Dell had hired a new manager to help her out so she could spend more time at home with Dinah. It was the one thing she had said she would never do, and now she had to do it. She interviewed only five people before she settled on the person whose spit-and-polish shined shoes had won him the job before he even opened his mouth. He was a young man who insisted that Dell call him Bobby. He had slicked-back brown hair that had an oily sheen, and he always wore a suit and a loud tie, and even after a month Dell could see the changes he was making, and she wasn't quite sure she liked them.

He had taken down all the photographs of feet in shoes. "It makes the place look bigger without them," he told her. He pulled up the worn carpet and washed and polished the wood floor.

"It looks bare," Dell said doubtfully.

"Naw, it's classy," Bobby said.

He climbed into the windows and took down her careful displays of Styrofoam figures perched among the shoes. He did the window so starkly, she wasn't sure at first that there were even shoes in it.

She stood frozen in front of the window. The window could hold up to twenty pairs of shoes, up to fifteen different props, too, if you handled it right, but she was looking in at three identical flats, all in different colors, all pointing toward each other.

Bobby came toward her, beaming. "Well?" he said. "Minimal art. Less is more. Very cool."

"Well," Dell said. "It certainly is different."

It was still her store, and less was never more, not with shoes and not with people. She let the window stand for one week, and then she came in early and spent two hours replacing it with the pumpkins and leaves. "Seasonal merchandise," she told him when she caught his stare.

He came out now when he saw Dinah. "So, this is Dinah!" he said. He smiled at her. Dinah shrugged. She was wearing black high-top sneakers that embarrassed Dell, but Bobby pointed at them. "Way to go! Converse All Stars!" he said. "Very today. Very now."

Dinah brightened. She flexed her toes.

She started looking at a display of black boots. She ran her hands over a pair of black pumps, and she looked at Dell.

Dell nodded to Bobby. "Get her the right size," she said briskly. "Whatever she wants."

Dinah looked up, startled. "I can't take these—"

Dell held up her hand. "You just did," she said.

"Size six and a half, am I right?" Bobby said to Dinah.

Dell turned. The air conditioner suddenly seemed unnaturally loud to her. The sound bothered her, like a bee caught inside her skull. It made her lose concentration for a moment. She rested one helpless hand on the back of a seat, and Dinah sprang forward to her.

"Dell, are you all right?" Bobby said. He placed one of his hands on her back and lowered her onto the seat. "Take it easy now," he said. "That's why you hired me."

"Oh, it is not," Dell said. Still, she tried to get up, then sank back onto the chair. The store was half empty right now. They didn't need her.

That evening they ate dinner on Dell's porch, corn on the cob and supermarket hamburgers and Cokes. Dinah was wearing her new black pumps. She kept arching her toes, taking sly peaks at the fresh new leather. The shoes weren't Dell's choice, but the shy, pleased look on Dinah's face was worth it. And she loved thinking of her granddaughter wearing her shoes.

"Very nice shoes," she told Dinah.

Dinah bit into the corn, studying it.

"You'll make lots of friends at school," Dell said, and instantly regretted saying it from the look Dinah gave her.

Dell touched her. "Listen, if you ever want to talk about anything—" She took a breath. "Believe me, I know how hard this is, I really do, and I'm a good listener if you just try me."

"I'm not much of a talker," Dinah said. She finished the corn, stood up, and then reached for Dell's plate. "It's okay, I'll do the dishes," Dinah said, turning into the house. She stopped at the door. "Thank you for the shoes," she said.

"How about a nice game of after-dinner cards?" Dell asked. She had a brand-new deck in her pocket. Dinah made a small face.

Dell watched Dinah go back inside, and then she laid out the cards for solitaire and thought about everything she had ever wanted and lost.

She stretched out her toes. There was that odd funny static in her head again. She must just be tired. She must just need to get to bed. Slowly she got up. She was still young, but her health wasn't wonderful, and things could happen. She had had a customer who was older than she was, seventy, in fact, who had placed a personal ad. "Fit and flirty," it said. "Solvent and seventy, likes to giggle." Dell had been amused, but the woman had gotten married just two months ago. Dell had clipped the announcement out of the paper and put it in her jewel box, and when she felt blue she took it out and looked at it.

Dell was almost through the game. She looked up at the sky. It was still early, and she wasn't yet tired. She shuffled the cards and started again.

Dinah couldn't fathom the depth of life's betrayal. Her grandmother's house was fussy and overheated, and the only good point about it was that it was three blocks from the Squirrel Hill shopping section, which had two bookstores, a video store, a movie theater, and a Gap.

There was no escape. Dell told her that the house in Akron had already been sold, to a family with a small daughter, and although there was money for Dinah, it was in a college trust fund. No one had asked Dinah if she even wanted to go to college.

She was uncomfortable in Dell's house, but she knew Lilly didn't want her, and how could she blame her? Her only alternative, to live with her mother, was no alternative at all. Every time she heard her grandmother crying at night, she was reminded of that day at the lake and her part in it. She heard Dell's cries, and then threaded through them, she swore she heard Lilly's. Two women crying, and because of her. Every time her grandmother tried to touch her, she moved back quietly. She didn't deserve kindness. She didn't deserve to be held or stroked or offered any sort of help. Every night she dreamed about the lake, and no matter what she did, she was always powerless to stop her father's flight toward the rock, always powerless not to hear Lilly screaming her name. She woke up trembling, the sheet gripped about her. She was sick and dizzy with the depth of her own fear. All this memory was surely punishment she had coming. Why should there be escape? Why should there be deliverance? She muffled her tears with a ball of sheet. I didn't see him buried, she thought. Sometimes it made her feel hot and shamed, but sometimes it made her feel comforted. He could still be alive, she thought. It could be a mistake. He could be with Lilly somewhere, the two of them mad at her, and even that would be all right— oh, please, God, that would be just fine by her, because he was her father, and she knew him, and she knew his angers didn't last. Dinah thought of the two of them speeding down a ribbon of road. She wrapped the sheet closer about her face and wept helplessly.

She did her own linens every morning so Dell wouldn't see how damp and sweaty the sheets were. She walked about the house as carefully as a dream that shouldn't be disturbed.

She didn't expect to feel at home, but her first day at school was more humiliating than anything she could have imagined. She wore New York black. A black band in her hair, a black minidress, and her new black shoes, and as soon as she strode into her homeroom, she heard the snickering.

"Hey, where's the funeral?" a boy said, and Dinah felt as stung as if he had struck her.

She had thought Akron was bad, but Schenley High seemed even worse. The cutest boys seemed to pair with the plainest girlfriends, and the prettiest girls ignored Dinah completely. She had made the mistake of saying she was from Akron only once, to a clerk in Dell's shoe shop. "My deepest sympathies," she had said, laughing. Now when Dinah walked into her homeroom she was ready. "I'm from New York City," she said.

Two boys in flannel shirts rolled their eyes at each other. "Big deal," said the girl in back of them.

Dinah didn't know how she made it through her first day. She felt wild and homely and unloved. She moved silently from class to class, grateful when the teacher didn't embarrass her further by making her stand up and introduce herself. She kept her head down, speaking to no one, feeling the whispers moving behind her back, like pieces of sharp glass. She was the first one out of a classroom and the first one in, and she almost always sat in the back corner, where she might be the most invisible. She bolted her lunch in two minutes flat and then left the cafeteria. She tried so hard to disappear that at the end of the day she actually felt lighter.

Dell was still at the store when she got home, but there was a plate of fresh-baked chocolate cupcakes on the table for her and a note. "Be back soon!" in a cheerful curlicued script. Dinah felt like weeping when she saw the cupcakes. She was starving, and she wondered if she should punish herself by not eating. She felt that she should make amends, but she didn't know to whom, and the cupcakes smelled delicious. She took one and bit into it.

She heard the mail flop in, and still eating the cupcake, she went to pick it up. Bills. Something for Dell from her friend Letty. Nothing for her.

Dinah put the mail on the end table. Her appetite had vanished. She went through the mail again. Nothing from Tonette, who was supposed to be her best friend. Nothing from Lilly. She felt suddenly sick and miserable and angry with herself for even caring whether Lilly kept in touch or not.

Lilly, she thought. You're clairvoyant, then tune in to this, she thought. I hate you. I wish you had been the one to die. She tensed, waited for the phone to ring, for Lilly to call and shout at her, but the house was silent. I wish you had died. She imagined it. Lilly dead. She could have comforted her father. They could have taken a long trip together, and then he would have been all right. Things would have gone back to normal.

She grabbed her books and went upstairs to study. It was an easy way to avoid her life. She stayed up until two in the morning, reading the assigned chapter of American history until she knew it by heart. She memorized geometry theorems and equations.

"Go to bed!" Dell called, and Dinah, exhausted, finally did.

The teachers began to like her, to smile when she came in, but the other kids rolled their eyes when they saw Dinah's hand shoot up. She felt their disdain when there was a pop quiz and she was the only one not sighing, not tapping her pen against the desk, willing an answer to come.

She knew Dell wanted her to come to the shoe store after school, but the way Dell kept watching her made her uncomfortable. Dell didn't think Dinah had done anything wrong. Dell was always beckoning her over to meet some customer, who would stare at Dinah and cluck sympathetically, and sometimes Dinah would torment herself by playing out a scenario in her head. She would blurt out the truth. She would say that she had caused her father's death, that she was responsible and everyone knew it, and then Dell's smile would fade and crack, then the customer would back away from Dinah as if what she had were catching. And then whatever would be coming to her, she would most certainly deserve it, and it would be a relief.

Today she walked all the way down to Shadyside and wandered in and out of the stores, looking for black clothing. She was determined not to buy anything that wasn't black, and in a poster shop she found a poster of New York, which she bought to hang on her wall.

She didn't tell Dell that the kids made fun of Hank's shoe shop, that no one would be caught dead buying those fuddy-duddy styles, and they made fun of Dell, too, who wore pearls when the temperature rose up to 104 degrees and who insisted on talking to them even though all they wanted were the shoes she didn't have.

Dinah was angry almost all of the time. She came home to an empty house and prowled the rooms. She went through all the drawers, taking everything out and putting it all back. She went through Dell's closet and took a beaded sweater from the 1930s that she had never seen Dell wear and decided to wear it to school the next day.

Dinah couldn't keep calling Tonette long distance, although Dell hadn't said a thing about the phone bill. Already Tonette seemed more and more distant. Names Dinah didn't know were cropping up in her speech. Ellen and Stacey and once or twice Rob. They used to be able to talk on the phone for hours, but lately she and Tonette stumbled into silence after ten minutes, and then there was nothing to do but hang up. If she wasn't going to go crazy, she would have to find someone to talk to.

Dinah ate her sandwich where she could, in empty classrooms, in the stairwell, and then she discovered the art room supply closet, which was always open and always empty.

She was eating lunch one day when she leaned too hard against a shelf and it came crashing down. The door flew open. The art teacher was an older man named Mr. Sgoras. He was used to finding couples locked together in the supply cabinet or one lone soul smoking dope, but finding this shy young girl in a beaded sweater, a jelly sandwich scrunched up in her hand, surprised and touched him.

"Well, now," he said. "Come on out here."

Dinah blinked at him. He had tufts of gray hair growing out of both ears. His face crunched up in a smile. "I'm sorry," she said. "I just can't eat in the cafeteria."

He nodded at her. "I can understand that," he said. He sat down at one of the tables. "Do you paint?" he said.

Dinah shrugged.

"Oh, I bet you do," he said. "You just don't know it yet." He got up and brought her a stiff piece of bumpy paper, a tin of watercolors, and a sable brush. Then he took out a pad and began writing.

"Are you sending me to detention?" Dinah said. She imagined a room full of dark hulking boys, spitballs whizzing down like hail.

"It's a pass," he said, tearing it off. "Every lunch period you want, you can eat here. But you have to paint when you're done." He grinned at her. "Deal?"

Mr. Sgoras was Dinah's first friend. He let her alone to eat her lunch and to paint. He was right. She did like painting. The colors soothed her, and she liked the way the bumpy watercolor paper felt under her hands. She liked it, too, that he didn't use her as an example to other art students. He told her how much he liked her paintings, but he never hung them up. He kept them in a folder for her. He had heard the stories about her father, but he thought she should be the one to bring them up if that was what she wanted to talk about. He had never even spoken to her until she began speaking to him first, asking him questions about what brushes to use, how to do a watercolor wash, and then he answered her questions and told her stories.

He told her when he was twenty he had caught a virus

that had almost destroyed his sight. The world began narrowing into blackness, and for two months, before the medications kicked in, he was almost completely blind. He told her how his first wife had run off with his best friend and how ten years later he had met the real love of his life. "You never know," he told Dinah, and handed her another, thinner brush.

Dinah raised the brush. She didn't tell him about her past. She talked about living with Dell, but she didn't say why that was, and he was polite enough not to ask. She didn't have to talk about feeling lonely or lost or guilty because every day she was painting it, and all Mr. Sgoras had to do was look at the gray wash she used in her paintings to know that she was hurting and know that his part might be as simple a thing as making sure there was always more paint, always more paper, and always, too, a place for her.

By fourth period Dinah's beaded sweater was a topic of conversation in school. She was wandering from G block math to H block science when she heard her name, shouted out at her, like a ball she was supposed to catch. She squinted, and then to her horror she saw Dell, in a bright red dress and matching hat, in those terrible ribbon-tied shoes Dell thought were so fashionable, waving energetically to her from the hallway.

At first Dinah pretended not to see.

"Dinah!" called Dell, and at least three kids looked up, their amused faces flashing from Dell to Dinah.

She wanted to die. She wanted to sink into the ground, that was how ashamed she felt. No one's mother came to school to embarrass them, let alone their grandmother in a dress so bright, it looked as if it might just catch on fire.

She was rooted in place. Let it just be over with, she thought. Dell tried to embrace her, a flurry of hands and perfume and hair. "Surprised to see me?" she said. She looked at Dinah, who had her arms folded tightly across her chest. "I know that sweater!" Dell said, but she didn't seem angry.

"Sure," Dinah said. A boy brushed by her.

"I thought I should introduce myself to your teachers," Dell said brightly. "Take a real interest."

"My teachers?" Dinah said. "You don't know who my teachers are." The room reeled before her.

"Your grandmother's a resourceful woman," Dell said proudly. "I went to the office and found out."

"I can't believe you talked to my teachers," said Dinah.

Dell looked shocked. "Of course I did!" she said. "And I'm glad I did. Did you know Miss Simmons thinks you could be a real writer if you put your mind to it? And your math teacher—my God, he said you're the only one who understands calculus in the whole class!"

Dinah wet her lips. "People talk to teachers at PTA," she said. She looked toward the door. "I have to get to class," she said.

"Could I go with you?" said Dell. She remembered Matt's fifth-grade class, a parents day she hadn't been able to attend because of broken pipes in the shop. Matt had come home so gloomy, he had shut himself up in his room and hadn't spoken to her for three days.

Dinah looked horrified. "No, no, not today," she said. She kept looking around. She wanted to bolt, but she was afraid of what Dell might do, where she might go. "You really should get back to the shop," she said desperately.

"This is more important," said Dell.

"You won't say that if someone robs the store," Dinah blurted. Suddenly Dell saw her face and stiffened. "Yes, I should go," she said. "I have to start our dinner."

She leaned forward to kiss Dinah, who stepped away from her, and Dell suddenly felt a thousand years old, just a stupid old woman who kept reaching and reaching and always, somehow, just missed.

"Who *was* that?" someone said to Dinah in last period history.

"No one," she said, and sank onto her seat.

Dinah took her time getting home. The house smelled of some kind of stew. There were fresh flowers on the hall table and beside them a box of cheap five-and-dime watercolors, a paintbrush, and some paper. Dinah picked them up, curious.

"I didn't know what kind to get," Dell said, coming into the room, wiping her hands on her apron. "Your art teacher said you were a fine painter."

"You spoke to Mr. Sgoras?" said Dinah. She felt suddenly unnerved, as if an earthquake were happening beneath her. She held on to the edge of the table.

Dell nodded emphatically. "He was a nice man," she said. "He sat me down and got me tea, but he said you were really quiet and he didn't know that much about you, just that you were a fine, fine painter.

Dinah quietly lifted up the paints. "Thank you for the paints," she said.

"Well—"

Dinah turned, cutting off her grandmother, and started up the stairs.

"My pleasure," Dell called out after her.

Dinah sat in her room. She had finished her homework, and she wasn't tired enough to sleep. She glanced over at the paints her grandmother had bought her. She got up and opened them and cautiously stroked the smooth creamy squares of color with her finger. The brush inside was a good one, sable, number 02, the kind she liked. She didn't have the right kind of paper, heavy with a bubbled surface. Dinah ran her hands over the paper Dell had bought her, and then impulsively she went to get a small cup of water.

That night Dinah painted for three hours. She forgot the time. She forgot she was living with her grandmother in a town she hated. She forgot everything but the wash of color sliding on the page, the smell of the paint.

When she finished she had a painting of her old room, of

a dog that had once boarded with her father and her for a while. She was startled to see how much time had passed. She felt flush and excited. Tomorrow she'd go get proper watercolor paper. Maybe she could find a cheap easel. She got up, and as soon as she stood, she was ravenous.

She took the stairs three at a time, and as she passed the front porch she saw Dell, sitting alone in her robe and pink sponge curlers, a game of solitaire set out in front of her. She wasn't playing, though. She was staring at the watch of Matt's she always wore, tracing one finger over the face, and she suddenly looked so frail and alone that Dinah stepped out onto the porch.

Dell looked up. "Hi," Dinah said tentatively.

"Hi yourself," Dell said.

"I was painting," Dinah said.

"Good," Dell said quietly. She stared out at the sky.

Dinah sat down beside Dell. She fingered one of the cards. "I'll play with you if you want," she said.

Dell picked up the deck and began to shuffle it slowly. "You don't have to," she said.

"It's okay," Dinah said. "I just don't know how to play."

"Well," Dell said, brightening, "gin's as good a place as any to start."

To Dinah's surprise, she began to like playing cards. She came home from school and did her homework and painted, and even though she told herself she was going to go to sleep, that she had to get up at six to make school in the morning, she'd gravitate downstairs. She and Dell played game after game of gin, keeping score with pencil and paper.

Dinah liked the night. The neighborhood was still and quiet, with only the occasional barking of a dog. She liked the sound the cards made on the table, she liked the fresh muffins Dell made, and she liked the tea Dell sometimes got up and made, deep fragrant cups that seemed exotic to Dinah.

"Another game," Dell said.

Dinah glanced at her watch. "It's nearly midnight," she said reluctantly. "School."

Dell squinted at her. "Are you tired? Do you want to stop playing?"

"No."

Dell shuffled the cards. "The body's a wonderful thing. It tells you what it needs." She handed the deck to Dinah. "Who are we to argue with it?" Dell said.

The night air felt cool and clean along Dinah's shoulders. "Are you sure?" she asked.

"If you want to stay up, and if you feel too tired to go to school tomorrow, I'll write you a note. One day won't hurt anybody," Dell said. "Want cookies? I'm getting some." She rose, and then she stopped suddenly, stumbling, gripping the edge of the door.

"Dell?" Dinah said, standing up, helping her grandmother, but Dell waved her off.

"Too much sitting, that's all," she said, waving Dinah away. "Just got to get my sea legs back."

Dell was getting more and more tired. She had never really wanted to before, but now she let Bobby take over more of the store. It didn't seem like the worst thing in the world not to have Styrofoam figures in the display windows anymore. It didn't seem so terrible the way he teased and flirted with all the young girls, especially when they walked out with boxes and boxes of new shoes. It was pleasant to sit down and watch Dinah dust, pleasant just to be in the shop, which in the end was more family to her than her family.

She hadn't heard word one from Lilly. She wasn't having the long heart-to-heart conversations with her granddaughter that she had hoped, but at least Dinah didn't flinch anymore when their hands accidentally touched in playing cards. And last night she had caught Dinah looking in one of her exercise books, *Great Grannies*. "What?" Dell demanded, but not before she had seen the chapter heading "Here's to Your Health."

Dinah slapped the book shut. "You stumbled last night," she said.

"I did not," Dell said. She took the book from Dinah and put it back in the shelf, but she couldn't help how pleased she felt that Dinah was worried, even a little.

"Come on," Dell said. "Let me beat the pants off you in cards."

It was turning toward winter. Already Dell was thinking or ordering the spring shoes.

Inside the store, the heater began to bother her more and more. "We have to get a plumber in," she told Bobby. "It's so noisy I can't hear myself think!"

He cocked his head. "It's as silent as a clam."

Still the sound bothered her. Her concentration scattered. Someone would ask for tan loafers and she'd be halfway to the stockroom before she'd realize in raw panic that she had forgotten what she was supposed to come for. She had to walk out again, smiling sympathetically. "Sorry, we don't have that style," she said.

"But you said . . . ," the woman said, her brow crumpling.

"I'm sure you misunderstood me," said Dell as pleasantly as she could.

But when it happened more and more, she called Dr. Lallo for an appointment. "Just a checkup," she told the nurse. She tried to keep her concentration, but she saw how she'd disappear for what she thought was only five minutes, only to return to find her customer gone.

One day she simply sat on one of the soft red chairs to rest her own feet. Just for a moment. She drifted. Something shimmered into her line of vision, and she looked up. Why, Hank, she thought, delighted. She was dreaming. Her husband was dancing in front of her, swaying in an army uniform, so snappy that he made her heart lift. She felt his hands on her shoulders, guiding her. "Oh, so nice," she murmured, and then his grip tightened, he grew a little rougher, and she protested. "Stop," she said, and then she suddenly felt something snap, and her eyes flew open, and the hands about her were Bobby's, and she felt so flooded with sadness, she felt she might drown.

"I must have dozed off," she said, trying to recompose herself. She tried to straighten, but her body felt weighted. Hank, she thought, and the scent of him suddenly drifted back to her. She sniffed at the air.

"Dell," said Bobby, his voice sliding. "Dell, this is too much for you."

She waved him away. He lifted her up. She had heard this conversation before. He wanted to buy her out.

"Dell, are you all right?"

Bobby's face spun toward her. "Dell," he said, and all the time she kept thinking how funny, she finally knew what had been buzzing around her head. It was a bee, large and furry, hovering about six inches from her, but so clear and sharp, she could see every tiny hair on its body and a small red mouth that moved, that seemed to be saying something to her, speaking an actual language.

"How amazing," she said. She tried to reach to grab it, and then she saw a sudden flash of red. "How pretty," she murmured, and then she shut her eyes.

It was only a small stroke. She was in the hospital just four days, and every day Dinah showed up to visit, her face white and tight with fear. "I made this for you," she said and handed Dell a small watercolor card. "Get well soon," it said.

Bobby beamed at her. Dell, watching his face through a haze of medication, through the blurred beat of her own heart, wondered about Bobby's mother. Did he go home on holidays? Did they talk? Did she carry his baby pictures and remember when he was the most precious thing she had in life?

"Rest," Bobby said, his voice so far away and soothing that, for a moment, she thought it was Matt's.

Dell came home in a cab with Dinah. "I'm perfectly fine," she told Dinah. "I just need to rest." She settled herself in the living room, on the couch so she could be close to everything, so she could call up the store and monitor every detail.

"I can't let things slide," she kept saying, but the truth of the matter was that somehow her interest had waned. She called Bobby every day. She insisted on speaking to the salespeople, and although she did everything an owner was supposed to do, she couldn't fake real enthusiasm. She couldn't fake concrete ideas. She sighed and ended up saying, "Well, I'm sure you're doing a wonderful job."

"Come back soon," said her stockboy, but when Dell thought of the rows and rows of shoeboxes in the back room, it made her dizzy. When she thought of the smell of leather, it sickened her. At home she got used to wearing nothing but slippers made of cloth, and she was happiest with a gift Dinah brought her—slipper socks, something she hadn't had since she was a child. Blue plaid with a soft blue padding on the bottom, like a cat's paw pad.

Bobby called every week, and for the first time Dell didn't pretend not to hear when he brought up buying her out again. She liked being at home. She liked having more time around Dinah. "The store will always be called Hank's," Bobby said. "And if you ever want to come back to work, you can." He mentioned a price, four times what Hank had paid for the shop. Dell, exhausted, finally agreed.

Bobby came over a week later with papers for her to sign, with two dozen red roses. He was boisterous. "I feel like family," he said. "And like family, I'll keep the store going."

"Good," she said, and signed away her husband's store.

Dell slept. She had to admit she was getting used to sleeping past ten, to puttering slowly around her own house, which now was filled with a girl. She began watching a soap opera for the first time in her life. *All Our Pretty Dreams*, because it took up the time before Dinah came home (putting her key nervously into the lock at three o'clock promptly, coming to see Dell first thing, imagine that!). She got to know the characters—Delilah and Maxine and that dreadful Grayson, who was cheating on both of them—and sometimes she got confused, sometimes she imagined she was living in the town of Mylodia Falls, too. Sometimes she swore she could hear Warwick stream, where everyone there went to have their affairs, to fall in love and be betrayed.

Her memory played tricks. She suddenly couldn't remember things about the store, whether she had sold it to Bobby or whether she still owned it. Had she ordered the new spring stock or done a new display? Sometimes, though she wouldn't dare admit it to anyone, she couldn't even remember what the store looked like or what it was called, although she pretended to. Hillary's, she thought. Hoyt's.

She waited a month and then finally just asked Dinah if she would go to the store and see what the windows looked like. "I always did the windows up," she said wistfully.

"Sure, I'll go," Dinah said.

It took Dinah an hour and a half to get to the store because the bus had a flat, and even when she got there, she wouldn't have recognized it if the name Hank's was not still above the door. She usually didn't want to go to the store, but now she did. She felt as if she were going to visit the real Dell, that the woman lying around in plaid slipper socks, avidly watching a soap, was an imposter. No, she'd walk into the store and Dell would be there in a starchy-looking dress, her hair set so carefully that you could still see the ridges of the rollers in it. Dell would smell of leather and floral perfume and sweat.

Dinah approached the store, blinking. The outside, which had been shiny red, was now stripped down to the brick. In the windows there weren't any of the Styrofoam figures Dell favored. Instead there was an entire window of black cowboy boots resting on a bed of shiny sharp spurs. In another window white boots were propped with jagged broken pieces of record albums. Dazed, she pushed open the door. Inside was new pale peach plush carpeting. The walls were peach also, and for the first time that Dinah could remember, music was playing, so low it took her a few minutes to recognize the Beatles' "Yesterday," a syrupy rendition with strings. The store was more crowded than she had ever seen it. "SALE," the signs said, startling her. "I don't believe in sales," Dell had told her. "People should be trained to want quality, and a sale implies that the shoes didn't sell, that no one of any taste wanted them."

"It brightens the place up, don't you think?" Bobby said, appearing suddenly. At first she didn't recognize him. The slick was gone from his hair, which was now long and soft and dusted his shoulders. He was in a suit, and he thrust both hands into his pockets.

Dinah was flustered. She didn't want to get her grandmother more upset, but she didn't like Bobby taking over the store, even though she herself was glad enough to be free of it.

"Right," Dinah said.

"Aw, honey, look," Bobby said, flipping his hair back with a toss of his head, and Dinah felt like telling him not to call her honey. "The name is still Hank's, for Christ's sake. But I mean, Jesus, you saw those displays with the Styrofoam dolls in the window—you saw the way she had things with nothing changed since 1920 or something. Who's attracted by that? Don't you think she'd be happy at how well the store's doing? I do."

"I don't know," Dinah said.

"It's my store now," Bobby said. "That's the bottom line." Behind him a woman held up a red pump, wanting her size.

"Excuse me," Bobby said, holding up his index finger. "Hang on a sec, Dinah." He pivoted smartly.

Dinah didn't know why she felt so lost. She turned and

walked out of the store, and when she got home she told Dell that the store was doing wonderfully, and if she forgot to mention the paint or the windows, she reasoned, how was that a crime? How was that any different a way of sugaring up the truth to make someone feel better?

Dell, watching her soap, clucked her tongue. "Amelia, don't!" she cried, and turned from Dinah.

Every night Dinah tried to cook dinner for Dell. She made hamburgers and frozen fish. She made instant mashed potatoes and packaged soups, and then she sat with Dell while Dell played with the food and dreamed.

She didn't know what to do. She didn't know whom to tell. Letty came over every few days and chatted with Dell, and when she left, she hugged Dinah.

"She's better!" Letty said. "You're a good little nurse."

But Dinah didn't think Dell was better. If anything, Dell seemed worse to her. All she ever wanted to do now was to leaf through magazines or watch whatever was on the television. She was sleeping more and more. She never set her hair or wore a dress, and all the expensive perfumes she used to spritz on herself were growing sour in their decanters from disuse. Dinah almost never saw her get up, except to go to the bathroom, and then she leaned along the wall for support unless Dinah ran up beside her and took her arm. "It's the medication," Dell told Dinah, but Dinah wasn't so sure. Dell's movements slowed. And the scariest thing was that sometimes Dinah suddenly felt that Dell didn't even know she was there. She had been used to walking through the door and having Dell practically pounce on her, having Dell buying her things she didn't want, laying them out on her bed; now, when she walked by Dell, all Dell showed was a mild and surprised kind of interest.

"When do you go back to see the doctor?" Dinah asked, but Dell just shrugged. "Don't you think you should go?"

"You're the best medicine for me," Dell said.

Dinah brought cards in on a TV tray for the two of them to play. Dell held the cards, fanning them. "This will be fun," Dell insisted, but after Dinah laid down her first pack, three aces, Dell's cards fluttered from her hands. "I'm tired," she admitted.

Dinah gathered up the cards. "It's fine," she said. She settled Dell in bed and dimmed the lights. She waited in the next room until she heard her grandmother's soft snore. She couldn't sleep. She lay in bed and thought and worried about her grandmother, and then finally she got up and sat out on the porch and played solitaire with her grandmother's cards, and she told herself it was the same. She put down a red queen and then a two of hearts, but she didn't feel any better. She didn't feel any less lonely, and she shuffled the cards back together in a pack and left them there in the night, and went back inside.

All day at school she couldn't concentrate. She had found a doctor's name in Dell's plastic flip-up book by the phone, but she couldn't remember if he was the one who had treated Dell in the hospital. She could call the hospital, but she didn't know what they would do. Doctors didn't make house calls anymore, and Dell wouldn't go to a doctor, no matter how Dinah pleaded.

Dinah began worrying more and more. She came right home from school. The most terrifying moments were right before she got her key in the door, right before she heard or saw her grandmother. Only then could she relax, could she reclaim her own self.

In the evening she did her schoolwork and watched Dell and looked out into the night every time a group of kids drove by.

She called Tonette. "Call someone," Tonette said. "Call Lilly."

"Lilly!" Dinah said. "No way."

"You have to call someone," Tonette said. "You can't be

expected to take this all on yourself. You can't be responsible for everything."

"Why can't I?" said Dinah.

She tried to keep neighbors from knowing anything was wrong. When she walked out the front door, she called, "I will, Dell!" loudly enough for the man across the street to hear, even though Dell was so soundly asleep, a rocket could have exploded and she wouldn't have heard it. She was careful not to let the newspapers pile up, and when the doorbell rang she tried not to answer it if she could help it. Once she heard loud, banging knocking, and then she heard Letty's voice. Dinah slid along the wall, careful not to move, her heart hammering inside of her, so loud that she was sure Letty could hear it, but Letty finally gave up and went away, and when Letty called that evening Dinah was careful to sound as cheery as possible.

"Oh, Dell's asleep," she said apologetically. "We were out all day, and she got tuckered out."

"I'll drop by tomorrow, then," Letty said.

"I'll tell her," Dinah said, and that night she sat down and forged Dell's hand on a note she would leave outside on the door for Letty the next day:

> Sorry I missed you. Had to take care of details about shoe shop. I'll call you. Dell

She watched Letty pluck the note from the front of the door and frown, reading it, and for one terrified minute she was sure Letty was going to bang on the door again, but instead she tucked the note in her purse and walked back down to her car.

She worried when she was at school, but she knew Dell didn't hear the door, and she just hoped that Letty would never call.

"You're such a help!" Dell said, delighted. She gave Dinah checks every week to do the shopping, to take care of things. Dinah was a quick learner, and in just two weeks she knew how to do the laundry, how to do the food shopping, and how to copy Dell's name on a check so neatly that no one would ever know it was a forgery.

The bills began to pile up, and for the first time Dinah began worrying about money. She paid as many as she could, and then they began coming back. Insufficient funds. The checkbook of Dell's she worked out of had a five-dollar balance, and Dinah didn't know what to do. She knew there was a lot of money from the sale of the shop, but she didn't know where that was or how to get at it. She had a trust fund, but she couldn't touch it until she was eighteen.

"Dell," she said, sitting next to her grandmother. Dell took her hand. "I need to put some money in the checking account."

"There's plenty of money in that account," Dell said, surprised.

"I spent it on groceries," Dinah said. "And the bills. I have to put more in the account."

Dell fingered the chenille spread, frowning. "Don't be silly," she said finally. "There's lots of money in there. And my check from the shop will come in automatically, the beginning of the month." She burrowed under the cover. The beginning of the month was three and a half weeks away, Dinah thought. "Just a quick nap," Dell said.

In the morning Dell had completely forgotten about the money, and Dinah was too nervous to remind her. Instead she told herself she'd just have to economize. She'd just have to make do.

This wasn't the same as being on her own. If she called someone, she might be sent someplace else, to a foster home or to her mother, but what worried her most was that as much as she had wanted to help Dell, she might be the cause of her grandmother's demise. She might be responsible in ways she had never intended.

Right before gym, still in her blue-striped suit, she called

Dell. She had let the phone ring twenty times and had even hung up and redialed, but there was no answer. She felt a flash of panic, and still in her gym suit, shivering, she suddenly walked right out of the school.

"Young lady!" a teacher called, but Dinah kept running.

She ran to the cab stop and cabbed home and dashed into the house. "Dell!" she screamed. She didn't know what she expected. Older women broke their hips all the time. It was possible to drown in three inches of water.

"Dell!" Dinah screamed again. She ran up the stairs, three at a time, and there was Dell, asleep in her bed, with the sheets soaking, the TV blaring a soap opera. The acrid smell assaulted Dinah's nose, but she bent and shook Dell, and even as her grandmother's lids fluttered open, and her grandmother looked at her in terror, all Dinah could think was that if she had been here, she could have prevented this.

"It's me," Dinah said. "It's Dinah."

"Deborah?" said Dell.

Dell had gotten terrifically heavy. It took Dinah nearly half an hour to get her into the bathtub, and even then she had to drag her grandmother's feet along the floor. She peeled off her clothes, doing her best not to touch her at all, and then gave up and soaped her grandmother as best she could. She powdered her and put her in a clean nightgown in a clean bed, and it wasn't until she was nearly done that Dell recognized her, just for a moment.

"Dinah," she said, and then she shut her eyes.

That evening Dinah stayed beside her grandmother's bed, just watching her sleep, monitoring every breath. She had a calculus exam the next day. She had an English lit paper on Chaucer due, but she didn't care. She could have gone to sleep herself, but then what would she have done, how could she have lived the rest of her life, if for the one minute Dinah was sleeping, Dell stopped breathing? She pinched herself to stay awake, she sang songs and dreamed, and by morning she felt as if she were half hallucinating, but it didn't matter. She waited until Dell woke with a start, stretching, and then Dinah got up slowly. She stayed home with Dell that day and then the next. She would miss school all year if she had to. She would stay awake forever if her body wouldn't betray her.

She stayed out of school for nearly a week and a half, calling the grocer's for deliveries, watching her grandmother, sometimes so preoccupied that she forgot to eat. She looked in the mirror, and she looked like a stranger to herself.

"You'll be fine," Dinah pleaded, putting cold cloths on Dell's forehead, but Dell's fever raged so that Dinah finally called her doctor, and then, too, because there was no longer any reason not to, she reached for the phone. She'd have to try to find the one person who probably hated her more than she did herself—Lilly. She didn't know where Lilly was. She'd call her New York number, or maybe she'd call Lilly's mother, if she could remember where she lived. Was it Maine? Vermont? Shaking, she dialed New York information, and then she dialed Lilly's number, bracing herself against Lilly's voice.

"Hello?" Dinah said, and Lilly's machine clicked on.

"I'm not here right now," Lilly's voice said, and Dinah felt as if she had been punched in the heart. Lilly's voice rattled off two numbers where Lilly might be reached, both of them long distance. Dinah grabbed for a pen, scribbling the numbers on her hand. She hung up the phone, and then, heart racing within her, she picked up the phone again, and she dialed.

chapter 7

Lilly did just about everything she could not to go back to Pittsburgh, short of getting in her car and disappearing.

"You have to help me!" Dinah screamed on the phone, her voice crimped with fear. "My dad wouldn't let this happen!"

Lilly gripped the phone. She saw a flickering image. Matt at the lake, shoring back Dinah's wet hair with his two hands, kissing the top of her head like a benediction. "I love my girl," he had said. Then he had looked up at Lilly, laughing. "Both of them," he said.

"Dell's back in the hospital!" Dinah screamed. "She had a stroke! What if she dies! What should I do!"

"Can you call someone there?" Lilly asked.

"Letty," Dinah said. "She's Dell's friend."

"Stay there. Or have her stay with you. You don't want to be alone right now." Lilly tugged at the phone cord. "Listen, you're going to have to help me," she said. "Do you know where your grandmother keeps her important papers? I want you to look around, see if you can find her health insurance policy. And something—anything—with a lawyer's name. Dell's going to need someone to take care of her," Lilly said. "And you can't stay alone, either. If there's any money, we can take care of those things."

"Who are you hiring for me!" Dinah said. "I can take care of myself."

"Dinah, you don't want to do that," Lilly said.

"How do you know what I want?" Dinah said.

Lilly could hear her breathing on the phone, hard and tight and fast. "If Dell has a nurse, the place would be too small for you. You'd have to pay rent yourself. You'd have to take care of bills. If your father didn't leave you money, you'd have to get a job. You don't want to do that."

"My father left me money," Dinah said hotly. "Of course he left me money. He loved me. I've got a whole trust fund for college. I can use some of that money to live on."

"Well, you'd still need a lawyer to get it."

Dinah was silent for a minute. "I don't know where the papers are. Dell had a lawyer when she sold the store, but I don't know who it was."

"That's okay," Lilly said. "Give me the name and number of the store. The new owner'll know. And I'm going to try to find your mother. That's the best thing to do."

"My mother!" Dinah said, astounded. "What makes you think I want to stay with her?"

"There's no one else," Lilly said quietly. The lines between them hummed. "Please," Lilly said. "Look for the papers. And look for photos of your mother. Or any information where she might be. Letters. Documents. Anything."

"What makes you think she wants to be found?" Dinah said.

It doesn't matter what she wants, Lilly thought. Instead she sighed. She said, "Dinah, please. Look."

Dinah could find only Dell's health insurance, which, to Lilly's relief, would pay for a nurse for a few months—long enough, she hoped, until Dell's money could be freed up. Then she called Hank's and spoke to Bobby, who expressed his sympathy and gave her the name of the lawyer who had closed the deal. "Cora Janet," he said.

Cora Janet was sympathetic and helpful, and in the end, she told Lilly, she could certainly free money for any live-in care for Dell that was needed and probably some for a detective, but it might take time.

"How long?" said Lilly.

Cora sighed. "Well," she said, "things like these aren't considered life-and-death matters by the courts. There's paperwork and petitioning the court, and it's pretty slow. But I could probably get you something in six months."

"Six months!" Lilly said, shocked. "What about the money Matt left his daughter? It was a trust, for college."

"If it's set aside specifically for college, there might be a problem." Cora paused. "Her grandmother was the sole guardian?"

"I think so. The only other one left would be her mother, but she hasn't been in touch for years."

"Well, would you want to be appointed guardian?"

"No," Lilly said roughly. "I can't do that." She was silent for a moment. "What happens if no one can be found to take care of her?"

"Well," Cora said, "she'd be a ward of the state. Maybe she'd get into foster care, but to tell you the truth, she's probably too old."

A headache fisted along Lilly's brow.

"Look, we'll just have to find out who the trustee is and take it from there," Cora said. "Dinah's a minor, so the trustee makes the decision about the money, but you could always challenge that decision. Of course, that kind of thing usually takes even longer. You could be looking at two years."

"That can't be," said Lilly.

"Come in and talk to me," Cora said. "We'll see what we can do. Set things in motion."

Lilly hung up, stunned. Six months. Two years. Dell

would need care before that. Dinah would, too. And how was she going to pay the lawyer?

For the first time in a while, Lilly was thinking about Dinah again, and she was edgy with energy. Anger could do that, could galvanize you, pulling you away from that deep place where the pain would be so intolerable, you might want to die rather than face it. Anger could even make you feel that you were living.

That night Tess came home with a video, a ritual between the two of them. "Come on, we'll watch," she said. Tess fell asleep, but Lilly stayed up past four, watching an old horror movie about giant spiders running amok in suburbia. She watched all the credits, and then she curled on the sofa and dozed.

She dreamed Matt was alive and indifferent to her. "Call me," he said, scribbling numbers in the air that she couldn't quite make out.

"Wait!" she cried, but he disappeared, waving good-bye airily. She ran to find a phone booth. She dialed fifty different numbers and never once reached him, and when she woke up she was soaked with sweat, tangled in ropes of sheet. Her heart amplified in her chest. It wasn't possible. He was alive. It was a mistake. The hospital had whisked him away from her, and all she had to do was find him.

If she wept, she knew Tess would wake. She knew Tess would talk to her and hold her, but it wasn't enough. Tess wasn't the person she wanted comforting her.

Lilly got up and turned on the TV, keeping the sound off. An old black-and-white cowboy movie flickered. A lone woman in a prairie dress was standing stubbornly in front of her cabin, a musket braced against her bosom. It was snowing, and behind her, wolves howled. Lilly tugged some sheet around her shoulders and watched.

Dinah stayed at Letty's, and every day Letty called Lilly. "What's going on?" she demanded. They wouldn't let her even visit Dell in the hospital. Dinah was an extra expense she couldn't afford on her husband's pension.

"I can't do this anymore!" Letty screamed hoarsely into the phone. "I'm not so young anymore!"

"Okay, okay," Lilly said. "Look, I'm taking care of it. I spoke to a lawyer. I'm going to hire a detective to find her mother—"

"I don't care if you hire the man in the moon. She'll have to stay by herself, then."

"She can't do that," Lilly said. "She's fifteen—"

"When I was sixteen I was married!" Letty shouted.

Lilly shut her eyes. My beautiful baby, Matt used to call Dinah. "I'll take care of it," she said wearily.

Lilly sat by the kitchen phone, twisting the cord in her hand. She thought of her job at the college, of the way it made the hours dwindle. She thought about Tess and about how being far away made memory much less distant, much less real. She thought about how all she had to do was have a five-minute conversation with Dinah and for the rest of the day she'd be nervous. She'd shatter plates when she tried to set Tess's table. She'd spill her glass of wine.

She was still sitting at the kitchen table when Tess came in, flushed with the night, bright and happy. "I have to go to Pittsburgh," Lilly said. "Just until they find Maggy or some money."

Tess set down her sack of groceries. She rested one hand on Lilly's hair. "I know," she said.

Lilly called Robert and begged him to sublet her New York City apartment. "I'll get you double your rent," he promised.

She went to the library and got a Pittsburgh phone book and hired a home nurse, a woman named Grace Stimple, who said she could start in three days' time, the day after Lilly would arrive in Pittsburgh herself. She called a detective in Pittsburgh, haltingly explaining the situation and how little money she had right now, but that there would be money later. He sighed and finally said, "Well, come in and talk to me. We'll see what we can figure out."

And when Robert called, smug and pleased, presenting her with a rent figure three times what she paid, Lilly got a Pittsburgh newspaper and called realtors because Dell's house would be far too tiny for her and Dinah and Dell and a nurse. She and Dinah would have to share a place, and Grace would have to live with Dell.

Lilly called Dinah to tell her. "These things might take a while," she told Dinah. "But I'll come out there in the meantime. You'll be all right."

"I know that," said Dinah, but Lilly heard her relief.

It was spring when Lilly came back to Pittsburgh. Coming here seemed the most insane thing she had ever done. She wanted to run back into the car before it was too late, before she was seen. And then the front door opened, and there was Dinah, her eyes dark and wild, her skin so pale that it almost looked translucent, and for a minute, before she felt sorry for it, Lilly felt a familiar pulse of anger, like a small, certain heart beating within her.

When Lilly came up the walk, Dinah stepped back into the house. The living room was dusty and disordered. Laundry was piled on the furniture. Dirty plates and cups sat on ledges. Lilly looked at Dinah in alarm.

"I tried to clean up," Dinah said. She led Lilly slowly down the hall, to Dell's room in the back. "You go in first," Dinah said.

Dell was sitting up in bed, dressed in a faded flowery dress. Her hair was curled clumsily, tied back in a red bandanna that Lilly recognized as Dinah's.

"Who are you?" said Dell. "What do you want?"

"This is Lilly," Dinah said.

"Very pleased to know you," Dell said suspiciously.

Dinah turned slowly back toward the door. "We'll be right back," she promised.

She turned helplessly to Lilly and then led Lilly back into the living room. "She goes in and out," she said.

Lilly sat on the couch, pushing aside a pile of newspapers and towels. "Does Letty still come by?" she asked.

Dinah shook her head. "Not lately." She rubbed fiercely at her hair. It was badly cut, as if she herself had taken the scissors to it.

"You have a tan," Dinah said, her gaze hardening.

"Santa Fe's hot," Lilly said.

Dinah nodded. "I'm sorry you had to come here. I know you didn't want to." She burrowed her hands in her pockets. "I wouldn't have called you, but I had no one else."

"It's all right," Lilly said evenly.

"This detective, does he think he'll find my mother fast?" she said.

"I haven't seen him yet. But I think he will." Lilly looked from Dinah to the window and back again. "Did you find any photos of Maggy? Any old letters or anything?"

Dinah stood up. "Finding her will solve your problem, won't it?" she said.

"It'll solve things for you, too," Lilly said.

"I looked," Dinah said. "There was nothing." She left the room.

Dell's house was small and cramped. Lilly made a bed for herself on the couch, but day and night she prowled restlessly. She looked herself for the things she could take to the detective, photographs, clues, anything that might lead him to Dinah's mother.

"I looked there," Dinah said flatly when Lilly scraped open a nightstand drawer.

"I'll look again," Lilly said, ignoring her. She opened all the drawers in the tables scattered about the house. She took a flashlight and went into the basement and opened box after box of old clothes and table linens, of tarnished silverware and books without their jackets.

Lilly prowled for almost four days and was almost ready to give up. She was in the basement, by the washing machine, when she saw a small white box, wedged behind a pair of man's heavy hiking boots. She grabbed for the box, but inside was just old faded articles about shoes and business. Disappointed, she set it aside. She picked up the boots to get them out of the way, and she noticed a sudden flash of white inside. She dug her hand in and pulled out a small packet of photographs.

She sat on the chilly basement floor, the photos fanning in her fingers. Why would Dell put photos in a man's boot? There were only three of them, black and white, the surface lined with creases like roadways on a map. There was a young woman with long dark hair that she guessed must be Dell by the 1940s style of dress. There was Dell again, picked up in some man's arms. The man was looking down at Dell, and Dell's face was shining with love, and Lilly's yearning was so great and clumsy, she quickly flipped to another photo. It was another pretty young woman with dark hair, but this one wasn't Dell. The hair was very short. She was wearing a halter top and short denim cutoffs. Lilly turned the picture over. "Maggy," it said. She tried to see the face, to imagine what this woman might look like now, but instead what she saw was Matt with the Maggy in the photo. Don't, she told herself. She picked up the photo and pocketed it.

She bounded up the basement steps, hot and dusty. Dinah was in the kitchen, swirling her spoon through a bowl of gluey oatmeal. She gave Lilly a fish stare.

"I found a photo," Lilly said. Dinah stopped moving her spoon.

Lilly fingered the photos. "I've got errands today. I'll try not to be late."

Dinah shrugged. She pushed her bowl of cereal away from her.

Lilly hated to leave Dinah with Dell, but Grace wouldn't be arriving until that evening, and she had to see the lawyer and start the paperwork. She had to keep her appointment with the detective. She had to transfer her savings into a local bank. And she had to see the places the realtor had set up for her. She scribbled out her appointments on a sheet of paper. She tucked it into her pocket, and five seconds after that, even though she had just written it down, she couldn't remember the detective's address. She dug the paper out again, smoothing the creases, reading her list. Pittsburgh, she thought wearily. I'm in Pittsburgh.

Needing a detective made her uneasy. She used to be the one who could place people in time, who could know where and how someone moved through space. She had found missing children living in abandoned cars and runaway husbands on vacation in Spain with their receptionists. Once she had even located a pet turtle that had burrowed deep into a winter boot in a closet, and now she felt so distraught, it was all she could do to find her house keys.

"Are you sure you don't want to come?" she said to Dinah.

Dinah shook her head. "There's nothing I could say about my mother," she said.

Neal Rodman had been a private detective for nearly twenty years. He kept a small office in Shadyside, close enough to home so he could walk to work every day.

He was his own boss. He could make his own hours, take what cases he liked. At first he had loved his job. He liked being given a mystery and then solving it, finding the facts and piecing them together in as orderly a fashion as he lined up his shirts in his closet.

He handled mostly domestic cases. He looked for runaway kids, though he seldom found them. He tracked errant husbands and wives, and sometimes he found out who was cheating whom in businesses, and if it wasn't as easy to dismiss one case and move on to the next, well, that was just because the cases built up—like floor wax—and all he needed was a vacation to refresh himself, to scratch back down to the surface where everything shone.

He thought he could do anything, that the whole trick was simply figuring people out, but after a while his optimism eroded. He didn't see the good things he could do anymore, the happiness when he found a lost child for a parent, the satisfaction when he helped someone uncover someone who was cheating them. Instead he began to notice all the things that could go wrong, all the unhappiness his work generated rather than cured. Oh, he could find people, but was it worth it, did it make things better? He began to notice that people were always squandering their happiness, choosing the thing that might make them the most unhappy, only because they were too frightened or angry or sad to see any alternative. And people were seldom grateful. He spent two months trailing the husband of a woman who insisted she wanted proof of his affairs. But when he finally provided photos of her husband and a blonde coming out of a hotel, her husband and a redhead dining by candlelight, her husband with a host of other lively companions, she looked at Neal, her mouth wobbling. "My," she said. She picked up the top photo, her husband on a beach, nuzzling a tiny redhead, and then she looked at Neal and slapped him so hard across his face, he felt dazed.

It didn't stop there. He found a man's son, but he found him making porno movies and not wanting to stop, and now when they met, the man crossed the street, pretending he didn't know Neal, pretending Neal didn't know him. No one ever seemed much happier for his work, and worse, it didn't seem as though he were creating any sort of order. It didn't feel that he had necessarily made one thing any better by his work. In fact, it all seemed as if he were eavesdropping on other people's lives, and it all made him more and more uncomfortable.

He was so tired of telling ugly truths, so angry with facts, that sometimes he began to lie a little, making sure to look people in the eyes, to keep his mouth steady, to seem sincere. He'd tell a mother that her daughter was living in a hotel

rather than shacking up with a junkie in a tenement apartment. He began deliberately to forget film for his camera or
shoot in the wrong light, because suddenly it seemed more
important that people had illusions. What was so healthy
about knowing all the answers, anyway? Wasn't a little mystery part of life?

The trick was not to want too much. That's where people got in trouble, thinking that wanting their spouses to love
them again might work as simply and cleanly as a chemical
reaction. Everyone was always disappointed, wounded by all
that unrequited wanting, badly enough to scar.

He was going to give it up. He had worked for twenty
years. He could retire and do something else if he wanted. He
thought that what he wanted to do was teach. Law enforce-
ment. Or even something completely different, like English as
a second language. Something people really wanted to learn,
something they'd be grateful for. And he wanted to do car-
pentry. Lately he had been building things for clients. Tables.
Chairs.

He liked being alone in his basement, building things
that might last. He had always been too busy, too self-con-
tained, to sustain his relationships for very long or to think
about a family, but now, all of a sudden, now that he was
thinking of retiring, he was noticing couples. He was noticing
kids with a kind of surprised yearning. When he went to dinner with friends, he held their babies close to his chest. He
played with their puppyish toddlers. And he began to look at
women with a fresh interest.

Every time he was just about to quit, though, another
case would come up, and he'd tell himself, Just this one, and
then Lilly had called, and he had decided impulsively to see
her only because she sounded as if she had been crying. This
is it, he told himself, the last case, his swan song.

Lilly came to his office wearing a short white dress and
sunglasses, her black hair in a braided spine down her back,

and as soon as she took off her sunglasses, he saw how red her eyes were, how tired she looked. She sat opposite him, her hands balled in her lap, hesitating as she told him the situation. "I hope you can help us," she said. "She can't stay alone."

Neal was silent for a minute.

"My—my fiancé really loved her," Lilly said.

"I'll find her mother," he said.

"Good," she said. "That's good. As soon as possible."

Lilly was so pale, he swore he could almost see the light through her, so beautiful, he felt himself suddenly wanting things he hadn't wanted in a very long while. You're tired, he told himself. She's a client, and this is ridiculous.

He took out his notebook. "Well, now," he said. "What can you tell me?"

Lilly bit her bottom lip. "I have a photo," she said suddenly. She undid the click lock on her purse and pulled it out. She handed it to Neal. "Is it okay?" she said anxiously. "It was all I could find."

The print was blurry, overexposed, with a pretty, dark-haired woman who could have been anyone, laughing, her hair thrown back.

"Well, it's just fine," he said doubtfully. "There's no reason for her to have changed her Social Security number. From what you told me, she doesn't seem to have covered her tracks." He shut the notebook. "Piece of cake," he said. "I'll start making calls today."

He stood up.

"Do you think it's going to take very long?" Lilly said.

"Well, you never know about time," he said.

He almost had the door open for her when he stopped. He didn't know why, but he felt he just had to speak to her again.

"So what do you do?" he said politely.

She blushed. "I'm going to start looking for work."

"What did you do?" he said.

She flopped her braid in front of her shoulder. "I was a clairvoyant," she said almost defiantly.

"A clairvoyant?" he said, surprised. He felt a pang of disappointment. He thought of musty Gypsy storefronts, of women wearing dirty pastel turbans, tucking dollar bills into their bodices.

"Well, I was," Lilly said quickly. "I'm not anymore."

He nodded, feeling himself foolishly brighten. "Maybe you should do my job," he joked, but Lilly flinched, and instantly he was sorry.

"You'll be in touch?" Lilly said finally.

"Every two weeks," he said. "Don't look so worried."

Neal looked at his caseload. Three suspected infidelities. A couple of runaways. He had to find a man who had been passing bad checks. Another woman wanted a potential boyfriend tailed. He thought of Lilly, her black hair, her eyes as deep as rivers. What the hell.

He kept Maggy's photo on his desk and tried to make up a list of places to call. He turned on his computer and stared at the screen. He had been trained. He believed in facts and details, in one tangible thing leading to another. He had never once in his life believed in clairvoyance or spirits, and he didn't believe in them now. He didn't believe in fate or chance or even a thing as simple and impossible as love at first sight.

The mortgage rates were down, and although the Pittsburgh realtor insisted she could have bought a place for what the rent was going to run her, Lilly just shook her head. "It's not going to be for that long," she said.

"Oh, that's what everybody thinks," the realtor said.

"Well, everybody's wrong," Lilly said.

The house was six blocks from Dell, a tiny two-bedroom furnished ranch that had been advertised as a "handyman special." The floors were chipped, but they were still wood. The ceilings and walls showed some water damage, but the house did have a broad, sunny porch. The furniture was hopeless. Colonial-style wood veneers. A heavy plaid couch.

"It'll be fine for a while," Lilly said.

"First month, last month, and you can move in immediately," the realtor said, giving up.

Lilly was back at Dell's by evening, before Grace arrived. "Well, we've got a place," she told Dinah.

"I don't want to move," Dinah said.

"It's only temporary. Just until we locate your mother."

Dinah nodded. "Is Dell going to die?" she asked abruptly.

"Die? Who told you that?" Lilly said. "Dell had a stroke, that's all."

"So she'll be okay," Dinah said.

"Of course she will," Lilly said.

Grace, the nurse Lilly had hired, showed up at eight o'clock that evening. She was small and lean and in her mid-fifties. She had been married once, running off to elope when she was just eighteen, and when she had found her young husband in bed with her best friend, she had packed her bags and never looked back. "I'm married to my work," she said. "I love nursing." She had references from women who considered her family, from men who had proposed to her even as she tended their sickbeds; but she always held something back. She always moved on as soon as they were healthy.

Although she was beautiful, the first thing Lilly thought when she saw her was the word *whitewash*. Grace was done in tones of white. She had blunt-cut cloudy hair and pale slate eyes, and she wore a nurse's uniform so stark that it was almost blinding.

"You don't have to wear a uniform," Lilly told her, taking her hand, which was large and warm.

"I want to," Grace said. "Sometimes people like to see the white. It's reassuring. And it's professional."

She surveyed the house and Dinah and then went to talk to Dell. She was gone only a few minutes, and when she came down, she was smiling. "Easy as pie," she said. "Now, where's the kitchen? I want to make Dell something to eat."

The house Lilly rented was not really big enough for the two of them. She couldn't bear it sometimes, rounding a corner and finding Dinah, as sudden and shocking as a dive into icy water.

Almost immediately Dinah began fussing with her room. "Can I have money to buy paint?" she said. "It's disgusting in here. The walls are all chipping." Lilly gave her money, and that evening, the house smelled of the yellow paint Dinah was using.

Lilly threw open all the windows, and in her room she set out her suitcases, their tops open like mouths. She took her clothes from it as she needed it, and if she had to launder anything, she'd put it back in the suitcase as soon as it was clean.

Dinah looked in at Lilly, her jeans spattered with paint. "I have paint left over," Dinah said. "Do you want it?"

Lilly shook her head.

"You don't?"

Lilly opened her window wider. "Nope," she said.

"But your room is as disgusting as mine was."

"It's just a room," Lilly said. "And it's fine."

Dinah hesitated.

"Leave the windows open," was all Lilly said.

Lilly woke at six, hearing Dinah's radio blaring in the kitchen. She got up and stumbled into the kitchen. Lilly blinked at Dinah, who was in a mask of makeup and the same dirty white beaded sweater, with her hair spiked with grease and her jeans torn carefully at the knees.

"I might not be home when you get home," Lilly called to her. "I have lots of errands again today."

Dinah stopped at the door. She looked at Lilly as if Lilly

were crazy. "I have a key," she said. "I don't need you to let me in."

"Fine," Lilly said shortly. She turned away from Dinah, away from the sharp closing slap of the door. And as soon as the house was empty and quiet, she felt relieved.

Lilly really didn't have any errands, but she was determined to keep busy, to not think. She walked from Shadyside to Squirrel Hill and back, stopping at the Bijoux for a double feature. She didn't care what the movie was.

The theater was barely full. Older women who couldn't quite hear rustled and talked through the films. Kids skipping school smuggled in pizzas, perfuming the theater with garlic and burned cheese. Lilly sat alone. The movie was called *Dogs,* and she had never heard of it, but it didn't matter. The dark felt companionable. She put her feet up and watched the film. She couldn't concentrate well enough to follow the story, but it didn't matter. The only time she was ever disappointed was when the film was over and the lights flashed on. She blinked at the sudden brightness. She wanted to call back the people who were slouching back into their coats, to tell them not to leave so fast. She glanced at her watch. Two hours gone.

She bought groceries, walking up and down the supermarket aisles, taking her time. In the checkout line she stood behind a woman who was unpacking a steak, a bottle of wine, greens, and two candles. She felt Lilly watching her and blushed.

"Big night," she said, and Lilly turned away. She grabbed for a tabloid and pretended to read, pretended she didn't see the small tin of caviar, the perfumed body lotion. BIGFOOT WAS MY HUSBAND! said the headline.

Lilly came home and tried to cook something for herself and Dinah—baked ziti, simple and filling. Dinah stormed in the house. "Not hungry!" she called from her room.

Lilly put a film of Saran Wrap over Dinah's portion of baked ziti and put it in the refrigerator. She ate by herself on the porch, staring out at the night. In the morning, when she opened the refrigerator, Dinah's portion was gone. The plate was washed and put away.

At night Lilly could hear Dinah moving around. She could hear Dinah opening and closing her bedroom door.

"You okay?" Lilly called, and the house was silent. Lilly got up and pulled on jeans and a sweater and stepped out onto the porch, peering into the street. Suddenly it seemed as though the simplest things were beyond her, and there she was, a onetime city girl who used to not be afraid of anything, now standing in the night, in a dark suburb, flinching at the moths whispering around the light by the screen.

Lilly did the laundry and folded it back in her suitcase, and then she went into the living room to watch whatever movies were on TV. Dinah was in her room, the door shut.

Lilly was watching Bette Davis, who was railing about the dump of a town she was stuck in. I know how you feel, Bette, Lilly thought. She settled a pillow against her belly. She sighed in the night, then suddenly felt someone behind her. "Dinah?" she said, but when she turned around, the room was empty.

When the movie was over, she was exhausted. She clicked off the set and went to bed, but that night she woke in the middle of a deep sleep, and as she blinked awake, she was certain she heard breathing. She got up and flicked on the switch. Her bureau was in disarray. A dollar was missing.

The next morning she approached Dinah. Dinah was grabbing for her schoolbooks, racing her fingers through her hair.

"Listen, do you need some money?" Lilly said.

"No," Dinah said. She bent to tie one of her high-top sneakers.

"Because if you did, you can ask me for it," Lilly said. "We can work out some sort of an allowance."

Dinah looked up at Lilly, her face clear and unreadable. "I don't need to ask you for anything," she said. She grabbed her purse from the chair and left, slapping the door behind her so it echoed in the house.

chapter 8

Dinah spent half her time worrying Lilly would leave and half her time willing her away. She hated the house and took her time coming home from school, but even as she was ignoring the bus and walking, she had a fleeting picture of Lilly taking her already packed suitcase and getting into her car and not looking back. Dinah hated herself for the curl of fear that buckled up inside her spine, for the way she speeded up her walk home.

As soon as she got into the house, she made noise.

She banged her books on the table. She slammed doors and coughed.

"Dinah?" Lilly called, and Dinah flooded with relief.

She followed the sound to the kitchen, where Lilly was reading. Casually, Dinah went to get a glass of water from the sink. The sink was filled with dirty dishes. The floor had crumbs all over it. Disgusted, Dinah turned on the hot water and started washing the dishes.

"School okay?" Lilly said, not even looking up from her book. "You're late, aren't you?"

"I have homework to do," Dinah said. "I have a test. Why do I have to do these dishes? Couldn't you have done them?" She turned to look at Lilly, lifting soap-foamy hands. Lilly gave a wry smile. "So don't do them," she said. She looked back at her book. "Things will get done or they won't get done."

Dinah continued washing the dishes angrily, making as much noise as possible, hoping to shame Lilly. Adults had always told Dinah she was a slob, but Lilly took the cake, Lilly was the biggest pig she had ever met. Except for her room, Dinah didn't consider this house her home, either, but that didn't mean she wanted to live with dirt.

"Oh, for heaven's sake," Lilly said, and got up and took the sponge. "I'll do them," she said. "Do your homework."

Dinah went upstairs to her room. She wondered if Lilly would do the dishes clean, but she didn't say anything. She stayed in her room with the door barricaded, staring at the newly painted walls, at the chipped wood floor. She fussed over it, because really it was the one thing that belonged to her now, even if it was only for a little while.

She got up and put on her radio, but she didn't use head-phones, because then she couldn't hear the swift sound of a door opening, the muffled roar of a car leaving her behind. She spread open her books, her notebooks, but she doodled with her pen in the margins, she ignored her homework.

At midnight, when she heard the lights clicking off, the water in the bathroom rushing on and off, all the sounds that meant Lilly was finally in for the night, Dinah did her home-work in a panic. She was exhausted.

She finished as quickly as she could, but even after she turned out her own lights, she couldn't sleep.

She tossed and tangled up the sheets. The house was too quiet. Anything could have happened. Finally she got up. She walked past Lilly's room. Lilly's door was open, and Dinah peered in, waiting for her eyes to get used to the darkness, searching until she saw Lilly's sheet rising and falling with her breath. She's alive, Dinah thought, and went back to bed.

Every few days, whenever she could, Dinah went to visit Dell after school. She didn't want to go with Lilly, who only dropped by occasionally. And she didn't want to schedule a visit, where Grace might have time to arrange things so it looked as if Dell were all right. Grace was always kind and friendly to her. She sometimes made Dinah tea and told her stories about growing up, but no matter how kind Grace was to her, how she smiled and fussed, she didn't trust Grace to tell her the truth.

When Grace started to follow her toward Dell's room, Dinah stopped. Grace hesitated and then suddenly nodded her head. "It's your visit," she said. "I'll be in the kitchen if you need me."

Dinah went to Dell's room. The room was barely lit and freshly clean, and for a moment it felt like an affront to Dinah. Dell was wearing a fluffy yellow robe, watching TV, and she frowned when she saw Dinah.

"It's Dinah," Dinah said. She sat on the edge of her grandmother's bed, taking her hand, feeling Dell's pulse beating. She fluffed Dell's pillow and brought her an extra blanket, putting it at the foot of her bed. "In case your feet get cold," she said.

She stayed over an hour, watching a game show on the television with her grandmother, holding her hand, and the whole time Dell didn't say one word to her. Not until Dinah finally got up to leave, when she snapped off the lights and was right at the threshold of the room. Then Dell looked at her.

"Dinah," she said clearly.

Dinah stopped. Dell patted the bed next to her. "Come here," she whispered. "Don't be afraid of the dark."

Dinah lay down gingerly beside her grandmother. The sheets were smooth and warm. "Aren't you ever afraid?" she said.

"There's nothing in the dark that isn't there in the light," Dell said emphatically.

"You believe that?"

"Sometimes," Dell said.

"You're never afraid?" Dinah asked Dell.

"Of what?"

"Dying," Dinah said.

Dell laughed. "Think about the pleasant things. Going to the beach. Having a picnic. Seeing people you love." She burrowed down into the bed. "I see you, it makes me feel better. I see Matt, it makes my day."

Dinah slipped from Dell's grasp and sat up, shocked. "Who do you see?"

Dell's eyes were suddenly roaming the room. "Matt. My Matty," she said. "He talks to me all day sometimes."

Dinah stood up awkwardly. "My father?"

Dell's eyes drifted shut. They rolled in dreams, and she sighed and turned away from Dinah. "Dell?" Dinah said.

The house was dark. Grace must be asleep, Dinah thought. She raced down the stairs. She opened the door carefully, and then, turning, she suddenly saw Grace, sipping tea in the kitchen, calmly watching her leave.

Dinah sat out on the front porch, curled against the banister, gripping it for support. Her grandmother was certain she saw Matt. Lilly, too, woke up some nights, tangled in a nightmare, calling Matt's name so loudly, Dinah would bolt from her bed. But Dinah herself never even dreamed about him, or sensed him, or felt any of the things people said sometimes happened when someone died, and the only reason she could think of for it was that she didn't deserve to. Dinah buried her head in her hands.

"Hey."

Dinah fanned her fingers open and looked up. Lilly was standing in the doorway.

"It's pretty late," she said. "Don't you want to go to sleep?"

"Dell talks to my father," Dinah said. Lilly flinched, drawing her sweater closer about her. "She says he's there."

"She's had a stroke," Lilly said finally. "She's been sick."

"You didn't call it sick when you did it," Dinah said.

"You didn't think it was impossible." She craned her neck around to look at Lilly. "I know you believe it," Dinah said. "You told me you did."

"Well," Lilly said, "I don't believe it now."

"Do you see him?" Dinah said. She stood up, moving closer to Lilly. "Would you tell me if you did?"

Lilly stepped back, pained. "Go to sleep," she said. "It's very late."

"You don't see him," Dinah said, "do you?" She moved around Lilly and went back into the house, letting the rusted screen door slap shut, leaving Lilly standing out in the night, rubbing warmth into her arms.

Lilly told herself she was being crazy, she told herself it was simply that she missed Matt so much, that that was the reason she began going to visit his mother every day, sometimes at lunch, sometimes right before dinner. Grace got to know that Lilly liked extra sugar in her tea, an extra cookie on her plate, and the rocking chair on the porch. Dell began looking forward to Lilly's visits. Some days Dell knew her, some days she didn't, but she always liked the company—no matter whose it was.

One Friday she came over and Grace, her hair in stiff pink plastic rollers, kneading bread dough over the kitchen table, waved Lilly upstairs. "Dell's upstairs!"

It was hotter as she climbed the stairs. She could hear the drone of the television in Dell's room.

Lilly paused at the top of the stairs. There was a clip of silence, and then Dell laughed. "Matty!" she said.

Lilly felt a line of ice forming on her spine. She wouldn't have been able to move if Dell hadn't turned toward her. She followed Dell's gaze as it flickered to the corner by the window, where a patch of light was dappled over the polished floor.

"Is someone there?" Lilly whispered.

Dell snapped up. "Who are you?" she said.

Lilly strained to see something through the light, squinting so hard that her eyes narrowed to slits. She could close her eyes and swear she smelled the lime-scented after-shave Matt loved, she swore she smelled the back of his neck, the clean gloss of his hair, but she knew as well as anybody that imagination didn't nourish the way flesh and blood and bone would. It wasn't the same, and all she had to do was open her eyes and she'd know it.

Lilly felt nauseated with confusion. She felt a hand on her back, and she whipped around, but it was only Grace.

"Lilly," Grace said, "come have tea."

Grace led Lilly downstairs and into the living room. "Sit," she commanded. Lilly sank onto one of the cushions.

"You all right?" Grace said.

"I got a little dizzy," Lilly said. "It's hot up there."

Grace studied her. She sighed. "You heard her talking to her son, didn't you? I know, it must be upsetting for you." She fluffed a cushion and held it, like a child, against her. "Dell thinks I don't know she talks to him," she said finally. "She doesn't mention it, and neither do I. It's her business, but of course I know. She's talking away, just as loudly as she does to me. I thought something was wrong, so I went upstairs, and there she was, carrying on her end of a conversation. She didn't even see me come into the room."

She sat up straighter. "Look, it makes her happy," she said. "Who am I to question a thing as pure and simple as happiness?"

"She's lucky," Lilly said.

"You call being sick lucky?" Grace said mildly.

"I used to talk to the dead," Lilly said abruptly. "I didn't even have to try. They just came to me."

"Did you?" said Grace. Unsurprised, she rubbed at her calves. "Did you want to?"

"I don't think it works like that," Lilly said.

"Really?" Grace said. "How does it work?"

Lilly shook her head. She leaned back, sinking against the cushions. "I don't know anymore," she said.

Lilly kept visiting Dell. She saw all the amber bottles of medicine lined up on Dell's bureau, she knew from Grace if Dell had had another sleepless night or another night so drugged with sleep that it had taken Grace half an hour just to rouse her. It didn't matter, though. Lilly couldn't stay rational. Every time Dell so much as smiled in the distance, Lilly started. She listened so hard, the silence was thunderous. She prickled from the weight of the air about her. She heard the fabric of her shirt when she moved. But I never hear you, she thought.

Lilly began to go back to bed after Dinah left for school. She tried to move stubbornly back into the oblivious dreamless sleeps she had been having, and every time her eyes flickered open she felt a disappointment so profound that she could have cried. She stayed in bed through the afternoon, through the occasional surprising ring of the phone. She was drowning in sleep, groggy and half dreaming. I have to stop this, she told herself in disgust, but she couldn't manage much.

She began spending whole long blocks of time on the phone again, talking and crying to Tess, who listened sympathetically, or to Nora, who was impatient.

"Lilly, come here," Nora said. "Why can't that woman who's taking care of Dell take care of Dinah?"

"She's got her hands full," Lilly said.

Nora sighed. "Things will be better," she said.

As soon as Lilly hung up from Nora, she instantly had to call someone else. She couldn't seem to get off the phone, to break the connection and be thrust back into her own life, so she dialed. She called people she hadn't thought of in years. An old college roommate took ten minutes to figure out who

Lilly was, but then ended up listening so sympathetically, Lilly called her the next day, too.

She stopped her phoning as soon as she heard Dinah coming in. She dragged herself up from bed. She tried to be busy. She never cared about cleaning the house or fixing it up, but now she needed projects, things with a beginning and a middle and a clear finish. She rearranged the kitchen cabinets. She dusted the shelves. Lilly thought that she herself should be the one to have a caretaker and not the house. Lilly would love it if someone would take charge of her for a while, would tell her when to get up and when to sleep, when and what to eat, anything that might help her get through it.

Dinah seemed to her to be getting wilder and wilder. She seemed angry all the time. She sometimes came home smelling of alcohol. "What do you think you're doing?" Lilly asked her.

"What's it to you?" Dinah said.

"What it is to me is that I'm responsible for you," Lilly said.

"A job you truly love," Dinah said.

"You're grounded," Lilly said, and when Dinah laughed, she grew so angry that it was all she could do not to take the three steps to Dinah and strike her. "You hate me? Fine. But you just remember that you asked me to help you."

"So what," said Dinah, but Lilly saw how suddenly small and unsure Dinah looked, how quiet she became. Lilly couldn't help feeling a flush of relief. I have her, Lilly thought.

Lilly had to do something more than cleaning to fill the spaces in her life, to keep busy until Dinah's mother could be found. She had to get a job, but she was qualified for almost nothing. There were no listings for psychics in the newspapers, for clairvoyants, and even if there were, that no longer seemed to include her. She couldn't very well hang out a shingle, because within the first two clients people would know she couldn't see beyond the next day, let alone into the future, she couldn't reach her own dead, let alone theirs.

She looked through the want ads every morning. She didn't have credentials to do very much, and the places she called—sales jobs, editorial, writing—were politely dismissive. She remembered Nora having to go door to door with Avon products, and she felt heavy with despair.

She needed the money. Maybe mindless work was the best thing for her now anyway. Mindless and as exhausting as possible. She walked through Squirrel Hill. She walked into dress shops, thinking maybe she could sell clothing, but the saleswomen were girls, not much older than Dinah and so well-dressed that Lilly felt ill at ease. They gave her glassy, contemptuous stares. She tried bookstores and restaurants. "We're not hiring," people told her.

In the end she finally wandered into the You Send Me card store in Shadyside, to buy a card for Nora. She was prowling listlessly through the cards when she overheard a woman's voice. "Well, the salary's a little low," the voice said.

Lilly edged around the corner. A woman was shaking a man's hand. The man wore jeans and a black vest, and his hair was long and shaggy. "I can't do much better," the man said.

Lilly waited until the woman had left and then impulsively approached the man. Up close he didn't look much older than Lilly. He lifted his brows at her. "Are you hiring?" she said.

He laughed and held out his hand to her. "Carl Johanson," he said. "And yes, we are, but it's just a clerk job, and the pay is embarrassing."

"I don't care," Lilly said. She felt suddenly new and buoyant with hope. "Anything is fine."

"You work the cash register. Dust the shelves. You sure that'll suit you?" He smiled apologetically.

"I need the job," Lilly said. "And it's perfect."

* * *

Having a job was wonderful because it forced Lilly to wake up mornings, to get beyond the numbing, eerie shock that there she was in her life and Matt was gone. It forced her to feel something as simple as the shower water on her body, to think about what she wore, how she brushed her hair, and best of all, it forced her to think of something, anything, other than herself.

She could wear jeans to work. The shop was almost always busy, and she found she liked the crowds of people. Carl taught her the register in less than an hour. He showed her where the charge slips were for really big purchases and how to work the phones, and every time he showed her something new, he apologized. "I just wish it were more interesting work for you," he said. "I can't see how you can be so cheerful about dusting out a display window."

"Trust me, it's wonderful," Lilly said.

The store was all wood and adobe tile and a few plants, too. Carl had an office in the back where he met with the card salesmen or the young artists who came in with ideas for lines. There was only one other person who worked in the store, a young silent man named George who sat at the register at the back and treated everybody with amused disdain.

Lilly was happy enough. She ran next door to the bank for change twice a day. She arranged the shelves and worked the register and fumbled with wrapping the few gifts the store stocked.

"Take a lunch hour," Carl encouraged her.

But Lilly didn't want to leave the shop. She liked the bustle of people, the rise and fall of conversations, as easy as breathing. And she was afraid as soon as she stepped outside, she'd remember who she was and what had happened to her. Instead she wandered around the shop. She told herself she was familiarizing herself with the stock, but actually, as she dusted and prowled, she was listening in on people's conversations, figuring out their lives just by the cards they chose. A new baby card in the wistful hands of a middle-aged woman

Chicago Public Library
West Belmont
6/18/2011   1:06:07 PM
-Patron Receipt-

ITEMS BORROWED:

1:
Title: Living other lives /
Item #: R0101140985
Due Date: 7/9/2011

2:
Title: Coming back to me /
Item #: R0174116696
Due Date: 7/9/2011

3:
Title: Winter garden /
Item #: R0423109348
Due Date: 6/18/2011

4:
Title: Winter garden /
Item #: R0423109348
Due Date: 7/9/2011

5:
Title: Winter garden /
Item #: R0423109348
Due Date: 6/18/2011

-Please retain for your records-

JSTHOMPS

with no wedding band. A Happy Divorce card held by a man with a sloppy grin. Lives going on, played out right before her, all commemorated with a card.

Lilly's neighborhood was filled with young families, giddy young working women sharing their own little rented house, and a few singles, and she began to recognize the same faces. Across the street was a woman with short red hair almost always kept in curlers. Down the block was a couple that almost never let go of each other's hands. She sometimes saw the young girls bopping by the bus stop, whispering when a handsome man walked by. Sometimes someone nodded hello at her, and although Lilly always smiled and tried to look inviting enough to talk to, no one ever stopped to speak, no one ever slowed down.

One day, though, Lilly was walking home from work when the red-haired woman ran out of her house and called to her. Lilly stopped, waiting.

"Kay Kendinsky," the woman said to Lilly. She pointed to her house. "My husband, Billy, and I live right there."

Lilly nodded. It was the first time she had seen Kay without her curlers, and Kay kept fussing her fingers through her hair, picking up the ends.

"Lilly," Lilly said.

Kay nodded. "I know who you are," she said. She shifted weight. She gave an awkward, loopy smile. "So," she said. "You give readings, I hear."

Lilly felt a cramp moving in her leg. "No, I don't," she said.

"Really?" Kay looked surprised. "Your daughter told me you did. She said you were one hundred percent accurate."

My daughter, Lilly thought. "Kids," she said, making Kay grin. "What imaginations."

She didn't talk to Kay for much longer after that. "I'll call you," Kay promised. "Billy and I should have you over for dinner." But she left without taking Lilly's number, and Lilly walked slowly into the house.

Dinah was in the living room, ironing a skirt, when Lilly walked in.

"Please don't tell people I'm clairvoyant," Lilly told Dinah. "It's not true anymore."

"I had to tell them something. They asked."

"Tell them I clerk in a card store," Lilly said.

"You don't want me to tell them that. God. A clerk."

"Why not," Lilly said. "It's the truth. They can walk in there and see for themselves." Lilly wrapped her hair around her hand, braiding it, getting it out of her way. "And anyway, I like being a clerk these days."

Dinah didn't know why she'd told Kay that Lilly was clairvoyant, and she didn't know why, even a few days after Lilly talked to her about it, she told a group of girls at school the same thing. She thought it was a thing so shocking and interesting that it would make people want to know her, but they'd want to know her because of Lilly, they'd be so intrigued that they might forget to ask one personal question of Dinah altogether. She didn't want them asking about her father, asking about who Lilly really was to her—and why.

She had gone and blabbed about Lilly in homeroom to a group of girls who were avidly playing with a Ouija board, ignoring her as they manipulated the finger piece so it would spell out the names of the boys they liked. Dinah told them that at night Lilly murmured things, spells most likely, and that she had potions and candles going half the time.

"Cool," said Denise Summers, who had just that week demanded that everybody call her Dinga.

"So does she have incubuses?" asked Leslie Farrah, applying red lipstick.

Dinah didn't want to admit she didn't know what incubuses were, so she gave Leslie a bored look. "Of course she does," she said, and Leslie hooted.

It wasn't until sixth period English that Dinah had a chance to look up incubus in the dictionary. A spirit that has sex with you, that drank the lifeblood from you. She felt ill and stupid. Every time she'd see Dinga or Leslie they'd be thinking that incubuses came to her house, and it would completely be her fault because she was the one who had told them.

What had she started? She couldn't take it back, she couldn't admit that she hadn't known what the word meant. There must be something terribly wrong with her, something that made her lie and want to steal and destroy.

That night she couldn't look at Lilly. She did all the dishes without asking. She swept the whole downstairs and folded all the laundry, and then she waited until Lilly was hunched over a novel at the kitchen table, and then she crept quietly out of the house, racing the few blocks to visit her grandmother.

Dell was sleeping, her chest rising and falling with breath, the TV still on. Dinah clicked it off, and Dell stirred, turning on her side. Dinah stood there for a few minutes, just watching. You're all right, then, she thought, and she placed her hands on her grandmother's shoulders, just for a moment.

"Hello?" Dell said. "Grace?"

"It's Dinah," Dinah said.

Dell's face cleared. "Well, now," she said. She didn't really say anything else to Dinah that whole time. She could have said "The man in the moon" over and over, and it wouldn't have mattered, because it was the quiet way Dell focused on her that Dinah needed and, more than that, the easy way she forgot every syllable Dinah revealed to her.

She stayed only until Dell fell asleep. She went down the stairs as quietly as she could, and when she got to the bottom she heard something stir.

"Walk home safely," Grace called out. "Keep by the streetlights."

That night Dinah was almost to her street when she heard a sudden low buzzing. A snap and spark of electricity.

Shivering, she stopped and turned abruptly, holding her breath, and there, whizzing past her, was a boy on a black motorcycle, his head thrown back, his hair nearly as long as hers. Dinah was stunned. She didn't need to get close to see how handsome he was. He reared up the motorcycle, like a cowboy on a horse, and then pivoted and took off.

The next day in school, the boy she'd seen on the motorcycle walked directly past Dinah into a classroom. He was wearing a black leather jacket so soft that it draped, black boots, and a black T-shirt, and as soon as Dinah saw him, she felt herself coming undone.

By third period she had woven all the gossip she had heard about him into a profile she could keep telling herself. His name was Mickey Riley, and he was seventeen and a senior. He had just moved from New York City to Highland Park. He lived in a small suburban house with his mother, and he knew everything there was to know about motorcycles. His mother was a waitress and, everybody said, a whore, too. She wore sheer leopard-print blouses and skirts so short and tight, she had to mince her steps when she walked, and it was rumored that Mickey practically lived alone.

The very first week of school Mickey had six girls in love with him, all of whom wrote his initials deep into the tops of their desks and sometimes in their own flesh, and an entourage of guys who already began to walk like him, and after school they all piled over to his house. Every one had a different story about Mickey. Tommy Sorta said that Mickey called his mother Annette and his father, who had remarried and lived in Connecticut, nothing at all. He said that Annette hadn't shown up at all, or even called, and that they had all sent out for pizza and beer at ten at night, and the only reason he hadn't stayed past midnight was that his own father would have skinned him alive.

While everyone wished secretly that they didn't have parents hanging around, the kids who frequented Mickey's were also a little shocked. Mickey's mother's bed had a fake leopard spread. You could eat whatever you wanted, and you could drink as much of the wine in the fridge as you wanted. Kids said she didn't care what went on in the house during the day, as long as it was quiet at night. Mickey never talked about his mother unless he had to, and that was usually just to say where she kept the booze or when she might be home, and everyone seemed to know enough not to ask about her. He can live on his own and I couldn't, Dinah thought, but she didn't hold it against him. Instead she yearned to know how he did it and how she could learn to do the same.

In school, Dinah stared at the back of Mickey so hard, she was surprised he didn't turn around from the heat of her glance. Shocks reverberated along her spine. Desire sounded a note she swore she heard. She memorized how his hair curled up at the back of his neck, how his shirts were sometimes not quite clean, and how although he told everyone he had five different denim shirts he wore all week, she knew for a fact it was only one because of the tiny ink stain just under his left shoulder.

In a crowded corridor, she shored up her courage and tapped him. He turned, beaming.

"I lived in New York City," Dinah said.

He lifted his brow. "Oh, yeah? Cool. Where?"

"Twenty-ninth Street," Dinah said, remembering Lilly's tiny apartment. She described the street to him, she stole Lilly's memories and told him, as much as it would take to keep him looking over at her.

"West Thirtieth," Mickey said.

"Oh, yeah, I know that street," Dinah lied.

She took her time getting to class, and she rushed out, in hopes of bumping into him. In Mr. Sgoras's art room, she painted motorcycles rearing like steeds. She painted long sweeping roads.

"And what's this?" said Mr. Sgoras, who knew perfectly

well, who had in fact found Mickey in the same supply closet he had once found Dinah, only Mickey was in there with another boy and the two of them were smoking dope.

"Expressionism," Dinah said.

"I see," said Mr. Sgoras. "Why don't you express something a little nicer?"

Dinah was at a loss what to do. She studied the fashion magazines, she held up the glossy photos of the models against her own face, and she knew that no matter what she did, she'd never look like any of them. She thought of interesting jokes she might tell Mickey, stories she could make up. She tugged at her hair, trying to pull length into it. She bought ten dollars' worth of Maybelline and a fake silver earring. She was even wishing on stars, praying to Saint Jude because she had read in the newspaper that if you said certain prayers for nine days in a row, you might get what you asked.

At the end of the ninth day, when nothing had happened, she started thinking about Lilly and her father. She remembered once, when she had asked her father how come he had fallen in love with Lilly so quickly, he had tickled her, joking that Lilly must have put a spell on him. He was making loving fun of her, but Dinah remembered the way he had leapt for the phone. She remembered how when he was with Lilly, she could have screamed and he wouldn't have heard her. Lilly. Jesus. Lilly.

She went out onto the porch. Lilly was reading and she looked up, surprised, when she saw Dinah.

"You know about love potions?" Dinah said.

"You think you can make someone love you?" Lilly said.

"Why can't you?" Dinah said. Her small shoulders sloped.

Lilly studied Dinah for so long, Dinah was about to give up, to turn away.

"All right," Lilly said abruptly. "Maybe I do know something."

Dinah started to follow Lilly in the house, when Lilly stopped. "No," Lilly said. "You can't know what goes in it." Dinah nodded.

Dinah sat out on the porch, waiting, searching the sky for the fiery wisp of a shooting star, a glimmer of moon, a planet, anything she might wish upon.

It didn't take Lilly long. She came back out, carrying a small silk bundle tied with blue ribbon, and then she handed it gravely to Dinah. "There you go," she said. "Be careful with it."

"What do I do with it?" Dinah said.

"Just carry it with you," Lilly said.

Dinah was very still. She hesitated, and then abruptly she bent down and just for one moment rested her hand on Lilly's shoulder. Lilly gave a small start and turned and looked at Dinah, her gaze so intent, Dinah stepped back.

"Thank you," Dinah said. She curved her fingers about the love charm, cradling it as if it were as precious as a life about to start.

Lilly nodded. "It's okay," she said, and then she turned slowly back to her book, but she didn't pick it up. Instead, she just looked first at Dinah and then down at her own empty hands, her palms curved up toward her.

chapter 9

Lilly never told Dinah that she had no more idea how to make a love potion than the man in the moon. She had prowled her kitchen, pulling out some sugar, some pepper, some odds and ends, and then had tied them up in a square of cloth. She had felt sorry for Dinah. She had seen belief carry countless clients. Belief had given her own life form and context for so long that now that she was without it, she foundered.

She watched Dinah, hoping for results. Dinah never mentioned the love potion, but Lilly noticed that now, when Dinah went to school, she usually wore pockets or she clutched her purse closer to her. She didn't know whom Dinah wanted to love her, and no matter how she felt about the girl, she wasn't mean enough to hope it wouldn't work.

Lilly got lost in the rhythm of work. She found out from Cora Janet that Dell's money, a much smaller amount than anyone thought but enough to cover Grace, was finally freed. She woke up in a better mood. Soon, she thought. Soon I can leave.

She kept calling Neal about Dinah's mother. She went to see him, because Neal was always happy to see her, and she liked the company. He made her sit down, and he made her tea, serving it to her in porcelain cups. "The leads say Texas." He was so sweetly apologetic that she burst into tears. "Hey," he said, his voice lowering.

She swiped at her drippy nose. "Bad day," she said finally.

"I'm a wonderful listener," he said. "Really. Things don't go beyond me."

"What are you talking about?" said Lilly, astonished. "Of course they do. People pay you to find out secrets."

"Not yours," he said. "I would never take money for your secrets. They would have to torture me, and even then I probably wouldn't tell."

"Probably?" said Lilly.

"Well, if they forced me to drink Drano, I might have a moral dilemma," he admitted.

"You're kind," she said.

He flushed, embarrassed. "Well, look," he said. "You have my number. All you have to do is dial it."

"I know," she said.

"Any time you want to know anything," he said. "Jesus. I sound like a fool, don't I?"

"I made Dinah a love spell," she blurted. He gave her a startled smile. "Speaking of fools," she said. "It's silly, isn't it?"

"Well," Neal said, "I don't think people need spells to fall in love. They do it well enough on their own."

"Oh," Lilly said. She had planned to stay a little longer today, but now she felt suddenly exposed, and she reached for her jacket.

Neal walked her to the door. "Check back with me," he said. "You never know when something will turn up."

When Lilly left his office, she felt more lonely than she had in a long time. No one was like her.

She didn't have any close friends here. Kay never said more than a breezy hello to her in passing. Kay probably thought she was snobby because she wouldn't tell fortunes. Well, Kay would be amazed to know that the woman she thought had all the answers actually cried herself to sleep nights, that the person she wanted guidance from was so lost, she couldn't even make out a coherent grocery list anymore.

Lilly looked for answers everywhere. She walked right into a church on her way to work, thinking she'd light a candle because it seemed such a simple, comforting thing to do. She hadn't expected a priest to be there, and when he saw her he gave her such a soft, compassionate look that she suddenly went over to him.

"Can I talk to you?" she said.

He sat her down in one of the empty, polished pews, and when she told him about Matt, he shook his head. He looked so sad, she felt like comforting him.

"The good are always taken early by God," he said. "It might help you to pray to the saints."

"I'm Jewish," she said.

He looked startled for a moment. "Well, the Lord sent you here to me for a reason. And prayer might help." He patted her back. "Do you know any prayers?" She shook her head. "Well, say what you feel. The angels will hear you. They're God's helpers. They're all around you."

She went home. She said what she felt, but if angels or God heard, they weren't communicating back to her, and she ended up feeling more alone than ever. She wouldn't give up, though. She called a local temple, which gave her an appointment with a rabbi they said was a specialist in grief. "He wrote a book on it," the woman told her. "Everybody just loves him."

Lilly mentioned to Dinah that she was going. "It's free," she said. Dinah was bent over a book. "It might make you feel better to talk," she said.

"I don't want to talk about anything," Dinah said. She got up and clutched her book to her chest. She wouldn't meet Lilly's eyes. "You want to go, you go without me."

Rabbi Sherner was in his sixties, with a drippy nose and an unzipped fly. He recited a litany of the burials he had had to preside over just in one week. "Little tiny babies barely warm!" he cried. "Newlyweds and sweet sixteens! That's what life is all about."

"But what will make me feel better?" Lilly said. No matter where she looked, she was aware of his damp nose, of his open fly. Zip it up, she told him mentally.

"What makes you think you're supposed to feel better?" he said. "We're here on earth to learn, and suffering is a wonderful teacher."

Lilly stared at him. "Why can't happiness teach?"

"I have a ten-step grief program," he told her. "I've written a book on it. In ten weeks we go through the whole process, you and me together, and by the end of the ten weeks—poof! You're fine."

"Ten weeks?" Lilly said doubtfully. "Then I'm fine?"

"Trust me," he said. "You know that airline tragedy, three hundred and fifty people killed in Philadelphia? You don't? Well, I called the authorities and offered my services free of charge." His face fired with passion. "The people I helped. I still get letters from them."

"I have to think about it," Lilly said.

"You call me, you'll see. Ten weeks."

She did call him. She went in for her second session, hoping his nose might be a little less drippy. She was relieved to see he at least had a huge clean handkerchief pressed up against his face. He made her sit on a wooden chair opposite him and nodded at her expectantly.

"I feel so alone," she said.

"You feel alone," he repeated, his eyes soulful.

She started feeling anxiety slithering up inside of her like a python. "I feel so useless."

"You feel useless."

"What am I supposed to do?"

"What are you supposed to do," he said sadly.

"This isn't helping," she said, her voice rising. "It's making me feel more hopeless."

He lifted a finger to his mouth. "Shhh," he said.

She started to cry. "Shhh," he said, leaning forward.

"I don't want to shush!" Lilly cried, her voice growing louder. "I. Don't. Want. To. Shush."

He stood up, alarmed, and tried to press her back down onto her chair, but Lilly wrestled free.

"I have to go," she said, wiping her eyes.

"The program is *ten* steps," he said. "This is only one. How can I help you if you don't commit?"

"I guess you can't," said Lilly, and was out the door.

She made an appointment with a psychiatrist, Dr. Sally Prunella, a name she had plunked out of the phone book, but as soon as Lilly walked into the office she knew she had made a mistake. Sally looked younger than Lilly. She was wearing a black leather mini and high-tops, and the first thing she did was hand Lilly a padded mallet and motion her to the couch.

"You won't hurt the couch," Sally said, "but you'll hurt yourself if you don't work out some of that rage. Come on, beat it out. Shout 'No!'"

Lilly sat listlessly on the couch, the cloth mallet perched in her lap. She couldn't imagine actually striking the mallet on anything except maybe the therapist.

"How old are you?" she said. "Did you ever treat anyone like me before? Did anyone you ever loved die?"

Sally frowned. "You have to work at this, Lilly."

"Just getting up in the morning is working at it," Lilly said. She stood, reaching for her purse. "I don't think this is working for me," she said.

"Same time next week?" Sally said brightly, her smile hard as glass.

Lilly went to a different psychiatrist, but before she sat down in the office she made sure there wasn't a cloth mallet in sight. The doctor was an older woman who listened attentively while Lilly shouted and cried and used up two entire boxes of Kleenex, and then she wrote something on a piece of paper. "This is what you might need," she said, and handed it to Lilly. "People who have been through it."

Every Wednesday night the Pittsburgh Bereavement Center had a Young Widows' Group. There were only ten people per group, and every one of them was between the ages of eighteen and forty. The meetings were in a small light-filled room at the old Elks Club, immediately after the Alcoholics Anonymous meeting.

"All right," the woman Lilly spoke to said, "but you have to commit to at least six meetings, because otherwise it's too upsetting to the other widows involved, it's another loss they're all too fragile to want to deal with."

"I'm going to a widows group," Lilly told Dinah.

"You're not a widow," Dinah said, putting tea on to boil. "You and my father weren't married." Her hair was longer now, and she had dyed a red strip into her pale blond hair that morning and was now fingering it anxiously.

"It's a technicality," Lilly said.

"I guess," Dinah said.

Lilly felt the familiar thrust of her anger, the pain at such easy cruelty. She's fifteen, she thought. She doesn't know. She's lucky she doesn't know.

"I've got to go," Lilly said. Dinah reached for the whistling kettle.

Lilly stood outside, watching the alcoholics leave. They were laughing and joking, in jeans and sloppy shirts, and she couldn't help it, she thought they looked interesting. She wanted to tag along, to go out with them for burgers or fries or bowling. A woman in the group turned and smiled at Lilly, and Lilly smiled back.

Lilly walked into the room, surprised by the neat row of elk heads mounted along the ceilings. There were brand-new couches lined along the walls, a few green card tables, and Lilly made herself as comfortable as she could on the stiff new sofa and waited. Five women walked in together, as familiar with each other as family, and as soon as they saw Lilly they came toward her. Lilly was in jeans and a faded black T-shirt, but these women looked as if they had dressed for the occasion, in silk shirts and suits, in heels and real gold earrings and makeup.

The smallest woman, a redhead in a brilliant floral dress, leaned toward Lilly. "Welcome to the club," she said wryly.

"What club?" Lilly said.

"Kelly Mace," she said. "How long?"

"How long what?" said Lilly.

"My husband died eight months ago," said Kelly.

"Oh," said Lilly. "Six," she said, and marveled at the months.

"Jesus, you're new," said another woman, a blonde in a tailored blue suit. "Rayna Rhodes," she said. "A year and a half. Colon cancer."

"If my husband hadn't died, I'd be in Hawaii right now and not in this stinking city," said Kelly. "We were arguing over a jar of mustard and he dropped dead. Took the ambulance forty minutes to make a two-block journey. I could have gotten to the hospital quicker if I had taken him myself." She shook her head. "If it wasn't fucked up, it wouldn't be life, would it?"

"Kelly's angry," said another woman, touching Lilly.

"Of course I'm angry!" said Kelly. "Jesus, what's the matter with you! What, are you delighted?"

"No," the woman said quietly. "I'm hardly delighted."

"How long?" said a woman with long black hair. She was carrying a clear container of salad from a Korean salad bar, and she began to open it, to poke out the cucumbers. "I hate to eat alone," she said. "Every Wednesday I'm guaranteed dinner companions." She gave a small, sharp laugh. "Oh, well . . ." She sighed. "Life is long."

The salad-eating woman pointed her fork at Lilly. "Stacey Rider," she said. "My husband was in a minor auto accident. Not a scratch on him. All he did was hit his chin. He came home, and that night while watching TV, he keeled right over. And the autopsy didn't show a damn thing was wrong with him. Not my perfect Paul." She started to giggle nervously and then to laugh. Her fork shook, dropping lettuce on the floor, and Rayna embraced her instantly.

"Hey," she said, rocking Stacey, who suddenly sat up straighter.

"I'm fine," she said, shaking her off, irritated. "I'm fine."

Kelly touched Lilly. "Don't worry," she said. "We may all seem a little nutty, but we're just what you need. We're all in this together, you know?"

Almost instantly a small, ferrety-looking woman in a green sweater and pants strode into the room, grinning broadly. "Paula Westie," she said to Lilly, taking her hand, separating her fingers with hers. She withdrew her hand.

Lilly sat down. There were only nine women, and they all positioned themselves about her.

Paula nodded. "Well, you must be Lilly," she said. "I'm the group leader, I run the show, but I'm not exactly chopped liver myself. I watched my first husband, Don, die from kidney failure. He was twenty-six."

Lilly balled her hands in her lap. If she wore a watch anymore, if all hours hadn't suddenly seemed the same to her, she would have looked at it now. She would have been counting out the minutes.

"Lilly," she said, "I'm living proof that there is life after death, because I just remarried six months ago!" She held up her ring finger.

"Yay, Paula," said Rayna, lilting her voice up. She rolled her eyes surreptitiously at Lilly.

Lilly blinked at Paula. She couldn't imagine her being married to anyone once, let alone twice. She knew perfectly well looks didn't matter, but there was something creepy about Paula. She looked as if she had secrets you didn't want to know, and she probably insisted on sharing them.

She looked around the room, at the women who were all looking at her, and she suddenly felt so tired, it was all she could do not to curl up under the chair and sleep.

"Why don't we all introduce ourselves," Paula said. "Lilly, how did you come to be here?"

By car, Lilly thought. "My fiancé died days before the wedding," she said. She wasn't listening to herself. She was floating up above the words. She was invisible.

"Fiancé? You're not a real widow, then," someone said.

"Oh, hell," Kelly said. "Fucking shit. What's the difference?"

"There's a difference." The woman, a redhead with tight curls, nodded at Lilly. "I was engaged. I ended up locked out of my own apartment because it was in my fiancé's name, not mine. I had to get a lawyer because all the money we had saved to buy a condo was in his name. His mother took it. We were going to change all that. As soon as we got married." She looked at Lilly bitterly. "That happen to you?"

Lilly shook her head, stunned.

"Wait until people say, 'At least you weren't married. At least it's easier for you.' That's one of my favorites."

"*Is* it easier for you, Lilly?" someone said.

"Everyone said I was a saint," the blond woman interrupted. She turned to Lilly. "Liver cancer. My husband was twenty years old. I never once complained. You know what it says on his tombstone? From your loving bride. I should have called a different doctor. I should have insisted he see a specialist. If I had, he would have made it, I know it." She started to cry, digging in her purse for a tissue. Kelly sighed.

"Susan, I thought we talked about how dangerous it was to keep blaming yourself like that," Paula said.

"I did everything," Susan sobbed. "I held his hand when he died!"

"That's right, you did," said Paula. "If there had been any other thing for you to do, you would have done it, but there wasn't."

Lilly felt herself retract. She felt as if someone were slowly ripping a bandage from her, except that the bandage covered her whole body.

"Don't you wish you could just be an amnesiac?" said Rayna.

A woman in the back straightened. "No," she said quietly. "I wish I could remember everything about my Eric so vividly, he would come right back to life."

"Lilly, what are you thinking?" Paula said.

"I'm thinking I'd rather be anywhere else," she said.

Kelly laughed. "Atta girl," she said. Susan leaned over and rubbed Lilly's knee.

Paula looked offended. "Listen, no one said this would be easy," she said. "But we're all here to help you." She looked around the room. "Every one of us has been where you are now."

"No, you haven't," said Lilly. She looked around. "There are no men here," she said, surprised. "No widowers."

Paula shrugged. "The men don't come," she said. "They bottle it all up. You know how men are."

Lilly lay back against her chair. For the remaining half hour she listened to a woman named Ada tell about finding her young husband dead in a Laundromat of an aneurism; she heard a woman named Betty tell of her husband dying of a heart attack while she was delivering her baby girl, a daughter that even now it hurt her to hold. She kept wondering, Did these women tell the same story week after week, every time there was a new member? She didn't think she could bear to hear it, let alone tell her own story. And then Paula stood up.

"I have a poem I'd like to share with you," she said. She lowered her voice and began reading. "Grief," she intoned, "is like a tree with long roots. Deep reaching into your heart. Your soul. Dead in winter. Gone, gone." She looked up dramatically and scanned the room before she turned to the paper again. "But by spring, buds bloom. Flowering into joy and the cycle that is life."

Lilly giggled loudly. A few women shot her looks, and Paula ignored Lilly altogether. Lilly pressed fingers against her laughing mouth, trying to quell the sound.

"I'd like a copy," Susan said.

Paula nodded at her. "Well, you call each other during the week," she said. "And remember, you can always call me, too."

The women nodded. A few started gathering their things, talking quietly together, making plans. "See you next week," she said, and Lilly bolted from her seat.

"You're coming back, aren't you?" Paula called.

Lilly stopped for a split second. She thought, Where else would she go? She heard the click and snap of heels behind her, and she quickened her pace. She didn't want to talk to anyone. She couldn't tolerate a second more of pain, anyone else's or her own.

All that week she thought about not going back. Her phone had rung at least once a night, a call from Rayna or Sharon or Kelly or one of the other women in the group she hadn't even made eye contact with, women Lilly had nothing in common with except for her grief. Lilly stood, listening to her answering machine.

"Just wanted to see if you were okay," Rayna said.

"Just wanted to know how you're doing," said Kelly.

"Just wanted to know what you thought of our little group. You seemed upset," said Paula.

Call me. Call me. Call me. Numbers after numbers that she didn't take down.

"Who's that?" Dinah asked.

"All wrong numbers," Lilly said.

She didn't care what she had promised; she couldn't be with all those women, with all that pain. But then Wednesday approached, and she thought about taking herself to a movie, about coming home to a house that was as empty as if she lived alone in it. I don't care, I'm not going, she told herself.

At five, right from work, she went shopping along Shadyside, wandering in and out of stores, thinking she was using up the evening that way; but when she had been in and out of every store, when she had tried on things she didn't like or need, she finally asked the salesgirl the time.

"Uh, it's just six," the girl said, and Lilly felt her spirit crumple like a ball of paper. Six. She had the whole evening to get through. She could go to a movie. Two hours. Eight. She could go shopping and then go to a movie. Ten. The group got out around eleven. All she'd have the energy to do was go home and sleep. She thought maybe Rayna read voraciously or Kelly loved movies. Maybe tonight might be different and they could talk about something other than the dead.

Dinah didn't know where Lilly was going that night, but her own mind was so full, there wasn't any room even to think to ask. Her thoughts were filled with Mickey. Her entire body shook when she saw him. Her blood seemed heated and wild. For the first time in her life she couldn't wait to get to school, and every minute that passed in school made her more and more depressed because it was one minute less that she would be able to see him. She knew that he didn't eat lunch but instead wandered around in the woods outside the school, smoking cigarettes and drinking beer by himself. And she knew too that he kept his motorcycle chained to a post behind the vocational school and another bike in his back-yard that he liked to work on, and she knew that if she wanted to see him one last time before he took off for home, she would have to hurry. She always wore her shortest skirts and her longest earrings, and she always carried Lilly's love potion in her pocket, but he never once seemed to notice her, even when she was sitting right there behind him. In study hall she rested her head in her hands and stared at him for forty-five solid minutes, so intently that half the school knew she had a crush on Mickey, but he never once looked up from the book he was reading, he never once seemed aware of all the fire she was generating.

He was as elusive as a ghost. She tried to trail him through the corridors, but he would suddenly disappear. She tried to find him outside in the woods in back of the school, but all she found was poison ivy, and she was itching for days afterward. He was a mystery she ached to solve. Every day he looked different to her, as if he carried all these identities within him. His hair was sometimes slicked back, a shade darker with all the oil in it. Other times it was loose and shaggy or pulled back into a stubby tail. He wore starchy white shirts or denim and jeans or tuxedo pants, and sometimes he wore wash-off tattoos. Occasionally he wore earrings or bracelets or bolo ties, and he didn't seem to care what people thought, and Dinah found herself falling helplessly more and more in love with him because of it.

She had been desperate to get away from Lilly. The nicer Lilly was to her, the meaner she felt, as if Lilly were being nice only to let her know who was the better person, the person who was not at fault. Now, though, she worried every time the phone rang. She never spoke to Neal when he called. What would he care if she got on the phone and begged him not to find her mother? What if Neal had found her mother and she had to leave? What if she had to leave before Mickey knew she loved him, before she had made him love her? How could she bear it if Mickey was going to be just another person she'd never see again in her life, another loss that would compound the other?

She began to take her time answering the phone, and if Lilly wasn't home, she wouldn't answer it at all. She carried the love potion everywhere she went. Sometimes she thought the love potion worked. It made her brave. It let her stand outside his classroom, waiting for him, and if it didn't also give voice to her thoughts, well, then maybe it just needed a little longer to work.

She took it out of her pocket and rubbed it. Mickey

would probably be home now. His house might be filled with kids. She held the charm up against her forehead, right where Lilly had once told her the third eye was, the place that saw the future. Dinah shut her eyes for just a second, and then, clutching the charm, she stood up. She started walking toward Mickey's.

When she was in front of Mickey's house, she stopped, stunned, and tucked the charm away deep into her purse. What kind of a crazy person was she that she would just show up at a house uninvited? What kind of abuse was she lending herself to? She could hear music blasting from one of the windows. Out front there were ten kids she didn't know drinking something pale from a pitcher, smoking cigarettes. Dinah wavered on her sneakers. She thought about going back home, about sitting in that lone empty house, the clock ticking behind her. She thought of her mother in some city she probably didn't want to live in, and then she thought of her father, and for a moment she heard the soft, solid flutter of wings. A dog barked from the backyard, and she jumped at the sound. She touched the charm and abruptly walked right toward the house, as if she had as much right to be there as anyone.

Mickey's house looked as though it should have been condemned. It was a small blue clapboard, and the paint was peeling so badly, it looked piebald. The windows didn't even need curtains, that was how badly smeared with dirt and age and living they were, and the porch had a few rotted steps, littered with newspapers and bottles, and the scrubby front yard was patchy with grass and faded dandelions.

She walked past the kids, invisible.

She didn't know what was wrong with her that she could just go inside a strange house as easily as if it belonged to her. She tensed, waiting for someone's grip on her arm, waiting for a voice to shout her back outside, but instead she moved deeper inside. The house was dark and musty. A couple was kissing on the plaid sofa, the girl's lean, long leg thrown over the boy's lap. In the corner was a starry blue ball. Dinah turned toward a girl she actually recognized, Cherry Wilson, who was in her gym class and who was the only other girl always chosen last for a team. Cherry had plopped down on a chair by the window and was fidgeting in her purse. When she spotted Dinah she narrowed her eyes for a moment.

"Dinah," she said, and then, triumphant, dug out a cigarette.

Dinah walked toward the kitchen, her heart thumping. Maybe Mickey was sitting at the table reading or drawing or making something to eat. Maybe he was at the back door, teaching his dog to fetch or beg or bark out a sound that could mean anything. She'd act casual. She'd pretend she didn't care about him one bit, that she had wandered here completely by accident. She'd be so cool, she'd make him want her right that minute, but she wouldn't give in. No, she'd walk away and leave him wanting more. She'd be cool. She would. The stereo was blasting from a far room, a voice shouting the song, the drums so loud, they pounded in her blood. The kitchen was empty.

She felt a pang of disappointment. Cautiously she opened the refrigerator door. Inside, something dank and soupy swam in a pot. A square of tinfoil was lumped into a corner. Wrinkling her nose, she shut the door.

She felt too self-conscious to sit still, so she prowled, doing her best to look cool and unconcerned.

She walked into one of the far bedrooms. Mickey's, she thought. There was one huge poster of the moon over his bed, a telescope by the window. She peered into it and saw a sudden span of highway, stretching to the horizon. She sat down gingerly on the bed, spreading her fingers over the spread, which was rough blue bumpy chenille.

"Hey." A boy wandered into the room. Dinah jumped up.

The boy laughed. He had long, perfectly white hair and pale, almost pinkish eyes. Albino, Dinah thought. He was dressed completely in denim. He was older than any boy she knew, but what horrified her were the jagged purple-and-blue bruises ringed about his neck.

"What did you think, I was a narc or something?" he said. He sat down amiably on the bed beside her. "Who are you?" he said.

Dinah looked at him. "Were you in an accident?" she said.

"A what?" he said, surprised.

She hesitated. "Your neck," she said.

He laughed. "You think I was in an accident?" he said.

"Did it hurt?"

He laughed again. "No, I wouldn't say it hurt." He grinned at her again. "Dan Fergus," the boy said. "And aren't you the sweet-potato pie?"

"Dinah," Dinah said.

He nodded and then looked casually over the headboard. There were ten small black lines. "Mickey's notches," he said, and laughed. He leaned forward to Dinah. "You hoping to be next?" he said, and Dinah suddenly smelled the sharp acrid scent of beer on his breath. She didn't like the way he was watching her, his eyes filling with her. "Someone's in the kitchen with Dinah," he sang. "Dinah, won't you blow." He put his hand, as light as a spider, on her thigh.

She stood up. "I gotta go," she said.

"Easy go, easy come," he said, laughing, and sprawled out on Mickey's bed, his boots plopped on the spread, his white hair spreading out. "I'll be here if you're looking for me, little Dinah-mite," he said. "Just ask for the accident victim."

Dinah wandered into the living room and sat down on a faded chair in the corner. Around her, everyone was talking or smoking or moving. She made herself still.

Dan suddenly walked into the room.

"Hey, here's the big man!" a boy called.

"Fuck you," Dan said cheerfully.

"I see Isabel left her calling card," the boy said.

"Man oh man," said Dan. "That chick ought to file her teeth." He looked at Dinah and winked.

Dinah told herself she didn't have to stay here another second if she didn't want to, she didn't have to explain to anyone why she might want to get up and go home. She bent down for her purse, only to find a girl she didn't know digging into it.

"You got matches?" the girl said, and then suddenly she lifted up a packet, Lilly's love charm, and the contents spilled out across the rug. A feather as pale as the morning sky, enough black pepper to set off a sneeze, some salt, a sliver of red ribbon, and a new green bud. The girl looked at it in astonishment and then looked over at Dinah, who was at her purse in three steps, who scooped up the spell and stuffed it into her bag and took off from the house.

"Hey!" someone called. "What kind of drugs is that?"

Behind her, Dan was laughing, calling for someone to open up the whiskey sour mix, because everyone knew that mixed with tap water, it made the best lemonade in the world.

Dinah kept walking. She hurled the love potion into the air, kicking at the flotsam as it fell. She felt as if something had exploded inside of her. She suddenly wanted to do something wild. She wanted to steal cars or necklaces or break hearts so badly, they might never heal. Maybe there was no forgiveness at all, maybe her father wasn't watching over her. Maybe it was all part of a punishment she deserved, something making her believe that she might have respite from her guilt, that she might have happiness, when all the time she was being set up to lose.

She walked past the grounds of Camp Whyhano and climbed the fence. Camp wasn't in session yet, but they had a pool, and she suddenly wanted to be in it. She shucked off her dress, her black cotton panties, and her shoes and dived into the water, staying under for as long as she could, until even her thoughts turned watery, until all she could see was a clear cool path of blue. She thought suddenly of her father, his face slammed up into her memory, and then she was suddenly crying, and she sprang to the surface, smashing her hands against the top of the water, beating it down, over and over, as if it were a living thing, until her hands burned from the force of her fury, until every bit of breath she had was exhausted. She turned on her back and floated, eyes shut against the sky.

She didn't know how long she was there. She was almost dozing, almost hypnotized, when she heard a noise. She sprang out of the pool and pulled on her dress. She was a fast enough runner to be out of there before anyone could catch her, a good enough liar for no one to be able to prove she had been trespassing. She grabbed for her shoes.

"Hey!"

She turned. Mickey was standing there in jeans and black T-shirt, looking at her in surprise.

"You break in?" he asked nonchalantly.

Dinah was too tired to be embarrassed, too wounded over a father who had loved her to care anymore about a boy who might never love her at all. "What if I did," she said.

He dug his hands in his pockets. "I don't know. What if you did?" he said. "I always do. You can be alone here."

The top of Dinah's dress was soaked from her hair. She sluiced it back with one hand.

"People say you live with a witch," he said.

"She's not a witch," Dinah said.

"Well, you'd be lucky if she was," he said simply.

"Ha. Lucky," said Dinah. "You go ahead and think that."

"A little magic never hurt anyone," Mickey said.

"There's no such thing as magic," Dinah said, thinking of the love potion, thinking of her grandmother talking to her father, of Lilly, who used to talk to everyone's dead.

She picked up her watch. Seven. Lilly would be home. Or maybe, too, Lilly wasn't even home at all. Or maybe she'd be relieved. She could take off then, do what she liked, which was probably anything that didn't have to do with Dinah. She looked up at Mickey, who was watching her.

"Dinah. That's your name, isn't it."

She nodded, lacing her sneakers.

"I'll see you tomorrow, Dinah."

"If I don't cut school," she said.

"Forget school. Here."

Dinah straightened. He'd go home, and the other kids would tell him about how she had just walked into his house as if she owned it, they'd tell him that she hadn't known the difference between a bruise and a love bite. She felt suddenly exhausted. It didn't matter whether she came here or not because wherever she was, he wouldn't be. "Sure," she said.

The next day she was at the pool by four, taking her time getting there, trying to subdue any dream she might have that he would actually show up. She had it all planned out. Thirty laps this time, so hard and fast that she might lose track of time altogether, she might be too exhausted to feel disappointment or loss or the keen propelling edge of desire.

The pool was empty when she got there. Of course. He had a houseful of beautiful girls, rooms full of guys with guitars and dope and cars and money. Why would he come here? It was stupid to expect anything, ridiculous to try for anything more than the comfort and cool of the water.

She had a black tank on underneath her clothes, and she was swimming almost her tenth lap when she heard something above her, and then she looked up and saw him standing there, watching her, and she was so startled, she swallowed a mouthful of water. "So I'm here," he said.

After that, all of life was nothing compared to three o'clock when Dinah could leave school and head for the pool, when she hoped Mickey would show up. He never promised to show up. He never discussed it with her, and the truth of the matter was that he was different day to day at school, sometimes talking to her, sometimes passing her as if she were no more substantial than a shadow.

She didn't know whom to thank for this miracle, the love potion or sometimes she wondered if it was her father orchestrating this, helping her forget. If Mickey would love her, it might be the promise of forgiveness. It might mean she wasn't completely evil. For the first time in a long while she didn't cry herself to sleep every night, her dreams weren't sour and full of violence and noise, and everything she saw didn't somehow act as a rebuke and remind her of what she had been responsible for and just how terrible a person she was.

Some days he didn't show up at the pool at all. She told herself she wasn't disappointed, she didn't care. She swam laps until she was exhausted, until it began to get dark.

But some days Mickey showed up, sometimes with his dog, Rick, and as soon as she saw the dog, her happiness turned sick with memory. The dog catapulted her back to her father's clinic. She remembered how he'd glide his hand on top of hers across an animal's coat, pressing down gently so she could feel the muscles. He showed her how to look in a dog's eyes so he wouldn't balk with fear, how to take a temperature and bind a wound. She could never remember being so absolutely happy as she had been then, and remembering those times made her miserable.

"Keep that thing away from me," she said roughly. She kept her distance from the dog, but it didn't matter, because the dog was as wary of her as she was of him. He snarled and bared his teeth.

"He doesn't like strangers," Mickey said. The dog dug at the grass.

"Maybe he'd be happier at home," Dinah said.

"Don't you want to not be a stranger to him?" Mickey said. He ruffed the dog's fur. "Good, Ricky," he said.

"Leave him at home," Dinah said, and Mickey shrugged. He tied the dog to a tree while they swam. Ricky barked once or twice and then scratched at the grass and hunkered down, sleeping.

Dinah and Mickey got out of the pool. They lay on the

grass, and he told her about his mother and how as long as he could remember it had been this way. Oh, he had had a father all right, it was just that no one seemed to know who exactly it was, including his mother.

"She was young," he said. "She had many boyfriends." He rested his chin on his knees. "She told all of them when she was pregnant, and they all gave her money, and one even offered to marry her, but she turned him down, and then when she was more pregnant, and more frightened, she changed her mind. And so had he. I guess it was too late then. She had me." He sighed. "She says she doesn't even remember their names, that liar."

"I don't have a father, either," said Dinah.

"No?" said Mickey.

"He died," said Dinah. "And my mother left us a long time ago." She waited, tensed, for Mickey to ask her how her father had died, but instead he hinged up on his elbows and kissed her, so gently that she wondered for a moment if she had imagined it.

"I'm sorry," he said, and then when she started to cry, he suddenly held her, rocking her against him.

"You had a father, though," Mickey said. "At least you had that." He stroked back her hair. "You know, sometimes I think the reason Annette stays away from the house so much is that I'm a man now. She hates men, but I'm her son and she can't differentiate."

He kissed her again, rolling her back down among the grass. The dog barked and whined. He lifted her shirt, swarming his hands over her bared skin, kissing her mouth, her neck, the edge of one shoulder, and all the time she felt the keen and steady beat of her heart, and all the time she kept thinking: I'm alive, I'm alive, I'm alive.

Falling in love changed everything. Mickey kissed Dinah in the middle of the school corridor, and people started paying attention to her. In the ladies' room, Cheryl Antomonia, who was tall and icy and beautiful, asked casually to borrow Dinah's lipstick. In math class, Billy Sol, who usually put his feet against the back of Dinah's chair, now passed her sticks of gum.

But people were as interested in Lilly as they were in Dinah and Mickey. "Why don't you have a séance at your house?" Cheryl asked. "Think of all the ghosts hanging around there." Dinah thought of her father and shook her head.

At night she couldn't sleep. She bunched the sheets in her hand and grabbed her pillow and tried to sleep out on the porch swing where it was cool, but even then she felt as though Mickey were there beside her, watching, touching, and she couldn't be still. She couldn't eat, and when she forced herself, the food tasted funny to her, somehow wrong, as if essence of carrot had gotten mixed up with essence of ice cream.

They weren't officially boyfriend and girlfriend. She knew that. He didn't call her every night or even every other night to talk. He didn't wait for her in school. She saw him coming out of history class, talking to Tammy Hopkins, leaning in close, and Dinah rushed toward him. She was out of breath when she got there. She tapped Mickey on the shoulder.

"Hey, you," she said. He looked at her, annoyed.

Tammy's eyes did a slow, amused roll, from Dinah's high-top boots to her black angora sweater. Dinah pulled her sweater down over her hips. "Want to get lunch?" she said brightly, looking at Mickey, ignoring Tammy.

"No, I can't," Mickey said.

"Oh," Dinah said. "Coffee, then. After school?"

Tammy looked at her watch. "Shit, we gotta go," she told Mickey. "Bye, Dinah," she said brightly, tugging at Mickey's sleeve.

"Mickey," Dinah said.

"Bye, babe," he said, rushing off with Tammy.

Dinah stood rooted to the corridor, watching the two of them leave. They weren't holding hands. They weren't kissing. They walked together, but there was a ruler of light between them, enough to keep them from being a couple. Babe, he had called her. Dinah repeated it to herself, as she walked back toward her locker. Babe.

He came to the pool the next day. She was so blindly grateful that she didn't mention Tammy, and neither did he. They walked around the camp and just talked, and when it got dark he tilted up her face to his.

"You," he said, and kissed her, so strong and deep that it made her dizzy, it made Tammy grow smaller and smaller in her mind until she was just a pinpoint. As soon as they parted, she felt an odd shock, as if someone had amputated her heart.

She had to tell someone, but there was no one to tell. She couldn't remember the last time she had called Ohio. Her friend's conversation had been filled with names she didn't even know any longer.

One night she bolted up, still in one of Matt's old T-shirts, and suddenly ran all the way to Dell's. She knew Grace went to sleep at ten, and she didn't want to wake her, but Dell's light was on, so Dinah climbed up a tree and this time, brave with love, rapped at the window.

Dell was sitting up in bed, looking at a photograph album, and when she saw Dinah, she smiled and opened the window. "Well, and who are you?" she said.

"Whisper," Dinah whispered.

She climbed in and sat at the edge of Dell's bed and suddenly hugged her grandmother.

"Dinah," said Dell, but her voice was far away and so soft, Dinah had to lean in close just to hear it.

"I'm in love," she told her grandmother.

"What a lovely thing that must be!" Dell said. She took Dinah's hands and stroked them.

"But I don't know if he loves me," Dinah said.

"He will," said Dell. "You bring him around. I can tell the moment I see him." She paused. "What's his name?"

"Mickey," said Dinah.

"Mickey," she repeated, reminded of another name, something still vague in her mind. "Dinah," she said, her voice firming around the sound, making it certain, and then her face blossomed into recognition. "Wait," she said. She got up and went to the dresser, and for a moment she looked up in the mirror, and Dinah could have sworn that her grandmother was growing younger, that the face that looked back at her was as smooth and unlined as her own, the eyes as bright. Dell opened the drawer and pulled out a string of glass beads and held them up so they caught the moonlight.

"I wore these when I was first married," Dell whispered. "No one could take their eyes off me."

Dinah took the beads, and when she put them on, Dell smiled. "You come back and visit me," Dell said.

Dinah and Mickey were lying on his bed. Her new glass necklace was set carefully on his night table, along with her shoes and socks. He was rolling her toward him, undoing her buttons so rapidly, some of them were popping off, when Dinah bolted upright, upset.

"Hey," Mickey said panting, sitting, too. "What is it? What's wrong?"

Dinah shook her head, miserable.

"No, come on, tell me," Mickey insisted. He leaned toward her, brushing the hair from her face.

Dinah pointed to all the notches on his headboard, bites into the wood.

"I'm sorry," he said. He draped his T-shirt over it, then let it fall down again. "I don't know what to do," he said help-lessly. "I wish they weren't there now." He rubbed Dinah's shoulders. He kissed her neck. "What should I do?" he said.

Dinah still felt his kiss on her neck. She felt herself

changing even as she sat on his bed. "Let's go to my room," she said. "Lilly's at a group until ten."

She led him back to her place, but once they were inside her room, Dinah was shy and silent. She knew he was used to girls calling his name, scraping their nails on his back to mark him as theirs, but she was barely moving beneath him.

"Dinah," he said.

She felt him trying to move her along with him, and then the rough tide of his passion made him greedy and he stopped speaking altogether. She felt him pushing inside of her, pulsing, and she shut her eyes. I love you, she thought. I love you, I love you, but she was silent. She spoke with her hands, spelling out her name across his back, down his thighs, on his belly. She spoke with her mouth, deep and dark against his.

He rolled from her and then grabbed her back to him, rocking her, stroking back her hair. "This was your first, right?" he said. "It'll get better. You wait."

Future tense, she thought. He'd used the future tense. Her heart bloomed inside of her. She looked at him. "You," she said, her eyes shining with delight.

He sang "Do You Believe in Magic," whispering the words against her soft hair, pulling her toward him again.

Lilly sat at her widows' group, thinking that this time was going to be the last.

This meeting, Paula had encouraged everyone to bring photos of their deceased. Lilly hadn't. She couldn't bear to look at photographs of Matt, time stopped on a print of paper even as it shot roughly past her. Paula was holding up a picture of her husband, Don. He looked like a male version of a Kewpie doll to Lilly, a short little blond with hair like the icing on a white wedding cake. He wore a plaid sports jacket and sherbet-colored pants, and he was waving into the camera. Waving good-bye, Lilly thought, and Paula hadn't even realized it. Neither had I, she thought.

"Wasn't he something?" Paula said seriously. Then she dug into her tweedy jacket and pulled out another picture. "Al," she said. The man was blond and small and looked almost exactly like Don. "My new husband," she said. "Remember, if I can do it, so can you."

It sounded like a pep rally. Lilly slunk on her seat. Why was that the goal, a new husband to replace the old? The topic was set for the night. Tales of fix-ups and ads placed in the personals. Photos passed around that Lilly couldn't stand to look at.

"Studies show," Paula said encouragingly, "that people who have had happy relationships are more apt to have them again."

That was fine, Lilly thought, but what if you wanted the same relationship, circling back to you, again and again?

"I know a good psychic," Kelly said abruptly, and Lilly straightened warily.

"The one I went to last week was fabulous," said Susan. "She put me right in contact with my Rick. I swear. She knew *pet* names."

Lilly didn't say anything. She knew how easy it was to pick up on a pet name, to throw out one or two before you hit the right one. Susan scribbled a name down on a piece of paper.

"I'm sorry, but I just think that's all wishful thinking," said Sondra, a new woman. "It's horrible, but dead is dead."

"You believe in science?" said Ada. "Matter neither being created nor destroyed? Well, aren't we matter? Doesn't it make sense that matter would come back?"

Kelly handed Sondra a scrap of paper. "See this man and then tell me that," she suggested. Sondra tucked the paper in her purse. "You go to psychics?" Kelly asked Lilly.

"Not me," Lilly said. She felt tired. No one ever asked her what she did for a living (and what would they think if they knew she was a clerk?), what hobbies she had, what her favorite season or color was. No one ever talked about anything but death and widowhood and their own secret society of grieving that would never, ever end.

A young woman suddenly appeared in the doorway, her eyes shrouded in dark glasses. "Is this the widows' group?" she said hesitantly. "I'm sorry I'm late—"

The other widows leaned forward, and suddenly Lilly couldn't breathe. She couldn't sit here and listen to another story about sudden and inexplicable death. She couldn't bring herself to hear Ada's story again, or Kelly's or Susan's, or Paula's, and the thought of having to talk about Matt, about having to relive it, even in words, made her heart stop. She stood up. "I gotta go," she said.

Paula looked alarmed. The new woman hesitated. "Lilly," Paula warned.

Lilly reached for her coat, but Kelly tugged it from her. "Hey," said Lilly, tugging it back.

"Lilly, what are you feeling?" Paula crooned.

"Panic," said Lilly. Sharon grabbed at Lilly's arm, and Lilly wrestled it free. There wasn't enough air to breathe in here. She reached for the door.

"Lilly!" shouted Kelly.

"Lilly, what are you feeling?"

"I don't want to be a member," Lilly said suddenly. The air thickened. "Every week the same horrible stories, and they all remind me of my own." She shut her eyes for a second. The new woman looked terrified and suddenly started to weep. "I just want to go to the movies," Lilly said. "That's all I want." She touched the new woman's arm. "Come with me," she said. "We'll see a comedy and eat buttered popcorn. We'll clap and stomp and have fun." The woman recoiled.

"Lilly," said Sondra. "You know that quote, um, 'Wherever I go, my giant goes with me'?"

Lilly stared at her, stupefied. Her heart was splintering, her breath had stopped, and this woman was talking about quotes and giants.

"No one will understand you like we do," said Sondra. She reached out her hand, her fingers unfurling.

"That's right," said Kelly. "Stay here."

Paula was walking toward Lilly, her smile gone, and suddenly something broke inside Lilly.

Lilly ran. She fairly tumbled down the stairs. Behind her, she could hear three sets of unidentified feet running after her. As soon as she got outside, she sprinted.

"Lilly!" someone shouted, and Lilly clapped her hands over her ears. "Lilly!"

A hand swiped at her sleeve, and she tore her arm free, so violently that she heard the fabric rip. Good-bye, good-bye, she thought.

She ran home. In her good shoes and good blouse. What are you feeling, Lilly? she thought. She felt good. She felt free. Huh. Huh. Huh. What are you feeling, Lilly? She had done the right thing. A thought edged into her consciousness. Matt. I miss you, she thought. Oh, God. You have no idea. Two more blocks, and then another. What are you feeling, Lilly? Huh. Huh. Come back, Matt. Just come back. Huh. Huh. Huh. What are you feeling, Lilly? Come back. Please. Come back, come back, come back.

She was drenched in sweat. Her hair was scrambled and crazy with curls. Her feet hurt and her eyes were wild and luminous and wounded. The house was completely dark. Dinah, she thought, and her chest tightened. She ran faster, into the house, up past the darkened living room, up the stairs to Dinah's room, where she jerked open the door.

Dinah, completely naked, her body pale and white in the moonlight, was trying desperately to step into her jeans. Behind her, a boy Lilly didn't know, already in jeans, was misbuttoning his shirt.

Dinah yanked up her zipper. She wouldn't meet Lilly's eyes. She stooped, collecting her shirt. The boy behind her stared at Lilly.

"What's going on here?" Lilly said.

"Nothing," said Dinah, reaching for her socks.

"Oh, look, we're really sorry," the boy said.

"Who are you?" Lilly said coldly.

"Mickey," he said.

Lilly was frightened by how angry she felt. She was hot and tired and worn out by grief and running, and she wasn't this girl's mother or legal guardian or even her conscience. She looked over at Mickey, who put one hand on Dinah's back, and suddenly Lilly recognized what else was traveling along inside of her, a sad, stubborn flicker of jealousy, a yearning so deep, it crumpled her to the edge of the bed.

"I'd better go," said Mickey. Dinah nodded at him.

"I'm really sorry," he said to Lilly again. He looked at her for a moment, then he slipped past her, making a racket down the stairs, slamming the front door.

Dinah waited. She looked lustrous, gleaming from within.

"I love him," Dinah said. "The love potion worked."

"I did this?" Lilly said quietly. "No, you did this."

Lilly leaned along the wall for a moment, bracing her hands there, steadying herself. "I really miss him," she said suddenly. "And I can't think of anything in my life to fix it." She didn't look at Dinah. She turned and went out of the room.

chapter 10

Grace sat out on the porch and needlepointed. Dell sat out in a brand-new dress that Grace had brought with her, a dress that made her think of summer, and she watched the stars and surveyed the neighborhood and wished her headache would go away. Dell peered out into the night. She swore she saw the slight young figure of a girl dashing past, hesitating for a moment before racing on. She squinted into the night. Nothing but parked cars and well-lit houses. Well, it was a perfect night for ghosts.

Her memory flickered like a candle. She thought of Matt, her son, full grown, coming to her house for dinner, and the perspective suddenly skewed. He receded in the background, and suddenly she was remembering what she had done in the store the day he had visited, how she had arranged twenty pairs of red shoes into a display.

Matt, she thought. Matthew. It was unnatural that she was alive while her son was dead. It was such a queer thing, to think that you'd never see someone again, that they had vanished, as simply as a magic act she had taken him to when he had been five. She remembered how Matt had been terrified. He had cried and carried on because the woman in the mirrored box had disappeared, and an usher had made her take him out.

"Please, he'll stop when the lady reappears," Dell had said, but the usher had been firm.

"The lady came back," she'd kept telling Matt all that night, but she didn't remember if he had believed her.

It wasn't the first time she had lied to protect his belief. When he was five he had pined for a game on the Pinky Lee TV show. He had wanted so badly to be the boy who had won it that she had gone out and bought the game for him herself, then forged a note: "Congratulations! Love from Pinky Lee!" She'd wasted five good stamps on it, too, and waited for hours until Matt was in the backyard to put it against the front door, just as if the mailman had delivered it. It killed her to remember how excited Matt had been, how he had torn at the paper. It killed her how much Matt had loved that game. And it killed her that she hadn't done more, that she hadn't once, as far as she remembered, ever sat down and played that game with him. It made her think she had somehow lived her life all wrong and that if she only had the chance, she could relive it right this time.

Dell's hands tingled. She rubbed feeling into them, carefully, so Grace wouldn't see. She kept her infirmities to herself. She wouldn't let on the way her sight was fading or the way she sometimes was so tired, it was all she could do to climb out of bed. She wouldn't let on that sometimes she forgot that Lilly was living practically next door, and she wouldn't let on that although she could see her granddaughter's mouth moving when she talked to her, she couldn't understand a word.

Dell didn't know why, but her boundaries seemed to be thinning. Already she knew that if she lifted her hand, she could move it gently through the wall, through the other side of the house, and remove it, as casually as if the whole foundation were made out of nothing more substantial than sweet cream. Some days she could see through the skin of her own hand, down through to the bone, pure and white and so smooth that she had to stroke her hand against her cheek.

She saw things in the air, drifting past her. Atoms, she thought. Or simply dust, sparkling with light and the promise of morning. She sighed, and Grace looked at her.

"Time for bed," Grace said, and both women rose and stretched and headed inside.

Dell woke in the middle of the night to find a figure, shadowy and still, sitting beside her. She sat up, blinking, and then her vision suddenly went so clear, it startled her.

Matt was beside her, grinning, his hair too long, in the clothes she had always hated, the denim jacket she'd told him time and again made him look like a hobo, the jeans she'd told him grown men didn't wear.

She sat up straighter. She felt the starchy sheets around her. She felt her own skin and heard her own heart. She looked at the clock by her bed, still ticking, still too loud. Three A.M. She reached out and touched his knee. It was solid and warm.

"How long have you been here?" she asked him.

"Long enough," he said, laughing.

"You deserved a better mother," she told him.

"Why, what did you do?" he said, politely interested.

"I don't even know your favorite color," she said. "I went through all of your things, and half of them were as confusing to me as Egyptian."

She looked down at her hands, shamed. It was a terrible thing to know so little about a life you had helped to create, and there wasn't a thing she could do about it.

"Blue," he said suddenly.

"Blue?"

"My favorite color," he said. "Now you know it."

"Oh," she said. "It's good to know."

She heard Grace on the stairs. Alarmed, she looked at Matt. Already he was thinning from her vision. "Please!" she said. "Don't go!"

"Don't you think I'll be back?" he told her, and vanished.

—

"All right in here?" Grace called, coming into the room. She had an old rose-print robe of Dell's, belted tightly about her waist. She was wearing big fluffy slippers that made her feet look animal. "I thought I heard you call me." She sat on the edge of Dell's bed, where Matt had been sitting, where it must still be warm, but she didn't seem to notice a thing.

Dell hesitated. She loved Grace, but she felt stingy. She wanted to keep Matt to herself, at least for a while. "I'm just fine," Dell said. "I was singing to myself."

"Good for you!" Grace said. "Keeps you young." She touched Dell's arm. "You need anything?"

"Just sleep," Dell said quickly.

"Happy trails, sleeping beauty," said Grace, rising, and she closed the door gently behind her.

Matt came to Dell more and more, nearly every day, but never at the same time, so she felt that she always had to be on her toes. She had to keep herself sharp. When Grace bounded in and said, "Okay, swap meet!" Dell got ornery. "Oh, come on, you big baby," Grace insisted. "Here's your sweater."

Dell looked around the room. She took her sweet time getting into her sweater, getting into her shoes, until she remembered that as a young girl, if she sat and waited for a phone call from a boy, it never happened, but if she walked two miles to the store for a magazine and back again, the call would be waiting for her.

"All right, you've convinced me," she said to Grace.

Grace drove like a maniac. You couldn't count on her to drive at a slow, steady pace, the way Dell used to when she drove, sometimes snailing along so that all the other drivers would honk and swear at her. No, Grace sprang into traffic and darted out again. She stopped for no reason at all and almost never was in the right lane for her turn. Dell put her window down all the way and threw her head back. The cool air rushed past.

They wandered among the aisles. Neither one of them had anything to swap, but if they liked anything well enough, Grace always talked the people into taking cash. Dell wandered until she saw a baby blue teacup and saucer. She lifted up the cup, so thin with wear, you could almost see through it. The saucer had a faint break, clumsily mended.

"It's lovely, isn't it?" a man said, bending toward Dell.

"Five dollars," Grace said, watching Dell. The man hesitated. "Come on, there's a chip," Grace said.

"Show me the five," the man said.

The whole drive home Dell kept the package balanced on her lap as delicately as if it were fine china. Blue. Her son loved blue, she thought. What a wonderful thing it was to buy a present for someone you loved and know it was exactly the right thing to buy. She turned to Grace. "I had a wonderful day," she said.

Grace beamed. "That's my job," she said. "Feeding you a future." She sat up straighter on her seat, and for the first time since Dell had known her, she edged into the right lane right when she was supposed to.

By the end of the month Dell knew Matt's favorite foods and favorite book, *David Copperfield*, which she made Grace get, and sometimes at night Grace would read to her.

She began to be more and more nervous about Dinah and Lilly visiting and coming upon Matt. He had never appeared anywhere but her bedroom, so when she had visitors she insisted they sit outside or in the kitchen or anywhere but where he might be. She didn't know if Matt visited them, and she was afraid to ask, afraid to put ideas into his head, and shamed, too, by her own ravenous heart, which wanted him, after all this time, all to herself. She told herself that Lilly and Dinah were young. They had their whole lives in front of them, while she was at the end of hers.

She tried to be casual, to find out if they knew Matt was still around. When Lilly was over, Dell asked her a million questions about her life. How was the house working out? "I bet it makes all kinds of noises at night," Dell said.

Lilly shrugged. "Well, it's an old house. Old houses keep settling, trying to get comfortable, I guess."

"Wonder if it's haunted," Dell said.

Lilly laughed. "I'm haunted, not the house," she said.

Immediately Dell felt guilty, but not guilty enough to tell Lilly that Matt came to see her each and every day. Instead she reached over and clasped Lilly's hand. She smiled at her, and the knot of guilt loosened.

With Dinah it seemed to be a little easier. Dinah didn't believe in miracles. And if Matt were visiting Dinah, Dinah would have told her, even as she pretended to sleep.

Dell gave Matt her total attention. It improved her mood. When he showed up last time, she could have sworn he looked younger, and when she asked him, he frowned.

"I'm almost in college," he said.

Dell blinked, trying to sort her tangled memories. And then, just as she thought she had it figured out, he vanished. She felt lonely. She called out to Grace. "Let's play cards," she said. "I'll let you win."

"Ha, you let me win," Grace said.

The two women sat out on the porch in the cool evening. Both of them cheated, but it was good-natured cheating, and no one really cared whether they won or lost. It was more the rustlings of the trees around them, the air against their hair, and all the dreams they never spoke of.

Dell thought she had never really lived with anyone in her house. Not really. Her husband had been gone before she had had time to get used to love around her. She had been too busy to notice Matt, and now here she was. She had in Grace a good card partner, a woman who loved both her and her house, who cared for them both as lovingly as if they belonged to her. She had a granddaughter who sneaked through the night to see her. She had Lilly, who sometimes, cautiously, visited. And best of all, most magic, she had Matt, her own son, whose favorite color was blue.

Lilly couldn't sleep. The house was silent and empty of Dinah when she got home, and although she had dozed off, clothed, on top of her bed, she had woken with a start to the beating of her own heart, accelerating crazily like a car gone wild. She had bolted up, thinking, This is what he felt. This is what happened when a life was ending. Did he think, Oh, my God, this can't be happening? Did he see her rushing toward him? Or was it a sudden, swift shock, life blanking out? What a fool she was. She put one hand over her heart, monitoring the beat. She was so desperate for life, it suddenly shamed her.

She turned on the TV. A woman with a blond bouffant and cleavage was taking calls from listeners and babbling advice. Underneath her flashed a legend: "Countess Dorella, Psychic 555-3319." Lilly moved closer to the set.

"Thank you!" a caller gushed. "You were right about my lousy ex-boyfriend, and you were right about my meeting someone in June. I did! And he's now my terrific new husband."

The studio audience cheered and clapped. "We *all* have the power to be happy," Dorella said, winking at the screen. "And that power is *here*." She tapped her forehead enthusiastically. "Call me with a question."

The number flashed across the screen, a bullet speeding into Lilly's chest, stunning her, propelling her up. She felt shaky with fear and longing. She felt like a fool, but she couldn't stop herself. She dialed the number.

"*Dorella Live*," a male voice rasped. "What's your question?"

Lilly, stunned at getting through, felt her vocal cords tightening. Sweat prickled along her back.

"Are you there?" the voice said. "What question do you want to ask Countess Dorella?"

"I want," Lilly said, forcing out sound. "I want—"

"Hello? Any day you're ready," the voice said, and then the line went dead.

Lilly held on to the receiver. I want, she thought. She looked back at the set, at Dorella, who was lightly touching her third eye at the center of her forehead in salute to the audience, which seemed drunk with happiness. "That's all we have time for today!" Dorella chimed. "Remember, the future is *now*." The music swelled and cut to a commercial for gourmet dog food.

Lilly clicked off the set. She didn't know what to do with herself. She wandered through the house. She went into Dinah's room, which was spotless. Dinah had makeup lined across the top of her dresser. She had two kinds of cheap cologne and a wire-bristle brush that said "Imported from France" on it. When Dinah had left that evening she had said she was spending the night at a friend's. She had a thick blue silk ribbon holding back her hair. It was longer, and Dinah had stopped dyeing it, and Lilly bet she didn't even realize just how pretty it was. Dinah was wearing glass earrings that caught and shattered the light, and a short black dress and small heels, and for a moment Lilly felt like a stranger, watching this young girl, and thinking, casually, How lovely she is, how brand new.

Lilly suspected Dinah was staying with that boy Mickey. Well, good for her, because everything could end, Lilly thought. In a million ways you might never imagine. Lilly had seen the two of them, jumping out of Dinah's bed. She had watched as intently as any voyeur, as longingly as any lonely person. Would anyone ever hold her again? Would anyone ever tell her that she mattered more than anything to him, that she was bright and funny and made him laugh? Would she ever be able to touch anyone and not wonder why it felt so queer and funny, why it felt as if everything in the world she needed was missing simply because the person she was touching wasn't Matt?

Lilly caught her reflection in the mirror. Her hair was in

shambles. Torn looking and tangled. Her skin was sallow, her lips were chapped, and she had smudgy circles under her eyes. She held her face in her hands.

"Look at you," she said to her reflection.

She thought of Nora and all those Avon cosmetics. "Two glamour pusses," Nora said. Lilly shook a reproving finger at herself in the mirror.

She reached for Dinah's face cream and smoothed it over her skin. She daubed on one of Dinah's perfumes on her pulse points. She carefully applied Dinah's lipstick, deep red, a small flame of color in her pale face. Her features shone before her. I used to be pretty, she thought. She remembered how it felt, walking into a room in a glow, inhabiting her own body with a pleased delight.

She turned and went into her room and opened up her suitcase and dug through it until she found a dress she had bought, the day before Matt had arrived in New York with Dinah. It was wrinkled from being packed up, but it was still special. It was a red velvet slip dress. Red to celebrate the fact that she wasn't going to be a New Yorker anymore. Matt had never even seen her in it. She had planned to wear it their first evening together at home in Ohio. She had wanted to surprise him.

She slid out of her clothes. She was prone to a pot belly, and she hadn't done a situp in months, but she hadn't really eaten, either. Even a steady diet of Twinkies wouldn't put on weight if that was all you took in. Naked, Lilly turned toward the mirror, standing in the careless puddle of her clothing. Heart and bone and flesh, she thought. She could count her ribs. She could cut someone with the angle of her hipbone. Her chest rose and fell with sips of breath. She reached automatically for the slip dress and pulled it over her naked body.

The dress fit her like her own shadow. She stared at herself, smoothing the lines, traveling her hands down her body. Then she took her own brush and brushed her hair out of its braid, spreading it across her shoulders. She crouched by her closet, fumbling for her one pair of high heels, pulling them on. She stood, two inches taller. She moved from the room.

Downstairs, she poured herself red wine in a wineglass. She put on the radio, and music floated into the room. "Blue Moon." Lilly stepped out onto the porch and looked across the neighborhood. All those lights in all those houses. All those wives not appreciating the husbands who loved them. She took a long, slow sip of the wine. She swayed to the music, in the dress she had bought to celebrate her new life. She moved her head so her hair swung down her back. She felt cloud-headed and woozy. She felt her body moving beneath the thin silky fabric of the dress. She lifted her glass. She was getting drunk. "To you," she said, and toasted the sky.

Mickey lay sprawled on his couch, Dinah beside him. His house was crowded with kids, but he'd be hard-pressed to pick out ten he knew. The old familiars were gone, visiting college campuses, already buying clothes for new climates. Roy. Nancy. All of them going. Even if he had any money, his own grades were so poor, he'd never get into college.

"So where are you going?" Tammy had asked him, tracing a line down the finger of his shirt. "Wouldn't it be a gas if we ended up at the same campus? We could really raise hell together."

"Berkeley," he lied. "California."

"I love California," Tammy said.

Liar, he told himself. Someone, a girl he didn't know in a backless dress and long, frizzy red hair, suddenly bent over him and handed him a pill. He looked up at her, and then, abruptly, he took the pill. "What is it?" he asked, swallowing, but she was moving back through the crowd. She was too far away. Beside him, Dinah stretched.

Someone tapped Mickey. He looked up, narrowing his eyes. He didn't even know this girl. "Your bathroom sink's stuffed up," she said.

"Jesus," Mickey said. He got up, shuffling Dinah from

him, but she followed him to the bathroom. She leaned along the wall and stared at him intently while he fiddled with the sink. "Washer," he said, reaching in the drawer of the vanity for the pliers he kept there.

"How did you know that?" Dinah said. She frowned. "Who taught you to fix sinks?" She moved closer, narrowing his light so he had to wave her away from him.

He tightened the washer and laughed. "Come on," he said. He stood up and saw the grease on his shirt. "Fuck," he said.

She followed him back to his bedroom. He pulled a shirt out of the dirty clothes pile and sniffed it experimentally. Not too funky. He pulled off his greasy shirt and pulled this one on, turning to see Dinah thumbing through his checkbook, scanning the balance of fifty dollars.

"What the fuck are you doing?" he said.

Dinah drew back as if he had hit her. "I don't have my own checking account," she said. "I was curious."

"You should be happy you don't need your own account," he said, and then he turned from her, walking back into his living room and all that restless sea of faces. Two younger boys stalled their conversation when he passed. They glanced at him with a reverence that made Mickey want to lay his head in his hands and never look up.

Dinah took his hand, and he threaded his fingers through hers. He sometimes thought it was Dinah's life he liked, and not Dinah at all, because her story was filled with as much sadness and uncertainty as his own. She had told him she had seen her father die right in front of her, that she had to live with her father's fiancée, a woman she didn't like, let alone know, a woman she claimed hated her, but she wouldn't say why. A detective looking for a mother she didn't know. A grandmother off in never-never land. Shunted from home to home. "I belong nowhere," Dinah told him.

"Me too," Mickey said, and he meant it. He didn't think he even belonged at his own home anymore.

"You belong to people," Dinah said.

They walked back into the living room. The drug was kicking in. He felt stiff and disjointed, and he slumped back onto the couch, Dinah beside him. There was whiskey sour lemonade spilled on the rug, dirty dishes in the sink and on the floor, and the whole thing suddenly made him tired, made him yearn for a log cabin with the floors swept clean every day, and maybe with a woman, maybe Dinah, he didn't know, but someone there to love only him. Or maybe someone who would stay with him and then leave the next morning without even saying her name. He was lost in reverie.

The music changed to Aerosmith. In the corner two people he didn't know were making out, all damp mouths and long legs and deep, tearing sighs. Two others were passing a joint back and forth, sucking in smoke, when the door suddenly opened and Annette, his mother, slammed in, her red heels snapping against the bare wood foyer. The music wailed, twisting around him. Mickey tried to grab a fistful of the notes and lift himself up. The air thickened. It held him upright, and he swooned back against it. He waved at his mother.

"Is this my own house or isn't it?" she screamed. "Didn't I tell you this had to stop? Didn't we have this conversation before? You don't listen, do you? You don't *hear*."

She stumbled over an ashtray full of cigarette butts. Mickey, dazzled, saw her moving, her arms and legs pulling like taffy. Hallucinogenic, he thought. Someone had given him acid. He heard a deep buzzing behind her as she moved, like the motor of a car. Colored lines sparked from her, like a body halo, like a Betty Boop cartoon he had seen once, and he couldn't help himself, he laughed. Even his laugh had shape, sparkling in the air like raindrops. He grabbed for a droplet of laughter, and then suddenly Annette lurched forward and struck him so hard, he smashed his head against the wall. Pain clamped in his stomach, the air crunched, and for a moment he thought he might throw up.

The music stopped suddenly. Silence blared. Kids rocketed to their feet, looking at the ground or the walls or any place but at Annette or Mickey. Dinah cowered by the wall.

"Get out," Annette said, nearly whispering, still watching Mickey. "All of you, get out of my house now."

Dinah hesitated. "You, too," Annette said.

The house emptied almost as quickly as it had filled. Annette's face bloomed with rage. When the house seemed silent, she strode across the room and slammed the door shut.

She moved toward him, and already he could smell the alcohol on her breath, but his legs felt weighted. He couldn't move, couldn't focus his eyes, and then she struck him again and again, and at each impact he felt his blood fireworking from him, so he had to cover his head with his hands. "I'm tired of coming home to this." She struck at him again, missing, swiping at air, which burned past him, hurting.

"You never come home, period!" he shouted.

"Well, I will be now," she shouted back. She dug at her hair, loosening it. Suddenly she slumped, faded. "I lost my goddamned job."

He pressed back against the wall. "They fired you?"

She looked at the room with disgust. She picked up a pillow. Underneath it was a pair of small white panties. She was suddenly full of furious energy again, and she flung them to the floor. "You disgusting little shit," she said.

Mickey stared at the panties. He didn't have a clue whom they belonged to.

"When you're eighteen, you're out of here!" Annette screamed. "On your own. You hear me? Because I've had it." She stood up. "Look at you. What are you on?"

She strode toward Mickey and dragged him roughly to his feet. She started to lift her hand again, streamers of fire racing from it. He tried to lock eyes, but hers were blank of love, blank of need or warmth, and suddenly something snapped inside of Mickey and he could move. He jerked from her. He pulled one leg forward, his bones turned to elastic, and although it seemed to span miles, his stride got him only to the door. He opened it, and suddenly, he didn't know how, he was running, a million miles an hour, a million miles away. She didn't have to tell him to go. He was already gone. And if he didn't have a destination yet, well, you could run and run, and then eventually you'd have to reach something. You couldn't help it.

"Mickey!"

Someone was shouting for him. He couldn't slow, though. Whoever it was had to speed up for him, had to grab him into a stop, and then he looked over and saw Dinah, slick with sweat.

"I'm getting kicked out of my own house!" he panted.

"It doesn't matter," she said.

"Of course it matters! Where am I supposed to go with no money? What am I supposed to do?"

Dinah chewed at her lip. "I have money," she said abruptly. "Or I will have money when I can get at it. My father left it to me for college."

"You can't give me your college money."

"I'm not giving it to you," Dinah said. "I'm—I'm giving it to us."

He looked at her through a druggy haze. He shook his head. He couldn't think clearly. "Us?" he said.

"Come on," she said. "We'll go to my house. Lilly's at work. We'll figure it out." He felt her arm hoop about his waist. He let his weight fall onto her, and when she started to walk he felt his legs moving. He felt himself walking, too.

Mickey and Dinah were stumbling toward Dinah's house when they heard the music. Mickey looked up. A woman, her long black hair floated about her, was swaying on the porch. Her body was a shadow, moving through her dress, slim and naked. He blinked, astonished. He had never seen anyone more beautiful.

Dinah stopped and looked up. "Oh, Jesus," she said.

She started to turn Mickey the other way, but he felt

pulled toward that image, that red dress. "Is that Lilly?" he said.

Lilly suddenly stopped swaying. She looked up at them, and then she wrapped her hair into a knot and folded her arms across her chest. "Dinah?" she called.

She ushered them into the living room, where Mickey promptly collapsed on the couch. He couldn't stop talking. He couldn't stop looking at Lilly, who was sitting opposite him, her elbows on her knees, watching him intently. He kept thinking of her naked body under her dress, the image of her in the moonlight.

"I was kicked out," he told her. Lilly nodded, waiting.

"What if I end up pumping gas in some station, what if I end up stocking groceries on shelves and everyone else is doing something, having something?" He sat up. A flame of color shot across the wall, and he rubbed his eyes.

"Shit," he said. He looked at Lilly. "Oh," he said. "Sorry."

She waved away his apology and leaned forward, resting on her palms, listening to him talk about his mother and his life. She didn't offer advice or interrupt or even say much. She didn't accuse him of being on drugs or reach for the phone in parental panic, and because she was so calm, he felt his words unwinding, as if they were thread on a spool. He was running down. His words broke off with an audible snap. He looked at Lilly.

"You know the future?" he said.

"No," she said.

"I do," Mickey said. "I know my life is going to be shit."

"No, it isn't," Dinah said to him, but he ignored her.

"I wish I could just get someplace warm," he said. "Someplace where no one even knew me." He rolled one hand over his thatchy hair. "Someplace warm," he repeated, and he saw it, he felt it. Sand rolling under his feet. A wash of heat.

"That's a future," Lilly said mildly.

"It is, isn't it," he said, cheering.

She smiled at him. "Go home," Lilly said. "I bet anything your mother's cooled off. I bet she's worried sick about where you are."

He shook his head, but he started to rise clumsily. Dinah helped him up, wrapping one arm about him.

"Someplace warm," he repeated. "A beach."

"It's going to be all right," Lilly said.

He stood there, unable to move.

"I'll walk you home," Dinah said to Mickey. She led him out the house.

He hesitated on the porch, pulled back toward Lilly. "I'm so fucking high," he told Dinah, but he didn't mean the drug. "I'm going to be up all night."

"I'll stay up with you," she said.

He bounded down the stairs. He stopped and kissed Dinah exuberantly. He felt like thanking her for living with such a woman. He looked back up at her house, at the lights going off, one by one by one. "What a great house," he told Dinah. "What a great, great house."

The whole way home he didn't hear a word Dinah said to him. Instead he thought about Lilly. Someplace warm, he thought. Someplace warm. That's a future, Lilly had told him. She knew. And then Berkeley, his lie, clicked into his mind. California. Why couldn't that be real? Why couldn't he make it all happen right now? He felt California beckoning to him. He didn't have much money saved, but he thought he had enough to gas up his motorcycle for at least part of the way, and when he ran out he could take some crummy job—a dishwasher, a waiter—anything at all, just to pay for the rest of his way out. No one would know who he was or who he had been, and you could do just about anything if it wasn't forever. He could get out there and find some job and save for his tuition. He wasn't stupid. Or hell, maybe he could be a mechanic. He knew about motorcycles. He could surely apprentice himself, do all the shit work, while he trained. He bet he could land a job. He could be somebody. He felt suddenly lighter. It dawned on him that thinking about the future actually might just mean that you had one.

He thought of Lilly. She knew, he kept thinking. She knew. He'd go back there and talk to her. Maybe she could tell him more. She could feed him hope.

The drug was dimming its power. Usually that stage made him edgy, made him want more, but this time the fix he was craving wasn't chemical. Tomorrow, he thought. Or the next day. He wasn't sure, but he'd go to see Lilly.

chapter 11

It was the summer, and Neal was still tracking Maggy. He had trailed her through her Social Security number, through three different states and countless jobs, until her trail ended in Santa Fe, New Mexico. He flew out there because he thought calling her on the phone would make it too easy for her to hang up on him, too easy to pick up and leave, and he wanted to end his career with some sort of clean finish. He wanted his last case to have no loose ends.

Maggy's house in Santa Fe was a small adobe surrounded by scrubby bushes. There wasn't a soul around, but there was an old beat-up blue pickup truck parked in front, and car parts, gritty with rust, were scattered on the browning lawn. When he got close enough to see inside her windows, to take in the fraying couch that looked pronged by countless cat claws, the mismatched chairs, and dusty floors, he thought that Maggy was either poor or simply uncaring.

He rang the bell. The door opened and a man stared at him. He was younger than Neal, in black sweat pants and a T-shirt. His black hair was cut roughly, and he was so thin Neal thought he must be a runner. "Who are you?" he said.

"I'm looking for Maggy Stoler," Neal said pleasantly.

"She's gone," the man said flatly.

"When will she be back?" said Neal.

"I told you she's gone." He looked at Neal with irritation.

"Who says I'm gone?"

Neal started. Behind the man a woman appeared, still dark and pretty, still the same face that had peered out of the old photo Lilly had given him. She was wearing a blue sleeveless dress, and on the third toe of her bare left foot was a small silver ring with a tiny silvery bell on it. She moved past the man, and the bell tinkled faintly. She squinted out at Neal.

"So, who are you?" she said.

She let him in. The living room was washed with blue sky and sun from the windows. The couch had a paler triangle of fabric where the sun had hit it once too often, and the chair Maggy beckoned for him to sit on had a broken spring that pressed against his back.

The man sat very close to Maggy, and every time she leaned forward, he did, too. "This is my husband, Earl," Maggy finally said.

"Well," Neal said. "Can we talk in private?"

"Why? We have no secrets," Earl said.

"He's right," Maggy said, picking at a piece of lint on her dress. "Sooner or later, everyone knows everything, don't they, Earl? Mail. Phone. Everything." Her eyes glittered.

Neal showed her Dinah's picture. Dinah at fifteen, with one earring and shaggy blond hair, standing with Matt, the two of them squinting into the sun. Maggy's face pinched up. She stared down at the photo.

Earl leaned forward and stared at the picture. "You know these people?" he said.

Maggy stood up. "Jesus," she said, and then sat down. "Did they send you to find me?" she asked.

"Who are they?" said Earl. "Maggy?"

"No," Neal said. "A woman did. She's taking care of

Dinah right now. Dinah's only relative besides you is her grandmother, and she's recovering from a stroke."

"What do you mean, her only relative?" Maggy said. "Where's Matt?"

"Are you going to tell me who they are?" Earl said. "Or am I going to keep sitting here like a fool?"

Maggy looked at Earl wearily. "My first husband. My daughter. I told you. You knew they existed."

"Swell," said Earl. "I thought that business was over and done with." He looked steadily at Neal. "Why'd they want to find Maggy? What's she done?"

Neal looked uncomfortable.

"Where's Matt?" Maggy said.

"He died," Neal said. "I'm sorry."

Maggy stiffened.

"A freak accident. Days before he was going to get re-married."

"Matt," Maggy said half in wonderment. "Matt dead."

"Dell's sick, so Lilly—his fiancée—took over, but, well . . . it's a rough situation."

"His fiancée," said Maggy. She shook her head. "How did he die?"

"Lake accident."

She seemed to be looking right through him. "I thought he'd always be fine," she said quietly. "People loved him. Animals. Kids. Women. I always knew he'd be okay."

"For Christ's sake, Maggy," said Earl.

"Do you want to talk to Dinah?" Neal finally said.

Maggy looked at him as if he had suggested she dance nude on the table. "What would I say to her?"

"She's your daughter."

"She hasn't been my daughter for a long time." Maggy said. "Earl's never even met her. She's what, seventeen now?"

"Sixteen," he said. "A really young sixteen. And you're her only living relative outside of Dell."

Maggy looked into the distance past him. "Look, I can't

take her, if this is what this is about," she said quietly. "I gave up custody a long time ago."

"That's right. We have our own life now here," Earl said. He reached for Maggy, but she jerked away from him.

Neal started to write something on a piece of paper, but Maggy stayed his hand. "Don't write her number," she said. "I won't call it. And don't write yours. I won't call you, either." She stood up. "You'd better go," she said.

Neal put the number on the table, under a glass ashtray.

Maggy was motionless, but Earl stood up briskly. "You heard the lady," he said. "I'll show you to the door."

He whisked Neal out into the bright outside. "Maggy won't appreciate your bothering her again," he said. Then he gave Neal a hard, slow smile and shut the door, clicking the locks shut, one by one.

Neal tried to call Maggy again, but she wouldn't come to the phone. "There's such a thing as harassment," Earl said.

Neal waited one more day, and then finally he took the next plane back to Pittsburgh. The whole ride home he had decided he wasn't going to tell Dinah that her mother hadn't wanted her—and that Dinah probably wouldn't have wanted her mother, either. He'd tell Lilly and hope she'd protect Dinah from the truth. It was at least a decent way for him to finish his last case.

When he strode up Lilly's lawn, she was reading on her porch, in shorts and a black top and bare feet, and she looked more beautiful to him than he had remembered. She sprang up with such delight that she made them both suddenly shy. "Is Dinah here?" he asked.

"Upstairs," said Lilly.

"Good," he said carefully, sitting on the porch with her. She looked at him, expectant.

Lilly listened quietly, and when he was finished talking, she rubbed at her arms as if she were freezing.

"What are you going to do?" he asked.

"I won't tell her."

"No, I mean about you."

Lilly gripped her elbows. "I don't know," she said. "Maybe Dell will get well enough for Dinah to stay with her again." She looked at Neal. She sat down on the porch. "I wish there were more money," she said suddenly. "I could hire someone. I could go back to New York." She stared out into the suburban road. "I'm going to call the lawyer again. I've got to get out of here."

"Is that where you'd go?" he said. "New York?"

"I still have my apartment there," she said. "I have a few friends." She drew her bare knees up to her chin and circled them with her arms. "That's where my life is."

"You have friends here," he said, but she laughed.

"You're kind," she said. "I like that."

The screen door slapped, and Dinah suddenly came out. Neal and Lilly were instantly silent. Dinah's gaze skipped from one face to the other. "You didn't find her, did you," Dinah said flatly.

"I'm sorry," Neal said.

"Are you leaving?" Dinah said to Lilly.

"No, of course not. Not yet," Lilly said. She dug her feet into the dirt. "We'll figure something out."

Dinah nodded and passed by them. "Where are you going?" Lilly said, and Dinah hesitated for only a minute.

"The library," she said. "Studying."

They watched her leaving. When she got to the end of the road, where she would have turned right for the library, Dinah turned left. Lilly turned to Neal. "Is she going to be okay, do you think?" Lilly said.

"Why wouldn't she be?" said Neal.

Neal closed up his office, as he had planned, and in the fall he got a job teaching history of law at the adult education division of the University of Pittsburgh. He loved his students, who were older and serious and actually took notes when he spoke, and even tried to make eye contact. He had a lot more free time, and he began coming over to Lilly's.

Lilly liked Neal, but she kept him at a distance. She couldn't have known that he was used to that, that every person he had ever followed had been at a distance from him. And detectives were used to waiting.

Neal knew how to find things out without people realizing that that was what he was doing. She didn't know he knew how she sometimes slammed out of work because he just happened to be in the book shop two stores away. She didn't know that the reason he knew to bring her tiger lilies was because one night he had watched her picking them. And she didn't know, too, that he had watched her reading on her porch; he has seen her fling the book disgustedly out into the night. He had seen her staring at her palm. He had seen her furiously scrubbing down the front steps, over and over, digging at them until the sopping sponge frayed into chunks in her hand.

One night he stood helplessly outside in the shadows. Lilly was rocking on the porch, crying. She swam out of a man's ratty red plaid bathrobe, desperately holding it as close and comforting about her as an embrace. It took everything in Neal not to bound up the stairs to her. It took everything to turn, to leave her alone.

Lilly watched Dinah being in love in a kind of yearning rage. She thought of Matt and cried. She thought about being cushioned by another pair of arms all night long, of waking up to a face you loved. She wept furiously. I want to be happy, she thought. I want a life.

She called Cora and asked her what was taking so long with the trustee, why they couldn't get a decision, a court date, anything at all.

"It takes time," Cora said. "Be a little patient."

Patient. Lilly roamed the house. She hated feeling that she wasn't in control, that she had to wait for something to happen. Widows' syndrome, she thought. An uneasiness with any sort of vacuum and a never-ending need to fill it. She remembered in the widows' group how at the end of a meeting everybody would take out their jewel-colored plastic day planners and make dates with everybody else, scribbling times and places under every day, filling up every spare second of silence with noise of some sort. They went to exhibits they weren't interested in, vacations they couldn't enjoy, and some of them even dated. Paula used to encourage dating.

"It's a landmark move," she insisted, "a sign you're moving on. You never forget, you continue." She got silent for a moment, and then she laughed. "What the hell, right?" she said. "What else are we going to do? At least it eats up the time."

Lilly jerked her robe tighter about her. She had hated the women in the group who said they would never love anyone the way they had loved their spouse, maybe because their feelings were the ones that terrified her the most. She had heard the other widows eulogizing their dead, refusing to find the nicks and tears in their relationships, and even when they were pressed to remember, they found excuses for affairs, reasons for long dull patches of loneliness. Lilly, though, wished for a bitter fight or two to remember. She wished for small cruelties, for an ebb and flow of love to hate and back again to love, instead of her own grand, giddy sweep toward a marriage that never got to happen. She wouldn't excise Matt's frailties as the other widows did for their own husbands. No, she'd dwell on them. She'd mark them and remember and maybe even embellish them, because then Matt would be human, and then maybe he'd recede a little, and then maybe any other man she might meet wouldn't pale before him.

Lilly didn't really expect to fall in love again, but she longed to be with someone, and she thought she might try dating. There was a man who kept coming into the card shop. His name was Spence, and he was an architect, handsome and funny and always buying cards for friends and, once, on her birthday, for her. Impulsively she asked him out to dinner.

"I thought you'd never ask," he said, and laughed.

She liked seeing him. It was loose and easy at first. He liked to go for drives and look at the buildings. He liked cooking elaborate dinners and seeing movies. And although he seemed interested in Lilly, he seemed more interested in Matt, and it began to scare her. He couldn't stop talking about Matt's death, wouldn't stop reminding her. "Did you and Matt do this?" he'd ask her when they were dancing in his living room. "Was Matt a good cook?"

"I don't want to talk about this," Lilly said.

"Of course you don't," he said sympathetically. "What's the matter with me." He ruffled her hair affectionately. "Come on, we'll go to a movie."

He spread out the paper, and they picked through the ads. "How about this one?" Lilly said, stubbing her finger against a promo photo of a couple throwing a blizzard of confetti at each other. *"All the Time,"* she said. "It's an independent film, but all I know about it is it's supposed to be fantastic."

Spence frowned. "Oh, no, we shouldn't see that movie," he told her, guiding her hand away from the page, clasping it in his own. He was looking at her as though she were a tragic heroine, and it made Lilly confused.

"Why not?" she asked.

He shook his head. "It has . . . uh, themes, that might make you feel terrible."

The way he kept looking at Lilly made her feel stubborn. "This is the movie I want to see," she insisted.

"All right," he said, sighing, "but if you want to leave at any time, you just tell me."

"Deal," Lilly said.

The whole time in the theater, she could feel him watching her, waiting for her emotions to break like an unstoppable tide. She didn't want to admit he had been right. The movie, about a young widow and her ghost husband, disturbed her. Behind her a woman started snuffling, weeping into a rustle of tissues. Spence patted Lilly's hand, and she removed it.

"Come on, let's leave," he whispered, and she shook her head. She made her hands into small fists in her lap. Get into a trance, she told herself. You know how.

Lilly blurred her vision. She concentrated, and after a while she didn't hear the movie at all. She didn't see it, and she felt a kind of steely calm.

When Spence touched her, she felt jolted. She blinked. The credits were sliding across the screen. The woman behind her blew her nose noisily. Spence ushered her out of the theater as if she were fragile china. "You poor love," he said. "It made you think of Matt, didn't it?"

He walked her home. "Are you okay?" he kept asking, and Lilly felt herself traveling, moving away from him as quickly as he was moving toward her. He stroked the length of her arm, and she didn't feel a thing until he had stopped. "You sure you're all right?" he said at her door.

"I think I'm just going to sleep," Lilly said.

Spence's mouth stiffened. "In the theater, in the dark, where you couldn't really see me, did you wish I was Matt?" he said.

"What?" Lilly said, shocked. "What?"

"No, I was just wondering. It's a perfectly human thing to wonder about. You're holding a hand, it's dark, it could be anybody's."

Lilly opened her door. "Good night, Spence," she said.

"Another time," he called out as she shut the door against him.

She wouldn't go out with him after that.

Lilly took two weeks, long enough for her hope to buoy her spirits, for her to want to give dating another chance. Then she started seeing a journalist Carl had fixed her up with. His name was Alan. He was tall and blond and so sun sensitive that he wore long-sleeved shirts even in the hottest weather. He didn't ask her fifty times a day about Matt; actually he didn't ask even once. He came to her door with flowers for her and a rose for Dinah, who winked at Lilly.

Lilly liked him well enough to keep seeing him. They saw movies and plays and sometimes just took long walks, and gradually she began to feel something when he traced the line of her neck, when he kissed her. She began to want to see him, to miss him when he didn't call.

He made her dinner at his apartment, one night when Dinah was camping at her friend Cherry's. He served veal chops and green peas, and he kept filling her glass with wine. He had oven mitts shaped like sea serpents, and he put them on like hand puppets and made them both sing along with the Italian love arias he had put on his stereo. He took off the mitts and scuttled one hand up her arm.

"Meet Mr. Crab," he said. His fingers unfurled. "Oh, he likes you," Alan said.

Laughing, Lilly slipped from her chair to the floor. She felt hopeful and light.

"Madame," said Alan, bowing deeply. Dinner was delicious. "Sit," he commanded. He wouldn't let her help him clear the table. He worked quickly, singing. She sat, beaming, and then when he was finished, he came out with a thin blue comforter and spread it on the floor. "Is this all right?" he said quietly. "Because if it isn't, just tell me, and we'll go for a walk." He crouched down and kissed her lightly before she could speak. He was silent, but she swore she still heard his singing; she still somehow moved to it.

He unbuttoned her blouse gently, taking it from her with as much care as if he were memorizing the fabric. He pulled her to her feet, swaying her to him in a kind of dance, his hand cupped to her hip. He was so slow and gentle that for a moment Lilly thought it all might work. He slid out of his clothes and helped her with hers, and then she felt the shock of strange skin against her own, the warmth and bone of an unfamiliar body. She was fuzzy with drink, and then he kissed her and she turned liquid, newly greedy with desire. She pulled him down onto the blanket, her heart keeping time with the music that was still singing within her. And that evening she fell asleep in his arms.

She woke to whispering. Someone was murmuring something against her hair, and for a moment she thought the dead had returned. She stirred, straining to siphon out words.

"Marry me," Alan whispered.

Lilly sat up and turned to him. He was leaning on one elbow, watching her.

"Subliminal suggestion," he joked weakly.

Lilly blinked. The air felt heavy and stale. Her mouth was cottony and her head throbbed, and the whole mood of the evening seemed to be vanishing, and she was anxious to escape before it was gone completely. "I'd better get home," she said.

"Absolutely," he said, kissing her on the forehead.

She felt better being away from him for a few days, and when he called her she was delighted that she wanted to see him. But something had changed in their relationship, and he began to pressure her.

"I'm forty years old," he kept saying. "I don't have time to play at life." He wanted to be married. He wanted kids. "Don't you want those things?" he asked Lilly. "What are we doing, then, if you don't want them?"

Lilly tried to nuzzle his shoulder. "We're dating," she said, and he pushed her from him.

"Kid stuff," he said.

She began to feel him looking at her in a new and different way, as if he were taking her measure. He grew reserved. She didn't miss his constant questions about their future, his prodding, but she missed the feeling that she wasn't alone in the world, that she was the center of someone else's life, and it made her think of and miss Matt more than she had in months. It made her feel as if she were being pulled backward, mired again in her past.

One night she was at his house for dinner, and when she went to use the phone to check her messages, she saw women's names scribbled in bold black ink by the phone. Diane. Emily. Alice. Dinner, it said. Roller-skating. She waited for jealousy or a flame of rage, but all she felt was a twinge of disappointment and then a sudden, frantic urge to find someone else to fill up the spaces Alan would leave. So that's what it was for her now, love. Busywork. It made her so sad and hopeless about herself that she walked into the kitchen, where Alan was chopping peppers for dinner. She leaned along the wall.

"Hey," she said, and he looked up, and she was so miserable, he stopped his cutting and came over to her and stroked back her hair. "Listen," Lilly said. "Maybe we should stop seeing each other."

He turned toward her, confused and unhappy. "It'll be better," she said.

Casually he walked back to the peppers and began mincing them up. "All right," he said, bent over his work. "We want different things, I guess."

She wanted to talk about it, but he refused. "Hey, we can't let dinner go to waste," he said. He didn't make the oven mitts sing. He didn't thrum his fingers on the table and say it was Mr. Crab, wanting to tell a bad joke. Instead he talked about everything but what either one of them was feeling. He told her about a story he was working on about wonder kids. He talked about a new reporter at his paper who wrote a gossip column. "Marissa," he said. He talked when he cleaned up and all through the drive back to her place, right up until the moment the car stopped and Lilly reached for the door, and then he was silent. Then he didn't even say goodbye.

She missed not seeing Alan, but she didn't call him, and he didn't come into the shop anymore. A week after she'd stopped seeing Alan, she began to get hang-up phone calls at home. Three and four times a night. And then one time she heard breathing, slow and restless, and she wasn't sure what made her think it was Alan, but she did. "Alan, cut it out," she finally said into the phone. "I know it's you."

"You used me," he said.

"I didn't mean to," Lilly said.

"Want to bet?" he said, and then he hung up.

Lilly got up and began cleaning the kitchen cabinets, taking down every dish and washing and drying it before she put it back up again. And when the phone rang again, when it was a man she had met in a movie line, wanting to know if she wanted to see a Truffaut double bill, Lilly felt paralyzed for only a moment.

"I'm busy," she said.

"Dating's not my forte," she told Neal.

"So don't do it," he told her. "Hang out with me."

He became an expert at being her friend. Late nights when Lilly couldn't sleep, she called Neal and they went to the diner for French fries and grilled-cheese sandwiches. Sunday mornings Neal sometimes showed up with bagels.

They were at dinner one night at a café, laughing, when he ate too big a chunk of chocolate cake and began to cough. It was just a cough, but Lilly dashed up from her seat, her face white.

"I can speak!" he told her. "I'm all right!"

She was frozen, pasted to her chair even after he had stopped coughing.

"Lilly, I'm fine," he insisted.

"I just overreacted, I guess," she said lamely. She tried to perk up, but he heard the panic, like an undertow, riding in her voice.

He watched her change. Whenever he ate, she tensed. They were at the movies one night, and he was starving. "Be right back," he said. He rushed to the lobby and bought two chocolate bars. He tore off the paper and wolfed them down at the back of the theater, finishing before he went and sat down next to Lilly again.

She looked at him. "You were gone so long," she whispered. "Are you all right?" Her relief at seeing him was so enormous, he felt somehow guilty, somehow responsible.

"Come on, relax," he told her.

After the movie they sat out on her porch and talked. She told him about her childhood, and about Dinah, and about the future she was trying to forge. "Why shouldn't I fall in love again?" she asked. "Spence was crazy, but Alan was pretty nice. Maybe Alan was just too soon."

"Maybe he was just the wrong guy," Neal said.

"I don't know. I kind of liked him," Lilly said. "He was funny. He sang songs to me."

I can be funny, Neal thought, I can sing. He started to hum, but his voice felt suddenly parched and empty.

"You got something in your throat?" Lilly said, concerned. "You want some water?"

"I'm fine," he said. He tried to make her see him. He draped an arm about her, and when she leaned against him he kissed her impulsively. She started as if she had been stung. "I'd better get going," he said, averting his eyes.

He lay awake in bed that night, making himself crazy thinking about her. When he finally fell asleep, his dreams flooded with her. He woke up cradling his pillow like a lover.

He went to see her the next morning, and when he saw her it was like a small shock, but she was so casual with him that his despair made him hostile.

"Guess what?" she said. "Carl thinks he has another fix-up for me. Should I go?" She smiled at him. Her hair was damp from her shower, and he could smell the baby powder she used, intoxicating and warm as her own skin.

"Sure, maybe this one's a mass murderer," he snapped.

Lilly's smile evaporated. She brushed her hair from her shoulders and frowned at him uncertainly.

"I gotta go," he said. "I just dropped by to say hello."

"I'll see you later," Lilly said. She turned from him. He wasn't five feet away from her house when he heard her humming. She has another date, he thought. And then: She has a right.

He didn't call her. He didn't want other women, but he began to think that maybe he was like Lilly. Maybe he just needed to get out there and see as many different people as he could, until all of them, or one of them, might fade from his mind the image of the one person he truly wanted.

Lilly waited for Neal to drop by that evening, and when he didn't she figured he just had something else to do. She went out on her date, with an accountant she had absolutely nothing in common with, and she came home and called Neal, but he didn't pick up the phone. When he didn't show up the next night, she called him. He was perfectly pleasant to her.

"Oh, I'm just busy," he said.

"Hey, a new ice-cream place opened up in Shadyside," she said. "Want to eat ourselves silly tomorrow night?"

"Can't do it," he said smoothly.

"My date was a bore." She laughed. "There's always the next time, right?"

"Sure," he said.

"So, want to see a movie later in the week?"

"Let me get back to you," he said. "My schedule's kind of confused."

"Is something wrong?" Lilly asked him. "Did I do something? Tell me what it is and I'll apologize."

"Don't be silly," he said.

She didn't know what to think until one day she decided to confront him, to find out what it was she had done to deserve his silence. "I thought we were friends," she practiced saying. "I thought we cared about each other." She grabbed her jacket and strode over to his place just in time to see him getting into his car with a woman with wild black hair and shimmering earrings. "Baby, don't forget the wine," the woman said, laughing, and Neal bent down and kissed her.

Lilly watched the car pull away. Love, she thought. She couldn't begrudge him the one thing she couldn't manage for herself. She couldn't expect friendship to burn brighter than romance. But she had thought they were close enough that he'd have confided in her about it, and it hurt her that he hadn't. She burrowed her hands deep into her pockets. Everything moves on, she told herself. Even you. You have a mind. Think what to do. You have legs. Use them.

Lilly kept as busy as she could. One day while she was at the card store, a vendor walked in when Carl wasn't there and asked if he could show the line to Lilly.

"Oh, I can't," she said.

He grinned at her. "Let me show them to you. I'll leave a brochure and you can show them to your boss."

The shop was fairly empty, and he sat down and showed her a new line. Computer-doctored photographs.

"The wing series," he said.

He had winged silverware. He had a woman with wings and a halo. A flying dinosaur glided with great amusement beside a spaceship. She liked them.

"Place an order," he said. "You can always cancel."

When Carl came back he was miffed, but he didn't cancel the order. "I bet you think I'm going to give you a raise, don't you?" Carl said. "But I'm much too cheap for that. Instead, I'm going to let you order more cards."

She felt better being at the cash register. She kept brochures by it to study, and she began taking more note of what people bought. Sometimes she brought the catalogs home to Dinah. "Tell me what you like," she said, and she and Dinah pored over the pictures, making fun of the ones they didn't like. The evening would stretch out.

Dinah was holding up black-and-white photo cards when the doorbell rang. "I'll get it," Lilly said. She opened the door, and Mickey beamed at her. "I was hoping you'd be home," he said.

"Really? Why?" said Lilly.

"I dropped by yesterday, but you weren't here. I . . . oh, look, I wanted to see you."

He stared at Lilly so long and hard, she felt as if he were boring a hole through her, and then she felt the air about her instantly cool. She turned and Dinah was standing there, her arms folded stiffly.

"Oh, hi," Mickey said. He looked from Lilly to Dinah, considering. "You want to get coffee?" he said to Dinah.

"I'm ready now," Dinah said, her voice sharp.

Lilly finished looking at the cards herself. She didn't know what was going on with Mickey, but whatever it was, she hoped it wouldn't hurt Dinah. She lifted up a card, a watercolor of a toothbrush flying in the air. Dinah'd love this, she thought, and it surprised her how much she suddenly missed Dinah sitting beside her. Well, she thought. If she missed Dinah, if she missed Neal, too bad for her.

Lilly didn't know what to do with herself. She needed something mindless, something involving. She got up and grabbed an old T-shirt she had forgotten to throw in the laundry and began to dust. She took the books out of the shelves and dusted them, and then she went into the kitchen and got a bucket and a mop and began to do the floors.

The place began to look clean, as if it had a life of its own. Lilly went outside and picked some flowers from the side of the house and brought them back inside. She rummaged through the kitchen until she found a glass vase, and then she arranged the flowers carefully, and they looked so lovely, she brought them into her room. They were beautiful. They were alive. They could give small comfort. And if you couldn't get what you needed, you should take what you could get. Lilly touched the petals, as soft as skin against her fingers, as blue as a pair of eyes that loved you.

chapter 12

Dinah couldn't be close enough to Mickey. She got to school early because she knew he did. "If you're not eating breakfast here, take money to buy it," Lilly told Dinah, and when Dinah shrugged, Lilly stuck ten dollars into her pack. "Buy lunch, too," Lilly said.

Dinah raced to school. She saw Mickey in the cafeteria, one of four people eating breakfast, his back to her, reading. She was starving, but she wanted to see him first, and she sneaked up behind him and planted a kiss on his neck. He whipped around, closing the book abruptly.

"What're you reading?" Dinah said.

"Nothing," Mickey said, but Dinah grabbed at the book. *California on Ten Dollars a Day*. He shrugged.

"California?" Dinah said.

"You know I can't stay here," Mickey said. He took the book back from her, tucking it into his pack.

"I can't stay here, either," Dinah said, her heart skittering inside of her.

"Yes, you can. You've got school here. You've got Lilly," he said.

"Lilly. Don't even mention that name to me," Dinah said.

"You don't want to go with me," he said. "I don't have much to offer you."

"You do so. You're amazing. You know things," she said.

Mickey shook his head. His face seemed to be telescoping away from her. She reached out to touch him, to make sure he was still there. "You don't want to get up and go someplace new alone, do you?"

"No," he admitted. "I guess I don't."

"I love you," she blurted. She suddenly didn't care who knew it. She felt reckless and wild and out of control. "You love me, too. I know it."

"Dinah," he said helplessly. "Listen to me a minute."

"Nobody loves you more than I do," Dinah said. "We understand each other. We have the same lives."

"Look, I know," he started, "but it's different for me. You may hate Lilly, but you can stay there. I can't stay with Annette."

"I'll have money," she said. She kissed him. "We'll be able to live on it."

He looked at her. "I thought I could get jobs along the way. Pay for gas that way."

"What if you can't?" she said. He grew silent.

"I don't know," he said. He looked around the cafeteria. Dinah's stomach growled audibly. "Go get something to eat," he told her.

She glanced over at the food line. She could smell the eggs, which weren't too disgusting if you were really hungry. The rolls were probably still warm. She looked at Mickey, and then she dug into her pocket and pulled out the ten dollars Lilly had given her to eat. Her stomach clamped, and she ignored it. "Look," she said. "I can get this much every day if I want. By the time we're ready to leave, I'll have enough for our gas, I bet. We can help each other."

"Dinah, I can't take your money," he said.

"*Our* money. It'll help pay for gas, for someplace to stay

until we get jobs," Dinah said. "Who knows how long that might take?"

Mickey studied her. "If I said yes," he said slowly, "and I'm not saying yes, then I'd have to pay you back. Every single dime. That's the only way it'd work. And I'm not saying yes, I told you."

She kissed him, again and again, until he lifted one hand and placed it against the back of her head, his fierce fingers drawing her close.

"Hey," a teacher called. "Break it up there!"

Mickey looked up, separating from Dinah. "Why?" he said. "We're not fighting."

Dinah began asking Lilly for a larger amount of food money, and in the next few weeks she had saved more money than she had ever had before, and all of it she kept hidden in a sock under her mattress. She was starving for most of the school day, but she wouldn't let Mickey know how hungry she was because then he'd make her eat, and she couldn't take food from the house to school because then Lilly would want to know why she needed the money. Instead she let herself buy two candy bars a day. She rationed them out, one in the morning and one in the afternoon, and if hunger made her nauseated, well, she convinced herself it was romantic. It's what I did for love, she thought.

She read everything she could about California. The next time she saw Mickey, she pulled out her newest guidebook from the library, *Los Angeles: La La Land for Lovers*. "I know the best places to finish high school," Dinah told him. "I know where we can learn to surf."

"Oh," he said. "Good."

"It's a great book," Dinah said.

"All right, all right, let's just stay cool about this," he said. "We'll have to talk about this more."

"You'll come to the house tonight, right?" Dinah said. "Come after four when Lilly's gone. We can figure out our money. We can plan. I just have to take a history makeup test and then I'll be home."

The bell sang behind them. Groups of kids broke up and streamed toward the door. "Come on," he said. "You don't want to be late."

Dinah took the makeup with one other person, Billy Porter, a boy so stupid, she used to whisper the answers to him. Billy was going to Harvard on a football scholarship, something that angered Dinah so bitterly that when she found out she refused to give him answers anymore.

The test was easy. Mrs. Marfoot, the teacher, stood in front of both Dinah and Billy and watched them. "I'm just making sure you don't even think about cheating," she said.

Dinah rolled her eyes. She finished in half an hour and rushed up from her seat, the paper fluttering in her hand.

"Wait," said Mrs. Marfoot, nodding toward Billy.

Dinah drew a small map of California across the top of her page. She inked "Los Angeles" in tiny block letters, and then she scribbled over it carefully so no one could see. Billy sighed and stood up.

"Go," said the teacher, and Dinah flew.

She ran home, checking her watch every five seconds. She was earlier than she had expected.

She was changed and remade-up and sitting on the front porch, wolfing down a sandwich, when she heard Mickey's motorcycle. She stood up. An image flickered into her mind: she and Mickey riding on his bike along a rocky coast, the ocean at their side, the water frosted with foam.

The motorcycle circled toward her, and then she saw Lilly riding behind him, swaying her body with the turn, her hair lifted on the wind. She shook off the image. She must be hallucinating.

Mickey pulled up in front of Dinah, and Lilly got off, her face flushed. "Hey, Dinah," Lilly said. "Mickey talked me into a ride." She dusted her hands along her jeans. "It was really fun."

"I thought you said bikes were dangerous," Dinah said.

Lilly laughed. "I've said a lot of silly things in my life," she said. She turned back to Mickey, her eyes bright. "Don't you ever feel like just riding and never stopping?" She panted, catching her breath. "I'd get on that thing and just keep going." She smiled at him.

Dinah touched Mickey's arm, and he started, as if he hadn't realized she was even there.

"We've got to go," Dinah said. "Come on."

Lilly pushed her hair from her shoulders. "Well, thanks again," she said to Mickey. She looked at Dinah. "See you later," she said, and then she bounded up the stairs, whistling, and went into the house.

Mickey was watching the front door. "Hey," Dinah said. "How come you gave her a ride?"

"She asked," said Mickey. "It was so funny. First adult I ever knew who asked. Most of them tell me about some friend of theirs who got a punctured lung or who died from riding a bike." He shook his head in admiration. "She was so fearless," he said. "We could have ridden forever."

They walked toward the camp. "How old is Lilly?" Mickey said.

"Old," said Dinah. "Do we have to talk about Lilly?"

Mickey shook his head. "Naw, she's not old," he said. "She can't be more than thirty." He looked at Dinah. "Does she tell you your future all the time?"

"That's a joke," Dinah said. "She's not psychic."

Mickey dug his hands into his pockets. "I don't know. I felt like she knew what was going to happen to me."

Dinah stopped walking. "Why? What did she say?"

"I don't know. I guess it wasn't so much what she said, it was just what I felt. She has this way of really looking into you. That's all I'm saying. It's pretty amazing." He looked at Dinah. "You're lucky."

"She doesn't know we're leaving, does she?" Dinah said.

"Dinah," he said, "I've been thinking on this—"

"What," Dinah said. "We're still going, aren't we?"

"I just don't know if this is a trip for two," he said.

"You said you didn't want to go alone," Dinah said. "You said it, not me."

"I know what I said."

"And what about the money? I've got so much saved."

He shook his head, silent. He led her to the camp fence. He crouched down, making a ladder rung of his fingers for her.

Dinah thought of Lilly getting up on Mickey's bike, and then she leaped over the fence and turned, making sure Mickey saw her. He thought Lilly was fearless. She'd show him fearless. She'd show him he couldn't leave without her. They ambled down toward the woods, and then she tumbled him to the ground. Mine, she thought, mine, mine, and then she branded him with her mouth.

"Mmm," he said, rolling on his back.

She tried to do the things Cherry had told her she did with her boyfriend, Harry Puccini, on the backseat of his father's car. Mickey sighed when Dinah undid his shirt buttons, when she stumbled over his fly, tugging down the zipper. He placed one hand on the back of her head, so gently she wanted to cry. She closed her eyes and tried to put his penis in her mouth. It felt cumbersome and rubbery, and for some reason she kept remembering this *Cosmopolitan* article on fellatio that kept using the adjective *velvety* to describe penises, but it didn't feel like that to her. Once his penis was there in her mouth, she wasn't really sure what she was supposed to do with it.

"Oh, God," he moaned.

She tried to retract her teeth. She let him do the moving, and when his hand gripped at her hair, she made herself be still, and then he flopped from her, spilling seed onto the grass, onto her. She scooted up the length of his body. She licked his stomach and stroked her initials over and over into his skin. Something's happened, she thought. Something's changed.

"Hey," she said. He stared dreamily at the sky hooded above them. She bit his shoulder, hoping to leave a mark. He laughed and tumbled her over to the ground and kissed her, so long and deep, she felt momentarily paralyzed.

"Oh, babe," he sang.

She wouldn't let him walk her home. She didn't want him seeing Lilly again, spoiling what she had done. He'd go home now and think of Dinah. He'd remember how she had held him right in her mouth.

She stopped him at University Street. He kissed her, and she felt desire pulling in her stomach. He walked away from her and then turned, watching her.

"What?" Dinah said.

"You're too good to me," he said. He walked over to her and cupped her face in his hands. He studied it, and then he kissed her and kissed her and kissed her again.

When she got home, Lilly was in the living room, staining an old cabinet someone had left in the house. She had on bright blue work gloves, and her hair was tied back with an old bandanna. She smiled at Dinah. "Mickey seems very nice," she said.

"Why wouldn't I have a nice boyfriend?" Dinah said, and left the room.

She took new note of Lilly. Lilly was wearing short cut-offs and a tight bare tank top. Her legs were long and pale. Her hair, pulled back, was still lush and shiny, and looking at it, Dinah felt wounded.

"What?" Lilly said, noticing her stare.

"You could get chemicals on your legs," Dinah said. "You should wear long pants."

"Oh," Lilly said, "I guess."

It didn't matter. After today Dinah had Mickey. He was going to Los Angeles, and she was going to go with him, and Lilly wasn't going to stop her.

The next morning, Mickey wasn't in school. She looked all morning for Mickey, and by noon, when she still couldn't find him, she began to worry. She used up all the change in the bottom of her purse calling his number from the school pay phone, worrying that he was sick or hurt or maybe even arrested for drugs. She worried so much, Cherry gave her a Valium that she had stolen from her mother, but all it did was blur the outlines of things. It was only third period, but Dinah couldn't wait. She walked out the front of the school, and then as soon as her feet hit the pavement, she ran to Mickey's house, banging on the door.

Annette opened the door, irritated. She stared at Dinah. "Who the hell are you?" she said.

"Dinah. Mickey's girlfriend," Dinah said, near tears.

Annette smirked. "Oh, really?" she said. "Mickey's girlfriend."

"Where's Mickey?" Dinah said.

"He left," Annette said. She flapped something in her hands, a piece of notepaper, a half of an envelope. Pencil scratched across blue paper. "California," she said with scorn.

"When?" Dinah said, her voice leaving her.

Annette looked at Dinah with hard new eyes. "You don't know?" she said.

Stunned, Dinah pivoted. He had left without her. He hadn't even said good-bye. She started running. She wasn't sure where she was going or what she would do, and all she could think of was getting the money she had and following him.

She ran home. She felt as if any moment she were about to throw up. She felt as if time had shortened and compressed. She dashed up toward the house when she saw Lilly in the backyard, talking to someone. Good. She wouldn't see Dinah leaving. Dinah wouldn't have to talk to her.

Dinah bounded up the stairs to her room and quickly gathered her money. One hundred and fifty dollars. She tucked it into the pocket of her skirt and raced downstairs and out the door. She tried to be quiet so Lilly wouldn't hear her. She glanced toward the side of the house to make sure Lilly wasn't in sight, and then she saw Mickey.

For a moment her heart soared. He's come for me, she thought, it's not too late, it's not. And then she saw Lilly come into view. They were talking. Mickey looked upset, and Lilly was gesturing. Shit, Dinah thought. Could Lilly have found out they were going to leave?

Dinah started toward Mickey, and then Mickey moved toward Lilly and kissed her, as softly as if a moth had brushed past Lilly's lips. Dinah stood frozen by the side of the house, for just one split second, before she pivoted and disappeared.

Dinah's heart was a small, hard, clenched fist. I don't need you, Dinah thought. Either of you.

As she walked along the road, cars beeped at her, a few voices catcalled, but she ignored them. Let them do whatever they wanted. Why did she need Mickey to be on her own? Why couldn't she go out and get a job as easily as he was going to? She could finish school, she could get her money and go on to college anywhere she pleased, and it didn't have to be in a place someone else had chosen for her. It could be where she really wanted to be herself.

A car beeped, and Dinah turned around slowly. A red convertible was slowing. A boy with shaggy blond hair grinned at her. You couldn't prevent some things from happening, but you could make other things happen instead. Maybe better things.

"Where to?" he said.

"New York City," Dinah said, and jumped in, brave and reckless, sliding across the red leather seat to her future.

chapter 13

It took Dinah twelve hours to get to New York City. The blond boy, whose name was Bob and who was a student at Princeton, had driven her as far as New Jersey. He was a bright, cheerful driver. His scattershot talk made her laugh, and he never once moved one inch from his seat toward her.

"Hungry?" he said, and she thought how polite he was, how considerate. Look for signs, Lilly had once told her— well, this was surely a sign that she had made the right decision.

They had stopped at a rest stop and were foraging through the food by one of the cash registers, crinkling the small plastic bags of chips, the waxy bags of cookies that were hard and stale to the touch. Dinah grabbed for some doughnuts.

"So," Bob said amiably, "you want to stop at a Best Western for the night?" His hand cupped a light crescent moon on the small of her back. "They've got nice rooms."

Dinah shook her head. "Come on," she said. He was too nice to push it. She wasn't really worried.

He smiled, unembarrassed. "No problem," he said. He undraped his arm from her shoulders and looked back at the cookies.

"Hang on a second," Dinah said, and pointed to the ladies' room. "I'll bust if I don't."

"I'm hanging," he said.

The ladies' room was clean and quiet. In the blurry mirror, her face loomed back at her, as foreign as a stranger's. She moved closer. If her face had changed completely, she wouldn't have been the least bit surprised, and she was a little disappointed to see that it hadn't.

She was in there only a few minutes, but when she came out, Bob was gone. He must be in the men's room, she reasoned. She gave him time, wandering around, in and out of the magazine store, in and out of the restaurant, waiting, expecting him to show up again with the same easy smile, the same loose invitations. She waited nearly a half hour, and then she finally walked out into the flat, hot parking lot and saw that his car was gone, too.

She couldn't allow herself to get discouraged or afraid. She sipped in a breath. She told herself it'd be easy enough to get another ride. All she had to do was stand by the exit and jab out a thumb. Look for signs, Lilly had once told her.

Sure enough, in three minutes a truck stopped, and she couldn't stop the grateful smile from blooming on her face. The driver was middle-aged, with a Phillies baseball cap tugged over his hair and cracked, blackened fingernails, and he made her sit in the back behind a curtained area.

"I'm not allowed passengers," he told her, "no matter how pretty they are." He didn't once touch her, even after she fell asleep, and when they reached New York he woke her gently.

"You got a place to stay, right?" he said. "You don't want to just be here alone."

"I'm meeting my sister," Dinah said.

"Okay," the man said, relieved. "You watch yourself."

Dinah leapt from the truck, stretching her legs. She felt

the heat of the pavement through her soles. The air smelled metallic, and the noise of the city was an assault.

People seemed to be thronging past her in packs, but she stood her ground. Every five seconds something snagged her attention. A flash of color. A snatch of sound. A face. Or simply the rustle and sweat of someone pushing roughly past. She was more exhilarated than afraid.

She wished Mickey could see her. She bet he'd love her now, in the middle of New York City and holding her own. She was his destiny, and he had been too stubborn and blind to see it. He'd regret the day he ever let his heart wander to Lilly. He'd regret the day he had ever left her.

She held up her hand for a cab as if she had been doing it forever. "The Village," she said with as much authority as she could muster.

The cabdriver nodded indifferently, and as she climbed in he slammed forward into traffic, sliding her across the vinyl seat. She stared out the window hungrily, feasting, enthralled. She had been here with her father. This was the place they should have stayed, the place they should have lived. Everything would have been different. A pain, small and hard and round as a nut, formed in her stomach, and she folded her arms over it.

"Village, lady," the cabdriver said, banging his horn, rounding a corner. "Where do you want to be left off?"

Dinah blinked. People were spilling out of an outdoor café, sprawled on chairs, smoking and laughing. Just to look at them made her feel instantly hopeful.

"Bleecker Street," she said.

The cab danced and swerved through traffic, tugging over to the side and peeling to a stop. Outside, a boy in black leather pants gestured.

"Five dollars," the driver said.

As soon as Dinah was out of the cab, the driver screeched away. She wandered over to a café and plunked down at one of the outdoor tables. She was glad she had worn black. She was glad she had grown her hair and had worn her best long silver earrings. She did something she had always wanted to do, order an iced espresso, and when it came she sipped her drink and watched the people. Even the waitress looked cool to her, dressed in a rubberized skirt that suctioned against her thighs when she moved, a diamond stud pin-pointed in her nose. Dinah studied the details, trying to memorize them. She waited, and when the waitress came back to ask if there was anything else she wanted, Dinah hesitated for only one minute.

"I could use a job," she admitted. "Do you need more waitresses?" She tried to appear casual. "I've got lots of experience," she lied.

"You know, I think they do," the waitress said. "Check back tomorrow when Frank's here. He's the manager. Big burly guy with a mustache. You ask him."

Dinah brightened. She had one hundred and fifty dollars in her purse. She could stay at the Y until she had enough for an apartment. How bad could it be? Anything was all right as long as you knew it was only temporary, as long as you felt it was a stepping-stone to something else. Already, in her mind, she saw her apartment. She wouldn't do it the way Lilly had done hers. No, hers would be filled with light and polished wood and painted a color, not just white. Hers would have a real kitchen, not just appliances lined up along the wall like stocky little foot soldiers.

She was polishing off the espresso, which was bitter and strong and which she refused to admit was anything but the most delicious thing she had ever tasted. She was thinking about the cheese snacks the boy had taken back in New Jersey, and was hungering for them, when a boy sat down opposite her, grinning expectantly. He had a long dark ponytail, and anyone could see he was ten times more handsome than Mickey, ten times smarter, too, she'd bet, and best of all he lived in New York City.

"Hi," Dinah said.

"Hi, yourself," he said, and he started talking immediately, unrolling his life story in such shotgun speech, she was sure she must be missing something. What she got was that his name was David and he lived on the Upper West Side with his divorced mother and his sister, Kate, who he claimed was a whore.

"She's got a real open-door policy, if you know what I mean," he said, and Dinah nodded sagely. He went to Dalton, and although everyone thought he would be a doctor like his father, what he really wanted to be was an actor. "I'm very, very good," he said, seriously.

"My name is Amy Fersten," Dinah lied, using the name of the prettiest girl at Pittsburgh High, a blonde who could go out with a different boy every day of the week if she wanted. He lifted one brow. "I live on the East Side."

"The Upper or the Village?" he said.

"Um, the Upper," Dinah said. "With my father."

David kicked out his feet and surveyed the crowd. "You like it up there?" he said, scrunching up his nose. "Isn't it a little—quiet? A little . . . um, clean?"

"I make plenty of noise," Dinah said. "And frankly, I'm a very dirty girl." She blushed. "Sloppy, I mean."

He laughed and stretched his arms up into the air. "Well, Amy, famey," he said, "you want to go to a party tonight? It's in my art teacher's loft. It'll be cool." He scratched his elbow, then lowered his arms back onto the table, narrowly missing a damp spot of spilled espresso. "Not that I'm asking you because I don't have a date, you understand."

"Of course not," Dinah said. She looked at him for a moment. She could go to the Y later and get her room, and if worse came to worst, if it was too late, she could spring for a room somewhere for one night. She looked at David. One hour in New York and a boy was asking her to a party.

She's brave, Mickey had once said about Lilly. His face had fired with admiration when he'd said it. He had focused beyond Dinah, seeing someone who wasn't there at all, ignoring the person who sat before him, imagining his kiss, yearning for it.

"Sure," Dinah said abruptly. "I'd love to go."

Dinah had never been to a loft in her life, but she didn't want this boy David to know it. She didn't want him to know that SoHo scared her a little because it was much emptier, because there seemed to be more alleyways and shadows. She kept thinking that if you didn't know this was New York City, if you didn't see anyone and you had just been plopped down, you might think you were lost in the worst tenement district in the world. One big crumbling downtown. That was what New York was like. The few people they passed glowered at her, except for a man with a green flowering branch strapped to his head and back who bowed deeply and then energetically asked them for money.

"Sorry, man," said David, but he gave the man a quarter.

"Mr. Kennedy," the man said, sneering. "Mr. Kennedy can afford a whole shiny quarter."

"Yeah, yeah," said David.

"I shoot you ass." The man sounded menacing, but he wobbled on his feet. He stayed back in the shadows.

David led Dinah down a side street, toward a dark, dirty building that had a sign on it that said "Ho Fat Noodles." "This is it," he said.

"Great," Dinah said, doubtfully.

He prodded one finger on a buzzer marked "Shorter," and a sudden garbled voice shouted something through the intercom.

"David!" David shouted, and the door suddenly buzzed open. The hallway was dark and smelled of cheese, and in front of them was a cavernous elevator. "After you," said David.

Lilly's brave, Dinah thought, and stepped into the elevator. David grinned at her and pulled the gate shut himself and prodded a button. The elevator stuttered and then rose up, and it seemed so rickety that she was stunned it didn't crash to the floor. It jerked to a stop; the door stumbled open.

"Cool, huh?" said David.

"Totally," said Dinah, forcing a smile.

"Right here," David said. There was another long hallway that smelled of cat.

Dinah could hear music. Loud and electronic, the bass pulsating. A large gray cat waddled around a corner, belly dragging, and Dinah sneezed. The door seemed to reverberate when she touched it.

He knocked on the door. The lock clicked four times, and then the door opened and a blast of sound assaulted Dinah.

There was one huge room, like a gym. People were dancing on a light wood floor, flailing their arms, pulsing like one living organism. There was lots of hair, lots of black, and Dinah saw, with a mixture of delight and dismay, lots of Siamese cats, too, all of them prowling around, mewling like babies, slyly approaching the silver dishes filled with cream that were scattered on the floor for them.

A man with a gray beard and a cat tucked under one arm grinned at David and Dinah. "Good taste," he said to David, winking at Dinah. "Mark DeVilbis," he said, wrapping one arm about Dinah. "Eat, drink, and be merry, but throw up on the Oriental and the rules are you have to clean it or we throw you to the cats." He laughed. "I don't know half the people here, isn't that funny? Lord knows how they got in."

Dinah laughed, but then his arm slid off and he was gone, lost in the party.

"Let's get wine," David said, leading her to a long wood table. She was starving. "It's all from Balducci's," David told her, and Dinah nodded, though she had no idea what he was talking about.

She picked at the roast meats, at the cold fish, and then took the wine David cupped in her hand. Below her, a cat snaked between her legs and she started so violently that she almost dropped her plate.

Dinah didn't remember how much she drank, only that she kept drinking. She danced with a wineglass in her hand, and every time she turned around, her glass seemed filled to the brim again. David talked to her nonstop while they danced, but she could hear only snatches of words above the music. Crummy rent. Bad vibes. Ace the course. Then, Pretty, she heard. Beautiful. Kiss you. Love you. She saw desire in his face. His features had gone soft and slack with wine, and when he leaned forward to kiss her, she leaned into his round, soft mouth. She parted her lips the way Mickey had taught her. She let her lids float shut.

"Mmmm," David said. "You are one delicious girl."

She thought she could dance forever. David held her to him tightly, and in her drunken haze she thought: What was to prevent the two of them living together, in a New York apartment, both going to school, both going out into the city every night? She imagined herself sending a postcard to Mickey, something showing the whole panorama of New York. David and I can see the city from our front window, she'd write. She rested her head against his shoulder. I'm a brave girl who takes chances, she thought. I'm braver than Lilly.

She was so drunk, she didn't really know when she lost David. She was dancing with a stranger, a boy with short black hair and a scruffy beard, and when she turned she saw David with his arms wrapped about a small redheaded girl, kissing her earnestly. She turned and the boy with the beard was gone, replaced with a blond. Dinah smiled. She whipped her hair around.

"I'm psychic," she told the boy, who winked at her.

"Psychotic?" he said.

"No, *psychic*," she said. He laughed and pointed to his ears, shaking his head. She fluted up the edges of her skirt with her fingertips and swung on the music.

She didn't know how long she had been dancing. She was still heady with wine, feverish from the music. The party had thickened. She had no idea where David was anymore, but she didn't really care. Being popular in New York was better than being popular in Pittsburgh. And each boy was a new victory over Mickey. She danced four dances in a row with a boy with a spiky haircut and a gold earring.

"Gregory," he said, thudding his chest like Tarzan, making her laugh.

"Who do you know here?" she shouted over the din, but he just laughed and shrugged. He danced so fluidly that Dinah felt left behind, and when he asked her if she'd like to see the stars from the roof, she said yes.

She climbed the stairs, four long flights, to the roof, behind Gregory, and behind her three other boys climbed.

"Hey," said one, grinning, when she turned around. He was wearing a blue-and-red-striped jersey safety-pinned at the shoulder.

"Hey yourself," she said. "We've got company," she said to Gregory.

"The more the merrier," he called back.

Gregory tugged her up. The other boys followed. They were all in jeans and T-shirts the color of rotting fruit. Dinah grinned at them, the center of attention. "Look, Orion!" she called, stretching toward the smattering of stars, but they were looking at her.

"This is Mack, Henry, and Paul," Gregory said.

"I'm John," said one boy.

"John," said Gregory. "Right. Sorry."

The roof was just a small tarry square with a beat-up-looking green chaise lounge in the corner. It was gated completely in chipping black iron, a low barrier that came just to her knees. Below, the city sparkled so much, she was surprised it didn't spontaneously combust. Dazzled, she leaned carefully toward the edge.

"Spit down," suggested Mack, who showed a chipped front tooth when he spoke.

"Okay," Dinah said, spitting a delicate thread of silver. The boys clapped.

Gregory closed the door to the downstairs. "Welcome to Tar Beach," he said. "So let's dance." He pushed up his sleeves, showing a small tattoo of a dove on his forearm.

"Hey," Dinah said, touching it.

He flinched back, surprised. "Come on, buttercup, dance with me," he said.

"There's no music," Dinah said, laughing, but he swung her about, passing her from boy to boy, all of them smiling at her, all of them glad to see her. Mack, Henry, John, Gregory. She wanted to remember, to tell Mickey. The night was clear and cold on her skin, and she never felt so popular or so pretty, she never felt so alive. She looked at John, who smiled shyly at her, who had wide blue eyes like chips of ocean.

Gregory slowed her dancing, swaying her against him. "You're not from here, are you?" he said.

"Of course I am," said Dinah. "Born and bred."

"Yeah?" he said. "Where's Twenty-second Street and Forty-fourth Avenue?"

"West of here," Dinah said.

"Hah. No such thing."

"Where's Clyde Street?" said Paul.

"Uptown," Dinah whispered. She felt her chest tightening. Henry touched the edge of her skirt, lifting it up a little.

Henry made a bonging sound. He hit an imaginary drum. "Wrong," he boomed.

"You look fifteen," Gregory said.

"You're wrong," Dinah lied. "I'm eighteen."

"Yeah, so's my mother," said Henry.

Nobody was dancing anymore. Gregory let her go and they formed a semicircle around her, waiting, poised.

"How old are you?" Dinah blurted.

Gregory laughed. "Eighteen," he said.

"So's his mother," said Henry.

"Let's go back to the party," Dinah said. She turned toward the door, but Gregory spun her to him.

"You're a runaway, aren't you?" he said, and then he bent to kiss her. His mouth tasted like metal.

She was drunk. She pulled back, laughing, when he tickled her ribs. And then she saw the knife shining in his hands, the other three boys hard and steady beside him.

"They'll hear you," she whispered.

"Oh, I don't think so," Gregory said pleasantly. "It's pretty noisy there. People are too blasted on coke to hear anything. And anyway, we're four flights up. Don't you remember the climb?"

"I came with David," she said.

"David who? You see any David?" He grinned. "David!" he called. His voice bounced and echoed back to him.

"Yo, David!" shouted Mack. He whipped his head around, so a spray of hair covered his features.

"Davy boy!" called John.

Henry, the one with the safety-pinned shirt, came forward and touched Dinah's throat. "Aren't you warm?" he said. "Don't you want to take off that hot shirt?"

Dinah panicked. She tried to turn. "No, come on—"

"Where to?" said Gregory, only now his voice didn't sound like his at all, now she was frightened.

He reached forward casually and, holding up the knife in his right hand, undid the top button of her shirt, and then he touched her, at the base of her throat, so gently that the hurt was unimaginable. She jerked back, and slowly, deliberately, he cut a button from her shirt. He tossed it in the air and snapped his fingers back around it.

She couldn't catch her breath. She couldn't see straight. She kept thinking that maybe with all the wine in her, she was misinterpreting. Maybe this was all a mirage. Maybe a million things, and then Mack stepped slowly toward her and Dinah swung one arm at him. He caught it neatly.

"Strong," he said admiringly, gripping her arm so tightly, the flesh turned white and bloodless.

She didn't know why, but she suddenly thought of Lilly showing her how fake psychics go into trance. "It's a real showstopper," Lilly had said. Dinah had never once seen Lilly in a real trance, but Lilly had shown her a fake one, and the memory flung itself forward in her mind. Dinah rolled her eyes into her head so the white showed. "Uhhhh," she moaned, making her voice guttural. Her heart was speeding a million miles an hour, but she flopped from Mack's grip onto the dirty rooftop. She made fish movements along the gritty floor, banging her feet on the roof, her lids fluttering crazily. She growled and tore at her skirt. She kept Lilly's face hard and clear in her mind.

"Shit! She's having a fit!" cried John.

"No, she isn't," Gregory said doubtfully. He bent down to Dinah, who thrashed on the ground, who foamed saliva.

Henry tugged at Gregory. "Fuck this shit," he said.

Gregory leaned down, so close to Dinah, she could feel the heat of his breath, stinging with alcohol. He reached down and put his hand up under her skirt, and in sudden terror she felt her bladder let go. She drew up her legs.

"Ah, *shit*," Gregory said in disgust. He flapped his damp hand. "Fucking shit."

Dinah felt a warm pool of urine washing below her.

"I'm out of here," said John. She heard his steps retreating. "I'm not that hard up."

"I'm gone," said a voice.

A finger prodded against Dinah's side, and she whirled, turning into the dampness, drawing her knees up against her chest, shutting her eyes so tightly that she saw smears of light.

"Nothing happened," said a voice to her.

Above her, Gregory loomed. He pointed the knife at Dinah. She shut her eyes, bracing for the knife. Here it comes. Here comes pain, she thought. Searing hot, a punch to the heart. She clenched her body. The world seemed to have gone white. She waited, and then she heard the door being jammed back open. She heard their voices, running down, softening into silence, and then the door banged shut behind them.

Dinah lay balled up on the roof, afraid to move. How much smaller could she make herself? How much more could she disappear? The back of her skirt was soaking wet. Her shirt was pasted to her back with sweat. She felt that if she sat up, she would vomit all over herself. She strained, but she couldn't hear a sound. Finally she struggled up, too terrified to cry. She patted her body, the small black purse she carried. She'd get up. She'd walk outside as though this were the most normal day in the world, and she'd find a Y. It hadn't happened. None of it. She'd forget.

Lilly's trance had saved her. Lilly, who was probably riding on the back of a bike, her arms looped about the person Dinah loved best in the world; Lilly, who might be lolling on a hotel bed somewhere, so brave she had run off with a boy half her age, a boy who probably wouldn't die for a long, long while after she would.

Dinah went to the door and tried to yank it open. It stuck. She pulled again, and when it still wouldn't budge, she banged her hands on it.

"Hey!" she screamed. "Open the door!"

She pressed her ear to the door. She could hear a humming, maybe vibrations from the party. She went to the edge of the rooftop. The windows in the other apartments were shut tight, covered with shades or blinds or in one case a heavy piece of cardboard. It was too high up for anyone to see her. She slunk down along the door, balling herself up, smaller and smaller, and then, helplessly, she started to cry.

A half hour before Dinah had left Pittsburgh for New York, Lilly had been gardening. She was working hard, humming, crouched down in the dirt, when she felt a shadow across her. She looked up and saw Mickey. He was wearing a leather jacket, and he had a heavy pack over his shoulder.

"I'm leaving," he said. "I'm going to California."

Lilly stood up, dirt dusted along her legs.

He stooped and picked up a flat stone from her garden, toying with it before he put it in his shirt pocket. "I came to say good-bye," he said.

"Good-bye? Dinah didn't tell me you were leaving."

"Listen—I know—can you tell Dinah . . ."

Lilly looked at him with amazement. "Tell Dinah—?" she said. "She loves you," she said. "You can't just disappear without saying good-bye."

Mickey hesitated. "I'm not doing anything to anyone," he said. "I just have to leave, that's all." He fumbled before her. "Listen," he said suddenly. "You said you wanted to just go someplace, to start fresh. You said you understood that."

"Everybody wants that," Lilly said.

He shifted weight, watching her. "So," he said, "do you want a lift?"

Lilly didn't say anything. She was thinking about Dinah, remembering the time she had come home and found the two of them together in bed. How serene Dinah had been, as if Mickey were a blanket she had wrapped protectively about her to ward off any chills. "Don't you do this," she said.

And then Mickey leaned forward and kissed her, and Lilly moved back as if he had struck her. "You write her," she said. "You let her know." And then Mickey was gone.

By midnight Dinah wasn't home, and Lilly panicked. She called Grace and Cherry and every one of Dinah's friends she could remember. She called the police. "Kids are always doing this sort of thing," an officer soothed her. "Let's give it forty-eight hours. You'll see. She'll be back."

"Forty-eight hours!" Lilly pleaded.

She didn't know what to do. She sat in Dinah's room and shut her eyes and willed herself to see where Dinah was.

She used to be able to find people. She used to be able to talk to the dead. Her mind tightened. She saw nothing. She was about to grab her jacket to run out and find Dinah herself, and then the phone rang and she jumped up, terrified. It rang again, and she picked it up. "Yes?" she whispered.

"Lilly Bloom?" said a voice. "This is the New York City police."

Lilly was stunned that Dinah was in New York City. She was terrified to go back there, terrified of how she would feel as soon as she was back in her past.

As soon as she landed in New York City, she felt ill. She stopped at a pay phone and called Robert, hoping a familiar voice might anchor her, but his line rang and rang and didn't catch, and finally she just hung up.

Every familiar thing hurt her. The smells of the city. The mixed grill vendors selling meats everyone suspected were stray cats. Hot dogs. Potatoes pronged open and slathered with butter for just two dollars. The noise. Shouts and cries and the clip of shoes on the pavement.

She couldn't get a cab. Traffic snarled and raced around her. She jabbed her hand up to hail one, and someone slapped her from the back, startling her, but when she turned around there was no one and the cab was gone.

She looked for a subway. But when she passed a subway station, the sign said A, E, and C. The C train? What was the C train? She felt a kind of dull panic. People were pouring out of the station.

"Delays," a woman in a fur coat snapped at Lilly, as if it were Lilly's fault.

Lilly walked. She was at Twenty-fourth Street. She could walk to Fourteenth in ten minutes and try to get a cab along the way. Briskly, she strode into the sea of people. She used to walk as fast as anybody here, but now it took some getting used to. She still knew the grid, but she couldn't remember the named streets. Was Bethune off Hudson? Worse, she had to ask directions of a young, cocky kid in a baseball cap and baggy jeans who looked at her disdainfully and then, abruptly, grinned. "You need a Hundred and Twenty-fifth Street," he assured her, pointing to the subway.

"Hey," Lilly said, annoyed. "I don't need Harlem."

He snickered and spit on the street with prideful disdain, then strode away from her, still laughing.

She passed through her old neighborhood. She walked past her old building and looked up. The window of her apartment was open, and a pretty young woman in a business suit was putting on makeup in the light. A yellow cat prowled in the crook of her arm. The fire escape, where she had once sat drinking wine with Matt, was now covered with potted flowering plants. Something had happened, everything had changed, and it wasn't her home anymore. She glanced across the street. Johnny Jerkoff's window was shut and cleaned. New white lace curtains were hanging there, a plant, green and leafy, showing through. Gone. Everything gone. The people, the places, and her life here, too. She turned, striding out of the neighborhood, and then, at the corner, she saw a cab.

She knew this police station. She had walked by it a million times when she'd lived here, on her way to a friend's, on her way to dinner with Robert, on her way to the life she was living, but she had never once been inside. All those years in New York and never mugged or robbed or hurt. As protected as if she had had her own guardian angel. She walked in, explained herself at the long front desk. A woman officer frowned.

"Oh, yeah," she said. "I'll take you." She thrust out her hand. "Debra Kent," she said.

Debra told Lilly that the police had found Dinah by accident. They had been responding to complaints about noise from a party and hadn't even noticed Dinah at first, not until Richard Corrigan, one of the officers, went up to the roof to check things out. He was looking for drugs. He was looking for just about anything but a thin young girl cowering in a corner. The girl was terrified, and she screamed and screamed the minute he tried to pull her from the edge of the roof. She shrieked, scrabbling away from him, veering dangerously toward the edge again.

"It's okay," he soothed.

He moved closer to her. Her dress was torn, and she looked pretty banged up. She reeked of alcohol, but her eyes were clear of drugs. She was so slight, he thought how easy it would have been for her to fall. He had a bad feeling about what might have gone on up here.

"Come on," he whispered, and then he had his arms about her. She had struggled and then had suddenly gone rag limp, almost in a trance.

"He tried to hurt me," she said in a small voice, and then she went mute, frozen in shock.

They brought her to the station, and the whole way down in the patrol car she had sat in the back, and every time one of the officers had so much as looked at her, she had shut her eyes.

They had given her hot coffee and had gently taken her wallet, with only her name scribbled inside it on a Pittsburgh Library Card, which at least was a start.

Debra talked to her. She was good with girls. She handled the rape cases, the beatings, and at least once every Christmas a card came for her from one of the people she had helped. Debra Kent sat Dinah down and fed her hot tea and chocolate from the vending machine and tried to get a statement from her.

Dinah, weeping, told her story in a loop, from beginning to end and then back to the beginning. She felt the hard cold roof against her back. She felt his hands grappling under her skirt, thrust up under her panties. Stop, she told herself, but the image loomed, so real she could smell him on top of her. Stop. Stop. Stop.

"I told him to stop!" she cried.

"Who?" Debra Kent said.

"He had a knife!" Dinah said.

Debra Kent was silent for a moment. "Listen," she said. "Can you give me the name of someone I can call for you?"

"David," Dinah said, weeping.

"David who?" Debra Kent asked gently.

"Mickey," said Dinah.

Debra Kent waited. "What's his number?" she said. "Who can we call for you?" she asked. "Just give me one name. Or give me your name."

"I want my father!" Dinah cried.

Debra Kent touched Dinah's arm. "I'll call him," she said. "All you have to do is give me his name and the number."

And then Dinah screamed and screamed so hard and so loud, another officer slammed into the room, his hand poised on his gun.

"We left her alone for a while," Debra said, pushing open a door and leading Lilly through it. "Then she gave your name and number, so we called you."

Inside the room, Dinah was sitting at a table, her head in her arms. "Hey," Lilly said.

Dinah looked up. "Lilly?" she said.

"I'll be just outside," Debra said, nodding at Dinah, then leaving the room.

"I've been looking all over for you."

"You don't have to be responsible for me," Dinah said, her voice flattening. "You didn't have to come here."

"What are you talking about?" Lilly said.

Dinah stared at her, her mouth rigid.

Lilly had started to move toward a battered leather chair when Dinah's hand shot out and gripped Lilly's wrist. Lilly felt stunned. She could feel both their pulses, storming up through their hands. "It's okay," she said. "I'm not going any-where."

Lilly sat beside Dinah the whole time Dinah gave her statement. And then Lilly quietly took Debra Kent aside.

"What happens now?" she asked Debra Kent.

Debra shrugged. "Nothing. Chances are we won't find those boys. The best thing to do is take her home."

Lilly took Dinah to a small hotel off Central Park. The whole time Dinah wouldn't look at her, and Lilly thought, She's in shock, that's all.

Dinah sat on the edge of the bed, fingering the cover, her eyes dark and hostile, and for a moment Lilly felt an old flicker of rage.

"Do you want something to eat?" she said. "Do you want to talk about any of it?"

"No."

"Do you want me to draw you a bath?"

"No."

Exasperated, Lilly stood up. "Do you want to be alone?"

"Isn't that what I am?" Dinah said. "Wasn't that your whole idea right from the beginning?"

"What's the matter with you?"

"What's the matter with you? Don't you think it's sick, going after someone half your age? You get a kick out of that? You get a real thrill?"

"What?" said Lilly. "What?" She shook her head. "Why did you leave?"

"I saw you with Mickey," Dinah spat. "You kissed."

Lilly sat down on the bed opposite Dinah. "He kissed me on impulse. It didn't mean a thing," she said. "I told him to tell you he was leaving."

Dinah stood up. "I knew he was leaving," she said. "I just didn't know he was leaving without me." She looked at Lilly. "Why didn't you go with him? You wanted to, didn't you? You kissed him, didn't you?"

"What's the matter with you?" Lilly said. "You think I'd go after your boyfriend? You think I'm like that?"

"It would have made things easier all around if you had

gone. You wouldn't have had to wait for my trust money. You wouldn't have had to stay. You think I need you, you're crazy." Dinah flung the pillow off the bed. "I don't need either of you. I don't need anyone. I'm fine right here by myself."

"If I had left, do you know what would have happened to you?" Lilly said, her voice hardening. "You would have become a ward of the state."

"I wish you had never met my boyfriend," Dinah said. "I wish you had never met my father. Everything would have been fine without your weaseling in where you're not wanted. You should have just left us all alone!"

"How is this my fault?" Lilly said.

"You came between us!" Dinah shouted. "You made it so I was shut out!"

"We were going to be *family*," Lilly said. "How is that shutting you out?"

"Don't tell me what we were going to have because I saw what we had," Dinah said. "I saw all right." She bent and grabbed for her purse, which upended onto the floor, spilling change and Kleenex and a wand of mascara. She fumbled for a cigarette at the bottom, and it crumbled into pieces in her hand. "I'd say something to my father and he suddenly wouldn't hear me. I'd touch him and he'd turn to you. I didn't have five minutes with him because of *you*."

"I was trying to include you—"

"Yeah, right, sure you were. I wasn't included in deciding to go to a goddamned lake. That was your idea, not mine. My idea was to stay in the city. And nothing would have happened if we had."

Lilly decided she was too angry to speak. If she even looked at Dinah, she thought she might strike her.

"It's your fault!" Dinah suddenly screamed. She started jamming things back into her purse. "It's all your fault! If it wasn't for you, my father would be alive!" She wouldn't look at Lilly. She jumped up and began searching frantically for her jacket. She tugged it on and had yanked the door open when, furious, Lilly grabbed her, slamming the door shut again. The sound reverberated through Lilly.

"Did I make him go on that rope swing?" Lilly screamed.

Dinah shrieked. "You made him go to the lake!"

"Did I push him?" Lilly shouted.

As soon as she said it, she went still. She felt as if a layer had been ripped from the air, thinning it, making it dangerous. Something seemed to move above her, coiled there, waiting. And then Dinah stopped screaming, and through the silence Lilly heard knocking against the wall, a muffled complaining voice from another guest. Dinah pressed against the wall and slowly rolled down to the floor.

Dinah lifted her head. She looked all of twelve, terrified and young and totally alone, and Lilly felt her anger burning down toward shame. "I didn't mean it," she said. "Not what I said, I didn't mean it."

Dinah looked up at her. "Yes, you did," she said. "But you can't hate me half as much as I hate myself."

"No, no, listen," Lilly said.

"I didn't mean anything to happen." She started to cry. "I loved him. He was my father." She swiped her hands across her face, smearing her mascara with her tears. "You had him all to yourself. Why couldn't I have him, just for a while?"

"This wasn't a contest," Lilly said.

"Yes, it was," Dinah said. She sobbed into her hands. "When do I get to be forgiven? I can say I'm sorry until the year three thousand, and it won't change anything. I can't change what I did. I can't bring him back. And you hate me for it."

Lilly felt everything in her body moving in slow motion. She could never remember ever feeling so tired or so heavy. She looked over at Dinah. "I can't bring him back, either," she said quietly. "And I can't forgive myself for it."

"You blame yourself?" Dinah said, stunned. She wiped her nose along her sleeve.

"I was the one who was supposed to see the future, wasn't I?" Lilly said.

"No one believed you could do that," Dinah whispered.

"I was the one who was supposed to talk to the dead."

Lilly thought she was laughing at how ridiculous her words sounded. The noise she was making felt that way, stuttering up through her throat, the effort of it making her shoulders dance. She sank to the floor, exhausted. She couldn't move, and then she felt something. Dinah's hand on her damp face.

Lilly's eyes kept pooling, her nose ran, but she let them. She felt Dinah sitting close, but it was a long time before either one of them said anything.

"My father carried this one picture of you in his shirt pocket all the time," Dinah said. Her voice, thick from tears, was a surprise in the silence. "It was a crummy shot. It looked like this cartoon to me. It might have been the Mona Lisa the way he carried on. I put the shirt in the wash by mistake one day," Dinah said. She looked at Lilly. "All right, it wasn't by mistake. The bleach faded the features right from your face, and I was glad. But you know what? He still carried the picture. He never asked me if I did it on purpose. He just kept looking at that picture."

"Really?" Lilly said, half smiling. "He did?"

Dinah shrugged and glanced away.

Lilly looked at her. "I know about the day you were born," she said, and Dinah met her gaze again. "Matt told me. He said your mother had been drugged so heavily during delivery that you had been born drugged, too. You were a groggy infant. You didn't cry once. You just kind of whimpered when you were hungry or wet. It worried Matt, no matter how the doctor reassured him. He took off work and stayed by your crib for nearly two weeks, just watching you. The first time you really cried, when a diaper pin pricked you, he started crying himself, he was so happy." Lilly wiped at her eyes.

"Your mother came home and found the two of you, crying in a chorus."

"He told you that story?" Dinah said.

"He told me thousands of stories about you," Lilly said.

"Tell me another one," Dinah whispered.

So Lilly told story after story that she could remember, stopping only when Dinah remembered a story about Matt that she wanted Lilly to hear. Dinah and Lilly sat against the wall, not touching, not moving, haltingly giving pieces of Matt's history back to each other, like gifts, filling in the places the other might be missing, telling Matt's life, making it real again, until morning.

Before they left, Dinah asked to ride the Staten Island ferry. "I always wanted to," she said.

The ferry was crowded with people, with tourists, their necks ringed with expensive cameras, and with a few bad guitar players, huckstering quarters. Dinah leaned along the railing while Lilly sat, watching her. They rode it back and forth twice, the breeze skipping back their hair.

They ate in SoHo. They wandered Bloomingdale's. In housewares Lilly suddenly began missing her Pittsburgh house. She thought of the floors she had just sanded. She smelled the flowers that she had planted in the backyard, that she had tended the way her father had once shown her. She couldn't believe she was homesick for a place she had never stopped to consider home, but it made her suddenly feel cheerful.

"Wait a minute," she told Dinah, and she bought a small blue rug that would set off the wood. She bought a ceramic watering can, and she suddenly considered both purchases pure acts of faith.

And before they left they went to Lilly's old café. It looked exactly the same, except there was a new reader in the back, a young, pale blond man who was flipping a quarter through his fingers and ignoring everyone.

She and Dinah sat and had tea and thick, sugary cakes, and the whole time Lilly half expected an old client to appear and recognize her, or the owner to drop by, but no one ever did. She finished her tea and stood up, and then the blond man suddenly noticed them.

"Hey," he said. "How's about I tell you two pretty ladies' fortunes?" He grinned. "Five dollars," he said.

Lilly said, "Oh, I don't think—"

"Come on, what are you afraid of?" He grinned again.

"Fine," Lilly said, and sat down.

He spread out the cards. It didn't take Lilly more than ten seconds to realize he didn't know what he was doing.

"Ah," he said. "I can see this is the best year of your lives." He looked up and winked at Lilly. "You're pregnant, aren't you?" he said.

Dinah started laughing, her shoulders crumpling.

Lilly stood up, helping Dinah, who was having paroxysms. "We have to go," Lilly said apologetically. She put down a ten.

"Wait, don't you want to know more?" he said.

"We know enough," Lilly said.

Outside on the street, they were both weak with laughter. Lilly was shaking. She felt wrung out. They held on to each other.

"The best year of our lives!" Dinah said, screaming with laughter.

"Pregnant!" Lilly laughed.

Dinah turned to Lilly. Her mouth tensed. "Listen," she said, halting. "I had a good time today."

"So did I," said Lilly.

Dinah waited for a moment. "We should have all done this, that day," she said.

"Well," Lilly said. "We're doing it now."

* * *

They went back to Pittsburgh that evening. Neither one of them talked about what might happen next, and as soon as they got home all they both wanted to do was sleep.

"Why don't we just camp out in the living room together tonight?" Lilly said. Dinah nodded.

They brought out blankets and pillows, and Lilly brought out tissues, too, although that night neither one of them used any. They made separate beds next to each other, and in the morning Lilly began to dream. Matt was sleeping beside her, spooned against her for warmth. She woke with a start and turned, rousing up from her dream, her heart jumpy with excitement, and there was Dinah, sleeping beside her, one arm thrown over Lilly's hip.

Lilly watched her for a minute. She pulled the blanket around Dinah's thin shoulders, and then she turned back around and slept herself.

Dinah now came and sat at the table and ate breakfast with Lilly, and Lilly found herself happier with some company. And one night, when Lilly had to do inventory at the card store, she came home at midnight, tense and irritable because none of the cards had been in the right slots, and Dinah had a cold dinner waiting for her. She had a tablecloth on the table, and two blue candles in silver holders, and she had poured wine for the two of them. She blushed at Lilly's surprised pleasure.

"I thought you'd be hungry, that's all," she said. "I remember Dell taking inventory, and I know what a drag it is."

The day before Dinah went back to school, she went to Mickey's. She wasn't sure what she wanted, if she expected to find him home again, or if she might run into Annette and hear news. She was halfway down his block when she heard Ricky barking, and then, from a distance, she saw the dog chained in the yard, licking repeatedly at his hind leg.

"He didn't take you, either," Dinah said.

She came closer, and the dog gave her a halfhearted

growl, and she saw that the leg he was licking looked infected. "You poor boy," she said.

She thought of her father. Let animals get your scent, see what you're about, he used to tell her. She held out her hand, and the dog sniffed at her tentatively. She was holding her hand out that way when Annette came out, her hands on her hips. Dinah looked up.

"He left that stupid mutt," Annette said.

"His leg's infected," Dinah said.

"He's licking it. That cures it."

"No, it doesn't," Dinah said.

The dog whined at the leash. "You hear from him?" Annette said, and when Dinah kept on looking at the dog, Annette shrugged and folded her arms about her. "Neither do I," she said.

"I can fix his leg up," Dinah said.

"Take him," Annette said. "What do I care."

Ricky was suspicious of Dinah. He growled at her when she put on the collar, and he snapped when she tried to wipe off his muddy paws. "Come on, you old abandoned boy," she said, and half led, half tugged him home.

She brought him in the house, and in the medicine cabinet she found the cotton and the antiseptic, and if the dog struggled, he at least looked at her with some trust. She made a dressing the way her father had shown her. She wrapped the bandage so the dog couldn't chew it off easily. She couldn't help it, every time she looked at it, she felt pride.

When Lilly came home from work, Dinah was on the porch, the dog sitting beside her. Lilly stopped short, confused.

"Mickey left him," Dinah said. "His mother didn't know what to do with him, and I saw his leg was infected. I fixed it up." She looped one arm about the dog. "I'll figure out what to do with him," she said finally.

Lilly resettled her purse and opened the front door. "Come on inside," she said. "Both of you."

Dinah spent a week at home before she went back to school. All anyone at school knew was that Mickey had disappeared, and Dinah shortly after, and nobody knew why, though they spent lots of lunch hours and class time conjecturing what was going on, plotting out dramas so inventive that even Dinah would have been impressed. Mickey had dumped Dinah, and feverish with grief, she had gotten herself sick. Dinah had dumped Mickey, gotten sick anyway, and Mickey had left. The two of them had run off and gotten married in the Elvis Chapel in Las Vegas.

Kids looked at her with openly curious faces. Boys were drawn to her pale, translucent skin, to the wildness and misery in her eyes.

"So, where's Mickey?" asked the boy who sat in back of her in homeroom.

Dinah was too exhausted to tell any sort of truth. "Where'd you think?" she said finally.

He was silent a minute, and then he shrugged. "Well," he said as if that explained anything.

She let people make up the story. She went along with whatever detail they came up with. When Anna Solarkin said that she had heard Mickey was in Europe, Dinah shrugged.

"Why didn't you go with him?" Anna said.

"I have his dog," Dinah said.

"I would have gone," Anna said emphatically, twisting back her heavily moussed bangs. "Machine-gun hoods couldn't have kept me away." She looked at Dinah. "You sure are brave to let him go without you."

Dinah lifted her chin. "You think so?" she said. "You think I'm brave?" She was thinking of a narrow New York City rooftop, of feeling so cold that it seemed her bones had turned to ice. She was thinking of how easy it was to switch gears from dancing on waves of music to shivering on a soaked roof floor. From a pirouette that was as crisp and sharp as a new knife blade pointed at your throat, as terrifying as trust. It was a story she'd never, in her whole life, tell another person and a story she'd never be able to forget.

"The bravest," Anna said emphatically.

chapter 14

Dell knew it was sinful, but sometimes she imagined herself dead. She lay in bed and thought about death, following the skip and slow of her heartbeat as if it were a destination.

When Matt had first told her that Lilly talked to the dead, she had laughed because she had thought he was joking. "Come on, what does she really do?" Dell had insisted.

"She's clairvoyant," Matt had said quietly.

This time Dell had hooted. "Now I've heard everything," she'd said.

She had promised to be on her best behavior when she met Lilly, although she told Matt she was going to ask Lilly how Aunt Bess, who had been dead for years and had believed that the moon landing was a Hollywood scam, was doing.

"Stop," he'd said patiently.

"You believe what she's doing?" Dell had said.

"It doesn't matter," he'd said. "I love her."

Dell had never changed her mind about Lilly. She had never once seen Lilly perform any miracles or know any sort of thing that anyone paying attention might know, too.

After Matt died, Lilly had sat opposite her, crying so softly, Dell barely heard her. "I can't reach him," she'd whispered to Dell, lowering her head, shamed, as though she'd been confessing a mortal sin.

"No one expects you to," Dell had said. She'd kept thinking that Lilly might as well have wished to sprout wings on her back.

"I'm so sorry," Lilly had repeated.

"There's nothing to be sorry about," Dell had told her, but even then she'd known she was lying to Lilly. The world was full of things to be sorry about. She herself was sorry about being cheated out of a husband and never having been able to relax enough to go out and find another. She was sorry that she hadn't raised Matt right, sorry that she had somehow made it so that her own granddaughter was afraid of her, sorry that Lilly couldn't wait to leave.

She had never really believed in anything. From the time she was five she'd known there was no such thing as Santa Claus or fairies or ghosts in the night, and nothing she had seen since had convinced her otherwise. Not family. Not any rabbi or priest. Not Lilly. Not the dead. Not until the day she had looked up from her bed and there had been Matt, no longer dead and no longer alive, either, and no matter how much she questioned him, he'd never get to be anything she'd ever get to understand until she was probably dead, too, and had reached the place he inhabited.

She knew her illness made her old. Her sight was failing. She used to be able to tell if a shoe was real leather or polyurethane from twenty feet away, but now sometimes it didn't matter whether she put on her glasses or not anymore. Everything smudged in front of her. Her skin was so fine and thin, it pleated across her bones. And her hair, once so strong you could have lassoed horses with it, was now as dry and fragile as house dust.

But as soon as she was with Matt, something happened. She felt a current of electricity spark through her veins. Her blood fired. Her heart beat as strong and as regular as a brand-new metronome. And sometimes when she was talking to

Matt, when he moved around in front of the mirror, just for a moment, behind him, her reflection shimmered back to her—a young girl.

But it wasn't just she who changed age. Matt confused and startled her with each new appearance. Sometimes he showed up and he was five, in dirty dungarees and sneakers. Sometimes he was a full-grown man, in his white lab coat, his name on a plastic pin. He was fifteen and eight and thirty-five, shuffling his ages as casually as a deck of cards.

"Matty," she said to him, sighing. She didn't care. She felt that each age of his was a chance for her to make amends, to do the things she should have done when he was flesh and blood.

When he showed up as a boy, she told him stories she remembered her own mother telling her, gesturing with her hands until he leaned forward on the bed, mesmerized. She patiently taught him his ABCs, singing the ABC song over and over until he could sing it with her, his high, clear voice belling out. When he showed up an anxious and surly teenager, she told him how handsome he looked. She listened when he talked about girls and grades and pimples. I'm a good mother, she told herself. She gleamed.

When he came as an adult, she asked him the difficult questions, she wanted the explanations. "Tell me about death," she said to him. "So is there really that column of light they write about? Do you see God?"

He laughed. "It's just death," he said, but he winked at her conspiratorially.

"When I die, will we be together?" she asked.

"Well, differently," he said, "and don't ask me how because you won't understand."

"You think your mother's stupid," she said, offended.

"It has nothing to do with being stupid, it has to do with being alive," he said impatiently, and she let it drop.

It was funny how elastic a thing the human heart was, how it could make room for one more, always one more. She had never in her whole life thought she could love another soul except for her husband. For years after she'd found out Hank had died, she'd trained her mind to remember only the good years, to stop herself when she stumbled over memories that were soft and painful, pulpy with grief. Hank loved me, she told herself. She remembered the long nights in bed, the two of them rolling and tumbling, so greedy for each other they couldn't stop touching and tasting; they couldn't sleep. She remembered working in the shop beside him because she couldn't stand to be more than a foot away from him. Even his smell could drive her crazy. She remembered his feet. Long and even toes, the nails perfectly trimmed because feet were his life.

She even remembered the first letters he had sent her from the war. "I love you," he'd written. She could trace the letters in the air. I love you. So what if there were later, bad memories? Who knew what had really happened? Who knew what had gone on in Hank's heart of hearts that he couldn't go back to his wife, who waited and subsisted on dreams? For years she had thought Hank was her one great love, but he wasn't the one who came to visit her, was he. She hadn't given much thought to Matt except as a burden holding her down, a bitter reminder of how she had failed, right up until the moment Matt had died and she had realized how much he meant to her.

Dell knew old age was a kind of flowering of her life. She knew things she hadn't known before. That time was elastic. That love could stretch. A lot of her senses were fading, but still she knew the important things. She knew without even looking when Dinah was right outside her window. She knew when Lilly was about to ring the front doorbell. And she knew that the time her son spent with her was always much too short, and that she always yearned for more, and that she was a woman who might do anything now to have it.

Dell felt more and more woozy. Things were gently and quietly leaving her, and she was content to let them. She'd wave them good-bye and bon voyage. Her sight blurred so that she began identifying things by their outlines. She heard the melodies Grace sang, but the words were hushed.

The house, too, was slipping away from her. Hank's house, which the two of them had christened by making love in every one of the rooms. The house she had kept nice waiting for him to come home. It didn't feel like hers anymore. It was Grace who fixed the drippy sinks, Grace who knew how to bleed the boiler. Weekends Grace hand-polished every stick of furniture in the house with lemon oil. She washed the windows and pruned the hedges and filled the vases with the wildflowers that grew just outside. Grace could spend whole days in the house, that was how much she loved it, and the one thing Dell knew was that she was going to leave the house to Grace.

She had something very different to leave Lilly and her granddaughter. The moment she died and left her body, she was going to lodge, just for a moment, in Dinah's heart and then in Lilly's. She'd touch there, lighting just enough of a spark so there would always be a warmth there, like a kind of visit, that Dinah and Lilly could connect right up to any time they wanted. It was the best thing she could think of to leave. And then she was going to fly right on out and up, pinwheeling toward Matt, going off just like a human sparkler to whatever new wonders awaited her. Death, she thought, was sometimes as much a miracle as life.

One evening Matt showed up and he was five years old, in the white duck sailor suit she had bought him just before he went off to camp. He grabbed for her legs. When he touched them, her toes wriggled.

"Come give your mother a hug," she said.

"Mama," he said, his voice light as breath. He sprang toward her and kissed her, downy baby cheeks against her own, and then he let her go; he seemed to grow fainter.

"Wait," she said, yearning toward him. "Wait for Mama." Matty, she thought. My Matty. Her heartbeat stuttered. It sounded to her like a lullaby she used to sing to him. She tried to hum along with the fractured beat, but her voice had left her, and then a sudden new heaviness crushed against her chest, sharpening, startling her. She was afraid for only a second, just until she felt Matt cradled in her arms. This time he was just minutes old, newborn small and as luminous as a pearl. He whimpered a little. "Mama's right here," she said, delighted. She wouldn't leave him. Not for anything. Not anymore. She held him tighter, waiting, flooding with love. She listened in wonder to her heart slowing its beat, to the whisper of her breath as it stalled and started again, and then, sighing, arms still around her baby son, she shut her eyes.

Dell was bundled under two blankets when Dinah walked in. Dinah rested her head against Dell's hand. "I decided something. I'm going away to college," she said. "I'm going to be a vet. Like my father."

Dell made a sound, low and guttural, and Dinah started. She knew her grandmother's sleep by heart. She knew the way she breathed, the way she moved and responded to Dinah's speech, and this wasn't it. Dell's breaths were too long and too pulled out, like taffy. Her skin was too cool. She grabbed at Dell's wrist, and a sluggish, labored pulse moved fitfully under her fingers. Dinah shook her grandmother, and when Dell didn't respond, she bolted to her feet. "Grace!" she screamed. "Grace!"

Dell was buried beside Matt on a brilliantly sunny day. A priest spoke. He said that Dell had had a good life, that she was ready to go, and that dying in her sleep instead of continuing to suffer was a gift from God. Grace stood very still, neither agreeing nor disagreeing, her features hidden by a veiled hat. Lilly held Dinah's hand, their fingers woven together tightly.

Grace stayed in Dell's house. Some nights Dinah came to visit, sitting hesitantly in the kitchen with Grace, the two of them sipping tea. The house creaked and groaned, and Grace cocked her head.

"Hear that?" she said. "That's Dell talking to us. I feel her all around me in this house."

Dinah sipped her tea. "Do you talk to her?" she said.

Grace considered. "I keep the furniture polished the way she liked. I buy her favorite flowers, and I love this house." She took Dinah's hands. "As far as I'm concerned, this house is yours, too. You come by anytime."

Dinah grieved for her grandmother in her own way. She began wearing one of Dell's rings, a red glass stone in a silvery band, and every time she looked at it she remembered her grandmother, and she was grateful she had gotten a chance to love her, even for a little while.

Dinah filled up her life with activity. She was at school. She studied at home, and she began going to the movies with Lilly at night. She ran Ricky more and more. They sprinted furiously, making them both exhausted and winded. She sprawled with the dog on a patch of cool green grass and looked up. Clouds swept above her, traveling across the sky. The dog pricked up his ears. He waited, expectant, and then Dinah sat up, crying about Dell, and wrapped her arms around him, hugging him to her. "You good boy," she said. He licked her face, delirious with love.

For a while Dinah had expected Mickey to call her, at least to ask for the dog. She used to walk by Annette's house, too, hoping to run into her, to hear news from Mickey; but the door was always closed, and she didn't want to knock. And then, as she and the dog got used to each other, she thought neither of them needed Mickey anymore. They belonged to each other.

His leg was perfectly healed. He let her stroke him and kiss him and rough his fur, and sometimes he let Lilly pet him, but when anyone else came near him, he bared his teeth. He made her feel completely safe. She loved running with him. He put his muddy paws on her, so she stopped wearing short tight skirts and began wearing jeans. He nipped at her hair, so she tied it back. And because they got so sweaty playing, she stopped wearing makeup.

At school she kept to herself.

"Hey, you sick?" Cherry said, offering her a lipstick in the ladies' room. Her friends stopped asking her about Mickey, and they stopped even asking her to go out after school with them.

"Bookworm," Cherry said in disdain. "Where's that going to get you?"

"Vet school," Dinah said. Cherry rolled her eyes.

The more Dinah took care of Ricky, the more she remembered her father. Every time she checked Ricky's ears or his eyes, every time she talked to him soothingly, she heard her father's voice shadowing her own. She felt his hands moving with her over the dog's muscles, almost as if he were there with her, as if he had never left her at all. Her hands trembled across the dog, and she felt him catching her nervousness, she felt him quiver. "Steady now," she told the dog. "Everything's going to be fine."

In the spring Carl made Lilly assistant manager of the card shop. "You do the ordering," he told her.

He gave her a sizable raise, and with it she put a down payment on a beautiful antique bed she had been yearning over. She liked the job, and Carl hinted that he was thinking of franchising and that Lilly might manage her own shop.

"Let's call it Lilly's," she said.

He grinned. "We'll see," he told her.

It was the spring, too, when Cora Janet finally called and told Lilly that Matt's money, and Dell's money, too, would be freed up by the fall. Dinah was sitting at the kitchen table, filling out early admission forms to college, and she stopped writing to listen. When Lilly hung up the phone, she came and sat down by Dinah.

"It took all this time," Lilly said. She looked at Dinah's applications. "Your money's in," she said.

Dinah clicked and unclicked the top of her pen. "Are you going back to New York now?"

"Well, I kind of like this old house," Lilly said. "I kind of like my job." She took the pen from Dinah. "And it's funny, but I even kind of like you."

Dinah looked down at the dog. "You don't have to be nice," she said quietly. "I have the money now. And in a year, I'll be away at school. You don't have to stay."

"Don't you want me to?" Lilly said. "I want you to keep living with me, right up until next year, when you go off to school." Dinah started, but Lilly kept speaking. "I like waking up and finding you eating cereal in the kitchen. I like taking walks with you. I even like this mangy dog."

"He doesn't have mange," Dinah said. She rolled the pen along her palms. "Do you think it would have worked out, you, me, and my father?" she said.

"I don't know," Lilly said. "But we both loved him."

"I know," Dinah said finally.

"This is your home," said Lilly. "When you go off to school, your room will still be here."

"My room," Dinah said, shy and pleased.

"For as long as you like," Lilly said.

Dinah watched Lilly resanding the floors in the hall. She leaned in the doorway for a moment, and then, without speaking, she crouched down, grabbed a brush, and helped.

When they were finished, Dinah talked Lilly into going to see outdoor movies at Schenley Park. They brought jackets and a small wicker basket packed with bread and cheese and a blue, starry ball for the dog. There were crowds of people. The movie, *Dracula*, blurred on the screen, but the night air was cool and clean and exhilarating. Ricky rambled back and forth, growling at patches of grass.

The movie broke down, and people began milling

around, when Lilly suddenly spotted Neal. She remembered all the nights they used to sit up and talk and laugh together, and as soon as she saw him, she missed him. She never thought about Spence anymore, or Alan, but she did think about Neal, and the only reason she hadn't called him was because he hadn't seemed to want to see her anymore.

She was about to get up, to go talk to him, when she saw a woman approach him, then kiss him on the cheek, and Lilly hesitated. I was his friend, I can just go over there and be friendly to both of them, she thought, but suddenly she didn't want to. Suddenly her pleasure wavered. She settled herself back down.

Dinah rested one hand on Lilly's knee. "Maybe she's his sister," she said.

Lilly laughed. "It's all right," she said to Dinah. "I just kind of missed him."

Dinah was silent for a minute. She picked at a hole in the knee of her jeans. "Don't you hate it?" she said quietly. "Missing people?"

"Yes," Lilly said. "I do."

Ricky loped over and settled himself by Dinah's feet. "Do you think it ever stops?" Dinah said.

"No," Lilly said. "But maybe it gets different."

Dinah plucked up a tuft of dry grass, crumbling it between her fingers. "Listen" she said. "I think you should go see Neal if you miss him."

Lilly looked over at Neal again. He was getting up, readying to leave. He helped the woman on with her jacket. "Maybe," she said.

One night, when Dinah was out running the dog, Lilly leafed through Dinah's college catalogs. Dinah highlighted the courses she liked in Day-glo pink. She doodled dogs and cats in every square inch of margin, the same kinds of scribblings Lilly remembered Matt used to do. She traced her fingers over the drawings.

She flipped pages. Math. Chemistry. Psychology. She browsed through the course descriptions, and the more she read, the more interested she became. She wondered what it might be like to take a course or two, to learn a whole new vocabulary. Group psychology. Abnormal psychology. She thought of herself sitting in a plush office, listening to clients who had been torn by life somehow, and suddenly she felt catapulted back to the Chelsea café, when face after face had leaned across the table to her and wanted consultation. She had had clients wanting her to break up the barriers between the past and the future. She had spent years talking to the dead and never once been able to reach the person she had wanted to reach the most, had never even been able to see him except in his daughter's handwriting across the catalog of a college that was halfway across the country. She thought suddenly of Neal, out on the grass, watching a movie with some woman, their hands so close, they might have been touching. She thought of him teaching at the university, less than twenty minutes away. Dinah was right. It was crazy to miss someone if you didn't have to.

Lilly went to the university the next evening. It was easy enough to find out where and when he taught. She drank three cups of tea in the student union, music drumming around her, before she made her way to his class.

The class was almost over by the time she got there. She wound her way to the back, unnoticed. Neal was in a sloppy blue sweater and jeans, in worn boots. "See you next time," he called cheerfully.

She didn't know what she wanted from him or even how she felt. She didn't know what he wanted, either, but looking at him now, she felt a sudden skip in her heart. She felt an indentation, like a seed being planted, like something that might take root and flourish, if she were lucky.

The same woman from the park, lean and pretty in the front row, her long legs flashing under the shortest dress Lilly had ever seen, was smiling up at Neal, and he was grinning at her, then laughing at something she whispered to him. Well, Lilly thought. Well. She could be just a flirtatious student, or she could be someone Neal loved. The future looped and danced and only sometimes let you see a glimpse of what your life might be like. Even at Lilly's best, when she could read a person so well that she might know what they would be doing at ninety, there was never a time when she ever saw anything in its totality. There was always surprise, mystery, and maybe, if you were lucky, for a very little while there might be magic. Who knew how many different lives could be held and experienced in one lifetime? Who knew what could break your heart and what could heal it?

Lilly waited until Neal turned. He looked out across the auditorium, as if he were looking for something, as if she had been sending signals, and then he saw that she was there, and that she was waiting for him. Lilly stood up. He stopped, and then something in Neal seemed to give way, and he couldn't help but smile, and then he started coming toward her.